Landon Taylor

The Battlefield Reviewed

Narrow escape from massacre by the Indians of Spirit Lake - Rocky mountain

history and tornado experiences. Also remarkable and amusing incidents

Landon Taylor

The Battlefield Reviewed
Narrow escape from massacre by the Indians of Spirit Lake - Rocky mountain history and tornado experiences. Also remarkable and amusing incidents

ISBN/EAN: 9783337287184

Printed in Europe, USA, Canada, Australia, Japan

Cover: Foto ©Andreas Hilbeck / pixelio.de

More available books at **www.hansebooks.com**

THE BATTLE FIELD REVIEWED.

NARROW ESCAPE FROM MASSACRE BY THE INDIANS OF
SPIRIT LAKE, WHEN PRESIDING ELDER OF
SIOUX CITY DISTRICT.

Rocky Mountain History and Tornado Experiences.

ALSO

REMARKABLE AND AMUSING INCIDENTS,

EMBRACING FORTY YEARS IN THE MINISTRY: INCLUDING FOUR YEARS IN
SOUTHERN OHIO, THIRTY YEARS IN THE TERRITORY AND STATE OF
IOWA, AND ONE YEAR IN VINELAND, N. J., IN 1863.

BY

REV. LANDON TAYLOR,

Member of the Upper Iowa Conference of the Methodist Episcopal Church.

Motto: No enterprise can fail with God to back it.

CHICAGO:
PUBLISHED FOR THE AUTHOR.
1881.

TO

All Lovers of our Savior,

AND ALL INTERESTED IN TRUTHFUL HISTORY,

AS WELL AS THE HAPPINESS OF THE HUMAN RACE,

To Them these Pages are Fraternally Inscribed.

BUT ESPECIALLY
THE AUTHOR SENDS WARM GREETINGS

TO THE MINISTERS AND DEVOTED MEMBERS

OF THE

Methodist Episcopal Church,

EMBRACING THOSE FIELDS OF MINISTERIAL LABOR WHERE HE MINISTERED
TO THOUSANDS THE GRACE OF LIFE.

PREFACE.

I have been for some time impressed that it was my duty to write out a history of my life and labors, of my trials and successes, and the great goodness of my Divine Master toward me through all of my history; but *more especially* through the many years in which I was devoted to the Christian ministry. But the duty never became a reality until the anniversary of my birthday, when I had reached sixty-eight years. On that day it was so forcibly impressed upon my mind, that not a doubt remained as to its being a present duty; when I left my room of devotion and entered upon my work. This occurred on the 6th day of December last; and from that time to this I have been engaged nearly every day (Sundays excepted) in writing out the present volume. It may interest my readers to know that the work of a lifetime is all written from memory. Not a scrap of memoranda have I had to assist me from the beginning to the end, and yet I have not wanted for names, dates, or even the language itself. Never before this had I fully appreciated the language of our Saviour in relation to the office of the Holy Spirit: "He shall teach you all things, and bring all things to your remembrance," etc. And I here record my gratitude to God for assistance so timely in this the day of my necessity, and for health and strength of body to enable me to complete my work. My Christian friends who read the facts and incidents contained in this history, may feel assured that they are not collected from doubtful sources, but such as occurred under my own eye; and the few received from others I can vouch for, without any hesitation. As I propose to devote all the profits arising from the sale of this book to purposes of benevolence, I come to my brethren in the ministry and in the laity and ask for *large patronage*, assuring them that its circulation among our people will produce a saving and salutary effect. With a view to interest and benefit the young, I have devoted one chapter of about ten pages to children and youth, which will be found of no less interest, even to adults, than the other history, and will give it a very valuable place in our libraries for the Sunday-school. For the title to my book I am greatly indebted to Rev. Maxwell P. Gaddis, of the Cincinnati conference, who is the author of the "Footprints of an Itinerant," and other valuable works. I have attempted to give sketches of Christian ministers, *only those* with whom I have been intimately associated in labor; many in my own conference are *equally worthy*, but for want of personal acquaintance, they are not included; and owing to the *number*, could hardly be embraced in a' work of this kind. As this is the first contribution of the kind west of the Mississippi, I trust that it may be the precursor to a more extended work, and that in the *great day*, when the results of this life shall be fully made up, this volume may share a part in the good accomplished.

LANDON TAYLOR.

BENTON HARBOR, Mich., April 27, 1881.

INTRODUCTION.

"Though ye have ten thousand instructors in Christ, yet have ye not many fathers, for in Christ Jesus I have begotten you through the gospel." So wrote Paul to the Corinthians, and so might write to thousands now living the venerable man whose long and successful ministry is described in the following pages. Among the great cloud of witnesses to the fidelity of that ministry I claim a place. More than thirty years ago, convicted of the Spirit in answer to his prayers, moved by his earnest appeals, and charmed by his triumphant faith in Christ, I rose, cast in my lot with the people of God, and soon found myself a fellow-citizen with the saints and of the household of God, sitting with the writer of this book and with many others in an heavenly place in Christ Jesus. This book is a loving epistle from Brother Taylor to his spiritual children scattered over the Great West, and to all those among whom he has gone preaching the kingdom of Jesus. Yet not to these only, but unto all the faithful everywhere this book will be a blessing. The title is thoroughly scriptural. Christ himself said "I came not to send peace, but a sword." Paul constantly used martial imagery in illustrating the intensity of the conflict in which the soldiers of Christ are engaged. He spoke of the shield of faith, the helmet of salvation, the sword of the Spirit; and at the close of life, from the Mamertine prison he sent forth a shout of victory which is to ring through all the ages: " I have fought a good fight, I have kept the faith." What conflict more sublime than this! The faithful minister of Christ is the

panoplied champion of every right and the hereditary foe
of every wrong. "He wrestles not against flesh and blood,
but against principalities, against powers, against the rulers
of the darkness of this world, against spiritual wickedness
in high places." What occupation more befitting a veteran
soldier than to pitch his tent on the margin of the river he
is so soon to cross and send memory backward over the
past that he may tell how the battle was fought and the
victory won! to linger fondly over many a scene of rejoicing when the powers of darkness were baffled and souls
were won to God and new joys were kindled among the
angels about the throne! David the shepherd king of Israel rejoiced when he rescued a lamb of his flock from the
power of the lion. God has put upon many of his ministers
the great honor of rescuing thousands of immortal souls
from the hand of the destroyer. Where is there a pleasure
so rich—so heavenly, as to look upon them in after life, and
remember what they might have been if the decision had
not been made for Christ and heaven! The greatest of all
itinerants said of his spiritual children, "For what is our
hope, or joy, or crown of rejoicing? Are not even ye in the
presence of our Lord Jesus Christ at his coming? for ye are
our glory and joy." Dealing as they do with individual
souls, faithful ministers are the real builders of the nation.
God has commissioned them to sow the seed of the kingdom, to awaken the conscience, and to preserve in the
human heart the memory of God—to remind men everywhere that the most precious of all possessions is the truth.
Upon the success of this work hinges the history of the
world. Nations taught of God are alone invincible. Luther
does the work; Bismarck gets the praise of men. What
would have been possible to the great statesman had he not
been preceded by the lowly preacher of that righteousness
which exalteth a nation! Statesmen are slow to see this.
Many of them are quite unwilling to acknowledge that
their work done in the gaze of the world is only *secondary*

to the work of that humble toiler concerning whom infinite wisdom has said: "He that winneth souls is wise."

An important place has been accorded to education; but intelligence without faith is a delusion and a snare. It will not save the people from the dry rot of moral corruption. The gospel alone can do that. Lord Brougham in a speech in reference to the appointment of the duke of Wellington as prime minister said: "Field-marshal the Duke of Wellington may take the army; he may take the navy; he may take the great seal; he may take the mitre—I make him a present of them all. Let him come on with his whole force, sword in hand, against the constitution, and the English people will not only beat him back, but laugh at his assaults. At other times the country may have heard with dismay that the soldier was abroad. It will not be so now. Let the soldier be abroad if he will; he can do nothing in this age. There is another personage abroad—a personage less imposing; in the eyes of some, perhaps insignificant. *The school master is abroad*, and I trust him, armed with his primer, against the soldier in full military array."

Concerning England as well as our own republic the facts would require a change in that statement. Let it be written thus: "The preacher of righteousness is abroad in the land; churches are being built; Sabbath-schools are being organized; family altars are being erected. These are the moral forces through which omnipotent power shapes the life of the republic."

Let the reader of this book pause a moment and reflect. If the work of this servant of God and all his fellow-laborers could be blotted out, with all the near and remote consequences of their toil, what would there be left worth having? We cannot think of such a destruction for a moment without dismay. Then let us honor them and break upon their heads the alabaster box most precious while yet they linger among us.

C. C. McCABE.

CONTENTS.

CHAPTER I.

FAMILY HISTORY.

CHAPTER II.

FAMILY HISTORY CONTINUED.

CHAPTER III.

A HAPPY SURPRISE, AND PRODIGAL'S RETURN.

CHAPTER IV.

PERSONAL HISTORY.

CHAPTER V.

REMARKABLE AWAKENING.

CHAPTER VI.

THE GREAT REVIVAL, WITH ITS INCIDENTS.

CHAPTER VII.

MY FIRST CIRCUIT.

CHAPTER VIII.

BURLINGTON CIRCUIT—STIRRING SCENES.

CHAPTER IX.

INCIDENTS CONTINUED.

CHAPTER X.

RESOLVED TO GO WEST—INTRODUCTION TO IOWA.

CHAPTER XI.

MY FIRST CHARGE IN IOWA—PIONEER EXPERIENCES.

CHAPTER XII.

PIONEER HISTORY CONTINUED—FIRST CIRCUIT.

CHAPTER XIII.

NEW TERRITORY AND NEW HISTORY.

CHAPTER XLV.

PIONEER HISTORY CONTINUED—CLEAR CREEK MISSION.

CHAPTER XV.

MINING DISTRICTS—ITS CEDAR CLIFFS AND CRYSTAL SPRINGS.

CHAPTER XVI.

DUBUQUE CIRCUIT—ITS INTERESTING HISTORY CONTINUED.

CHAPTER XVII.

DUBUQUE CIRCUIT CONTINUED—ITS LABORS AND VICTORIES.

CHAPTER XVIII.

DUBUQUE STATION—DEPRESSION AND TRIUMPH.

CHAPTER XIX.

DAVENPORT STATION—ITS SACRED HISTORY.

CHAPTER XX.

CHAPTER XXI.

· CHAPTER XXII.

CHAPTER XXIII.

DUBUQUE CITY—CENTENARY HISTORY—SECOND APPOINTMENT.

CHAPTER XXIV.

SUNDAY-SCHOOL AGENT FOR UPPER IOWA CONFERENCE.

CHAPTER XXV.

HISTORY OF SUNDAY-SCHOOL WORK CONTINUED.

CHAPTER XXVI.

PIONEER HISTORY— NEW AND RICH EXPERIENCES ON
SIOUX CITY DISTRICT.

.

CHAPTER XXVII.

PIONEER HISTORY CONTINUED—BISHOP AMES MY TRAVELING COMPANION.

CHAPTER XXVIII.

MAQUOKETA STATION—HARD LABOR BUT RICH REWARD.

1*

CHAPTER XXXII.

MISTAKEN VIEWS OF MOUNTAIN AIR — NEW KNOWLEDGE GAINED.

CHAPTER XXXIII.

IOWA CITY—ITS THRILLING HISTORY—WAR COMMENCED.

CHAPTER XXXIV.

CEDAR FALLS AND DAVENPORT.

CHAPTER XXXV.

INTERESTS OF VINELAND, N. J.

CHAPTER XXXVI.

CLINTON STATION—1863.

CHAPTER XXXVII.

A SHORT REST—THE CONFERENCE FOR MY PARISH—BIBLE AGENCY.

CHAPTER XXXVIII.

LE CLAIRE—ITS PROSPEROUS AND PLEASANT YEAR.

CHAPTER XXXIX

LOW MOOR—ITS LABORS, TRIALS, AND VICTORIES.

CHAPTER XL.

CHAPTER XLI.

CHAPTER XLII.

CHAPTER XLIII.

ENDURING MEMORIALS.

CHAPTER XLIV.

CONCLUSION, OR PARTING WORDS.

THE BATTLE FIELD REVIEWED.

CHAPTER I.

My gratitude cannot be expressed when I reflect that I had my birth and education in a Christian family. My father preached the gospel of Christ before I was born, and the first things that I can remember are the words of prayer and the voice of song arising from our family altar. My father's name was James Taylor, and my mother's Julia A. Hathaway—the former born on the Mohawk, and the latter near Elmira, in the State of New York. The name of my grandmother, on my father's side, was Anna Landon, and thus it is easy to see how I secured the name. Of my father's family there were three sons and four daughters; the names of the first, James, Robert, and Harvey; of the second, Olive, Fanny, Sally, and Amelia. Four of this family are still living—Olive, in Elmira, N. Y., aged 84; Sally, in Ohio, 82; Amelia, in Michigan, 80; and Harvey, in Iowa, 78. I give these names and ages, as it is a remarkable occurrence to see so many of one family spared to reach the ages to which they have attained. In the early history of my father's family, they emigrated to Elmira, then called Newtown, when the country was almost a wilderness. Here they were subject to all the inconveniences of a pioneer life. Without any religious privileges, and very limited as to education, they were called to battle with all the difficulties of a new country, and resort to almost every expedient to provide for the wants of a large family. At the age of nineteen my father was brought to see the necessity of a renewed life by a very peculiar providence. Residing at that time with a family of Friends, an old missionary put up for the night. When starting away the next morning, as he mounted his horse he said to my father, "Remember now thy Creator in the days of thy youth," and said no more. But it was enough. The Holy Spirit made those words effectual in reaching his heart, and within a few months he was brought out into the "light and liberty of the children of God." "A word fitly spoken, how good is it!" Truly was it so in this case, for within a short time after this happy change in his life, he began to look around to ascertain where he could unite with the people of God. The nearest organized church was at Johnson's Settlement, near Ithaca, and to this place he traveled on foot, that his name might be enrolled in the church of his choice. His visit to this settlement was well-timed, just as their camp-meeting was in progress, and they received him as a brother beloved. At its close he returned home and at once commenced in the work of his Master. As he called the people together and told them what the Lord had done for him (and He was ready to do the same for them), the good work of revival commenced and many were brought to the saving knowledge of the truth; and thus the first Methodist church was organized in that part of the State. As that old missionary went on his way, how little did he think of the gracious results growing out of those few words which he had spoken. But the mustard seed had sprung up and was now bringing forth fruit, "some thirty, some sixty, and some an hundred fold." Having no regular preaching at this time, my father continued his labors, first as an exhorter, then a licensed preacher, having charge of the society until a pastor was sent them by the Genesee conference. This was the beginning of Methodism in and around Elmira in 1807, and thus the good work has continued from year to year, until the Methodist

Episcopal Church now holds an honorable position among her sister churches.

My father's children consisted of seven sons and one daughter, and as the former were in unbroken succession, we had a *doctor* among us by inheritance ; but the fruits of his medical skill, as I am aware, never came to light. Three of my brothers, besides myself, became ministers of the gospel, and served in the different conferences ; two of whom have passed on to their reward, and the other two now hold a superannuated relation in the Upper Iowa conference. My grandmother, Anna Landon, being left a widow by the death of her husband, David Taylor, married a man by the name of Abijah Batterson, a wealthy farmer; and as she gave me my name, at the age of nine I went to live with them, and remained until I was twenty-one years of age. Here I found a good home, with good influences, lacking the practical forms of Christianity; and yet, so far as morality could go, they were almost without fault. Being raised in the land of the Puritans, the Sabbath must be strictly observed; truth must be strictly adhered to, profanity never tolerated, and loyalty to parents promptly rendered. Very few Christians were more exacting touching the exteriors of religion than they; except in the season of *chestnut gathering*, when this labor was regarded as a virtuous act even on the Sabbath. I never in my boyhood could exactly reconcile this service to the sacredness of the day, and its consistency with their other requirements, except that it was numbered among the works of necessity, having no time to attend to it during the other days of the week. Since that time I have learned that conscience has some curious freaks, bending almost double at times to accommodate itself to self-interest. But, upon the whole, my training and counsels were good. My grandmother was a model woman in every sense of the word, save in this important one—devoted loyalty to God. At the age of fifteen, there was a great work of reformation in the com-to passing hours. I continued in this employ for some weeks, when I was engaged to teach a district school, at twenty-five dollars a month. This was in French Grant, on the banks of the Ohio river. Whilst on my way to Portsmouth, to be examined, previous to my commencement, riding along on the river bank, a fowl flew up and lit on the fence, which startled my horse; when, *whirling instantly*, he struck his fore feet down the steep bank, and threw me at least fifteen feet towards the water's edge. The only thing which saved me was the *sliding fall*, corresponding to the *slant* of the bank; but, as it was, it tore the buttons off from my coat, and bruised my arms; but I was thankful that the injury was no worse. In looking around for my horse, I found that he had rolled near to the edge of the stream, and was waiting patiently his master's orders. Finding a place where we could ascend the bank, we started on our way; but horse nor rider had the least ambition to repeat the history. In this district, I taught two winters, making my home at Mr. and Mrs. Folsom's. My brother James having married a sister of Mr. Folsom, I felt very much at home.

On Christmas morning of the second term, there occurred a very amusing incident. Among the interests of that early day, was that of turning the teacher out of doors. As a rule, plans of this kind were kept a profound secret, upon the part of the scholars interested, in order that the surprise might give value to the victory; but in this case, some friendly scholar revealed the project, and thereby I was the better prepared to make my defense. The leader in the enterprise was so certain of success that he had heralded the result, before the day of trial had arrived, and by this means I was the better qualified for the occasion. Christmas morning came, bright and beautiful; an early breakfast was prepared to suit the occasion, when I started about day-dawn for the school-house which was to be the battle-ground of defeat or victory. Fortunately, our school-house was more highly favored than many at that time, for there was an attic, and a space near the chimney sufficiently large to admit one person, *i. e.*, of the lean kind, and through this I squeezed my way, and was soon beyond the reach of human vision. Scarcely had· I reached the place of concealment, when my meditations were disturbed by a shrill whistle, and as I looked out through the cracks of the building, about sunrise, who should I discover but the captain of the undertaking making his way, with confident step, toward the house, with axe and wedges in one hand, and a rail on his shoulder, prepared to fortify door and windows against any force that might be brought against them. He soon struck up a fire, in which I was *personally interested,* and then he went to work securing the doors and windows, and in preparing for a siege defense. I need not say that it was quite a task for my impulsive nature to maintain a strict silence, but the spice of the occasion depended upon it, and I must not eat the fruit until it was fully ripe. About this time some of the scholars began to come in, to be in readiness to see the fun, and as they questioned him as to his ability to " hold the fort," he said that " no one man, even if he was a Yankee school-master, could enter in and keep school that day, unless he agreed to give the school a *good treat.*" And as questions were asked, he became more positive in answering them; and the nearer the hour when the teacher was expected, the larger the crowd within, and the greater the excitement. I can say, to this day, that I have been in a great many tight places in life, but seldom in one where it required so much nerve to maintain my gravity as this. But the crisis had arrived, the school-hour had come, and, as with all of the enthusiasm of his nature he exclaimed, " If Mr. Taylor gets into this house to-day, it will be *through a shower of bench legs,*" in the burst of laughter which arose from the scholars, I could not restrain, and cast in my contribution with the rest. This was the first intimation they had received that I was among the defenders and prepared to keep the fort. The surprise and capture which had been prepared for me was transferred to other parties, as the reaction seemed to carry everything before it. Never, in my life, have I witnessed such a merriment as when I came out of my hiding-place. The scholars nearly all seemed in sympathy with their teacher, and the victory was so skillfully won that not a treat was again mentioned, nor a holiday demanded. The school commenced at the usual hour, and continued through the day. At noon I purchased about one bushel of apples to please the children, and thus the day closed in peace and harmony; but the leader of the plan was so often annoyed by the scholars as to his preparations of defense and fearful failure, that the pressure was *too great;* he left the school and did not return. In my call at noon at a neighbor's to purchase my apples, the old lady said that " She had often heard of Yankee tricks, but this was the first one that ever took place near their door." As I repaired to my home, they were still ignorant of the success of the day, and here we had our second jubilee. This was the first and last experience of mine of this kind in olden times. There are many bright spots in my history of school teaching in days long past. Many of my warmest friends living are among my old scholars. Some of them have gone to their reward, and I am glad that I have lived long enough to see this relic of barbarism pass away.

CHAPTER III.

At the close of this term of school-teaching, my brother having taken a large job of nail-kegs for Portsmouth, I became a partner, and continued with him during the most of the year. My brother at this time was a bold and earnest skeptic, well read up in the arguments of that school, and

a very able debater. Though at that date I was not a
Christian, yet we had many arguments for and against the
truth of revealed religion. In one instance I recollect, I
brought him to an answer which he required one day to
consider. The question was this: "Why is it, if the Christian religion is false and a delusion, that in proportion as it
is embraced and its influence prevails among nations and
communities, that they become *refined, intelligent, wealthy*
and *powerful*, and vice versa?" And the history and maps
of the world attest this beyond a doubt. At the end of
twenty four hours he was no better prepared to solve this
question than at the beginning. As we were engaged in
our enterprise in the woods getting out timber, who should
come upon us suddenly but our father from the state of
New York. He had sold out his farm in that state and followed his children to the land of promise, induced not only
by the hope of bettering his condition as to temporal interests, but beyond this: that of bringing back his prodigal
son to the good and right way. His emigration proved
successful at this time, inasmuch as he had the privilege of
purchasing a small farm within a few miles of my brother's,
and thus he moved to his new home. But I soon discovered
that my father was not satisfied so long as James was a
professed infidel; and his teaching and influence was poi-
sonous to the other members of the family. He was a man
of much prayer and of very strong faith, and in every important undertaking his rule was to apply to the source of
all wisdom for divine instruction and guidance. This was
the plan which he had adopted in order to recover his wandering boy. And in this he had the strongest confidence
that he would succeed; having tested it in so many instances
in the history of the past, and it had never failed him,
he believed that it would not fail him now. That divine
power that changed a Jacob to Israel, a prisoner to a
prince, that gave him such "power with God and with
men," would speedily change the mind and heart of his

wayward son, and bring him off victorious. And thus he plead and pressed his suit from week to week, until he obtained the *witness* that his prayer was honored of God, and that his child would be reclaimed. He also recognized the importance of personal effort accompanying prayer, and thus he proceeded at once to make us a visit. We were busily engaged at work in our shop when my father arrived, but I discovered at once that something had occurred of more than ordinary interest. Just *what*, I could not tell. He introduced the subject gradually and yet prudently; referred to past days and former history; tenderly informed him what an untold interest he had recently felt as to his spiritual condition and eternal welfare; and then ventured to ask him if a "change had not already taken place in his views and feelings." To my surprise he answered "yes." "I was aware of that," said my father; and here the fountain of feeling opened. In the arms of affection they embraced each other, and their tears imparted an interest to the scene. The great deep of human sympathy seemed to be broken up—the one in penitential tears, and the other in overwhelming joy. It reminded me of the meeting of Joseph and his father in the land of Goshen. No brighter spot in all of my father's life was ever reached than this. "Sorrow endured for the night, but joy came in the morning." Though not a Christian, my own heart was moved in sympathy with the occasion, and the impression on my mind will last whilst memory endures. The result is soon told. My brother then and there pledged to renounce his infidelity, return to his long-rejected Saviour, and consecrate the remainder of his life to the service of God. In this covenant he was true to his trust. Within a few months he united with the Methodist Episcopal church and went to work in earnest in recovering the ground which he had lost. But the struggle was a severe one; for having wandered so far away, sinned against so much light, it was meet that the penalty should be severe, and painful it was.

For nearly one year he wept and prayed before he was re-stored to the favor of God. But I must pass on from this scene of thrilling interest—from my father with his joys, and my brother with his penitence, and bring them forward again at the proper time.

CHAPTER IV.

In concluding the former chapter I was engaged at work with my brother, but at the close of the year I was solicited by Mr. John Squires, who was then manager of Franklin Furnace, Jr., in French Grant, to engage as clerk in their store; and as this position was more desirable than any I had held in Ohio, I gladly accepted the offer and entered at once upon its labors. In this employment the days passed pleasantly away. My new home brought with it new friends and new amusements, among which was the playing of cards for pastime when the day's labor was ended. In this way our winter evenings were spent with some favored associate until far in the night, when our wasting energies ought to have been replenished with sleep; and thus the interest increased until one evening in the month of May, as the clock struck ten. At that moment the bell seemed to have a *warning* voice which we had never heard before. Each stroke seemed to speak of the sinner's coming doom. The warning was not to be trifled with, for it spoke to all present; and the next moment we were on our feet taking the solemn vow that it was the last game of cards that we should ever play. This night wound up the history of these amusements, and led at once to a life of consecration to God. The next day we sought a place for prayer in the consecrated grove, and this was continued through the week, in which sacred retreat, in my own personal experience, I realized all that is included in the language of the poet:

"The joys the dear Redeemer brings
Will bear a strict review;
Nor need we ever change again,
For Christ is always new."

The following Sabbath being quarterly meeting, I united with the Methodist Episcopal church in Wheelersburg, Ohio, and bade farewell to such amusements forever. This happy event took place in the year of our Lord 1837, and at once I commenced a life of labor for the Master. I was appointed class-leader the same week that I gave my name to the church. Our ministers at this time on the circuit were Wesley Rowe and Daniel T. Wainright, true and faithful men. In the office of class-leader, without any experience, I felt more like being led and taught, than to lead others, and especially so as the class were old and experienced members of the church, among whom was the mother of Rev. James Gilruth. But as an obedient son, among such teachers I knew I could learn; so a travel of three miles found me every Sabbath in my place.

During the fall of this year, having formed the acquaintance of Miss Jane Vincent, a sister to Mrs. Squires, the wife of the manager, we were married and lived very happily together for nearly three years, when an adverse providence, as I then regarded it, put an end to our domestic bliss during life. Shortly after the birth of our second son, her health failed, and with it the loss of her reason, and within three weeks became totally insane. This was a trial coming on so suddenly, and of such a character, that at times it seemed as if it were greater than I could bear. It was a shock so unexpected and severe that I seemed totally unprepared to meet it. A few weeks previous, an affectionate, amiable and sensible wife, respected and loved by all who knew her; but now, all that is left is but a *wreck* of what was. Just starting out in life, buoyant with hope and expectations for the future, home brightened with the reception of two bright and promising boys, and rendered the more so by our mutual love. But now all is dark and dreary, with scarcely a ray of light to cheer or a hope to comfort. With two helpless babes on my hands, where shall I find a mother? With an insane companion to control and watch over constantly, where shall I find relief? The change was so great, and the sorrow so deep, that tears, though sought, refused to flow. This unfortunate occurrence took place in February, 1840. Having tried every source for relief at home for nearly four months without any success, I started for Columbus, to the Lunatic Asylum, and after four days of exciting and dreary experience, I arrived there, and left her in the care of the superintendent, Dr. Awl. I found the doctor very kind and obliging, and he did everything within his power to comfort and encourage me in this hour of domestic affliction. Having complied with all the legal requirements I started for home. Left to myself, all alone in my carriage, relieved of the burden of four months' cares and anxieties, its history now coming up before me like a *map spread out*, I could no longer refrain. The tender remembrances of the past opened anew the sympathies of my heart, and the tears flowed like rain. For a time I exhibited more of the traits of a child than of a man. The forces had been so long collecting, that when nature gave way the tide of feeling seemed to carry everything with it, and like Joseph, when he made himself known to his brethren, I " wept aloud." But what painter could describe my feelings when I reached home! Here was the house, the vacant rooms, the chairs, the stove, the bed, the table and bureau, with some remaining apparel; but not a whisper to be heard, not a face to be seen, not a child's prattle nor a mother's song to sweeten the joys of home. Even the domestic cat had left, and the impress of melancholy reigned supreme. That hour, shall I ever forget? No, not whilst memory lasts. It is written *indelibly* upon that page of my history, and the ravages of time will never erase it. But let me turn to another page of history.

What an inspiration there is in hope, said "to spring eternal in the human breast"! Being now at home again, and relieved of the weight of labor and care so long resting upon me, I resumed my place at the Furnace. The best provision possible was made for the children for a time, in the hope that the mother would soon be restored to the bosom of her family; for all other interests were trifling when compared to this. For this we waited, for this we hoped, and for this we earnestly prayed. At the expiration of three months I received a letter from Dr. Awl, that my companion was recovering and in a short time would be able to come home. These tidings inspired me with a new life, and in my rapture I could almost realize the hour when my domestic happiness would be restored. But like the sun coming out from behind the cloud to be hid again soon by one *darker* and *larger*, so it was with my transient joys. I waited and wished, but no more tidings came for months, and finally when they came her case was decided incurable. In addition to this the Furnace company failed about this time, my only source of dependence, indebted to me twelve hundred dollars, and left me without a cent. Thus did one misfortune follow upon the heels of another, and I found myself upon the approach of winter without money and without a home. But this was no time to despair, and gathering courage from my trying situation, I launched out into the country and was successful in securing a district school at twenty dollars per month. What an important lesson I had learned within the space of a few months: that however promising our prospects in life, how soon they may be blasted. But there was one source of comfort remaining; one Friend that would not fail me; and supported by this assurance, I knew that relief would come at last: And in this I was not disappointed, for as soon as this school was closed I was applied to for another; and thus I continued for the space of two years—the most of this time in Haverhill, on the banks of the Ohio river. How mysterious are the workings of Providence; and though the ordeal be severe through which we pass, it is the most effectual in reaching the end to be accomplished. How limited were my views at this time as to the end to be reached whilst passing through this painful experience. For more than two years I had prayed daily for the recovery of my companion, and yet her condition was not changed, but the more confirmed; and often did I inquire: "Why is this so? *Why*, in the morning of life, have I been shorn of everything dear to human hearts? Companion a blank, home vacated, children scattered, money gone, and I like a lonely exile upon the wave of uncertainty." In fact, I could not comprehend the past nor read the future; but through all of this domestic darkness a cheering ray of light would shine upon my path, and I could read: "Though human hopes may fail, the crown in heaven is sure." Amidst all of the uncertainties of life, I was conscious of this, that the discipline through which I was passing was bringing me to think less of earth and more of heaven.

CHAPTER V.

In my last chapter, I was passing through the shadows into light, and this change was very much assisted by one or two peculiar circumstances connected with my life at Haverhill. The first was the most remarkable manifestation of *divine light* of which the human mind can conceive. This was about nine o'clock at night, after I had retired to rest, and continued several minutes. I had read of such revelations in the history of Christians, but to me it was entirely new. The light was " above the brightness of the sun," and my spiritual joy and rapture corresponded to the

brilliancy of the night. This was not a dream nor a vision,
but a divine reality, as I had but just retired, and reasoned
long afterward as to the grand design of this visitation.   I
did not at that time pretend to understand its teaching, but
I was filled with wonder and with awe, and I treasured it
up in my heart, waiting for the future to interpret its
meaning.   For this I did not have long to wait.   My home
at Haverhill was at Benjamin Butterfield's, a farmer from
New England, and a life-long Universalist.   He was a man
honored and respected by all who knew him, and he was
also one of our school directors.   During my stay with the
family the first month, I became greatly interested in their
salvation, and made the *father* especially a subject of
prayer; for I was conscious if he were saved, the rest of
the family would follow.   This interest upon my part was
continued but a short time, when I was overheard by him,
who understood the burden of my petition.   On the following morning, after breakfast, sitting by the fire, I discovered that he was *all alive* with emotion; his lips quivered,
the tears started, and he was laboring for sufficient com-
posure to introduce a *new subject.* "Mr. Taylor," said he,
" I have been anxious for some time to have a talk with
you.   I have known you for years, and I have had all confidence in your honesty and sincerity, and now I wish you
to tell me, as a *candid* man, whether there is any reality in
experimental religion.   I have been a professed Universalist nearly all of my life.   I have tried to be honest and
do right, but if there is a better way, where true happiness
is to be found, I wish to find it."   This was the coveted opportunity which I had sought, and I spared no pains to improve it to the best advantage.   After a frank conversation,
I left him for my school-room, an honest inquirer and a
weeping penitent.

The next quarterly meeting was to be held in this place
within a few weeks, and I knew that this would be a suitable time to improve upon the good impressions made.

Isaac C. Hunter was our presiding elder upon this occasion, and he preached with power and with effect. On Monday evening, as the meeting was continued, after a short sermon by Rev. Charles Ferguson, the junior preacher of the circuit, six of my oldest scholars came forward for prayer, and among them was the daughter of Mr. Butterfield. Being their teacher, the pastor called upon me to pray for their salvation, and within a short time they all became the subjects of saving grace. I now began to understand the reasons of that previous light. It was but the precursor of that great *awakening*, which had now commenced already in my school-room, and in the salvation of my own scholars. Among the brightest and the happiest was the daughter of my friend, and my own joy was so full and my spirit so free that all of life's sorrows had passed away. Not a cloud was left; not a semblance of gloom remained. All sadness from this hour of blessing disappeared, and I was brought out into a plain where all was sunshine and "joy unspeakable and full of glory." I could now read the pages of my previous life. I could now understand the reason why my path had been so thorny, and all of my earthly prospects cut off. I had been led by a hand divine, and disciplined in the school of Christ; and in this teaching I had been shown the poverty of earthly things, that I might place a greater value on things eternal. So great was the change, and so complete the victory, that I hardly dare speak of past affliction; it was a term *too harsh* when referring to myself. How I now realized that they all had been blessings, and I was now prepared to work for Him who had done so much for me. On Tuesday night the meeting was continued, the invitation given for seekers, and among them was Mr. Butterfield. This was a great surprise to his old neighbors, and *especially* Universalist friends; but the decision was made, and he was not the man to falter when eternal life was at stake. The next day at home he found the " pearl of great price," and rejoiced in the witness of a

3

new life. The joy which he now felt was too good to keep,
and he related to others what a Saviour he had found. And
thus the work went on, until fifty were numbered as the
fruits of this revival. Mr. Butterfield lived a very happy
man for a few weeks, and then passed away in great peace.
I stood by his side and received his last testimony; closed
his eyes in death, and rejoiced with his children in his
triumph through divine grace. His funeral sermon was
preached by Rev. Charles Ferguson, now a member of the
Cincinnati conference, and near his old home his remains
now sleep awaiting the resurrection morn.

With my new and glorious experience, I now felt that a
wider field of usefulness was before me, and that duty would
call me from the school-room into the more enlarged work
of preaching the gospel of the Lord Jesus Christ. With
this conviction, I began in earnest to labor in the work of
saving souls, and, though I continued to teach, every spare
day and night found me laboring to promote the blessed
work going on through French Grant circuit. Brother
Andrew Murphy was senior preacher for this year 1841-'42,
and with his colleague, Brother Ferguson, labored like
men of God. Such was the character of the work that
during the conference year over one thousand persons were
added to the M. E. church on that circuit. In the month
of June, A. D. 1842, I received license to preach the gospel.
Though I had been doing a minister's work for many
months, the time came when I must receive authority from
the church. During the quarterly meeting, I was requested
by the preacher in charge to preach my trial sermon, giving
me about two hours in which to make my preparation.
This was one of the greatest crosses of my life, to appear
before a large audience *on trial*, in the presence of my
father, my brother, and pastors of the charge. Soon the
hour of service arrived, for me *too soon*, when the church
was crowded to see and hear what the young man had to
say. This was the time, if ever in my life, that I trusted in

Christ for strength to bear me successfully through. I did not trust in vain. My text was this: " He that overcometh shall inherit all things." My main divisions were: " What we were to overcome;" and then, " What to inherit." I had not proceeded far, before a curious assembly and criticising ministers became as " small dust in the balance." I truly realized during that sermon, that I had overcome through faith, and that the gracious promise belonged to me. As I came down from the pulpit (for they were high in those days), I was met with congratulations, and I think that no one was more grateful for the success than my father when the suspense was past and grace had triumphed. He felt, as well he might, that the trials and discouragements through which he had passed for the cause of his Master in early life were now being rewarded in the salvation and useful life of his children; and as he was closing up his labors in the church, they would continue to honor his name and bless the world long after he had entered upon his reward. The service of the quarterly meeting now ended, I repaired to my sacred home in Haverhill, with fresh resolutions to employ all my powers in the service of God. No earthly home could have been more highly favored than mine in the prosecution of such a work. Though Mr. Butterfield was gone, two daughters, Ellen and Eliza, and two sons, John and Benjamin, still remained as members of the family; and as they had recently united with the church, it was a " household of faith," a little Bethany, where the Saviour and his disciples ever found a hearty welcome and a happy home. How many who have partaken of their hospitality in past years, will heartily endorse this tribute, and among them Brother Ferguson, who passed at this home so many happy hours. I continued with the family nearly three years, and often live over again in memory those precious hours passed on the bank of the pleasant Ohio. Ellen has joined the church triumphant, but Eliza and the brothers still live. O that they may constitute a family *unbroken* in the kingdom of heaven!

CHAPTER VI.

I must now return to the history of my brother James. I left him several pages back, after his interview with father, having renounced his skepticism and pledged fidelity to Christ. And now opens up for him new scenes and new experiences. It was all well, and friendly greetings with daily exchange of visits, whilst he remained true to their cause, but so soon as it was known that he had forsaken the fold, and embraced the faith of the gospel, persecutions began. His former associates not only forsook, but would even mock and deride him whilst passing by their dwellings, and even circulate false and evil reports as to his character and motives. In this way he had a fine opportunity to test the value of their friendship as well as its origin; but none of these things moved him, for a life of eight years under the gloom of skepticism had wrought a perfect cure; and now that the final resolve had been made there was no compromise. The first opportunity, under the pastorate of Wesley Rowe and Daniel T. Wainright, he united with the church, and thereby pledged fidelity for life. Our connection with the church began about the same time, but as he had to undo the influences of eight long years of error, his first religious progress was very slow. His repentance was long, deep and painful, but he struggled on until pardon came, and the evidence of his restoration to the favor of God. He now became a power for good. His long schooling in unbelief made him familiar with all the strongholds and arguments of infidel writers—so much so that he would meet and repulse them at every turn, then carry the war into their own camp. Not long after his restoration, he began to officiate in public as an exhorter, then a preacher, and finally he became an important helper in the great work of revival in Scioto county, Ohio. In a short time he removed with his family to Rock Island, Ill., when he became a member of the Rock River conference; then agent of the American Bible society, and in this work he continued until the Master called him home. His end was peace. His widow and three sons are still residing in Prairie City, Ill., all members of the M. E. church.

But let me return to the gracious work in progress on French Grant circuit. I have already referred to its origin in Haverhill, and the results attending. The next quarterly meeting was held in Wheelersburg, embracing the holidays, which continued nearly six weeks and seemed to carry everything before it; even infidels who did not attend service were arrested by the Holy Spirit in their houses, and messengers were sent out for Christians to come and pray for them. In one instance, a man by the name of Power, who was a vile opposer of the work, about the hour of midnight was struck under such conviction that he was led to the chapel, and I was sent for, among others, to labor with him; and we continued our efforts until he rose from the altar a converted man. I still remember his subsequent testimony. Said he: "No longer than last week I despised the very name of those Taylors; but *now* I love the very ground they walk on." He continued a faithful member of the church for more than thirty years, when, about the age of eighty, his history was transferred to heaven. During this revival Brother Murphy preached many able and effective sermons. The work continued all through that year, and as meetings were appointed, the community seemed to be waiting and expecting a gracious ingathering. In one instance, accompanying Brother Ferguson to one of his appointments, we met a man on the way by the name of Strauther. As I was introduced to him by the pastor, after learning his spiritual condition, he informed me that he would willingly give his team and wagon if he could obtain saving grace during that meeting. I informed him that he could secure it, if he was ready and willing, with less cost; that he could obtain grace and keep his team besides. On Sabbath afternoon, with others at the altar of prayer, he was soundly converted, and among other things which he said, he stated "that Brother Taylor was right, for he was now saved and had his team in the bargain." This instance only shows the readiness of the people to receive the gospel of Christ. At one of our services during the summer, at Vesuvius Furnace, when the invitation was given for seekers of religion to come forward, they came by *crowds*, and there must have been at least one hundred at the altar for prayers. I never witnessed such a scene in my life, for many fell over the seats before reaching the altar. The meeting continued four days and there were 132 accessions to the church. During this great awakening our pastors appointed by the conference were highly favored with ministerial help. Here was Rev. Daniel Young, an old and talented preacher from New England, Revs. Howell, Brewer, Scott, and my father, all baptized into the spirit of the work, besides a host of lay brethren well qualified for the place assigned them. Among the latter, I cannot pass the name of Thomas O'Neal without notice. He was a remarkable young man, about twenty-five years of age, and though he had an impediment in his speech, he was a power wherever he went. All had confidence in him, and he was ever ready, anxious and seeking opportunities to lead some lost soul to Christ; and although it was often difficult for him to converse, yet when he sang, or when he prayed, all impediment was gone, and every one felt the divine inspiration. For many years he resided at Ironton, Ohio, with his brother William and widowed mother, and from this city he went to heaven, triumphant to the last. Blessed man. In that community he still lives in the hearts of his brethren, and by the power of his influence, and when the

Saviour " comes to make up his jewels," Thomas O'Neal will be found among the *most precious.*

During this year a meeting was held at Scioto Furnace with the same gracious results which attended them at other appointments. Among the interesting items, I here met a man, an old acquaintance from the State of New York. I had known him from a boy, and during that acquaintance he had run through a very good farm by a life of dissipation. I had no knowledge of his removal to that part of Ohio until I met him there, and his surprise upon seeing me was as great as mine. He seemed to be overjoyed at our meeting, and requested me to sit down with him, as he had good news to tell me. I gladly complied with his request, and he proceeded to say to me that he had " become a new man." " You knew me," said he, " in Chemung, N. Y., and how I drank up all I had, and left my family in poverty and in want. After you left New York, matters grew worse and worse, and as a last resort I concluded to move to Ohio, in order to get beyond the reach of my old associates. Two years ago last spring I came to this place, with hardly a penny left, determined, now as I was in a new place, I would live a different life, and I have done so. I went to work to redeem my character, and the first opportunity I united with the church and embraced religion. I then joined the temperance society, and from that time to the present I have not tasted a drop. I tell you, Mr. Taylor, I am a happy man, and my wife and children are a happy family; but I cannot recall my misspent life." As he gave me this short history of the great change in his experience, at times he was too full for utterance, and my own heart beat in unison with his, for I knew it all to be true. As he left me I gave him words of encouragement, and urged him never to falter. This interview was in June, 1842. He continued faithful until the following November, when, having some business at Lucasville, he found some of his old whisky associates. They prevailed upon him to take a social glass with them, assuring him that a little would do him no harm, and succeeded. This was the *crisis* in his reform—*this was the fatal step!!* He started home toward night with a jug of liquor in his hand, and the next morning he was found near the road-side a *stiffened corpse.* Thus ended the earthly history of Mr. S. Upon this occasion, had he *stood firm* he might have triumphed through all the future; he might have secured a name for fidelity grateful to surviving friends. But by this one indulgence, truly it may be said:

> "Ruin ensues, reproach, and endless shame,
> And one *false step* forever blasts his fame."

But whilst we record this painful history, we have many things amusing and *inspiring*, and there is no better opportunity of becoming acquainted with human nature, and of treasuring up stirring facts, than during the progress of such a gracious work. At these times, what there is in a man will come to the surface, and not unfrequently what has been hidden for years will be made known. At Franklin Furnace, Jr., after such a revival, it was said that Mr. B., a desperate sinner, who had professed conversion, " would remain faithful until his oxen ran away "—to which they were accustomed,—"and no longer." There was much interest as to the result, especially among the outsiders, when the *trial-day* should come. He was loading up his sled upon the hill-side for coal purposes, when all at once his team started, overturned his sled and made for the road home. For some little time he stood and watched their progress, then broke out in song:

> "And I don't feel anything like getting tired. Hallelujah!
> For *I hope to shout glory when this world's on fire. Hallelujah!*"

This event, witnessed by one of the prophets who had prophesied evil concerning him, was too good to keep, and Mr. B. was adjudged capable of living religion, with an

unruly yoke of oxen. A short time since I was informed
by a friend living near him, that he is still true to his trust.

Among our previous ministers on this circuit, I must not
omit the names of Revs. Wm. R. Anderson, E. V. Bing,
A. M. Alexander, Brother Longman, James Donahoo, and
McVay. Though these ministers served us previous to the
time embraced in the above history, yet their names and
faithful labors have not been forgotten. Brother Anderson
was a fine preacher, an excellent scholar, and a noble man.
My first license to exhort I received from him in 1838. Six
years after this he was stationed in Portsmouth and preached
my father's funeral sermon. Through the remaining years
of his ministry his record was the same. He died in the
vigor of manhood, but he was ready. In after years, Sister
Anderson married Rev. Charles Ferguson, my old friend,
where I ever find a welcome home. Rev. E. V. Bing, at
this date, was a *fine singer*, and of pleasant address. On
the circuit there lived at one of his appointments a noted
infidel, but he was very fond of music. Hearing of the
young minister's reputation as a singer, he went out to
meeting. After preaching, Brother Bing opened the doors
of the church with the usual invitation of coming forward
and giving the preacher their hand. The preacher sang
one of his best, when the skeptic became so *charmed* that
he was the first to go forward. The friends were surprised,
and concluded that they had secured a valuable accession
to their ranks, when the infidel apologized and politely
backed out. Rev. A. M. Alexander was everybody's friend.
He had a smile and a pleasant word for old and young. I
never saw him ruffled in the least. His sermons were plain
and practical, a vein of good common sense running through
them all. On one occasion he preached on the Transfigu-
ration, in my presence, which was truly a masterly effort.
He still lives, a member of the old Ohio conference, ripe in
years and rich in blessings. Brother Longman was an
Englishman, retaining much of the English brogue, but not

unpleasant. He was a very good preacher, and socially a very pleasant man. He enjoyed a pleasant joke, and carried with him a good degree of sunshine. The only fault I have to present in our labors together is this: After preaching from "The Lord God is a Sun," etc., the exhortation so covered up the sermon that it was nowhere to be found. He remained two years on French Grant circuit, very much beloved, and useful on the charge. Rev. James Donahoo was a plain, solid preacher. Like many others among our pioneer preachers, he possessed great physical strength; and in some instances scoffers and opposers felt the virtue of his muscular arm and brawny fist. He generally ran in advance of the Saviour's command, inasmuch as he suffered not the "right cheek to be smitten." On one occasion he was attacked on the road by a great bully, sitting in his buggy. Without stopping to pull off his overcoat, one blow from his *mighty arm* left him sprawling in the road, whilst he passed on, singing in spirit:

> "Sure I must fight if I would win;
> Increase my courage, Lord."

He was transferred to his heavenly home many years since, and some of his children are now living near Davenport, Iowa, members of the M. E. church. Many precious seasons did I enjoy with these faithful men of God, and soon I trust this history will be continued in a more interesting form, when we "shall see as we are seen, and know as we are known." This chapter closes up the labors of 1841–'42 on old French Grant circuit. In my next I will introduce my readers to other interests.

CHAPTER VII.

The last year wound up gloriously, and at the coming conference Rev. A. Murphy was returned to us with Rev. Joseph Morris, and Brother Ferguson was sent to Coal River circuit, on the Kanawha district. Before I part with Brother Ferguson, as he was a kind of colleague of mine all through the year, I must give a parting tribute. He was then just starting out into the ministerial work, and thus his character as a preacher was still before him; but already the signs were visible. He was studious, blessed with a good memory, and loved to *quote* eminent authors. I think that he excelled in quoting Young and Pollok, and in his discourses would often make them tell on his audience. I recollect that on one evening in the grove, with a large congregation, he preached on the Coming Judgment, when he used Young's description with wonderful effect. Some present thought it had come, surely enough, and rose up to their feet to be ready for orders. His powers of exhortation at that date were of the first class. He had a fine commanding voice, power with God in prayer, and was filled with the spirit of his mission. He was an extra evangelist, and wherever he labored souls were saved. He possessed all the social qualities to constitute him a pleasant associate and a true friend. His companion is not in the least behind him in all of those qualities to interest and brighten the family home. This conference year (1881), they are stationed at Wilmington, Ohio, in the Cincinnati conference. Rev. Joseph Morris, his successor, was also a true friend. We labored together like brothers during the year, and I found in him all the attributes of a true counselor, and a never-failing friend. He was a good thinker and a very efficient worker, and when the year closed, I felt that in the separation I had sustained a great loss. Nothing beyond

the usual interest took place this year on the charge, excepting the reaction which usually attends such great in-
gatherings, and a few interesting meetings upon different
points of the work. As I had intended to close up my
school this summer and enter upon the work of the ministry, I was recommended by the quarterly conference to the
traveling connection, and received an appointment with
Rev. John Dillon to this circuit. I was now at home among
my many friends, which made it pleasant; but as I had told
the people about all I knew, having been laboring for the
past two years right among them, I found the study to be
much harder than it would have been among strangers; but
having a multitude of praying friends, and an excellent
colleague, I went forward and found my strength equal to
the task. Our circuit included twenty-one appointments
besides extras. As I started out upon my work, I found an
excellent adviser in the person of Rev. Daniel Young,
familiarly called "Uncle Dan." He had been favored with
a long experience in New England, was a very talented
minister, and took a great interest in my welfare. In the
list of advices which he gave me, I will mention a few; as
they proved a blessing to me, they may be of service to
others. *First*—Always be at your appointment in time;
failing in this, you will soon lose your influence with the
people. *Second*—Be yourself, *i. e.*, be natural. Some young
ministers seem to think they must assume a kind of *preaching tone*, which is unnatural, and thereby injure themselves
and destroy their usefulness during life. *Third*—Be short.
Never tell all you know in one sermon. *Fourth*—Spare
the Bible. Do not pound it, for it is God's book; in this
way you will show your reverence for his word, and your
good sense. *Fifth*—Quit when you are done, and don't
annoy your congregation with useless repetitions. *Sixth*—
Be kind and pleasant always to the children, and don't
abuse the dogs, lest you might insult the owner. *Seventh*—
Beware of foolish apologies, for they indicate vanity and a

want of good taste. I will add no more. Let me say that
as I was young and inexperienced, the counsel of this aged
minister was of great service to me in following years. He
continued his residence in Scioto county until his death,
having attained to more than four-score years. He died at
the residence of his son Jesse, near Portsmouth, in the triumphs of faith.

The majority of our appointments on this charge were at
the furnaces, and having had several years of experience as
clerk at one of them, I was the better prepared to labor
successfully among them. At one of our furnace homes at
Ætna we put up with the owner and manager, whose name
was Dempsey. After our evening service he said to me:
"Would you like to hear me read Brother Dillon's last
sermon, preached at our place? If you would, I have it
here, all written out, and I will read it to you." Being
anxious to hear it, he gave it to me, word for word, as it
fell from the lips of the preacher, as acknowledged afterward by Brother Dillon himself. I was astonished at such
powers of memory, he having written it out after they returned home. At Pine Grove, another of our appointments,
we were favored with a thrilling incident. Our presiding-
elder, Samuel Hamilton, and Wm. R. Anderson, then stationed at Portsmouth, were returning from quarterly meeting. Having left an appointment to preach on their way
out, during the sermon by Bro. A. a man by the name of
Wood was struck under powerful conviction. When he
returned home he was in such distress that he sent for the
ministers and O'Neals to labor with him. They all came
speedily, and as they entered the room Mr. Wood lay pros-
trate upon the floor, crying for mercy. They all prayed
round, occasionally singing an appropriate hymn, until far
in the night, when *suddenly* he rose to his feet and shouted
the praises of God. As his friends began to rejoice with
him over his supposed conversion, he said to them: "I am
not yet converted, but I am praising God because I have

faith to believe that he *will convert me.*" And surely enough,
true to his faith, within a short time they all rejoiced together in the victory achieved. About two years from this
date old Brother Wood departed in peace for the church
triumphant. Rev. Hamilton wrote his obituary, and among
other things he said: " I have witnessed a great many conversions, but no one have I ever known to shout over such
a small amount of grace as Brother Wood." Such stirring
facts as these are among the minister's spoils, " fighting the
good fight of faith," and to him they are of more value than
gold or silver. And especially are such experiences as the
above of peculiar interest to the young minister, in order to
strengthen his faith, and assure him that, though unseen,
there is a power with him upon which he may depend when
all human agencies are unavailing.

During the labors of this winter (1844), I passed through
a trial well calculated to confer a future benefit. We had
concluded to hold a week's meeting at Lawrence Furnace,
and on Saturday we commenced it. After the usual services on the Sabbath, on Monday morning my colleague
was on his horse about to start for home, a distance of
twelve miles. His reasons for going he would not give,
and to me they are unknown to this day. Whether it was
one of those constitutional depressions, or the discouraging
prospects in relation to a good work, I could not tell. I
plead, I entreated him, reminded him of the disappointment
of the people if the meeting were not continued; but all to
no purpose; *go he would.* Well, said I, if you *will go*, I
will give you the benefit of an old fable before you start.
" Very well," said he, " let me have it." I give it here, in
brief: Two friends, setting out together through a dangerous wood, mutually agreed that in case of an attack they
would assist each other. They had not proceeded far before
they saw a bear making toward them with great rage. One
of them, being very active, sprang up into a tree; the other
threw himself flat upon the ground, having heard it asserted

that a bear would not prey upon a dead carcass. The bear came up, and after smelling of him for some time, left him and went on. When he was fairly out of sight, the man from the tree cried out: "Well, my friend, what said the bear? he seemed to whisper to you *very closely.*" "Yes," said the other, "and he *gave me this good piece of advice, never to associate with a wretch who in the hour of danger will desert his friend.*" Brother Dillon laughed and said "that the moral was very *pointed*, and he would endeavor to profit by it." He left, and I remained to conduct the meeting. Very seldom during my labors in the ministry have I felt such a spirit of loneliness as at this time. I knew that my only dependence was now in that blessed Saviour who had promised help in time of need, and to him I looked and prayed for success in this trying hour. The meeting continued till Thursday evening, when, upon invitation, the altar was filled with earnest penitents, and it was a season of victory and rejoicing. On Friday, and in the evening, the interest was renewed, and embraced among the number the owner of the furnace, Mr. John Culvertson, and one of his daughters. On Saturday, my colleague having an appointment at Center Furnace, within three miles of us, a Brother Brewer, local preacher, went over to meet him and request that he should come at once and assist in the great work. As he was nearing his place of destination, he heard a voice by the roadside in a little thicket of bushes, as if some one was earnestly engaged in prayer. What was his surprise when he discovered that it was Brother Dillon. He was engaged at this moment confessing to the Lord "how he had acted the part of Jonah, run away from the work, after all of Brother Taylor's entreaties, when his help was needed; how sorry he was that he had done so, and that if the Lord would forgive him for this, he would never do so again." This was more than Brother Brewer's impulsive nature could bear, and he cried with ringing response, "*Amen! Hallelujah!*" I need not attempt to describe the scene, for it was one of those that cannot be described. Truly, there was *fire among the bushes*, and yet they were not burnt. Whilst the one shouted relief, the other shouted victory, and full of this spirit they returned to the scene of interest to do battle for God. As they entered my room, there we had a second edition of the scene in the woods. They were *too full* to delay the description of the surprise and capture, whilst tears and praises blended with joy and rejoicing. This to me was history entirely new, and its salutary teaching was never lost. Upon the return of the pastor, forty-four had been converted and added to the church. The meeting continued over the Sabbath, and wound up gloriously. In the brighter history of the better land, I expect to remember and adore the blessed Redeemer for his saving power bestowed during my *trial day* at Lawrence Furnace in the winter of 1844. My dear Brother Dillon and Brother Brewer have gone home, and I shall soon be there, but how we will renew the stirring remembrances of earth when we meet in that land beyond the river. Brother Culvertson, the proprietor of the furnace, and his daughter Mary, long since have passed over, and how my heart rejoiced when I read in the *Advocate* that their end was peace.

About this time I was called to part with my oldest child. He was suddenly attacked with the croup, and all remedies were tried in vain; and thus at the age of five years he went to live in that pure clime where sickness never comes. The day of his burial, to my soul, was like a summer's eve, and I was unspeakably happy, knowing that in Jesus he had a home and unfailing protection. His little grave is in sight of Wheelersburg, Ohio, and within a few rods of where I united with the Methodist Episcopal church. The emblem of beauty and immortality blooms every summer upon his grave, and reminds me of a sublimer land, and never-fading flowers. During the ensuing summer I had a violent attack of the bilious fever, and for a time I was not expected to live. But my work was not yet done. Through the kind attentions of my friends, and the blessing of God, I was again raised up, and with renewed determination, resolved that all of my powers should be employed in winning souls for Christ. The conference year closed up with prosperity, and when the time came, I parted from my colleague with deep regret. We had been united in love like David and Jonathan, and now we were to enter upon other fields of labor.

CHAPTER VIII.

This fall our conference was held at Gallipolis, and at its close Brother Dillon was continued on French Grant circuit, and I was appointed to Burlington, above, on the Ohio river, with Rev. Moses Milligan in charge, and Rev. John Ferree continued as my presiding elder. Very few men secured a warmer place in my affections. He seemed more like a father to me than a brother, and during three or four years' acquaintance, not one word escaped his lips in violation of the spirit of dignity and ministerial propriety. I loved him on earth, I shall love him more in heaven. As this was the year (1844) of our presidential election, political matters ran high. I was interviewed in several instances as to my politics, but invariably answered " that I had not been sent upon the work to canvass presidential candidates, but to preach the gospel of Christ." This closed up the chapter. Had there been at that time as much at stake as at the present, duty would have pointed out a different course; but the great question of loyalty to the Union at that date had not been raised. The friends upon this charge gave me a warm reception, and I commenced my labors with opening prospects for a year of usefulness. Old Rome, the home of camp-meetings for many years, was on this circuit, and this gave me a fine oppor-

4

tunity to improve upon this text: "So much as in me is, I
am ready to preach the gospel to you that are at Rome
also." It was not long before a gracious work commenced
at what was called Father Keeny's appointment, and nearly
swept the neighborhood. Such was the intensity of interest that no weather nor discouragements kept the people
from the house of God. Mud and rain prevailed, but
through thick and thin they came in multitudes, pressing
the question, "What must I do to be saved?" One morning, during this meeting, we witnessed a scene never to be
forgotten. After a hard struggle, one of the prominent
men of the place came out into divine light. The manifestation of the Holy Spirit was such that it filled the
house, carrying everything before it. In the height of this
influence he turned to Mr. Rowley, his neighbor, and
exclaimed: " Thomas, five years ago I was under conviction for my sins, and to drown that conviction I went to
your patch and stole watermelons! Will you forgive me?"
This was news to Thomas, but as soon forgiven. He then
turned towards his aged mother: " How often have I heard
you pray for your wicked son when you were all alone and
did not know that I heard you; " and clasping her in his
arms he asked, " Mother, will you forgive me?" Then
turning to me—" Brother Taylor, you are the first preacher
that ever visited me and prayed in my house, and the instrument in the hands of God in my salvation; God bless you!"
when from his *warm embrace*, I felt it great relief. Such
confessions and benedictions as these were enough to melt
all hearts. The interest continued about six weeks, and
resulted in giving new life to the membership, forty accessions to the church, and in the erection of a new house of
worship. An interesting feature in this revival was, that
no one thought of uniting with the church until they were
converted, and because of this, the work was of a permanent character; and so far as I know, all remained faithful
during the year.

Whilst our meeting was in progress, we had a case of
interest well calculated to amuse, as well as present the
workings of human nature in connection with God's grace.
The daughter of Mrs. Simmons became very happy, and
went through the room praising the Lord, and saluting
every person she met. Upon her return home, the mother
sharply reproved Elizabeth for her behavior during the
evening, as not orderly and in harmony with good taste.
Said the mother—who was a regular Baptist—" I will be
there to-morrow evening, and I will see if you can't behave
yourself." True to her promise, sure enough, she was *there*,
looking very wise and watchful. As usual, the blessed
Spirit came down upon the assembly, and the first one to
rise up and give utterance to her joy was Mother Simmons.
Through the house and over the benches she went, praising the Lord for his goodness, leaving the daughter completely in the shade. Accompanying the family home that
evening, as we were all seated by the fire, I said to her:
" How is this? You went to meeting to-night to watch
over your daughter, to keep her *straight*, and lo! it needed
some one to watch over you." The facts were such that
no logic or skill on her part could relieve the case, when
after some little hesitation she answered: " Well, well,
Brother Taylor, I'll tell you what it is, there was no hypocrisy in that shout." After this incident the old lady's criticism was all exploded, and her soul filled with gratitude
in the salvation of three of her children. During such
religious awakenings I have found it difficult, in some
instances, to have everything move in accordance with our
views and wishes, but it is better to bear a little, for the
time being; then, at the *proper time*, correct any impropri-
eties that may have taken place, by some kind remark. In
this way I have never failed.

About this time I was called to visit my father for the
last time on earth. He was attacked with the typhoid
fever, and I was sent for in order to comfort him in his last

days and receive his farewell benediction. Though my
work was urgent, duty called me to honor him and administer to his wants in closing up a useful life. I found him
much reduced, but his spirit was joyful and happy. I continued with him for several days, received his last testimony
and counsel, and then returned to my charge. His confidence in God was unshaken to the last, and his remains
were deposited by the side of my little son in the cemetery
of Wheelersburg. He died at the age of fifty-six, having
been a minister of the gospel thirty-four years.

As I wish to be correct as I can in the order of time, as
well as true to history, I must here record a circumstance
of no ordinary interest. It relates to a young man about
my age, who embraced religion a short time subsequent to
my own conversion, and was in fact almost a bosom friend.
Being of an ardent temperament like myself, and very
warm and zealous in the cause, and often together in religious meetings, there sprang up an attachment between us
of unusual strength, which continued for some years. His
temporal interests were in connection with the iron furnaces
of this county, which his business talent rendered him capable of conducting with success. As I started for Burlington circuit I was favored with his benediction and prayers,
and I looked forward to the day when he would stand in
the first position in the church. But now I learned that
he was about transferring his iron interest to the purchase
of a steamboat for the Ohio river. Being fully acquainted
with the nature and the hazard of a boatman's life, I almost
trembled at the thought. At once I sat down and wrote
him a letter, warning him of the dangers of such a step,
and the probabilities that it would result in the *loss of his
soul*. In a few days I received an answer to my letter,
thanking me kindly for the interest manifested for his welfare; at the same time assuring me that he had weighed the
matter well; that whilst all I had stated as to its dangers
were true, that his religious principles were settled, his

habits were established, and that he could live a "religious life on the water as well as on the land." I kept the letter in my possession for sometime, awaiting the final result. But I did not have long to wait. All that I had feared, *yea more*, followed in this new enterprise. A high life, embracing ungodly associates, card-playing and dissipation, took the place of humility and devotion to God, and soon it became known that all of his religious tendencies had departed. In after years, when I was stationed in Davenport, Iowa, his new boat struck the railroad bridge in passing through it, took fire and burned up, when the earnings of many years passed away in an hour. He prosecuted the railway company for damages, but recovered nothing. After other reverses, having been placed in charge as captain of a new boat, on his way south, the boiler exploded, blew him, with many others, up into the air, and not a single vestige of his person could ever be found. Thus ends the history of my once much esteemed, noble-hearted and beloved friend. When I take into account the *great contrast* between his promising youth, his hopeful prospects, and his pledge of fidelity to duty, with his after failure and unfortunate end, how am I reminded of the language of St. Paul: "They that will be rich, fall into temptation and a snare, and into many foolish and hurtful lusts, which drown men in destruction and perdition." Had he been satisfied in doing well, his name might have remained among the first-born sons of light; his memory might have left a sweet fragrance to surviving friends, and his influence for good salutary in coming years; but ambitious to launch out into the deep of uncertainty, his fall was as great as his anticipations had been glorious. Let all ambitious youth who read this short sketch of his life beware of such a history and such an end.

During the holidays Brother Milligan and myself held a series of meetings in Rome chapel, with much interest and success. Among the number brought into the church was

a youth whose parents lived in the vicinity, and were old
members of the church.   When we took his name, and
looked upon his youthful countenance, we were little aware
of the historic page just opening.   Had some one said to
me, "That youth of fourteen will stand up in future years
as a faithful herald of the Cross," I could hardly have en-
dorsed the prophesy; and yet it has now become actual
history.   I was then a young man, and this young convert
but a mere boy; but I have lived to see Rev. J. W. Wake-
field not only rise to manhood, but to embrace a ministerial
history of twenty-three years.   This was the mere boy who
said to us at that meeting in 1845, by coming forward:
"Here am I, an offering unto the Lord, for time and eternity."   It is my ardent wish and earnest prayer that if I
contributed in the least as his pastor to raise him to his
high and holy position which he now occupies, that he may
represent the interests of his divine Master more successfully than I have done.   The inviting fields of usefulness
are still before him.   In the very prime of life, with a
strong physical frame, and a heart purified by divine grace,
he has many victories yet to gain, and many souls yet to
win.   May the blessed Saviour who called him to labor, be
privileged to crown him with eternal honor.

In entering upon a new field of labor, the itinerant minister has a double benefit, not only that of making new history for himself, but in gathering up many interesting items
from his predecessor and adding them to his own.   How
often have I been interested, yea, benefited, by the relation
of some thrilling incident in the labors of the pastor the
year previous.   And this is one of the secrets of the grand
success attending the Methodist ministry.   Moving among
the people, and reaching *all the people*, he is benefited, not
only by his own personal influence, but in addition to this,
he is enabled to collect together those practical facts that,
when needed, he can bring out of his treasury things *new
and old*, and thereby give to "saint and sinner each a por-

tion in due season." Logic is good in its place; I mean logic in theory; but there is none so telling, so salutary upon an audience, as the logic of facts. Whether this salutary influence attended the one I am about to relate, I am not positive, but I am sure it was so intended. One of my predecessors upon this charge was Elijah Fields, so well known throughout the state of Ohio. It appears that at one of his putting-up places, the lady of the house was not famed for neatness, and he being careful in this respect, concluded that he would try an experiment. So, upon his first visit to that appointment, he called at the house, was welcomed by the good sister, requested to put up his horse and make himself at home. This being done, he took a seat in the sitting-room whilst the main work was going on in the kitchen. Discovering that *his* was also the dining-room, with its cupboard and fixtures, he went to work taking out the dishes. Having prepared water and pounded brick for the occasion, he began scouring the cupboard, its knives and forks, and upon a cleaning-up generally. About this time Sister ——, having heard the friction of the machinery going on, came into his room, and to her surprise, the transforming process was in *full blast*. "Why, Brother Fields, what in the world are you doing?" He pleasantly answered: "I saw, sister, that you had so much work on your hands that I concluded to turn in and help you." He continued until his task was finished; dinner was prepared, the husband returned from his work, the sermon was preached, and then he went on his way rejoicing. Whether this lesson had the desired effect whilst he remained with them I am unable to say; but certain I am that during my stay with them there was still room for improvement, and another visit from Brother Fields would not have been out of place. Elijah Fields was a noble man. He served the church as a minister of the gospel forty-two years in the Ohio conference; died Oct. 1, 1878, in St. Paris, and there he is buried. "He rests from his labors, and his works follow him."

CHAPTER IX.

In my last chapter I furnished my readers with a practical proof of obedience to this scriptural command: "Diligent in business," even to culinary interests; and now I will add to the history of Burlington circuit some additional items. At one of the appointments of my predecessor the society had not prospered for years. Means had been employed from time to time to remedy the difficulty, but all to no purpose. Quarrels, contentions and old grudges, with hatred, was about all the religious capital of which the members could boast. The pastor was not *the man* to be content with such a state of things, so at the close of the sermon he remarked that he was about to invert the usual order of things. "In opening the doors of the church it was customary to invite persons to *come in*, but he was now about to ask them to *go out*." So he gave them the opportunity, and about sixteen left at once. This process ended, "Now," said the minister, "all of you present that will determine to serve God *faithfully* and cease *forever* your old strifes and contentions, to you, and *to you only*, I will open the doors of the church and invite you to come in." Quite a large number came forward, a new class was organized upon the ruins of the old one; some of the old offenders became ashamed of themselves and united also, and the society enjoyed peace and prosperity. Whether this would stand the test of *legal* criticism may be doubted, but for skill and real strategy in managing such a difficulty it was a *masterly stroke,* and the final result honored its approval. At this date, even in Ohio, we had but few chapels, and many of our appointments were at school-houses and private dwellings. At one of the last, the pastor referred to above had an appointment to preach at 10½ o'clock A. M.. when the porch also was filled with interested hearers,

Our minister could not bear the least disturbance, it would totally disconcert him; so about the time he started out in his sermon, an *old hen* having a nest in the porch above, came to the front, asserting her rights, cackling at the top of her voice. The minister, at the risk of eggs for dinner, bade Mr. S., the proprietor of the house, " *to drive away that old hen.*" The mandate was instantly obeyed, when Mr. S. returned and took his seat; and about the same time returned the *old hen.* Louder and still louder she cackled, when Mr. S. out and after her again. This second scare he drove her some distance away, hoping it would prove effectual; when he returned to enjoy the sermon. Scarcely had he resumed his seat, when, lo! here comes the old hen, re-enforced by the old *rooster*, by the excitement their voices *raised to higher notes*, when *away* went the owner, with *raised club, hen and rooster*, who kept guard at a distance until the discourse was finished. I venture to assert that Mr. S. did not get very happy under that gospel sermon, but it furnished a fine opportunity for amusing history in our winter hours. Many a good laugh have I enjoyed with Mr. S. over what we called our " *cackling sermon.*"

Very few men were as calm in affliction as my predecessor. His family motto was: " My grace is sufficient for thee;" and through all of his domestic trials, *this* was a " balm for every wound and a cordial for every fear." In fact, any show of feeling in seasons of distress, as in the loss of earthly friends, was regarded by him as wanting in resignation to the divine will. In the family was a favorite son, some five years old, the father's pet, and when he returned home from long rides on his circuit the joy of the meeting was inexpressible. During an absence of some two weeks, the little boy sickened and died. After his burial, a messenger was sent to meet him, carry the tidings, and request his return home. The minister giving me this account, and bearer of the message, knowing the father's love for his boy,

expected, when his death was made known, to witness strong
manifestations of grief. But instead of this, he simply turned
aside his face—gave one solemn sigh—and remarked: " It
is hard to part with little Johnny, but *God's grace is sufficient.*" He then inquired into all the details of his sickness and death as calmly as a Christian philosopher. Reaching the door of his dwelling, his beloved companion met
him with a sorrowful heart, and as they entered the room
he addressed her thus: "Ann," pointing to his motto, " do
you see that? Johnny* was *dear* to us, but grace will be
dearer than ever, as we shall now need it." This was Christian heroism. We may talk of patriotism for our country,
we may honor the spirit which enables the soldier to march
up to the mouth of the cannon in order to protect his
home and achieve his liberty; but even such patriotism
must stand in the *background* when compared to that manifested by this herald of the Cross of Christ.

> " When through fiery trials thy pathway shall lie,
> My grace *all-sufficient* shall be thy supply;
> For I will be with thee thy troubles to bless,
> *And sanctify to thee thy deepest distress.*"

The history of our labors upon Burlington circuit was
very pleasant and prosperous, winding up with a blessed
camp-meeting at old Rome, with a report of two hundred
additions to the church. Permit me to state, before taking
leave of this charge, that among the many fields of labor
to which I have been appointed, I have never found a more
cordial and generous-hearted people than many on this work.
With what joy and gladness I shall greet them on the other
shore. Scores of them whilst I write are among the redeemed in heaven, to whom I ministered in the years of
1844–45, and I am still left awhile to tell of saving grace
and how eternal crowns are won; but soon with me the last
militant song will be sung, and over the desolations of the
last enemy I expect to raise the notes of eternal triumph.

---

* I am not positive as to the name, but the facts are the same.

CHAPTER X.

At the close of this year, inasmuch as the Ohio conference was crowded with laborers, I was impressed that it was my duty to go West. In addition to this, the Ohio valley was not favorable at that time to persons of bilious temperament; and as this was a standing difficulty, I decided to emigrate to the territory of Iowa. However, before fully deciding the question—as it has always been my rule in matters of importance—I presented the whole matter to Him who has promised to guide and in the path of duty to prosper. The answer to my petition came not only in power, but in these words: "Go; thy youth shall be renewed like the eagle's, and in this work thou shalt prosper." The answer could not have been more convincing had I heard these words from a human voice, as they were accompanied by the blessed Spirit. From this hour I knew my duty, and prepared at once to perform it. It was a trial to leave the home where I was converted, and the many dear friends that I loved, to tell of redeeming grace in distant lands, and among strangers; and that, too, with the prospect of small compensation. As I was making preparations for my journey, how did these words come home to my heart:

> "Home, thy joys are passing lovely,
>   Joys no stranger's heart can tell;
> Happy home as I have proved thee,
>   Can I say at last farewell?
> Can I leave thee, can I leave thee,
>   Far in distant lands to dwell?"

In the month of August, 1845, I placed my horse and trunk on board of a steamboat at Portsmouth, Ohio, and started for Burlington, Iowa. At that time we had no railroads across the states from Ohio to the West, but we went

down the river to the mouth, then up the Mississippi, via
St. Louis. The Ohio river being very low, we had a long,
tedious passage, but I reached Burlington a few days previous to the session of the Iowa conference. A camp-meeting being in progress within a few miles of the place, I
repaired to it at once, as I was aware that it would afford
me a fine opportunity for an introduction to some of the
preachers· of the conference. On Saturday the presiding
elder came, whose name was Bartholomew Weed, and in
the division of Sabbath appointments he assigned me the
hour of nine o'clock the next morning. Being a total
stranger to all present, and having come a long distance
with the intention of making this my home, I felt that much
depended upon making a favorable impression in preaching
my first sermon. As I had previously learned the only way
to success, I applied to him for strength who said, "Lo, I
am with you alway," and I was not disappointed. My
theme was "The highway of holiness;" and before I concluded, we all felt that our position was an elevated one.
At the close the presiding elder congratulated me on my
successful effort, and I doubt not but that it had its influence in assigning me to my field of labor the coming year.
Brother Weed preached at eleven an excellent sermon, but
during the greatest interest he seemed all at once very
much embarrassed. When the congregation was dismissed
he said to me that it was caused by the impression that his
son had returned and was seated before him; and this mistake
had so confused his mind that he was not able to rise above
it. This son had caused him much trouble. If I mistake
not, he was their only child, and at an early age he became
an outlaw and entirely beyond his control. He had been
arrested and sent to prison, but by some means made his
escape. He concealed himself in a ledge of rocks and de-
fied the officers of justice, being armed with deadly weapons;
but he was finally taken and delivered up to them by his
own father. At this date he was totally ignorant as to his

fate, and this increased his anxiety and suspense in relation
to his son. It was no wonder that the parent was embarrassed under such a pressure, and the more so in the belief
that he had returned home. We can hardly imagine a more
severe trial to an affectionate parent than one of this character. Elder Weed was a very worthy man and an able
minister of the gospel. He had left his own home, the New
Jersey conference, two or three years before, to face the
winds and brave the hardships of a new territory. He had
greatly endeared himself to the preachers and people of
this new country, and now, at this conference held in Burlington, he transferred to his own home.

The ministers attending this camp-meeting were: Revs·
A. Coleman, E. S. Norris, Joseph and Thomas Kirkpatrick,
J. W. Brier, David Crawford, Michael See, and Wm. Hurlburt. The camp-meeting closed on Tuesday, and the same
day we repaired to conference. On our way, three of us
riding on horseback, we were greeted with such a salutation as I never witnessed before nor since. The sun was
shining brightly, without the appearance of a cloud, and we
were engaged in lively conversation, when a flash of lightning came with such force that our middle man was very
much stunned. Whether this strange phenomenon was
ominous of good or evil has not as yet been revealed. But
I have no doubt, if rightly understood, it was in perfect
harmony with nature's laws. On Wednesday morning conference convened in old "Zion," Bishop Morris presiding.
This church was the first, I think, built in the territory, and
was well entitled to its honorable name. At this date it
would have been an easy matter "to walk about Zion, and
to tell the towers thereof;" but since that time it has been
so surrounded and hedged in by other buildings, that the
circle would have to be greatly enlarged. But we that
were there "can tell it to the generation following." This
building was used for years by the legislature of the territory, as they had no other convenient place; so you see it

was law through the week, and gospel on the Sabbath, and in a qualified sense, it might have been said, "Justice and mercy met there and embraced." The conference session was a pleasant one, and it may be of interest to our brethren of the present day to know the names of the men that composed the original Iowa conference at this time. I give them from memory, inasmuch as we have no minutes from that body in 1845. Here is a list of the names: H. W. Reed, Samuel Clark, Joseph Kirkpatrick, John Hayden, Joel Arrington, I. I. Stewart, A. Coleman, Wm. Hurlburt, Wm. Simpson, J. B. Hardy, Milton Jameson, David Worthington, E. S. Norris, G. B. Bowman, L. B. Dennis, U. Ferree, Thomas Kirkpatrick, and Moses F. Shinn. Rev. Joel B. Taylor, as well as some others, was not yet admitted into conference. As I depend altogether upon my memory, having no memoranda, I may have omitted some name. This was the little host who represented the interests of the M. E. church during that fall west of the Mississippi. Rev. Joseph Kirkpatrick having transferred to the Rock River conference at this session, reduced the number to about sixteen. There were about twenty-five received on trial at this time, and all that remain of them in Iowa, to my knowledge, in 1881 (including the writer), are John Harris and Michael See, members of the Iowa conference. Rev. J. W. Brier is still living, somewhere in California. This is what time does in sifting, testing, and disposing of its laborers, and in a few more years that little company of about forty-five who went out from Burlington into different fields of labor to do work for God will be sharing the rewards of that toil, where tempests will not drive, and where sickness will not blast. But as I have rather transcended the bounds of the historian by looking into the future, I will return to the conference still in session. Among our visiting brethren was Richard Haney and Rev. Tippett. Brother Haney preached a very interesting sermon from "God forbid that I should glory save in the cross of the Lord Jesus Christ." The outlines were

about as follows: "If any man, St. Paul might have gloried:
1. In his intellectual attainments. 2. In his knowledge and
conformity to the Jewish law. 3. In his spiritual gifts. 4.
In his citizenship. 5. In the abundance of revelations.
But he gloried in the cross of Christ. When speaking of his
citizenship, he stated that one reason why he cautioned his
son Timothy not to forget his cloak, left at Troas, was, that
it was the *token* of his *citizenship*." I thought then, and still
think, that the statement was more beautiful than true. I
should sooner suspect the "parchments" which he empha-
sized than the "cloak." The Sabbath of the session is now
past, business is now finished, the last prayer is offered up,
and here we are sitting to hear the reading of our appointments. What an interest and suspense hang upon a few
minutes' reading. It was so then, but in this age of progress
most every one knows his field of labor before they are read.
Perhaps this is best, but it takes away all the luxury of the
surprise. In the division of labor for this year I was appointed to Mt. Pleasant circuit, with Wm. Simpson in charge.
He had served the church on this circuit the previous year,
and now we unite our strength for the year to come. As I
came within about five miles of the village, I ascended a
little bluff, so common on the prairies, and here in *full
view* was the flourishing town and surrounding country. I
stopped my horse in order to take a brief survey, and enter
upon a few minutes' reflection like this: "Before me lies
the beautiful country over which I am to travel the coming
year, and there live the souls that I am sent to benefit. The
character which I am to make in this new country will last
whilst history has a page and Christ has a church." Then I
asked my divine Master for a *pledge* to my success, when it
came in the *freedom* and *fullness* of his love. I was completely melted down into tenderness and filled with grateful
joy in the assurance that my labors would be blessed of the
Lord. With this divine assurance I made my way to Mt.
Pleasant, where I met with a warm reception from the

brethren who had been anxiously looking for my arrival, and was now ready to minister to them in things pertaining to the spiritual life.

CHAPTER XI.

My arrival in Mt. Pleasant was on the Sabbath. I listened to a very good sermon in the morning from a Baptist minister, who announced my appointment, when at three P. M. I stood before the audience to deliver my first message. I selected for my scripture: "Then were the disciples glad when they saw the Lord." The manifestation of the Spirit was such that all present felt its power, and Rev. A. J. Heustis, the president of the college, became so happy that he praised God aloud. I think it quite important in our introduction to a new charge, especially a stranger, to make a good impression in our first sermon, but if I had any *sugar-sticks* I would rather reserve them for future use; for in ministerial progress it is much easier to begin at the foot of the hill and climb upward, than to commence at its summit and incline downward. I have known a few such cases in my ministerial history, and in one the preacher was never able to conquer the reaction. This sermon was preached at camp-meeting, where the religious interest was high, and of course he must give them his best. The people were so delighted with the sermon that they requested the presiding elder to have him sent to their circuit. Being on the way to conference, the request was honored, and he was appointed their pastor. But, oh what a difference between his sermons *now* and at camp-meeting! There is no resemblance. They are disappointed, and he is mortified, and at the end of six months, by request of the quarterly conference, he was removed, paying him in full for the year. And thus I would say to my younger brethren in the work: "Beware of sugar-sticks, unless you know just where our people need sweetening."

Mount Pleasant, my home for this year, was a pleasant village of seven or eight hundred inhabitants. It was here that the Iowa seminary, as it was then called, was located, with Rev. A. J. Huestis as principal, which has since grown up into the "Iowa Wesleyan university," and bids fair to stand eventually alongside of· the first institutions of learning. From a small village the place has continued to prosper until it has reached a population of about six thousand, and still looks forward to a brighter future. A large proportion of the citizens of Mt. Pleasant being recently from Ohio, I felt much at home among them. Brother Simpson, my colleague, gave me a warm reception and adopted me as a fellow-laborer into his family during the year. He was of Irish descent, six feet and two inches in height, of a warm, impulsive nature, and a *fast*, unfailing friend. In his early days he enjoyed no advantages for an education, but had learned to read and write in connection with ·his preparation for the ministry. By dint of close application to study, and an intelligent companion to assist him, at this date he managed the English language very well, and was acceptable and useful on this charge. In the early part of this year the principal of the institution of learning and myself entered into an arrangement which I could commend to all others occupying a similar position. We agreed through the year to criticise each other after our pulpit efforts, for our mutual benefit. If either erred in pronunciation, or in doctrine, at our first interview we agreed to call it up and correct it; and thus we continued our *friendly criticisms* through the year, greatly to our advantage. In no one year of my ministerial labors have I received so much benefit in correct pronunciation as this, growing out of our mutual aid society.

The first week after my arrival was taken up in visiting the friends, and in adopting plans for the year; but as Saturday arrived, I mounted my horse and started for my work on the Sabbath. I was informed that it was fifteen miles

5

to my place of destination, and that my way was through
"Jefferson City," about eight miles on my road. Having
passed over the eight miles, as I supposed—for prairie miles
are very long ones—I began to inquire about Jefferson City.
"Two miles," said one; and hopefully I plodded on. The
next one I met, I repeated the question: "How far to Jefferson City?" "Three-fourths of a mile, sir;" and on I went
with renewed speed. Having measured the distance, as I
supposed, I met a boy on the road. I said to him, "My
boy, how far is it to Jefferson City?" He looked a little
surprised, and answered: "Sir, you are right in the midst
of it." This was my first introduction to a Western city.
It consisted of one log-house and a stable, and all the rest
belonged to Shakespeare's "baseless fabric of a vision."
After viewing the spot where the city might have been, I
proceeded to the place of my appointment. I was favored
with four earnest hearers, and after the sermon they informed me that sickness in the neighborhood was the cause
of the small attendance, and wished me to go *at once* and
visit Sister Livermore, the wife of the class-leader, who was
very low. I honored their request, and found her apparently very near home. As I conversed and prayed with
her and the family, I found her ready and waiting. She
seemed to be on the very borders of the good land. I have
looked upon many calm and happy faces in sickness, but I
think I never saw one that appeared more heavenly than
hers. I left, with the promise that if she recovered her
health in four weeks, I would repeat the visit and put up
with them for the night. As I left, I thought how privileged is the Christian. Here is that lady, more than one
thousand miles from her native home, with but little of this
world, and yet in possession of a treasure which enables her
to rise above the weakness of the body, bid defiance to
death itself, and raise the notes of victory in the certain
prospect of a better home. What theme more inspiring to
the faithful laborer, and what motive more elevating and

sublime. As I came round in four weeks her health had greatly improved, and I found her, as I expected, one of those Christian ladies who had been blessed with a good home, and favored in early life with good society. During my stay I obtained a short sketch of her early life, and the circumstances which led to her conversion. They are so remarkable and interesting that I am sure I cannot entertain my readers any better than to give the outlines as she gave them to me.

She was raised near Binghamton, in the state of New York. Her father's name was Pease. Being in good circumstances, and under no religious restraint, she, with others, as they grew up, became very fond of dancing; and being a kind of leader among the young people, of course she must be present and lead the way. At the age of fifteen, in company with a cousin of the same age, as they were engaged in making their dresses for the Fourth of July, they were arrested, both at the same time, by the *peculiar sound* in drawing their thread through the cloth. Each stitch seemed to say: "*It is the last.*" The impression was so strong—and equally so with both—that they suspended their work about nine o'clock in the evening and retired to rest, *but not to sleep.* The unseen Messenger divine had undertaken an important work, and all through the night his whisperings seemed to say: "This is the way that leads to death." Morning came, but the work of preparing for the dance was laid aside; and soon it was known through all the circle of their youthful friends that the Miss Peases had decided not to attend the coming ball. The cry of *turning Methodists* was raised and circulated through the community; but they had settled the question on that memorable night, and no taunts nor persuasions could turn them from their purpose. The fourth of July came, the ball went off, but they did not attend. But a new trial was to come. The uncle of these ladies, chagrined at the defeat, determined to recover lost ground if *possible*, and so he laid his plan in order to deceive and decoy them. The plan was this: To request Miss Pease, the subject of our sketch, to spend one or two weeks at his house, assisting in making up some garments for the family, during which time a pleasure party would be given, and in this way carry out their plans with success. True to the arrangement, the whole programme was faithfully executed, and the day of the select party was near at hand. The morning previous, however, the cousin alluded to came over to spend the day with her, and to fortify each other for the coming trial. The better to carry out their purposes, in the afternoon they took a walk out into the grove in order to implore divine aid, and make the final resolve what course to pursue in the coming dance. It was this: Knowing that they would be selected, as usual, to lead off on the morrow, that when the fiddler announced that he was ready, instead of danc- ing, they would drop on their knees and *pray* with all the fervency of spirit within their power, and depend upon God for results. Well, the day came, bright and cheerful; the company of about sixty met, and the hour of interest had arrived. As they had anticipated, they were the first ones led out upon the floor to head the dance. The eventful moment had arrived, and, standing there, awaiting the sig- nal, the *suspense was fearful*, and it seemed, said Mrs. Liver- more, "that I should *drop* in my tracks." But as it is said that "fortune favors the brave," more truthfully may it be said, "God honors the faithful." True to duty, as the fiddler announced that he was ready, those two young ladies of fifteen bowed in humble prayer. Shall I record the result? The transition from dancing to praying was *perfectly overwhelming*. Within a few minutes almost every person present was bowed before God in the attitude of prayer. The two young ladies were instantly converted; the sister of the proprietor of the house, an old backslider, was reclaimed, and went through the room shouting the praises of God. The fiddler struck the chest with his fiddle and broke it into pieces, and was soon converted, and the prayer-meeting lasted through the night, resulting in the salvation of about sixteen souls. But the good work did not stop here. It went on through the community for weeks to come, and resulted in the accession of sixty members to the church. Among the converts was Mr. Pease himself, who afterward became a local preacher in the M. E. church. Can the history of the church furnish any more true and noble example of youthful fidelity and heroic courage than is here presented by these two young ladies of fifteen? And oh, what a *precious crown* our divine Master will place upon their heads when he comes to make up his jewels. This was the sister whom I found so calm and so happy, looking into the face of death. Is it any wonder that a Christian, possessing such a spirit, triumphing over the enemy in the first conflict in early life, should raise the notes of victory as she came almost in sight of the promised land? These were some of the rich experiences which I now began to gather up in cultivating Immanuel's land; and though in this early history of my work in Iowa I could not look for much in the shape of dollars, yet the riches of divine grace in human hearts richly compensated for all that was lacking in temporal good.

After making one or two rounds on this circuit, and becoming acquainted with the people, I was brought to the knowledge of another fact. It is thought by many in the older states that the first settlers of a new country are a kind of uncultivated *border ruffians*, and that about any kind of preaching will do for them. But let me say, "Be not deceived." It is the last place, with my present experience, that I should search to find persons of this character. Instead of this, I can truthfully say that I never labored among a more refined, intelligent and enterprising people than I found in the first settlement of Iowa. The mistaken view that many in the older states entertain as to the privileges and character of Iowa in its early history is well ex-

pressed by a Methodist lady in love-feast at this date:
"When we concluded to leave Ohio for this new country,
the thoughts of leaving my old meeting-house and class that
I had enjoyed for so many years, and going to a place where
I should be deprived of them, I could hardly endure. But
we left and came determined to run the risk. When we
arrived it was all new, and our neighbors few. So we went
right to work putting up our cabin; and what do you think!
before it was *half finished,* here came along a Methodist
minister and put up with us, and before he left, preached
for us; and here we have had the same gospel, the same
Saviour, and the same saving grace that we enjoyed in my
old home." In fact it is this element of enterprise and real
worth which prompts them to launch out into the world in
order to do something for God and humanity, and the majority of the early emigrants to this territory and state,
though poor when they came, are now among the wealthiest
of the land. It is quite amusing, as you travel through the
state, to witness the memorials of gradation. On almost
every farm you will see them standing as follows: Cabin,
number *one;* improved, number *two;* and permanent building, number *three.* As a rule the crude ones are not destroyed. They are not preserved for ornament either, but
converted into practical use. The first is often used as a
crib or a stable, and the second for an agricultural or a wash
house; and beyond this, they stand as living memorials of
family history; reminding them how poor and humble they
once were, and now how comfortable and wealthy they
have become. There is another commendable element in a
new country—the acknowledged equality of the people. So
few there are who possess enough to be proud of, that, by
common consent, in aristocratic stock, they "share all
things in common;" and this spirit prevailing, the social
element is warm and friendly. In old settled communities,
the tendency is to "caste," to divide off into cliques, numbering from upper-tendom down to 0; but here every man

and woman stands at *par*, if their good sense and good behavior deserve it. The late Bishop Thomson remarked
" That it is said somewhere out West that they have an institution which goes by the *force of circumstances*." Had
the bishop passed through the experience of some of us
who have enjoyed the luxuries of a frontier life, he would
have found not *one*, but many such institutions; and it was
almost marvelous to see, in the case of an emergency, how
soon they could be got into active operation, and then how
self-adjusting they were. In the absence of flour, came on
the corn-dodger; when Rio ran out, we had our crust
coffee; and when our wells ran dry, we had the slough water.

> " In the absence of chairs we had puncheons for benches,
> And bedsteads were made without varnish or wrenches;
> But peaceful we slept, for angels in numbers
> Protected our dwelling and sweetened our slumbers."

So you see we had poets in those days, inspired by the
force of circumstances.

CHAPTER XII.

I must not forget, that at this date, Rev. Wm. Simpson
and myself are laboring pleasantly together on Mt. Pleasant
circuit, with Rev. Andrew Coleman* for our presiding elder.
Brother Coleman had been transferred from the Rock River
conference, stationed at Burlington the year previous, and
now in the fall of 1845 he was appointed to Burlington district. He was a very devoted minister of Christ, and in
some instances preached with great fervor and effect. He
was faithful and unswerving in that which he considered to
be his duty, and compromise was out of the question. He
was a man of deep devotion, communed much with God in
secret prayer, and was very conscientious in reading and

---

* Deceased a few weeks since.—L. T.

treasuring up the word of life. His sermons and prayers
all gave evidence that he had been with Jesus on the mount
of blessing and learned of him. After serving the church
as an effectual laborer for nearly half a century, he asked
for a superannuated relation, and is still living at Oskaloosa,
Iowa, in a good old age, ripe for heaven.

During the present year I formed the acquaintance of
Joel Arrington, I. I. Stewart, and L. B. Dennis, who were
among the first members of Iowa conference. Brother Arrington was short and fleshy, weight about two hundred and
twenty pounds, round face, a musical voice, and a ready
speaker. He was as fine a specimen of "Laugh and grow
fat" as I ever saw. Always genial and pleasant, he had a
little spice for almost every occasion, and carried sunshine
wherever he went. Being stationed at Fort Madison, he
remarked that he was glad that his people had poor memories, for he had but twelve good sermons; so that when the
last was preached he began the second series, and by so
doing he gave them "line upon line, and precept upon precept." But his labors soon closed. He was called away
right in the vigor of manhood to his Master's work in a
purer clime.

Rev. I. I. Stewart has been transferred also, but he lived
and labored many years after the death of Brother Arrington. He was a fine specimen of a Christian gentleman—
about medium height, fair complexion, frank and open
countenance, neat in his person, and of cheerful disposition.
His friends were many, and apparently his faults were few.
In preaching he spoke quite rapidly and smoothly, with a
pleasant voice and easy gestures, his theology sound and
sermons good. He served the church honorably and successfully; a portion of the time as presiding elder of the
district; afterward, as chaplain in the army of the Union;
when, his work being finished, he passed away from earth
supported by the consolations of that gospel which he had
preached to others. His remains are now reposing in the

beautiful cemetery at Mt. Pleasant, by the side of loved ones who had passed on before.

Rev. L. B. Dennis is still living and laboring in the state of Illinois; and labor he *will*, I think, until his divine Master tells him to stop. He is a complete embodiment of zeal and perseverance. His appointment to a charge is almost always the signal of a blessed revival, for he seldom fails. He stands about six feet high, straightly built, light complexion, and at this date his hair is perfectly white; walks with a quick *firm* step, as though he meant business. He is a fast friend, a genial companion, and a despiser of mean things. In preaching he sometimes reminds me of a friend in the Ohio conference, who used to say, in the warmth of his zeal in preaching: " Brethren, I will leave my logic at any time so that I can go out and catch a sinner." Brother Dennis labors for results. He is not so careful about his discourse being "*planed* and *grooved*" as he is that souls may be saved; and having this end in view, his exhortations are crowned with success. Not that he needs the skill in sermonizing, but he prefers the fire. As an evidence of the character of the man, a few years since his horse was stolen. He pursued the thief night and day, leaving his aids behind him, until he recovered his horse and the thief was secured. "That Methodist preacher," said the thief, "would have followed me to perdition in order to secure his horse." May his days be many, and his end triumphant.

Thomas Kirkpatrick was another of those pioneers who came to Iowa in its early history in order to cultivate "Immanuel's lands." He was one of the original sixteen who met at Burlington, and for many years was a devoted and successful minister. He sat by my side when preaching the first sermon in the territory, and to this day I feel like returning him thanks for his encouraging responses to a stranger in a strange land. I am under the necessity of giving a limited sketch, as we were not intimately associated together in our labors. I can say this, however, that on some of his charges he was very successful, and he has made an honorable record in advancing the interests of the Redeemer's cause among men.

Perhaps no two men ever labored more harmoniously together than Brother Simpson and myself. The season for extra efforts came on, and the spirit of revival prevailed all over the circuit. As we had at that time but one chapel on our work, our meetings were held in private houses, and by scores sinners were saved and added to the church. In those days of simplicity it seemed much easier for seekers to enter into spiritual life than at the present day, for often the change took place in listening to the gospel's saving truths. I think that this readiness in accepting Christ was owing chiefly to the fact that there were not then so many influences at work to dissipate the mind and draw away the affections from God. In this age of inventions and progress it requires a vast amount of labor on the part of the church to remove obstructions, and counteract opposing influences, before we can put forth direct efforts with hopes of success. And especially is this the case with our young men who are drawn away into those haunts of vice. But at that time it was not an uncommon occurrence to see the altar crowded with young men, many of whom are now faithful heralds of the cross of Christ. At one of our appointments we were much annoyed with an old infidel by the name of Grimsby. He had taken great pains to secure all the books of that character which he could procure, and professed great knowledge and skill in quoting Volney, Payne, and Hume. He had succeeded in some of his attacks upon our young and inexperienced preachers previously, causing them to give up that appointment, and in poisoning the minds of the young men of the neighborhood. During the progress of our meeting, *surely enough*, here came the old champion to the meeting, loaded with books and papers, all ready for battle. The services ended for the hour, the old man remained for dinner, expecting a fine opportunity to demolish the whole Christian system at a blow. It was not long before he squared himself for my colleague, and opened his battery. The congregation, knowing the purpose for which he came, and having heard him again and again state that he could silence all the Methodist preachers of Iowa, remained in the room, awaiting the result. Not receiving much encouragement for an argument with Brother Simpson, he turned his attention to me. I first questioned him as to his authors—whether he had ever read Faber, Watson, Butler, and "Leslie's Short Method with the Deist," and Benjamin Franklin's letter to Thomas Payne when he was about to write his "Age of Reason." I then quoted from those authors, and inquired if he was familiar with them. To my astonishment, he was as ignorant as a child. After leading him on to the right point, I then turned upon him, charging him with the presumption of coming to our religious meeting to attack the truths of Christianity, when he acknowledged that he was not acquainted with the first evidence upon which they were based. This method of an aggressive warfare upon his skeptical tactics was altogether unexpected, and, the whole audience present acquiescing in his defeat, he gathered up his favorite volumes and left us in peaceful possession. This was a great victory in view of its effect upon the young people, and in its restraining influence in keeping him at home. There was universal joy and rejoicing among the people of the neighborhood over the result, and no one enjoyed it more than my colleague.

The winter passed away pleasantly and profitably, scores of souls were converted, and there seemed to be a general awakening all through the community. Our last interest was in the village of Mt. Pleasant, where, assisted by the presiding elder, the work went on gloriously. I must here record one circumstance which fully proves that "our sufficiency is of God." The good work was progressing finely, and souls were saved at every service. But the brethren thought that if the services of Brother Norris, stationed at Burlington, could be procured, wonders would be accomplished. Honoring their request, he was sent for, and he came in the assurance of success. His sermon, the first evening, was able and moving, and all the audience seemed to be affected; but when the invitation for seekers was given, not a soul moved, and all the urging afterward seemed to be unavailing. Finally, the meeting came to a full stop, and darkness seemed to shade all minds. Had it not been for the power and inspiration of song that some hopeful brother at that moment struck up in these words: "How tedious and tasteless the hours," etc., the enemy might have recorded the victory; but all uniting in that beautiful hymn, it seemed to relieve the embarrassment, and give us a show of success. I am aware that to feign a victory when we are really whipped does not secure many spoils, and yet in some instances it may deceive and retard the progress of the enemy, and encourage the hopeful to renewed efforts. Having stood a kind of leader of reserved forces on that memorable night, I can truly say, in the language of Napoleon, "A few such victories would have ruined us." Brother Norris preached the two evenings succeeding, and not a soul was converted whilst he remained; but as soon as he left for home, the interest revived and continued as usual. About this time the brethren of the charge seemed to wake up to the fact that they had been depending upon man for success, rather than upon God, and the failure was legibly written in results not to be misunderstood. How often, since that time, have I benefited by that item of history; and whilst an able minister in such a work is a great blessing, we are to be careful to remember that *he is able only* through the blessing of our divine Lord.

We were favored at this time with a case of sublime interest, showing the power of divine grace. One of our young converts, Sanders by name, with whom, a few evenings previous, the brethren had labored until midnight to secure his conversion, now lies at the point of death. His attack was sudden and fatal. When asked, in his last moments, if he feared to die, he answered: "How can I, when I see before me such a *great light!*" And now, having been just "translated out of darkness into the light and liberty of the sons of God" on earth, he is translated from the church militant to the church triumphant in heaven. Such witnesses to the truth of the gospel are not to be set aside. Having given my readers this beautiful incident in the case of this young convert, I will now furnish you with its contrast.

About the hour of midnight a messenger arrived at my lodging, requesting me to visit a sick man about eight miles out in the country. He wished me to come *at once*, as his case was a desperate one. I made no delay, but hastened to his residence as soon as possible. He was one of my hearers at church, and considered to be a good citizen, but he had been neglecting the great salvation; and now, at the age of fifty-four, he was suddenly called upon to look death in the face. As I witnessed his agony—more in mind than in body—my heart was moved within me. He was so honest to confess his failures and neglects, that if I could have secured the cup of salvation I would have pressed it to his lips. I presented the only remedy for a dying man— the promises of the Saviour, and his power to save to the uttermost and in the last moments of life. He acknowledged it all, but he met every motive by saying: "*It is too late!* The time was when I could have found pardon, but I have passed the time, and now I have no hope." I prayed with him, and still urged the mercies of Christ, but all to no purpose. I left him with feelings and impressions never realized before. Here he had lived and enjoyed all the means of grace for more than fifty years, convinced of sin and his obligations to God; and they were urged upon him through all of those years, and still he had neglected them, and hoped for a "more convenient season." And now, suddenly called to an account, all the comfort remaining to him is the conviction that "*It is too late !*" Let all who read this who are procrastinating their return to God profit by his sad history.

We have passed through some of the stirring scenes of revival interest during the winter, and now spring, with its sunshine and flowers, has come, and the voice, not of the turtle but of prairie-birds is heard in our land. One of the interesting events of this season was the arrival of the Rev. Alcinous Young, a transfer from the Pittsburg conference, with his family, who settled in Mt. Pleasant. He came with the intention of making Iowa his home. We found him and his family a valuable accession to our church, and his ministry was appreciated during the year. We shall have occasion to notice his character and work more extensively on some future page. The labors of the year wound up with a successful camp-meeting on the circuit, and the report of one hundred accessions to the M. E. church. Before taking leave of this charge, I must not omit to mention that the brethren and sisters were of that class who were ever ready to assist and encourage their ministers in every good work, and though, in that early history, they had but little means for their support, yet that *little* was more for them than hundreds at the present day. Among the many, I may mention the names of Brothers Kilpatrick, Bird, Rathbone, Rockhole, Rogers, Teas, McCoy, Snyder, and J. P. Grantham. Brother Grantham went to Mt. Pleasant in 1837; was county recorder eight years, clerk of the district court sixteen years, one term in the legislature, mayor of the city, and county judge, besides filling many other offices. In the church, he was honored with all he could carry and execute, and for the last twelve years he has occupied the position of clerk in the land office in the city of Washington. Some of these brethren above mentioned are still living, whilst others have passed on to their reward. My salary for this year's faithful service was thirty-five dollars.

CHAPTER XIII.

Our conference for this year (1846) held its session at Muscatine, Bishop Hamline presiding. Rev. H. W. Reed was elected secretary, and I was chosen his assistant. The bishop's method of transacting business was such that some of the members of the conference took exceptions, but they soon became convinced that he was right, and they were wrong. Having had some acquaintance with him in Ohio, his presence and superintendence were quite cheering to me in a land of strangers. He was not only a very able minister, but one of the most devoted in all the history of my acquaintance. I was present at Chillicothe, Ohio, when for the first time he witnessed *publicly* the power of Christ "to save from all sin," and I remember well the influence of that testimony in the morning love-feast. It was such as I have seldom witnessed, and in its moving effects seemed to sway all minds. To meet such a herald as this at our conference in Iowa, and to be privileged to enjoy the benefit of his counsels and example in my youth, was a great blessing; and how richly did I enjoy it. He said to us: "Young men, think not that with a little Greek or Latin you can go out into the world and convert sinners. If you expect success in this work, you must be baptized with the Holy Ghost." Some of us who listened to those moving words, went out, I think, from that Jerusalem "endowed with power from on high." We were favored with a pleasant and profitable session, and in the appointments I was assigned to Clear Creek mission in charge, and Rev. John Jay my assistant.

On my return to Mt. Pleasant, in company with Rev. Alcinous Young, now stationed at that place, we enjoyed a kind of episode whilst fording the Iowa river, more strange than edifying. In the middle of the stream our horse

choked down, by the pressure of the water, and having no
time to spare, I was under the necessity of leaping out into
three or four feet in depth, to save our animal from drown-
ing.   By the time I had relieved the pressure, the mercury
had gone down to *sober consideration*, but the success out
of our perilous position gave us such inspiration that I felt
like saying "None of these things move me;" and when I
considered that St. Paul had been a "day and a night in
the deep," I felt that a little water bath of this kind would
only steady my nerves and enrich my experience.   And so
I found it, for in a short time we were among kind friends
and seated by a comfortable fire, where the perils of waters
were forgotten, by the warming influence of a good supper
and a refreshing night's rest.   Having learned from Rev.
Wm. Hurlburt, who labored on Clear Creek the year previous, that the people were nearly all sick with chills and
fever, I remained on my old charge until the week following.   I mention this, it being the only instance during my
ministry in the state that I did not fill my appointment the
next Sabbath after I received it.   I was conscientious in
this, knowing that a charge suffers loss, and the minister
also, in being a long time reaching his work.   Reports are
afloat as to his ability; some ranging *too high*, and others
too low, so that it may require weeks to remedy them after
he reaches his work.   The best rule, *if possible*, is to carry
your own good qualities with you, and appear before them
in your own person at once.   This will remove the uneasi-
ness of suspense, and the occasion of any injurious reports
going before you in advance.   Well, the week following, I
left my former charge with the salutations and prayers
which generally attend separations of this kind, and especially so in the case of my colleague and his companion.
Such had been the harmony and attachment between us
that it seemed like the farewell of St. Paul from his brethren
at Ephesus; but duty called, and I started for my work, a
distance of sixty miles.   When I reached it, surely enough,

I found nearly all sick with the ague and fever, several families in some instances collected together in one, in order that there might be well persons enough to wait upon the sick. On my arrival I found Brother Jay, my colleague, at his post, ready for duty. Brother Jay had been raised a Quaker, but was now thoroughly converted to the doctrines and discipline of the M. E. church. He was one of those genial, hopeful spirits that took every event for the best as it came, and always looked on the brightest side. If matters at times looked a little gloomy, by some cheering remark and hearty laugh he would bring sunshine out of it if he could. If I entered his room when he was shaking with the ague, the first salutation would be a hearty laugh. To give my readers a more accurate idea of the man, at one of our camp-meetings, being very fond of singing, and anxious to see things move, he entered into a tent and began one of his favorite songs; but things did not move. He then went to another, and another, with the same results. Having nearly completed the circle of tents with no better success, he finally gave it up by saying: "Well, well, there is no use of trying to shout for a whole camp-meeting."

We arranged our work and entered upon its duties immediately. But few could attend worship, but we served these few, when in about two weeks I came down with the ague and fever. Had this been my first experience of the kind, I might have been greatly alarmed, but having become familiar with its onsets in Ohio, I was very well qualified to grapple with its strong arm. I soon checked its progress, but laboring in a malarial valley it soon returned, so that I could say with General Green, of the Revolution, whilst warring in the South: "I fight, get beaten, rise and fight again." In some instances, before my sermon was half through, I would feel the cold chills crawling up my back; then reach my next appointment at the height of a burning fever. But such inspiration did not furnish " thoughts that breathed and words that burned." But my appointments

. 6

were out and I must fill them. Our mission extended south into Washington county, and seventy-five miles north to Montezuma, and the regions around and beyond.

On my second round on this work I overtook a man whose countenance I thought I recognized, but I was not positive. I thus addressed him: "Stranger, I am inclined to think that I have seen you before." "Perhaps so," said he; "where are you from?" I answered "From Scioto county, Ohio, near Hanging Rock." Said he: "What is your name?" I gave it, and then I requested him to give me his. He did so, and what was my surprise to find my old friend and classmate of former years. I knew him well. Our first acquaintance was near Hanging Rock, Scioto county, Ohio, a short time after I united with the Methodist Episcopal church. We professed religion about the same time, and often did we meet in the same house of worship, and in the same class-room unite together in singing the songs of Zion and in relating our Christian experience. Our acquaintance continued for some years in Ohio, until after he became a licensed exhorter. A short time after this he moved to the West, but as to the place of his destination I was not informed. But well do I recollect the many expressions of solicitude for his welfare in a strange land. Several years had now passed and I had heard nothing concerning him until the present interview. My heart began to swell with warm emotion as I grasped his hand, in the thought that I had met an old acquaintance, and, as I supposed, a Christian brother, in a land of strangers. But my ardor was soon cooled as I inquired: "Brother B., how do you prosper in religion?" "Religion!" said he, "that is all nonsense; a delusion of the brain; mere animal excitement." "But," said I, "did you not once profess religion and shout aloud the praises of God, and did I not hear you say that you enjoyed such peace and happiness as the world could not give? And was not that the happiest part of your life?" He admitted it all, but still persisted in its being a delusion, using very profane and unbecoming language. I warned him of his danger. I entreated him to come back to the Saviour. I reminded him of those days when he enjoyed such heavenly communion in the house of God, and spoke so confidently of a blissful immortality beyond the grave. When I referred to the past it touched a tender cord, yet he made an effort to stand it out. Before I left him he invited me to visit his family, which I promised to do in four weeks, feeling that if it were possible to do him any good, I would spare no pains. The visit I made according to promise, and then I entreated him again. I reminded him of his family—his promising children—the influence he exerted—his welfare in time and eternity; but he seemed to turn a deaf ear. I bade him and his family adieu, and I never saw his face again. The nearest I came to it was to look upon his grave the day after he was buried. Shall I give an account of his death? My pen hesitates to write it. A few weeks after my visit he went to a liquor shop about eight miles distant, and whilst in company with an infidel companion of his, together blaspheming the name of God and ridiculing the Christian religion, they were both struck by lightning and sent into eternity in a moment! O, what a fearful death was this to die, with the words of bitter profanity upon his lips! those lips that a few years before had been employed in prayer and praise, but now forever sealed, ere the last curse had died away on mortal's ear. What a warning is this to backsliders; and how does it speak to professing Christians to shun the company of the wicked. A few weeks after his arrival in Keokuk county he handed in his letter, and for a time met with the people of God, but by associating with skeptical men his mind soon became poisoned, he was shorn of his strength, neglected his religious duties, became an infidel himself, and in the prime of life was cut off without a moment's warning. Had he been faithful, he might have been a blessing to the world and an ornament to the church — his earthly sun might have set radiant with the glories of a brighter day; but by forsaking God, all that remains is the record of his folly and his fearful fate.

The work of an itinerant is such, passing regularly around his field of labor, preaching sermons and leading class, that were it not for these striking instances of personal history, it would be hard to collect material for a biography; but favored with these, and the many incidents in our revival work, I am led to think that no class of men are so highly favored with rich and striking histories as the successful evangelist. As the winter season came on, the health of the community improved and our labors embraced the usual interests through this season of the year. I have already stated that our mission extended north to what is now Montezuma, but then it was a city only in name. A little later a young brother was sent to that circuit which embraced Montezuma, and in his revival notice to the *Western Advocate*, he stated that he had swept the city; that every man, woman and child had been converted. We learned about this time that the city contained *in all* but seven houses, and these were cabins, so that the taking of a city like this was not equal to "ruling his spirit." After this notice my good Brother Simpson always called him "Cortez," as he captured the great Montezuma. Nothing of unusual character transpired on our work until the return of the summer, when we began to enjoy some of the luxuries of a new mission. The first was on this wise:

A small colony settled this year on English river, a distance from us of about thirty miles. Some of the families being Methodists, they sent word to have us visit them, and, if expedient, form a class. We returned a favorable answer, and in the latter part of August, with horses and saddle-bags, started for the new settlement. There being no traveled road, we struck out into the open prairie in the direction of our destined place. It was a long and tedious

ride, but toward evening we saw signs of civilization in
reaching a little grove, and a few wandering cattle, and we
took courage. We arrived at Brother Rodman's, our stopping place, the sun about an hour high, tired and hungry.
As we rode up to the door of the house, Sister Rodman
came out and welcomed us to their cabin home with all the
warmth of a pioneer. But she remarked: "As glad as I
am to see you, we haven't a mouthful of anything to eat in
the house. My husband has gone to mill, about twenty-five
miles distant, and will not return until to-morrow." Rather
hard fare thought we who had been fasting all day; and
now for skill and courage to triumph over difficulties.
"Sister Rodman," said I, "you have corn in the field." She
answered "yes." "And an old milk pan that I can obtain?"
"Yes; one lying out yonder in the yard." "And cows
near by?" "Yes." "*Well, now for business.* Brother
Jay, you go and bring the corn. Sister Rodman, send
the boy after the cows, and you hang on the kettle and
boil the water, and we will have a *feast of fat things
after all.*"

Having secured a hammer and a nail, I went to work and
made the mill (grater), and by the time that my colleague
had arrived with the corn the mill was all ready for grind-
ing. Within a few minutes we had four or five quarts of
as nice meal as we ever saw. The pudding was soon made,
table set, and milk ready. But now there is another difficulty. Said the good sister, "We have but *one bowl* and
one spoon, having broken our dishes moving to Iowa."
"Never mind, we can manage *that*," said I. So, being
preacher in charge, I ate at the first table. Brother Jay
was a very pleasant and pliable man, but the severest test
of his patience, I think, during the year, was in waiting until
my bowl was empty; but the good time came, when he took
his turn at the second table. Had there not been mush in
abundance, there might have been grounds for fear at this
point, on the part of those coming after, but as we had laid

in a good supply, each one took his turn until the last child was satisfied, and some fragments remained. Whether this was the kind of table in the "wilderness" referred to by the psalmist, I am unable to tell; but one thing I know, that never was there a meal of mush and milk more heartily and gratefully enjoyed than *this*, though meted out in a single dish. In this service our visit was attended with a double benefit, not only in helping ourselves in this emergency, but in providing ample supplies for the family. And now the neighbors were called in to enjoy another kind of a feast; and though there was not much inspiration in a supper of milk to give elasticity to a sermon, yet the recent triumph which we had just enjoyed was better by far than any artificial stimulants. The text to suit this occasion was very appropriate: "The Lord is my Shepherd, I shall not want." Should I tell you that we had an old-fashioned Methodist meeting, I should be true to history, for our success in the unseen was equal to that of the visible and temporal. The next morning we were treated with some fine corn-bread, made from that same *mill;* when, all being in readiness, we started for home, exulting like St. Paul: "Poor, yet making many rich; having nothing, and yet possessing all things." Do you call these hardships? and do you wish to be excused from making such a history? You may do all this; but permit me to say these are the *rich spots* in the history of my life that ease and luxury could not purchase, and gold could not buy; and I doubt not, in the rewards of the better land, the Master will crown these with the richest estimate, and the highest honor.

CHAPTER XIV.

One of the greatest interests of the M. E. church in the United States, from its first organization, has been its camp-meetings. Thousands who would not attend divine service anywhere else would go to these gatherings in the grove where they knew they would not be restricted by walls or pews. And though they were induced to go through novelty or curiosity, yet, being placed under the influence of divine truth, they were arrested by the Holy Spirit, and returned home witnessing " what great things the Lord had done for them." How often have we heard in our meetings for religious testimony, one and another state that "at such a camp-meeting I was convicted for my sins, and sought and found the 'pearl of great price.'" Some of the brightest stars in our church are witnesses to such experiences. The late Bishop Thomson and Dr. Dempster were striking examples, with scores of others. And though they may furnish occasion for bad behavior on the part of some, yet *these persons* would not be doing any good elsewhere; so that these objections weigh but little in view of the great good accomplished. Toward the close of the summer we held such a meeting on our charge, which was attended with great interest and success. About thirty professed conversion, and the church was very much blessed. I must record a circumstance which took place at this meeting, for the benefit of young people. A very amiable young lady who had been accompanied to this place by her intended husband, became interested during the meeting and went to the altar for prayers. Having learned subsequently that he had been making light of the altar services, she gave him a gentle rebuke by permitting him to return home alone, and it was some little time before the matter was

reconciled. But it was finally adjusted, and I had the
pleasure of performing the marriage ceremony, and ultimately enjoying their hospitality in their own home, both
zealous and useful members of the church. I think they
are both living and faithful, and should they be permitted
to read this they will know what I mean, and appreciate
the history from their old pastor and friend. The firm stand
which this young lady maintained in this conscientious
step taken, raised her in the estimation of the community,
and I doubt not in that of her future husband. Nothing is
lost in doing right.

Not far from this time, by invitation, I attended a German camp-meeting on Dutch creek, within the bounds of
my circuit. It was conducted by Dr. Jacoby, the presiding
elder; and as many of my congregation were present, I was
requested to take part in the exercises. The services
progressed with interest until Sunday afternoon, when it
was known that efforts would be made by the *roughs* in the
vicinity to break up the evening meeting. For weeks, not
a drop of rain had fallen, and not a cloud to be seen above
the horizon indicating an approaching shower. But the
elder knew that some way must be devised to meet the
emergency, and that within a few hours, for the tokens of
war had become already visible. How many Methodist
ministers know something of the suspense between a good
meeting and the devil's parade on Sunday night. This was
his experience and his dread; but he concluded that the
power which brought the cloud out of the sea and watered
the land of Samaria was sufficient to secure victory to him in
this season of trial. Being thus assured, he resorted to
earnest prayer; beseeching God that he would send the
rain in such quantities that his enemies might be defeated
and his small church enjoy the benefit. Not a sign in the
heavens was visible until about six o'clock P. M., when at a
distance the lightning was seen, the distant thunder was
heard; the storm approached nearer and nearer, when,

shortly after the lamps were lighted, the shower came, and with it all of the gracious results asked for. I am reminded to this day of the inward satisfaction expressed by Brother Jacoby as the rowdies ran from tree to tree to find shelter, saying: " Don't you see them run?" And run *they did*, many of them until they reached home. The rain continued pouring until every tent was soaked and the camp-ground literally flooded with water. The young Arabs who had come out to disturb Israel were discomfited, and the surrounding country blessed with refreshing. The only reflection in this case was the *quantity* of rain which fell, amounting to a flood, even surpassing the expectations of the petitioner himself, furnishing additional material for the old lady who remarked " that rain was a very good thing, but these Methodists are always overdoing matters." I remained some two months on that mission after this event, laboring with the people; but the truth remained on their hearts, and with those who are living to this day, that *that* storm was sent of God in answer to the prayers of Elder Jacoby. Farewell, ye old veteran! You have now reached a land where enemies and storms cannot annoy— the home of that God who then protected you and who will be your portion forever. We have now reached a period in the history of this year's labors when we must bid adieu to Clear Creek mission with its many friends and stirring incidents, and repair to our conference, but not until I say that my salary for this year's labor was fifty dollars.

CHAPTER XV.

Our annual conference for this fall (1847) was held at
Mt. Pleasant, my former home. Bishop Waugh was with
us, and by his fatherly counsels and genial spirit endeared
himself to all of its members. Rev. H. W. Reed was
elected secretary and I was chosen as his assistant. We
had a very pleasant and profitable session; and especially
so to me, as I was among my old friends. This was our
first introduction to James W. Harlan, who had recently
graduated at Greencastle, Indiana, and came to Iowa with
the intention of making this his final home. His history is
so well-known in the state, as a public man, that it will be
unnecessary to extend it. On the Sabbath the bishop
preached a good practical sermon on the extension of
Christ's kingdom, and John T. Mitchell preached in the
afternoon. I think never, up to this date, had I felt such
an inexpressible desire for the salvation of souls; and I was
ready to go anywhere within the bounds of the conference,
so that I might accomplish this great work. Our session
closed on Monday, and I was appointed to Dubuque circuit,
my charge embracing the mining district where the "pure
waters flow." Elder H. W. Reed, residing within the
bounds of my circuit, conducted me to it and made me
welcome to his own home. The good friends on my former
charge had asked for my return with a strong petition to
the appointing power, but they thought it not best, in view
of my severe experience with the chills and fever. And
now located among warm friends, pure air, and clear water,
I soon felt like a new man, and was fully prepared for the
fall and winter campaign. I shall ever feel a debt of gratitude to Brother Reed for his influence at that time in
removing me from that sickly valley on the Skunk river
into a more healthy atmosphere.

Our first quarterly meeting came on within two weeks after reaching my new field of labor at Cook's chapel. Rev. George B. Bowman was presiding elder of Dubuque district. This was our first acquaintance, inasmuch as we had labored in different parts of the state. I found him true, kind and faithful, and never could I ask for a warmer friend. He was an embodiment of untiring energy and devotion to the work in which he was engaged, and he loved to have the preachers on his district profit by his example. He had a *full round* voice, and when fully interested in his sermon it became quite loud, and at our camp-meetings could have been heard nearly one mile. I have often thought that he could perform more pulpit work within the same time, taking into the account the amount of labor laid out, than any minister of my acquaintance; and his sermons and exhortations were oft-times attended with gracious results. On the Sabbath of this quarterly meeting above alluded to, he preached one hour and a half on the Coming Judgment. After service we went home with old Brother Houps, a Wesleyan from England. As dinner was preparing, the old brother accosted the elder thus: " Brother Bowman, what made you preach so long to day? Why, you preached one hour and a half!" "Was it that long?" inquired the elder. " Well, if I had attempted to shorten it, I should not have known which end to shorten." " Cut a piece off from both ends," said the Wesleyan, "and it will be long enough then." This dear brother had listened to the ministrations of the sainted Wesley. I need only to say that the counsel of Brother Houps was followed by a hearty laugh, which prepared us to relish a good dinner. Monday morning came, when the elder went home, and I continued the meeting during the week, which resulted in forty-four professed conversions and accessions to the church. During this week of revival I witnessed a very touching scene. A promising young man came forward to the altar, and after a long struggle came out into spiritual light, and a happier man, appaently, I never witnessed. In the midst of his unbounded joy he thought of his unconverted mother. He made his way down the aisle after her, but she saw him coming, and started for the door. Passing out into the dark, his mother a little in the advance, he cried out: " O mother, *how can I give you up!*" but she hastened home and eluded the pursuer. This is a striking proof of the power of divine love in the human heart when made a partaker of God's grace, and in perfect harmony with the language of our Saviour: "There is joy in heaven over one sinner that repenteth."

It is interesting to witness in such a work of divine grace as this, its influence in different directions. Truly, "Godliness is profitable unto all things." Some old grudges of long-standing were removed, and the chapel, having stood for years about half finished, was completed within a short time. Yea, "The wilderness and solitary places became glad, and the desert rejoiced and blossomed like the rose." Not having been favored with a revival of religion on this charge for several years, and this one being so remarkable, it stirred up the community for miles around, and its influence extended into the city of Dubuque. Rev. E. S. Norris being stationed in that city engaged my services for one week, promising to assist me in return. The meeting commenced in a mining district, about two miles from the city, now called Rockdale, and the same results attended it, even at the first service. Ten were forward for prayers, and the power of the Spirit was manifest. On Monday evening the interest was still greater. Sixteen were at the altar, and after a short season of prayer, they all rose to their feet *at the same moment of time* soundly converted. But what was still more remarkable, for three successive evenings the same number were forward, and on each evening all were converted at the *same moment* of time. This was the most striking manifestation of divine power ever witnessed by any one present, and it seemed to carry everything before it. The revival services lasted eight days, and the pastor reported seventy-five saved and added to the church.

The awakening was now such that it commenced in different places on my circuit and bid fair to sweep in its influence my entire charge. Such was its prevalence, that for five months I was constantly in the work of laboring to save souls night and day. I was astonished, as well as my friends, that I had strength and vigor to labor during that time without breaking down; but the Holy Spirit that created the necessity strengthened and inspired me and brought me out unharmed. There was one little drawback, however, in my physical man, owing to constant change in my sleeping apartments, which brought on the inflammatory rheumatism, so painful that in some instances I required help to get on and off from my horse, and in the greatest religious interest I was under the necessity of standing on one foot whilst presenting the glorious message of salvation. But I could well endure a little bodily suffering that I might witness the escape of scores from the death that never dies. How little this world looked to me at this time, except as a short stopping-place, to qualify for a higher and holier destiny beyond, and in my sleeping hours, often would I awake and find my soul soaring around the borders of the land of pure delight. These are some of the first fruits gathered by the faithful laborer, and they indicate unmistakably the character of his coming reward. At one of our meetings I witnessed a rare occurrence. Two aged persons came forward as seekers, one of them seventy-five and the other over eighty years of age. What a sight to witness! two such men, standing upon the edge of time, pleading for the pledge of life eternal! They had been spared to live through more than three generations without God and without grace, and now, just ready to depart, they ask for mercy to prepare them for their final passage.

> " Depth of mercy, can there be
> *Mercy still reserved* for me?"

Yes; there was mercy even for them, and within a short time they could realize

"The clouds disperse, the light appears;
My sins are all forgiven;
Triumphant grace hath quelled my fears.
Roll on, ye suns, fly swift, ye years,
I'm on my way to heaven."

One of these *old* ·young converts had been for many years a soldier in the army of Wellington, and in almost every expression he would use military terms. As he arose from his seat, filled with praise and gratitude to God for his wondrous love, he remarked: "My friends, this is not a *forlorn hope.* I have been in a great many dangerous places, fought in many battles, rejoiced in many victories, but I have never before met such an enemy and gained such a victory as this to-night; and no reinforcements of the enemy shall wrest it out of my hand. The Lord of hosts is with us; the God of Jacob is our refuge." It was perfectly thrilling to hear him use his patriotic phrases and then make scriptural applications. My memory fails in retaining them all, but does not fail in recording his final triumph. Within four months from the time that he stood at the divine altar inspiring our hearts with his clear testimony, I stood by the side of his coffin magnifying the grace that saved him, and proclaiming his final victory through faith in the blood of the Lamb.

And right at this point I had an experience so new to me, and yet so glorious in the outcome, that I will give it in brief for the benefit of my brethren in the ministry. At this place, where these two old veterans were saved, I appointed a meeting with the understanding that it should continue through the week. It began on Sunday and continued up to Thursday evening, and at every service many were forward for prayers. It seemed that there was so little faith in the church that we were at a stand-still and could go no further. I proposed, before the audience retired, that as many as would pledge themselves to spend the ensuing day (Friday) in fasting and in prayer until three o'clock P. M., for the success of our next service, *to rise up*, when nearly all in the house arose. This pledge was faithfully kept. The following evening I preached about twenty minutes, standing on one foot (being lame with the rheumatism), on the excuses, and then invited seekers forward. Without any urging thirty came instantly—I think every unconverted person in the house *save one*,—and within ten minutes' time they were all on their feet adoring the Saviour for what he had done for them. The reason that this *one* did not go forward was this—he was the father of three little children, and they were present. Said the wife to her husband, " You hold the children until I go forward, and when I am saved I will hold.them for you." Accordingly she went, but soon I saw her returning with joy beaming from her countenance, and as she returned she exclaimed: "O, George, I have found Jesus; now I will hold the children, and you go and seek salvation, too." *No sooner said than done;* and in a short time he returned, also rejoicing in possession of the same treasure; and two happier persons I never looked upon. O, could you have looked into the eyes of those dear children, as their father and mother were rejoicing in their happy state, as I did, it would have touched the tenderest sensibilities of the soul. They seemed to say, anxiously and inquiringly: " Mother, is there not some of this left for me?" I am sure if Jesus had been there personally, as he stood before the multitude, he would have taken them up in his arms and blessed them, too.

There was present at the altar on this occasion an individual of much interest. His name was Loomis. He was reared among the respectable families of the city of New York, and his parents were members of the Methodist Episcopal church. He had passed from year to year through the most extensive and stirring revivals of that city, and was still unsaved. He had recently come to the mining regions

in hopes of securing a fortune, and was there at work when
he heard of this meeting. He had traveled several miles
that evening to reach it, and as he placed his hand on the
door-knob to enter, some passage of Scripture which I was
then quoting—I think this: "Behold, I stand at the door and
knock," reached his conscience, and as a consequence he
was first among the seekers, and among the first converted.
He remained with us during the year in church fellowship,
and was an honor to the society of which he was a member.
The last sinner present was now saved, and such a pentecost as followed is beyond all description. Every heart was
filled with gladness, and every tongue active proclaiming
the praises of the divine Master. We remained until near
eleven o'clock P. M., when we adjourned and repaired for
home to reflect upon Jesus' power to save, and his skill in
teaching us how immortal crowns are won. Brother and
Sister Nolon, whose hospitalities I shared that evening, still
cherish that season as one of the most remarkable in their
religious life. Two of the converts who embraced religion
at this revival, before the year was closed went home to
unite in singing redemption's song in heaven. This matter
of taking pledges from the members of the church, alluded
to above, should be very carefully guarded. There are
times and occasions like the one referred to, when they are
appropriate and necessary, but when of too frequent occurrence, they lose all of their virtue or binding force. I have
now in my mind a zealous minister who labored on a charge
to which I was afterward appointed, that had nearly worn
the brethren out with his call for pledges, and they had become a burden instead of a blessing. How much discretion
is needed in this work of saving souls. My interchange of
service with Rev. E. S. Norris, pastor in Dubuque city, was
pleasant and profitable. He was an able minister of the
New Testament, and earnestly devoted to his charge in
building up its spiritual interests. He preached at times
with great ability and effect, and was much beloved by his

people. In no work since my entrance into the ministry, had I noticed the practical effects of the Christian religion as I saw it here. Families which I had previously visited by invitation, where the good taste and sometimes the good appetite of the pastor were *severely tested*, after embracing religion were entirely changed. And why not? "If any man be in Christ, he is a new creature. *Old things* are passed away; behold, all things are become new." And here was proof at hand. Grace had not only changed the heart, but every interest about the house presented a different appearance; so much so, that one would be led to suppose that the whole premises had been converted to a new faith and a new life. This is what the Christian religion does for the human race. It not only lays the "rough paths of peevish nature even, and opens in each breast a little heaven, but by its transforming influence it changes old habits into new virtues, and causes the wilderness of sin to bud and blossom as the rose."

CHAPTER XVI.

In my last chapter I concluded with the marked change that godliness produces in the practical affairs of life. I now present *altogether* a new item of history. During my first year on this circuit, I took in a new appointment, and formed a very prosperous class. The leader being a Wesleyan, recently from England, and well instructed in all the interests of the church, made my visits to that place both profitable and pleasant. It is well known, however, that our Methodist brethren who come from the old country are not so careful, as a rule, in relation to their temperance habits, as the Americans. This was the case here, and I did what I could to correct it. Meanwhile we had been favored with a large accession of young converts, and a

7

growing interest at every service. As I was on my way to preach to them the day previous, I was informed that the class-leader had purchased a barrel of liquor since my last appointment, that many members of the church had been intoxicated, and that it was spreading havoc through the community generally. At first I could not credit it; but having been fully confirmed, I was filled with surprise and a kind of indignation to think that a work of such promise, and to accomplish which I had expended so much labor, should be blasted in a day, and that through the influence of liquor. On Monday evening, as usual, I went to the place of preaching as though nothing had happened. The congregation gathered; but oh, what a change! The spirit was there, but it was the spirit of whisky; and, like Egyptian darkness, it could be *felt* as well as *smelt*. I selected a text for the occasion that had edge as well as point, for I was conscious that I should need both in order to do justice to my audience. It was the language of Samuel to Saul, who had been sent to Amalek to destroy the city and everything connected with it, but had disobeyed God's commandment by saving the life of the king, and the best of the sheep and the oxen. On his return home, he was met by the old prophet, whom he addressed as follows: "Blessed be thou of the Lord; I have performed the commandment of the Lord." And Samuel said: "What meanest then this bleating of the sheep in mine ears, and the lowing of the oxen which I hear?" This last scripture was my text. I proceeded to show how God had honored Saul by raising him from his low estate to that of being king over Israel; how his enemies had been subdued before him, and nothing was in the way of his elevation to the highest position among men.

I then gave some of his commendable characteristics, his prompt obedience in starting out, his undoubted courage, and his ultimate repentance. Then the nature of his crime and his miserable apology. First, he attested his innocence when Samuel visited him, before he was pronounced guilty, with flattery and deception. Further, he laid the blame upon the people; and as if to palliate the crime of disloyalty to God, he proposed to offer them as sacrifices to the Lord. Then I dwelt upon the final result; which was his degradation and death. Then came on the application. In this I reminded them how highly they had been favored all their lives with the teaching and salutary influences of the gospel; and especially so *recently*, in raising up a large class of professed Christians, where a short time previous no herald's voice proclaiming salvation had been heard, or the songs of Zion sung; and how the Lord had prospered them spiritually and was ready to prosper them more. I referred to the fact that the pastor's reception among them had always been of the heartiest kind. They were ever ready to welcome him with the salutation "Blessed be thou of the Lord," and the leader to report favorably as to the spiritual condition of the membership. How reciprocal was the welcome, and how I rejoiced to hear it. "But how is it now? What is the spiritual record to-night? Has Christ been honored and his word obeyed? If so, what means this *barrel of whisky* under the bed, and these *smelling bottles* all through the audience? Are these evidences of spiritual prosperity and growth in grace?" Never had I preached and never had they listened to such a sermon before. Nathan had visited David, and with his finger pointed exclaimed "*Thou art the man!*" Had there been at that moment a clap of thunder, I am satisfied that it would not have startled and surprised the audience more than this. No responsive amens, no hallelujahs followed, but one *solemn silence* seemed to say: "Lord, I have sinned and done this evil in thy sight." This faithful message had performed its work. The next morning the leader made a hearty confession, promised amendment, rolled out the barrel of liquor into the street, knocked in the head, and the last of its stimulating qualities sank away into mother earth. But the work of that week could never be undone. Its shameful record had passed into history, and even an angel's hand could not wipe out the blot. And there it will stand as a part of earth's doings until eternal interests shall be substituted for time. The facts above related were sufficient to satisfy all parties, and no experience of this kind was repeated during my labors upon the charge. A chapel was subsequently built near the scene of interest, and stands to this day as a memorial of battles fought and victories won; and I doubt not that when the Master comes to gather up his own, some precious jewels will hail from the neighborhood of R's chapel.

I have already referred to the variety of subjects and incidents which come within the sphere of ministerial experience. Within the bounds of this work an excellent brother was always present at preaching, and took his seat in the " amen corner." The programme was so well laid out and so faithfully kept, that I knew just what to expect. About fifteen or twenty minutes of the sermon was employed in nodding and snoring, until the minister became fully engaged, when all at once he would awake and begin to praise the Lord as if warmed up under the inspiration of divine truth. I never blamed him for gratitude to God in enjoying a good nap, but for his pretensions of getting very happy under the discourse, when everybody knew that he had been fast asleep. The shout would have come in with better grace had it been an intelligent one. I suppose that I could have obviated the difficulty for the time being had I taken for my text: " What meanest thou, O sleeper!" or pursued the course of one laboring near me, in a hot day in June. Discovering many of his congregation asleep, he paused in his sermon and remarked: " We will change the order of exercises for a short time, for the especial benefit of those who are asleep. We will sing one

or two verses of a hymn, and for convenience sake we will
line it, that you may all sing." He began as follows:

> " My drowsy powers, why sleep ye so?
> Awake, my sluggish soul!
> Nothing hath half thy work to do.
> *Yet nothing 's half so dull.*"

The second stanza was not needed, for the first was not
finished before every one was wide awake and ready to hear
the remaining part of the discourse. I recollect in one
instance, having reached a new charge, one of my most influential members came to me before preaching and remarked:
" Brother Taylor, you must not be afflicted if you see me
asleep during services, for it is a constitutional difficulty,
and it would be the same if I were listening to Bishop
Bascom." And I doubt not whilst we have to contend
with frail bodies and a sluggish atmosphere, we shall need
grace to endure this infirmity, and have abundant reasons
to be thankful that they are sleepers *merely* and not dis-
pensers of T. J. both at the same time.

About this time my attention was called to another subject. Having lost in Ohio, by the failure of the company
for which I was engaged, all I had to depend upon, I
arrived in the territory with but very little means. Receiving but eighty-five dollars for the services of the two past
years, I had but little to expend in making provision for
the future. And yet I considered it a religious duty to do
all that I could for those depending upon me, and for my
own support in the failure of my health or the decline of
life. Though I was young, I had already known quite a
number of Methodist ministers whose health had failed, left
without support, and had to depend upon their own feeble
exertions and the charities of the church. Fully realizing
this, every dollar which I could spare was laid out in the
purchase of a little piece of land in a good locality which I
knew would be valuable at some future day. And thus I
saved and economized until I was the owner of about four

hundred acres, part in Muscatine and part in Dubuque
county, which I afterwards sold at a good profit; and in this
way I was soon above embarrassment, and had something
besides to assist my friends and the cause of Christ. I
have ever recognized the blessing of God in enabling me
to secure temporal good—seemingly without much effort
on my part—as in any other department of Christian work,
my faith fully embracing the promise of Jesus, that if we
"Seek first the kingdom of God and his righteousness, all
other things will be added." Such has been my faith and
such has been my portion. And now in the sixty-ninth
year of my natural life, I can gratefully say, "The Lord
is my Shepherd, I shall not want. He maketh me to lie
down in green pastures, he leadeth me by the side of still
waters;" and in looking into the future, I can with confidence exclaim: "Surely goodness and mercy *shall follow*
me all the days of my life, and I shall abide in the house of
the Lord forever."

During the great spiritual interests of this year, I was
occasionally favored with the visits of Elder H. W. Reed,
who was now in charge of Iowa City district. His visits
were always welcome and his services always appreciated
on this circuit where his family resided. He was originally
a member of the Rock River conference, and in this relation was stationed two years in Dubuque city. In its
division, he was appointed to Iowa, presiding elder of
Dubuque district, which position he held when I first formed
his acquaintance. As he is still living and laboring in Kansas, I must be careful how and what I write. For several
years he was the standing secretary of the conference, and
constantly in the district work. He was of medium size, had
a pleasant but not very strong voice, was clear-headed, *far-
seeing*, a good student, an able preacher, and an efficient presiding elder. He was also very kind-hearted, a fast friend,
and very popular with the preachers on his charge, and in
the conference generally. Being intimately associated with

him for several years, living within the bounds of my work, as well as his assistant secretary, I had a fine opportunity of becoming acquainted with him. His sermons were practical and interesting, having something new to present in almost every subject. His powers of amplification belonged only to himself. Oftentimes as I listened to him when seeming to have finished the proposition, he would sally out anew, and present some peculiar phase of the subject which I had never thought of. Upon one occasion, having invited him to preach for me, just after a church trial of two or three members of my charge, prosecuted and conducted by a local preacher in the community, he took for his text, James v. 20: " Let him know that he which converteth the sinner from the error of his way shall save a soul from death, and shall hide a multitude of sins." It was truly a masterly effort. When dwelling upon the nobleness and grandeur of converting the sinner from the error of his way, and saving a soul from death, his description of this work was sublime. But when he drew the contrast—how unmanly, low, and mean, and even *fiendish* it was to use every effort to *destroy* a soul, and that oft-times to gratify some old grudge, or to carry out some unreasonable prejudice, he gave such a portrait that no one could help seeing it. The advocate listened as interestedly as though the original of the picture had not been present, but the flashes of divine truth were so numerous and forcible that my sympathies began to run out toward the lawyer instead of the prisoners; and I was not quite certain but the pastor himself was included for entertaining the charge. The matter, however, was satisfactorily adjusted and the end was peace. But at our annual conferences, in some instances, when some of our young " *sprigs* " were wont to criticise his movements or opinions, it was really amusing to see how soon their laurels would be changed into willows. Upon one occasion a brother arose and charged the elder with being guilty—" not of open-handed

accusation which could be met in an honorable way—steel
answering to steel—but a kind of hypocritical dissembling,
that of whispering a man's character to death without his
being able to make a show of defense." He concluded by
saying "that he did not wish *to die in that way.*" The
elder listened very calmly until his speech was ended, then
he arose and remarked " That he was at a loss to know
what the brother was driving at; that he was not aware
until then that his character had been arrested and passed
through such a *trying ordeal;* that he had not heard of the
decease of any one's character *in that way;* but that if *his*
condition was dangerous, and death probable, he would
advise him to go to work and *make such a character* that it
could not be whispered to death;" concluding his remarks
about in this way: that it was a little suspicious touching
the real value of a man's character, to see it die so easy
a death. My readers will not be surprised when I inform
them that this short speech put a quietus upon the logic of
the young man eloquent, and it was the last time that he
ventured to criticise the "old chief." This last title—" the
old chief "—the elder secured by being sent by the government as agent of the Black Foot Indians, where he
remained for some length of time. In this position, like
all others in which he had been placed, he acquitted himself
with honor, several times having been elected delegate to
General Conference; and though at this date, like the writer,
the "Almond tree" is in blossom, I doubt not but that
his virtues, even in old age, will shine on increasingly unto
the perfect day.

But let me turn aside for a few moments from my narrative and examine this memorial. It is a letter just received
from a dear friend residing in Winona, Minn., with words
of encouragement and gladness that I have decided to write
up the history of my life and labors. You will recollect
that upon a former page I spoke of a gracious revival at
Rockdale, near the city of Dubuque, where sixteen were

converted during four successive nights. Among that number of sixteen, I think on Wednesday night, there stood a promising youth of light complexion, about twelve years of age, his countenance radiant with divine light, rejoicing in the assurance of life eternal. As he was quite young, and low in stature, he was easily singled out from all the rest. That youth went out from that consecrated altar within a few years to engage in the duties and meet the responsibilities of life. The church, in its wisdom, set him right to work, and at the early age of thirteen he was elected Sunday-school librarian, and when fifteen years of age recording steward for the charge to which he belonged. At the age of seventeen he was the employee of Rev. E. S. Norris, and stretched the first chain on the government surveys in Minnesota west of the Mississippi river. Upon the resignation of E. S. Norris the contract was turned over to him, and for more than two years, with twenty-six men engaged under his control, the Sabbath was sacredly kept, not a drop of liquor was used, neither profanity nor card playing allowed. Such a surveying record as this it is a pleasure to record. In 1856 he settled in Winona, then a small village, commenced the study of law, and for a time engaged in the land business and in the loaning of money. About this date he was appointed class-leader and Sunday-school superintendent in First church, Winona, which office he has held for twenty-five years. In the years of 1865 and 1866 he filled the office of state senator, and was for many years president of the Normal school board, which includes three state normal schools, which position he fills at the present time. To sum it all up: In every interest pertaining to the growth and prosperity of the city, and especially the interests of the church, he has been in the front ranks. From a handful, when he settled in the city, the M. E. church now numbers about six hundred members, with seven hundred children in their Sunday-schools; and from a little village, the city contains a population of ten thousand. Thus I have given my readers a short and imperfect sketch of the history of *that boy* who stood among the converts in Rockdale in November, 1847—now Hon. Thomas Simpson, one of the first men in Winona, Minn. In the winter of 1875 I paid him a visit as conference evangelist, when I had the pleasure of a reunion of old friendships and that of an acquaintance with his intelligent companion and interesting little household for more than two weeks. In my labors among that people, during my short sojourn, I still cherish the remembrance of their friendships and generosity with grateful pleasure, and, with very many others, hold dear in my memory and love Brother and Sister Gage, who were converted under my labors at Old Centenary, Dubuque, in the winter of 1855. How joyful will be our meeting as we join immortal hands on the heavenly shore!

Whilst traveling Dubuque circuit the second year, I enjoyed the privilege of visiting Brother Rowley, whose father and brother lived on Burlington circuit, Lawrence county, Ohio. I enjoyed with him a very pleasant season, and it seemed like meeting a former acquaintance. His aged father had just departed, which brings me to record my last visit to him and family before I emigrated West. Many interesting spots there are in personal history to which the mind will ever after refer with gratitude and delight, and such there are also in the history of the devoted Christian; and though age and infirmity come on, the mind may be enfeebled and the memory weakened, but the day of his conversion or sanctification remains so sweetly enclosed within, that the hand of weakness or decay can not disturb its calm repose. Delightfully indeed do I reflect upon this visit made to that old veteran of the Cross when traveling Burlington circuit. So exceedingly infirm was he (having attained the age of ninety-six years), that he was unable to distinguish his own children. But when I asked him if he knew the Saviour, immediately it touched a cord that seemed to vibrate backward to the vigorous days of youth. He

carried me, in his interesting relation, fifty or sixty years
through the history of the past to the day of his conversion.
He informed me that through that long and varied course
he had known the Saviour well, and up to that time he had
been a "friend that sticketh closer than a brother." He
then, by a sudden transition, took an upward flight toward
heaven. He spoke of a country where old age will not dim
the eye, and where the rush of numerous years will no more
affect the memory. He spoke of the crown of life, of a
glorified body, of happy society, the rapturous joys of
heaven, and the prospect of soon entering upon their enjoyment; and whilst I listened to his stirring relation, I was
constrained to say: "If such be the power and excellence
of religion, let me always enjoy it." Since then this venerable father has gone to rest. He finished, I am told, his
five score years, then closed his peaceful eyes amid the
brightening rays of eternal day. Many highly favored interviews have I enjoyed with Christians among the old and the
young; many have been the hours which have been spent
in holy converse; but never, I think, was I raised to a more
elevated view of the pure joys of the "Eden above," than
under that short but interesting sermon. I was forcibly reminded that whilst the "outward man is perishing, the inward man is renewed day by day," and though nearly lost
to earth, so far as it regards the body, the soul may be
gathering strength and preparing to fly away to its destined
home. Thirty-seven winters have passed since I bade adieu
to that good old man and the quiet vale in which he resided,
but still do I see his sightless eyeballs turned upward
toward heaven, the tears of grateful joy tracing the furrows
of his cheek; and still do I hear his shattered voice ex-
claiming, in the language of faith, "All the days of my appointed time will I wait till my change come." Labor is
still mine; and *gladly* will I labor in a cause which presents
such immortal beauties, and such undying glories. Yes,
labor is mine, whilst rest is his; but the day is not far dis-

tant when I shall meet him and many others with whom I have labored and rejoiced, in that pure clime where old things shall be done away, and all things new become.

CHAPTER XVII.

The labors of the past year on Dubuque circuit closed with an interesting camp-meeting in which the church was greatly blessed, but such had been the thorough work of grace in the community that not a soul was converted; yet there were about two hundred reported saved during the labors of the year. Our conference session this fall (1848) was held in the city of Dubuque, Bishop Morris presiding. Nothing of unusual occurrence took place during this session, save that the merits of secret societies were pretty well discussed, and a resolution offered and passed advising the members of the conference not to unite with them. This action having created some unpleasant feeling during the year, at the ensuing conference all restrictions were removed and peace fully restored. Joseph Brooks was elected secretary and served without any assistant. The bishop, on the Sabbath, preached one of his plain, practical sermons, but his theme I cannot call to mind. The appointments being read, I was returned to Dubuque circuit, as I expected, the quarterly conference requesting it, with my old presiding-elder Bowman. And now came on a new experience. I found it much easier to get the people converted than it was to have them "stay converted," and thus I labored hard in order to maintain the ground that I had gained. But the Lord was with us, and gave us during the second a very pleasant year. Rev. E. S. Norris was continued also in the city. About this date there was nothing more prolific of evil among the first settlers than the claim interest. Some would encircle too much land; one would invade the rights of another either by jumping or entering his claim; and thus for years the minister on the charge would have more difficulty with the brethren to adjust matters satisfactorily than in almost everything else. Then, again, in the matter of pre-empting, the law required a cabin to be built, and actual residence, in order to be entitled to its benefits. And such cabins were enough to amuse any one. They were often built with sticks, hardly of sufficient size for a man to lie down in to sleep during the night; no chinking nor plastering; and yet they called these cabins; and in one instance, I was told by one of our pioneers that he passed a man in the prairie, lying down in a barrel with his feet sticking out, and when asked what he was doing there, answered: "I am satisfying the pre-emption law." Then they would repair to the land office and affirm that they had filled its demands by actual residence. These were some of the drawbacks to a healthful state in the church during its first settlements, and it needed much grace and wisdom in order to satisfy all parties, and to preserve harmony and peace. After the usual labors of the winter were past, the elder requested me to visit Maquoketa and Dewitt, left vacant by their pastor, Rev. J. W. Brier, emigrating to California. This was the period (1849) when the great gold excitement broke out there, and very many went from Iowa to make a fortune in its golden sands. I was requested to remain over two Sabbaths, baptize the young converts and receive them into the church. Having passed the Sunday at the former place, on Monday I started for Dewitt, in company with Brother Cook. Reaching Dewitt, the friends gave me a warm reception, and after preaching on the Sabbath, I baptized a large number by immersion. It being in the spring season, the water was very cold and the service rather chilling to the subjects, and very much so to the administrator. In no one instance in my life did I realize the benefits of *skill* in this mode of baptism as in the present. Some of

the converts were of good size, and I needed the benefit of
all the wisdom in my possession in the *cold*, swift-running
water. As I had previously witnessed some narrow escapes
in this ceremony, by placing the subject *straight* with the
stream, and then raising him by main strength, when all
was ready I adopted this method: I asked the candidates
to kneel in the water; this covered most of their person;
then all I had to do was to immerse the head and shoulders.
But the *best of all* in this form, they are standing on their
feet, and spend no *time* in raising themselves out of the
water, and all the pastor has to do is to steady them. In
this way I can manage a person weighing three hundred as
well as one of ordinary size. I have given this method to
scores of ministers in Iowa, including a number of Baptists,
and I never found but one who had adopted this form; but
were very grateful for the information, and ever adopted it
afterwards. I give this what I call very *interesting item*
for the benefit of those ministers who are ignorant of its
value. However we may prefer other modes of baptism
rather than immersion, as a church we give the candidates
their choice. This being the case, we shall have this work
to do, and this method is such an improvement on the old
that I trust all Methodist ministers may adopt it both for
safety and convenience. My work being finished on this
charge, I returned home greatly enriched by many newly-
made friends and interesting experiences. I was favored
at this time with the assistance of three or four local
preachers on Dubuque circuit, who rendered me all the aid
within their power, viz: Simeon Clark, Richard Greenley, Ira
Stimson and Wm. Taylor. The last named was my brother,
recently from Ohio. And now, before taking leave of this
circuit, I must pause to return my heartfelt gratitude to
my divine Lord and Master for the health, the divine power
and success given me in this amazing work of grace. And
thankfully do I call to mind such names as these among the
laymen who took an active part in its accomplishment, viz:

Paul, Nolan, Cousin, Cook, Greenly, Taylor, Johnsons, Simpson, Raw, Houps, and very *many others* whose names are written in the "*Book of Life*," and I think of the hearty reception they will give me when I have said the last farewell to earth and greet them upon immortal shores.

CHAPTER XVIII.

Our annual conference this fall (1849) was held at Fort Madison, Bishop Janes presiding. I had the pleasure of his acquaintance for several days, as Elder Reed conveyed us with his carriage from his home through the state to the seat of conference. He preached twice for us by the way, once near Mt. Vernon, and again in Iowa City. The first from Romans xii. and 1: "I beseech you," etc.; and at Iowa City from Acts ix. 31: "Then had the churches," etc. They were excellent sermons, and it gratified the people very much to think that they had been privileged to listen to a bishop. Bishop Janes was a very pleasant traveling companion, very genial and sociable, and no unprofitable words ever came from his mouth. In every sense of the word he was a model bishop, and in all of his movements he magnified the grace of God. This was his first visit to our state, and in his short stay he endeared himself to the members of our conference and to the citizens of Fort Madison. His sermon on the Sabbath from "Who is this that cometh from Edom," etc., was one of great ability and power, and many of us yet living still remember its salutary effects. In the very height of feeling—all captivated by the power of divine truth, he exclaimed: "Brethren, will you ever again prefer philosophy to the glorious gospel of Jesus Christ!" In his address to the candidates for ordination, he made some telling remarks "Brethren," said he, "some ministers are expecting that their station will give them *character*, but I will tell you what is far better: labor to give *character* to your station. In the first you may fail, but in the other *never!*" Such words as these were words of wisdom, and though thirty-one years have fled since they were uttered, I can still see his piercing eye, and hear his shrill voice sowing seed for eternity. H. W. Reed was elected secretary at this session, with L. Taylor for his assistant. We were favored with a gracious religious influence during its continuance, and I think as " laborers with God" we went out to our charges with increased zeal and a higher spiritual life. In the distribution of labor at this conference I was appointed to Dubuque city, with Rev. John Harris, recently from England. Brother Harris was a fine preacher, with a musical voice, was a little cross-eyed, possessed a vivid imagination and was well read up in the history of the church. As there had existed some little difficulty in the city between the elder and stationed preacher, and this affecting other parties—both having their friends,—I did not consider my reception as cordial as I had been accustomed to in my appointment to a new charge. But trusting in that Friend who had never failed me, I had no doubt but that I should be enabled to triumph before the close of the year, and that all prejudice would give way before the power of love. And thus I went to work to promote the interests of the charge. One month had not passed, before a gracious reaction took place, and I was raised above the highest wave of opposing influences. In fact the victory came sooner and the triumph was greater than I had expected; and from this onward I could realize in my own religious condition what the poet meant in this language:

> " And placed on high above the storm's career,
> *Look downward where a thousand realms appear.*"

Brother Harris being preacher in charge, and quite sensitive in relation to his ministerial rights, came in contact often with opposing forces, which at times were not very pleasant; but one of the most strange and interesting features in the history of this year, a blessed work of grace commenced right in the warmest and highest state of the difficulty, and *went right on* as though it had nothing to oppose it, and souls were converted at every service. It is said that every revival of religion has some *new feature*—different from others; and certainly this was the case during this winter. The divine rule is that difficulties must be adjusted, enemies made friends, and old grudges buried, before the Lord will come with refreshing and saving power; but here was joy and rejoicing in defiance of contention and strife. And thus it continued throughout the most of the winter. As near as we could learn, about one hundred souls were converted during this meeting.

And here again a contrast was presented which created a deep and lasting impression. Through my solicitation, a family by the name of Wright attended this meeting, and Mr. W. came forward to the altar for prayers. During a season of great interest in the services, he arose a converted man. I stood by his side and saw the glow of heavenly joy beaming from his countenance, and heard the offering of praise from his lips. He was not aware up to this time that his family—wife and two daughters—were bowed at the same altar. Looking around in the height of his rapture, he saw his companion and two children saved and happy as well as himself, and it almost overpowered him, and he exclaimed: " Good Lord, the blessing has come all at once!" This was a befitting scene not only for joy among saints, but for " joy in the presence of the angels of God." Here was an entire family—all saved—and the recording angel wrote their names in the Lamb's Book of Life at the same time. How different were their feelings as they returned home, from what they were when they came to the house of God. They *came* burthened with a sense

8

of sin, but they returned rich with the treasures of redeeming love.

The other instance, occurring about the same time, was a young man recently from the South, by the name of Nutt. He was what might be called "*a fast young man*," whose father was quite wealthy; and owning a large number of slaves, he had been raised in idleness, which led to gambling and dissipation. And yet he was talented, of fine appearance, and knew how to act the part of a gentleman. Attending this meeting, he became awakened, came forward to the altar as a seeker, and professed saving faith through the merits of Jesus Christ. What astonishment, and yet what rejoicing, when his name was enrolled with the people of God. He continued very fervent and faithful to duty for several weeks, until he fell in company with some of his former comrades in vice; was persuaded to take a social glass, and in doing this, opened the door for further indulgence. As he came to himself, the sense of shame, and the consciousness of having disgraced himself and dishonored the church, bore upon his mind so heavily, that having procured a revolver, he ascended to the top of a steamboat at the landing, and blew out his brains. He was found in this condition soon after, with a letter nailed to the boat, addressed to Ben. M. Samuels, a member of our church. Mr. Samuels gave the letter to me and I preserved it a long time. Had I then known that at some future day I should be engaged in writing up this history, no motive would have induced me to part with it. The next day was a *solemn one*, as the funeral services were held in our church, and this closed up the earthly history of that talented and lamented youth. Let all who read this, beware of such a history and fearful end.

Through all the history of the past, in my ministerial labors of over forty years, nothing has been so detrimental and *ruinous* to the cause of Christ as the *liquor influence*. It not only hedges up the way for doing good, but causes more backsliding and disgrace to the church than all others put together. An individual under its influence, is mentally insane, and is prepared for every shameful and abominable work; and I am more than ever convinced that both *liquor dealing* and *drunkenness* ought to be treated and punished as any other crime; and not until the people of these United States, and our law-makers, regard it in this light will its *withering, destroying* influence come to an end. There seems to be at the present time an awakening up to this view of the subject, and to the devoted women of our land *all praise is due*, and the prayers and efforts of all the good should unite, as one *mighty power*, to banish forever this scandal from our race.

Perhaps in no city of the same size in the state of Iowa has the Methodist Episcopal church so small a membership compared to its population, as that of Dubuque. This is owing, doubtless, to the prominence of the Catholic element. This has been for many years the home of the bishop, and as a result, a kind of center for Catholic power and influence. Very few persons, unless they have lived and labored among them, are aware how ignorant they are upon almost every other subject save their temporal interests, and devotion to their church. They believe that their bishop possesses great power on the earth, even to the raising of the dead to life. As an instance, Mr. W., an old citizen living near the city, had an Irishman in his employ, with whom he had this conversation: " Pat, you believe that your bishop can raise the dead, do you not?" " O, yes, Mr. W.; the bishop can raise the dead." " Well, Pat, if you will get the bishop to come down next Monday to our graveyard, and do this, so that I can see it, you may tell him that I will turn Catholic, and at my death I will leave the church all of my property." Pat replied, "I will do it; I will see him to-morrow morning, and *be sure* he'll come." True to his promise, the next morning found him knocking at the bishop's door, anxious to deliver his message. He

was invited into his room, when he made known to the
bishop Mr. W.'s very generous proposal. He listened very
attentively until Pat was through, then he remarked, " Pat,
don't you know what the Bible says about this matter? It
says that if they will not believe Moses and the prophets,
neither will they be persuaded, though one should rise from
the dead. So, Pat, you see it's of no use." Poor Pat went
home greatly disappointed; as Mr. W. was quite wealthy,
he had hoped that he had furnished the bishop the opportunity of catching a *big fish*, but now all his hopes are
blasted. This he reported to Mr. W., and I received the
relation of facts from him. Was this honest? A man
occupying such a high position in the church, practicing
deception upon a poor Irishman—one of his members—in
order that he might still believe a lie? I think that in the
great day of exposition such works will be found among
the *hay, wood* and *stubble*, and the flames will consume
them.

In the arrangement of this charge at the commencement
of the year, we alternated in our preaching, giving the city
two sermons on the Sabbath and Rockdale one. This being
my first station in the state, and there being an able corps
of listeners—if not critics—I had to *man up* all of my talents in order to edify and feed the flock. Here was Rev.
E. S. Norris, who located the last conference; Jas. R. Goodrich, of the Rock River conference; Brother Spaulding, an
old missionary, and Brother Wallace from the Wesleyans—
all strong men; and for a comparatively young minister to
interest and bless such competent judges of divine truth,
as well as a large force of laymen equally competent,
required every exertion, assisted by divine grace. It was
not long before I had the satisfaction of knowing, by
increasing congregations, and encouraging words from the
old ministers, that my pulpit efforts were appreciated more
and more, and this inspired me with new zeal to make
every new sermon " *a critic on the last*," and thus I applied

myself with similar results until the close of the year. What knowledge is so valuable as that secured by experience! In this work of study, preparing for the Sabbath I learned this important lesson, which may benefit those just entering upon the work, *i. e.*, to begin your preparation on Tuesday and continue up to Saturday, and let this be a *review day*, realizing that if you make Saturday a day of hard mental labor, the reaction will be sure to meet you on the Sabbath, and in many instances take away the interest from your sermon. How often have I paid the penalty on Sunday for excessive mental labor on Saturday, and at the time did not know the reason why. But above all things, " Study to show thyself approved unto God, a workman that needeth not to be ashamed, rightly dividing the word of truth."

Among the interests of this year (1850), what is now the Main Street church was commenced, its foundation laid, and walls built to a height of several feet, which was completed subsequently under the labors of Rev. F. W. Cowles. It has undergone several changes and improvements since that time, until it is now a model of church architecture.

I have neglected to notice one interesting event connected with the many of this conference year, without which our history would not be full and complete. I refer to the debate between Mr. Levan, a minister of the Campbellites, and John C. Luccock, a traveling preacher in the M. E. church. The Rev. Levan was holding a series of meetings in the city, and in some of his sermons he took the opportunity to criticise and ridicule the altar exercises of our church; defying any man to controvert his assertions in relation to baptism. Our people were so annoyed that they concluded to send for Luccock, who was a member of the Rock River conference. He came, and the discussion lasted about three days. The only difficulty in the discussion was this, that there was not enough of Levan to draw him out, and instead of meeting an equal, with whom

he might measure swords, he found a mere dwarf, which
required him to stoop down to find. I have witnessed
many debates, but *this* was the most unequal contest within
the range of my experience; yet it doubtless exerted a favorable influence in promoting the interests of our great revival.
About this time my brother, Harvey Taylor, arrived in Dubuque from Ohio, and the following spring took work under
the presiding elder preparatory to entering our conference.
The revival spirit still continued up to the close of the
year, at both of our appointments, and our labors closed in
the spirit of harmony and peace. My colleague and myself
labored together in the spirit of love, and the work of the
Lord prospered in our hands. I shall never forget the
names of Farley, Samuels, Goodrich, Hetherington, Earhart, Rogers, Karrick, Decker, Waller, Manson, Pratt,
Simpson, Bonson, and in fact a host of others not named,
who held up our hands, and whose prayers followed us as
we took our final leave and repaired to another field of
labor, to form new friendships and gain new victories. This
is the portion of the traveling preacher. He labors upon
a charge until the bonds of friendship and love become
strong; he then bids them a kind farewell and enters into
new relations, and goes forth to make new history, and
before he again returns, some precious spirits have been
released from earth to enter into purer joys and greater
honors. But the time of reunion will come by and by,
when friends long separated will embrace each other in
that pure country where no farewell will be heard nor tear
of regret ever flow.

CHAPTER XIX.

We are again on our way to our next annual conference, to be held in Fairfield, Jefferson county. Rev. H. W. Reed has kindly proffered a seat in his carriage, and we are moving onward to the seat of interest. On our way we put up at Brother Price's, in the city of Davenport, where the elder is to hold his last quarterly meeting for the present year. It is the last Saturday and Sunday in July, and the mercury stands about one hundred above zero; but it matters not, the quarterly meeting must be held and the preaching must be done. I was not as well versed in the policy of presiding elders at that early period as I am now, or I might have suspected that he wished to introduce me to the people, in order that they might see how they would like their new preacher. But so it was. I took my turn in the pulpit service; and the meeting passed off pleasantly. On Monday morning, as we were preparing to start, we found that our satchel, containing conference records, had been stolen. If the thief had only known that its contents belonged to Methodist ministers it would have remained undisturbed; but he supposed that he had seized a prize until he examined it, when lo! its principal wealth consisted in reports and resolutions. He was so chagrined and *sold* when learning the character of his prize, that he threw it into a pile of brush, and it was afterward recovered, but not until we had suffered much inconvenience. On our way to Fairfield, passing through different pastoral charges, I was interested and amused to see how the elder was labored with in relation to the new preacher for the coming year. There happened to be a *peculiar crisis* in the condition of almost every circuit, which required a very competent minister to meet, and unless they were favored in this way the charge "*would suffer great loss.*" To me it was quite singular that this pressure had occurred on so many works *at the same time*, but I could discover by the twinkle of the elder's eye that it was a kind of philosophy which he perfectly understood. I had no charge to present against the persons so interested, when so much depends upon the character of the man. It is a great misfortune, however, in many instances, to the presiding elder, in view of the wants of the people, that he has any but No. 1 preachers in his district. Very many think that it is quite an elevation to be promoted to this office; but when the elder happens to have two or three preachers on his work, ambitious to have the best appointments, whilst at the same time the people desire some one else, the position is not so enviable after all; and yet, notwithstanding all their crosses and embarrassments, very few among us seem to think that it is a "punishment *greater than we can bear.*" I have been persuaded, for many years, that the church is not always as prudent in receiving applicants for the ministry as the necessities of the case require. Many times, through the influence of friends, or *personal* favor, young men are licensed to preach the gospel, and admitted to conference, who, as subsequent experience proves, have no qualifications for the work; and now it is hard to *remedy* what might have been avoided. Better close the door than suffer the penalty. I must give you a little scrap of history right in point. On one of my charges, not far from this date, there lived one of those uneasy spirits, applying every year for license to preach, and growling and whining that he was oppressed by the " brethren." We gave him a permit to try his hand once; then if he succeeded *well* he had the promise of a hearing in the church. His appointment was about six miles from home, had been well circulated, and at the appointed time the log school-house was filled with curious and interested listeners. As to the *merits* of the sermon, I cannot state; but something may be gathered in relation thereto, by the closing exercises. Before dismissal, one of the audience arose and stated that he thought it too much for a man of such splendid abilities to come so far and give his time without some remuneration; and he therefore made a motion to take up a collection for his especial benefit. The motion was approved, two hats were passed around and the contents very politely presented to the new preacher, when lo! buttons, chips, pebbles, and quids of tobacco, all came in for a share to assist in compensating the speaker for his very valuable services. I suppose after this effort no one doubted but that he had "*gifts and graces.*" This was a kind of quietus, which cooled off his ardent zeal and closed up his labors for that year. He afterward emigrated to Indiana, but whether his call was renewed in after life I never learned, yet I doubt not he long remembered his first sermon and liberal collection on —— circuit. In this case the remedy was fitted to the disease and met it effectually; but whilst there are some extreme cases of this kind, very many timid and humble young men, had they a little encouragement from the pastor, might render valuable services to the church as heralds of divine truth, who through lack of this influence content themselves in a more humble relation. My readers will pardon me for this digression and return with me to the seat of our annual conference.

Here we met Bishop Hamline, who was in feeble health. His personal appearance was quite different from that when he presided at Muscatine, and it was with great difficulty that he attended to the duties of his office. At this session the writer was elected secretary, with George H. Jennison for his assistant. The conference records not at hand, as noticed above, we proceeded as best we could. This was our first introduction to Henry Clay Dean, who was introduced to the brethren and was appointed to preach on Tuesday night preceding the session. He preached an eloquent sermon, and many of the brethren were elated that we had such a valuable accession to our ranks. As this was my first experience as secretary, the bishop, as well as Elder Reed, was very kind in rendering me all the assistance I needed. The citizens of Fairfield did everything within their power to entertain the conference, and we were favored with a good religious influence. The reports of the brethren from the different charges were very favorable in the increase of members to the church, and our borders were greatly enlarged. On Monday the appointments were read, and within a short space of time these messengers of mercy were making good speed toward their new fields of labor. My field of labor was Davenport station, filled the year previous by Rev. J. L. Kelly, who was now stationed at Rockdale, Dubuque district. Brother Kelly was a transfer from Indiana to ours, reaching Iowa in the fall of 1848. He was a very good preacher, a fine singer, genial and pleasant in all his intercourse with his fellow-men, and had an incident and a joke for almost every occasion. He labored for many years in Iowa, when, his health failing, he took a superannuated relation, and is now living near the city of Dubuque.

The introduction of a minister to a new charge is attended with a peculiar interest. He has a history to make, and the question arises, will that history be a failure or a success. This question is not only of interest to himself, but to the people for whose welfare he has come to labor. Such were my impressions as I reached this young and growing city, and commenced the labors of the year. But among the things unknown, of one thing I was certain, that the same Almighty power which had attended my labors in the past would not fail me in Davenport. Yea, I felt this assurance, that no enterprise *could fail with God to back it*. With this faith I entered upon its labors, knowing that I should find as willing hands and warm hearts in this station as I found in my former charge. Rev. Alcinous Young, the presiding elder of Davenport district, having chosen this place for his home, would make it still more pleasant for the pas-

tor in his relation to the work. But a few weeks had
elapsed when the elder wished me to assist him at a quarterly meeting on an adjoining work, at Cooper's chapel.
The meeting continued for three or four weeks, during
which time I labored constantly, and it resulted in the salvation of many souls. Brother Young and Rev. James
Gilruth, visiting the city, filled my place whilst I was laboring in the country. I felt the more inclined to assist at this
revival, as it commenced under my labors, and Rev. R.
Swearingen, the preacher of the circuit at that time, being
young and inexperienced in work of this kind. I saw at
this meeting what I never saw before or since—a husband
and wife at the altar for prayers, the one eighty and the
other seventy-six; and, if I mistake not, both professed
conversion the same night. It is such a rare occurrence to
see aged persons embrace religion, that this scene possessed
an interest beyond the power of language to describe.
Truly this awakening was a wonderful work of grace, and
caused one of the citizens of the community to think that
the millennium was near at hand. The history of Sabbath
evening, the second week of the meeting, will be remembered not only in time, but in eternity. Such was the manifestation of divine power that it seemed all hearts must
yield to its influence. At the highest interest I was requested to go out into the congregation and see if I could
not induce a man and his wife to come to the place for
prayer. I went, and after some solicitation I prevailed
upon them to come forward. In a few minutes they were
both converted and happy. I then made an effort to induce
another to take the same step who was under very deep
conviction. I used every motive of persuasion within my
power, but failed; the only promise which I secured was
that he would come forward to-morrow night. The meeting
of that evening closed with the most glorious results.
About twenty professed faith in Christ, and Zion shouted
aloud for joy. Monday evening came, and I looked anx-

iously for my friend whose pledge I had taken, but he was
not there. Tuesday night came, but he was not present;
and finally the revival services closed and we saw him no
more. Shall I relate the history? The same night that he
went home from that meeting he was taken suddenly ill,
lived a few days in great misery, and died, giving no evidence to his friends that his end was peace. When I
learned his fate, how forcibly did this truth come to my
mind: "He that being often reproved, hardeneth his neck,
shall suddenly be destroyed, and that without remedy."
Here were two persons, labored with by the same minister,
enjoying the same means of grace: the one improved them
and was saved, the other rejected them and was lost. I
may add that the first died triumphant during the year, and
I was called to attend the memorial services. Such is the
history of human life. "Blessed is that man who maketh
the Lord his trust."

During the progress of this labor, our presiding elder
with his family moved into the parsonage, and I was invited
to make his house my home. This I gladly accepted, and I
could not have felt any more contented and happy in my
own father's house. Sister Young was truly a " mother in
Israel," of strong faith, very able in prayer and in exhortation, and all alive to the interests of religion. Very few
females of my acquaintance combined so much Bible
knowledge and Christian devotion as Sister Young, and in
our prayer-meetings her presence was always like an angel
of blessing; and how did her prayers and influence inspire
me with new faith and courage during all of my labors in
this charge! In fact, in this station we were peculiarly
favored "with honorable women *not a few*," and the spirit
of revival commenced with the services of the new year.
The names of the brethren at that time who stood up
squarely by my side in every good work are quite familiar
to many of the members of our conference. Quite a number of them are still living, but, like the writer, the "almond

tree " is in the blossom and their movements are not quite so rapid as they were thirty years ago. Hiram Price, Rev. Wm. Burris, Rufus Ricker, Wm. Cook, Israel Hall, and some others, not named, were then young men, just entered upon the practical interests of life. But a few more years, all that will remain will be—like that of Brother Morton—a record of the past; yet it is pleasant to call up those old reminiscences and friendships of days gone by, and enjoy the short luxury of living life over again. Our revival during the first winter was not as rapid as it had been in some of my former charges, but it was progressive, and a large number found peace in believing. There was one new feature in *this*, as well as in the former revival, and as I never before witnessed it, I will give it a place in this history.

During a season of unusual interest, one evening I opened the doors of the church, and very soon I saw an individual crowding his way out of the slip, and as soon as he reached the aisle he started for the altar where I stood *upon the run*. I had before witnessed thousands fleeing from the dominions of Satan to Jesus for refuge, but this was the first instance of "*flying for life*" with such speed. It reminded me of the young man in the Gospel who came *running* to the Saviour inquiring what he " should do to inherit eternal life." In a subsequent conversation in reference to it, when I asked him why he ran, he answered, "I felt that I had not one moment to spare." Oh, if all who unite with us in church fellowship were as *ripe* for duty as this brother there would be no necessity of urging them to take one step in the path of life.

In the early part of this year Rufus Ricker, a member and steward of this station, had an interview with me in reference to his entering the ministerial work. He informed me that up to that time, though he had felt it to be his duty, and presented it to his brethren in the ministry, he had received but little encouragement. I gave him the

best counsel within my power, and he went to work preparing for the openings of divine providence. His case
was presented to the quarterly conference, and before the
close of the year I had heard his first sermon, and he was
recommended as a suitable person to be admitted into the
annual conference. In doing this I was aware that I should
lose a good faithful brother from my charge, "but what
was I, that I could withstand God." If He had a work for
him to do, with all of my preferences I must stand aside.
At the ensuing annual conference, held in Davenport, he
was admitted on trial, and now he is in his thirty-first year
in the traveling connection. God has blessed his efforts on
almost every field of labor, and in the coming day he will
share a rich reward. This is one act of my life which I trust
I shall never have cause to regret. It was at the commencement of this conference year that the Miss Gilruths
opened a seminary for the education of young ladies, which
continued until the death of Harriet, the elder sister. She
went to Ohio to visit her relatives, was taken sick with the
cholera, and died within a few hours. So ends the history
of human hopes.

It has been wisely said that "coming events cast their
shadows before," and this is true in the history of coming
men. It might have seemed quite improbable to very
many at that date, that Hiram Price, filling the office of
class-leader in the church, and recorder of Scott county,
just starting out to make history as a public man, would,
within thirty years, fill so many positions of honor and
public trust as have been conferred upon him. But the *elements* were there, and required only the occasion to bring
them into exercise. His unswerving fidelity to duty, his
zeal in the cause of temperance and every good work, his
detestation of everything little and mean, combined with
unusual business ability, and an excellent companion to aid
him—all these were the shadows or precursors of the *coming man*. And I am glad that a kind Providence raises up

here and there such a man to honor the church and bless the world. Very few know him better than the writer, and perhaps few appreciate him more. When the time comes that his *full record* shall be written up for *both worlds*, I trust that *in capital letters Success* shall be written in the beginning and at the end. In my brief tribute to the prominent men in Davenport at this time (1350), I acknowledge with gratitude the services of Rev. Wm. Burris, a graduate from Lane seminary, Cincinnati, Ohio, who stood by my side as a true and faithful friend. He was a good preacher, of easy address; kindness and cheerfulness were written all over his face, and his presence contributed greatly to our social interests. A short time after the breaking out of the rebellion he received a position in Washington City, and resides there at the present time. Wm. Cook, afterward Judge Cook, was one of the first pioneers in and around the city, and still takes great pleasure in relating many of its stirring incidents and experiences. He was a member of the *first class* organized here, and has filled the office of class-leader or steward in the M. E. church over forty years. He is now looking with much pleasure toward his enduring home. I know of no man who takes more enjoyment in singing such stanzas as the following than Judge Cook:

> "The Lord has promised good to me,
>   His word my hope secures,
> He will my shield and portion be
>   *As long as life* endures."

About this time a "Macedonian cry" came up from Muscatine. Rev. Wm. Hurlburt being stationed in that city, wished me to come and assist him in a series of meetings. The presiding elder being very anxious for me to go, and promising that he would be responsible for my appointments on the Sabbath, I went, and remained two weeks. The first week of the services the work of grace commenced in a very remarkable manner, and the entire village seemed moved under its influence. On the Sabbath I preached from " The great salvation," and in no one instance in my life—seemingly—with greater effect. At one period in the sermon, such was the remarkable power of the Spirit attending it, that some rose to their feet unconscious of the act. In the evening, my text was, " Son, remember," etc., and when the offer was presented for seekers to come forward, I never witnessed such a scene. Every nook and corner of the house was filled with the vast crowd; and yet they pressed their way to the altar by scores. It was supposed that fifty persons were present. It was a night never to be forgotten for deep convictions and clear conversions. The meeting continued with unabating interest all through the week following, when duty called me to return to my charge. The pastor, Mr. Hurlburt, reported at the close of this revival, near one hundred who had consecrated themselves to God.

At this meeting I formed the acquaintance of a worthy and devoted sister of that station, who gave me a very touching and remarkable fact, illustrating God's care and faithfulness in providing for the wants of his children. The history occurred in her own family. As I know that it will interest others as well as myself, I give the incident as she related it to me. It was at the close of the war in 1812. Her father having fallen in battle, her mother was left a widow, with several small children, and very little subsistence. Crops having failed also that year, to a great extent, and the winter severe, they found themselves reduced to the last loaf of bread. The mother divided this among the children for supper, and they retired to rest without a particle of food for the coming day. The prayers of that mother, however, were overheard by this daughter—who gave me this relation—through the night, pleading God's promises, that if the little sparrows " were not forgotten before him, that he would remember the widow and the orphan in this the hour of their extremity." The morning came, the fire was built, but no bread nor meat for their morning meal. About sunrise there was a knock at the door. A farmer entered who lived about one mile distant, called very penurious in his dealings—and after taking his seat inquired of the mother if there was anything peculiar in the condition of their family; that all through the night he had been so troubled about them that he could not sleep; and with this last expression the tears ran down his cheeks. He stated further, that he had come in this early morn, that if they were wanting in anything for their family in the way of provisions they should be provided for. The facts were all made known to the farmer; their wants were supplied, and the faithful widowed mother lived many years afterward, and never neglected to impress upon the minds of her children that the " Righteous are never forsaken." I would here state that I have occupied more space in writing up my first year's labors on this charge than usual, because it was one of much interest. As our annual conference was to convene in Davenport, it required no little labor to provide places for the members and visitors to our conference. But in a short time this work was completed; and in August, from every part of the state, were to be seen these hardy pioneers flocking into our young and growing city. Bishop Waugh arrived the week previous and was at Brother Price's waiting the reception of his brethren. The only peculiar feature attending this session was this: The weather was very hot. Among the many ministers arriving, whom should I greet but my brother, James Taylor, a member of the Rock River conference. I had not seen him for many years, and I greeted him with the warmth of a brother. But I hardly knew him. He looked lank and worn, his countenance not natural. In my surprise I said: " James, *what in the world is the matter?*" Before answering—as he doubtless felt the pressure of the question—I answered for him. James.

9

it is the excessive use of tobacco that has done this work. He acknowledged it; said he had been hard at work in his conference studies and had used it to stimulate him. He then took from his pocket the last he had, cast it to the earth, and said, "*Farewell, forever.*" I will tell you the result in the next chapter, as I must now provide for the preachers coming in from their fields of labor. At the commencement of this session Rev. J. G. Dimmett was elected secretary, and, I think, Michael Hare assistant. Among our visitors we were introduced to Mr. Delazon Smith, who had recently renounced infidelity, embraced religion, and had united with the M. E. church. An afternoon was set apart for him to lecture, and he occupied some two or three hours showing up the workings of skepticism in a masterly manner. His speech and concurring testimony contributed much to the interest of our session. On Saturday afternoon, after a practical sermon by a member of the Rock River conference, we were favored with one of the most remarkable visitations of the Spirit in our conference history. Strong men who had never quailed, were prostrated by its mighty power, and its influence continued nearly two hours. It was nothing more nor less than a Pentecostal visitation, and the old brick church resounded with the praises of God. The session continued until Monday—Bishop Waugh endearing himself to all the brethren —the appointments were read, and then every man for himself. In a very short time the city was as quiet as though no new history had been made. This is *history* repeated every year, and notwithstanding its repetition, it seems to lose none of its charms. And thus winds up the history of my labors in Davenport station for the first year.

CHAPTER XX.

As I had expected, I was returned to Davenport, and now begin the labors and responsibilities of a new year. In starting out upon its history I have decidedly the advantage of the past, inasmuch as I am now acquainted with the people and they are acquainted with me, and nothing is wanting but to go to work to promote the interests of the church. In the accomplishment of this purpose, during the first quarter, I preached a series of sermons designed to promote the attainment of a higher spiritual life, accompanied with a prayer-meeting on Tuesday evening to aid in its success; and from that date the work seemed to take new inspiration, and continued through the year without the least abatement. Such was its influence, that some persons came to me and asked for the benefit of our prayers and admission to the church. It reminded me of ancient times, when the people said: "We will go with you, for we have heard that God is with you." Among the number embracing religion at this time were Miss Pauline Gilruth, Miss Mary Price, and Mrs. Dr. Stephenson. Miss Gilruth is now the wife of Dr. Kynett, corresponding secretary of the "Board of Church Extension;" Miss Price became the wife of Robert L. Collier, a member of our conference, then stationed at Davenport, and Mrs. Stephenson still lives in the city, an ornament to the church. Sister Collier was a model Christian lady, but her work is done, and her home is among the pure above. So far as the influence of divine grace is concerned within the church, this may be set down as the *crowning year* of my ministerial life. It was nothing more nor less than a little heaven "on earth begun;" and as above stated, there was no declension during the year. If I were asked to account for this state of religious prosperity, instrumentally at least, I would say that it was in erecting a high spiritual standard, and then living up to its demands. My long experience has proved to me—and this is the Bible rule—that results will be glorious in ratio to our faith; for the stream never rises above the fountain. If we have strong faith, our courage, our efforts, our power with men will be in like proportion, and thus our success; but if we have no faith, we have no courage; we put forth no effort, and of course nothing is accomplished. I once saw this scriptural rule so beautifully and so forcibly illustrated that I will here give it in brief. Two boys, about twelve years of age, started to the pasture one evening to drive home the cows. There was a stream to cross, spanned by a small log—and as the recent shower had raised the creek, the crossing appeared a little dangerous. Said John to Charles, " I can cross that log;" and as faith always inspires courage—no sooner said, than *over he went*, and waited for his companion. Charles came up to it and looked, and began to doubt, and as doubting always begets fear, he faltered, backed out and returned home. John brought the cows home and was rewarded with success. Now, what was the overcoming element in this case?—about the same age, apparently about the same physical strength, and both of fair talent. My reader answers: "John had *faith* and Charles had none," and here was the difference. And this little incident in its practical lesson will account for the differences—in a good measure—in the success of men and women in every department of human life. Many professed Christians have faith, providing the circumstances are favorable in the advance. Charles would have had no difficulty in this case if there had been a good hand-railing across the log; but for want of this his inspiration was gone. I must here give one of the most striking scraps of history to show up this faith of favorable circumstances, within my knowledge. And as the fact occurred *here*, it will be right in point. And though a few of my brethren of the Upper Iowa conference have heard the relation in some of my sermons, it is as true and pertinent notwithstanding. A devoted minister living in this city, like many others, had his seasons of doubt and depression, which often affected his personal enjoyment. His companion was just the reverse, and often chided him for his want of faith in God when the promises were so full and free. Being on a visit to a neighbor's one afternoon, there came up a heavy shower of rain, and on their return home, the roads had been gullied out by the running water. Descending a steep hill, the wife expressed her fears in relation to their safe descent. And now it was his turn to exhort her in reference to her lack of faith. Said her husband: " Can't you have faith in God in going down this hill as well as anywhere?" etc. " O, yes," she said; " I can trust God whilst the *harness holds*, but if the harness breaks I don't know what will become of us." Through subsequent years, I have had much to do with this kind of faith based upon the strength of the harness, reaching no further than favorable appearances, instead of relying upon the great and precious promises of the gospel.

> " 'Tis mighty faith the promise sees,
>   And looks to that alone;
>   Laughs at impossibilities,
>   *And cries It shall be done!*"

Perhaps it was to administer a word in season to these pleasant-day and *smooth-road* professors of religion, that Brother Price's local preacher came to Davenport in its early history. His text was: " Wherefore, the rather, brethren, *give diligence* to make your calling and election sure," etc. The *burden* of his discourse was to show the peculiar traits of those *rather-brethren*, and if any of this class above referred to were there, there is no doubt that they came in for a share. It requires considerable credulity to believe that an authorized minister of the gospel should be so ignorant as to impose upon sensible people in this way, but I suppose he belonged to the same class and had his call about the same time of that brother in Ohio, mentioned in a former chapter, who received such a liberal collection, and as he emigrated West, he might have pitched his tent near the young city, and this may have been his second sermon, minus the collection. But whilst we may smile over those *rather-brethren*, the blunder is no worse than one in our own day. His subject that evening was: "Can the Ethiopian change his skin? or the leopard his spots?" When he came to the leopard, he entertained his congregation with a short history of the leprosy; how it broke out in *spots*, which no human power could change or remedy, and then the application to the sinner was sharp and forcible. Being stationed near the place where this wonderful sermon was preached, I received it fresh from the pulpit. After such expositions as I have here presented, should we not be more careful in saving the interests of the Christian religion from such reproach?

Henry Clay Dean this year was stationed in Muscatine, and wrote me again and again this winter (1852), to assist him in his protracted meeting in that city. Having some knowledge of the man, I declined to go until I received a letter from the official board urging me to come, and Elder Young being very anxious, I went, intending to stay two weeks. The time having expired, the last night of the services was such that I consented to stay one week longer. On that night I witnessed what I never saw before—twenty-five young men at the altar for prayers, and not one female or aged person. You will not be surprised that I consented, with such a motive, to remain a while longer. The meeting continued with such increasing interest through this week also, that I was no nearer ready to return home than the week previous, so I remained another week, making four weeks in all. I consented to this as my presiding elder agreed to see my pulpit supplied in Davenport. At an interesting period of our meeting an intelligent young man came to me for counsel as to what he should do to be saved. Learning his history and convictions, I advised him to arise in the congregation just assembling, declare his purposes, and in that act consecrate himself to the Lord, and I believed he would be blessed before he sat down. In a few minutes the meeting opened, and at a proper time he arose to his feet. He strictly followed my advice, and in expressing his purpose to devote all of his powers to the service of God, then and forever, the blessing came, standing on his feet; and as he was naturally eloquent, I hardly ever witnessed such a moving effect. Being a young man of good standing, and well known in the community, his conversion was the savor of life to many others. He united with the church and is still a faithful and prominent member in Chicago.

But I am now to present, if possible, a more touching scene than that of the young man. One evening, just at the close of my sermon, a messenger came *in haste*, requesting me to visit a sister at the point of death. I hastened to the sick room, and as I entered the door, she was shouting to the top of her voice. Her husband, a sister and two friends were bowed in prayer at the sofa, and the room was filled with the glory of God. She requested me to sing one of her favorite songs of praise, in which she joined until her voice failed, and then continued the action of holy rapture with her hands until her spirit left its clay to find a welcome in the heavenly home. I have witnessed many death scenes, but this of Sister Borland was the most triumphant in my ministerial history.

Having closed up my four weeks' labor on this charge, and witnessing about one hundred conversions, I returned home and found everything prospering. The good work of revival was still going on and converts added to the church. About this time I received a letter from my brother James in Illinois. I had been quite anxious to hear from him, as he had resolved to close up on tobacco, as to his success. I had known so many failures that I was almost afraid to hear his report, lest he might be among the rest. But the first line of his sheet opened with gratitude to God, whose grace had enabled him to conquer his enemy; and now he says: " Thank God, I am a free man. It is now about six months since I renounced its use and pledged loyalty to my conscience, and I am free. I weigh twenty pounds heavier than when I left you at Davenport, and in every respect I feel my life renewed." I will say here that he remained *true* to the last. I should greatly rejoice, if I could persuade all of my brethren who use it to do the same. A few months subsequent to this date, I had one of the most remarkable experiences of my life. It was in relation to this same brother. Some five months had passed since receiving this letter, and I was quite anxious to know how he was prospering. One day, enjoying my season of devotion, suddenly my mind became burthened as to his spiritual condition; so much so, that I was mysteriously drawn out to pray for his liberation. The picture was so vivid to the eye of my mind, that it became a reality. The next day it was renewed with still greater intensity. But on the third day the picture drawn was *so real*, and attended with such a weight of *intense* interest, that I lost all sight of the visionary, and it became a reality; and I did not cease praying until the victory was complete. The blessing which I received, as the evidence of victory, was *past all expression*, and I arose filled with *wonder*, *love* and *praise*. I said at once, " I will now test this matter, by writing to my brother, and inquiring if there had been anything peculiar in his experience." I did so; and in answer to my inquiry, he informed me that " he had just passed through one of the greatest trials of his life, and that on *that day* at camp-meeting he had come off victorious, triumphing over all his foes." When I received his letter confirming the reality of my experience, the refreshing came again with renewed power. After such an experience as this, amounting to a demonstration, could I ever doubt the doctrine of

the " communion with saints!"   Within three months from
this remarkable circumstance, another occurred of a similar
character, which many of the friends in Davenport still
remember.   At the close of one of our prayer-meetings on
Thursday evening, Sister Young came to me and stated
that she had been strongly impressed during the services,
that an old friend and brother in California had just
departed.   I said to her, " *Mark the date* until you hear
from them."   She did so, and when the letter came bearing
the intelligence of his death, the time corresponded exactly
with the previous impression.   That the Holy Spirit does
at times make such revelations to the human mind is beyond
a doubt, when some important interests are involved.   And
is it any more strange that they should sometimes occur
under the Christian dispensation, than in the days of Joseph
and Daniel?   Those who have read the writings of James
Caughey, the great revivalist, remember the revelation
made to his mind which induced him to go to England and
there labor for years in the great work of saving souls.   So
far as the *mystery* is concerned, it is not any more so than
that the All-Wise hears and answers prayer.   That this is
no uncommon occurrence, the Word of God and the history of the church unite in their testimony; *i. e.*, in *direct
answers* to the prayer of faith.   I record an interesting case
of this kind in the history of this year's labors, which will
close up the page of incidents on this work.   The most of
our older ministers were acquainted with John Morton,
a member of this charge; and how many have enjoyed a
pleasant stay at his home!   During the past winter he was
brought low with the rheumatism, and his friends entertained but little hope of his recovery.   At the worst stage
of the disease, when not expected to live, a few minutes
before Sunday evening's service I stepped into his room to
see him.   He was very sick, and doubtful whether he would
survive the morning.   As I was leaving, Sister Morton, with
deep emotion, requested me to " remember him in the

prayers of the church." Just before dismissal, I brought up his case, and requested that if it were God's will that he should be restored to health, that we would all unite our prayers, *then* and there, to this end. I then requested an able brother to lead, when all seemed to unite as *one* for the recovery of our dear brother. It was the victory of faith; and as the assembly arose all seemed to be impressed that our prayers had prevailed. After service, I called in again, but what a change! Said Sister Morton, " About an hour since, a great change took place for the better, and he appears like a new man." He continued to improve rapidly until his health was restored, and lived, like Hezekiah, about fifteen years after this event, to comfort his friends and bless the world. From that memorable evening I have not had the least doubt but that Brother Morton was raised up in answer to the prayers of the people of God; and when we meet him in the land of light, where the pages of Divine providence are better understood, we shall realize, as we never shall be able to in this life, " That the effectual fervent prayer of a righteous man availeth much." I would still love to linger around this sacred spot, where so many friendships were formed, and where so many souls were blessed, but I am called to new duties and new interests in other fields of labor, where conflicts are to be met, where faith is to be tried, and victories are to be won. But I still remember my motto: *That no enterprise can fail with God to back it.* Before entering upon the history of a new charge, however, I must state that during my term of two years and three months in this city, the population had more than doubled; our membership in the same ratio; we had no church trials or any difficulties of this kind, and not one death in the society. Rev. James Gilruth and family, from the state of Ohio, moved to this city during this year and became members of this station. We shall refer to him again.

"Scenes of sacred peace and pleasure,
    Holy days and Sabbath bell,
Richest, brightest, sweetest treasure,
    Can I say at last farewell?
Can I leave thee? Can I leave thee?
    Soon in other lands to dwell!"

This language of the poet embodies about my feelings as I left these friends, and the old chapel, to enter upon a new field of labor.

CHAPTER XXI.

We met this fall for our conference session at Burlington, once more in Old Zion, Bishop Ames presiding. The state of feeling was not as pleasant as at some of our former sessions, owing to some preferences of men in the station. Some were for Paul, and others for Apollos—so much so that the state of party feeling ran quite high; and where this spirit rules, it must necessarily conflict with the Spirit of God. Bishop Ames also pursued a different course from that of his predecessors in letting every man know as to his coming work. These two elements combined created much confusion and unpleasant feeling during the conference, and caused the appointing power much trouble. The pastor for the past year was Rev. Joseph Brooks, an able minister, formerly from Ohio, and the question to be settled, among others, was, should he be returned to the charge, or some new man in his stead. I was not aware of my appointment to the station—as the charge had been recently made—until just before the reading of the appointments, and was taken a little by surprise. But the "die was cast," and my appointment was read out for Burlington city, with David Worthington presiding elder of the district. To be the better prepared for the work before me, aware of its plenitude, I called the official board together in order to learn the true state of things before entering upon it. We found at this meeting such a state of finances as to discourage almost any man or official brethren to remedy. Matters stood about as follows: Parsonage purchased the last year, twelve hundred dollars. Interest at twelve per cent. for one year, one hundred and forty-four dollars. Incidentals unpaid during the past year, one hundred and seventy-five dollars. Making in all fifteen hundred and nineteen dollars; and to meet this, not one cent in the treasury. I give these items that my readers may know something of the nature of the work before me. Before we adjourned I was elected general collector and treasurer, as well as secretary, and thus I had *honor* enough for one man. Pastor on Sunday, and Thursday evenings, and financial agent through the week. Not a hill, nor a valley, not a nook, nor a corner throughout the city, but I traveled over and over to relieve the church from embarrassment and save our religious credit; and had I not been favored with help above the arm of man, I most certainly should have failed. But the Lord gave me aid, with the people I found favor, and before my term was closed the cloud had passed away and we were rejoicing in the light. I must here record my gratitude to God, and to those faithful brethren who stood by me through all this ordeal, and among them I must name Jedediah Bennett as not among the least. In the darkest day he hung out the *signal of hope*, and thus we plucked victory out of seeming defeat. But the burden and responsibilities of those two years I shall never forget. They are so indelibly engraven upon my memory that the changes of time will never be able to efface them.

On the second Sabbath I chose for my text: " Lord, wilt thou not revive us again, that thy people may rejoice in thee?" The spirit of revival was manifest; after the discourse the class-rooms were filled, and the songs of praise resounded through almost every part of the house. In the evening I preached from "None of us liveth to himself," etc.

The sermon ended, I opened the doors of the church, and six persons honored the invitation. From this date all the interests of the church seemed to improve; the chapel was crowded with hearers, and there were new accessions almost every week. So, you see, whilst we were laboring for dollars to relieve the temporal, we were gathering souls to enrich the spiritual and eternal. This station, through many past years, had about the same history—revivals in the winter until every foot of space was occupied, and they could go no further, and then a thinning out in the summer until they reached about the same level. Realizing this difficulty, and knowing that the prosperity of our church greatly depended upon aggressive movements from the beginning of the year, I used all of my influence in order to prepare the minds of the brethren for a division of the charge at its close. The effort had been previously made, but failed, owing to the reluctance in the separation of old class-mates and tried friends. Having convinced them that the spiritual interests of Christ's church were far above that of our own preferences, and that it was a Christian duty to do all in our power to promote that interest, when the matter was presented to the last quarterly conference for the year, it passed unanimously and the lines were established.

David Worthington, our presiding elder on this district, was one of the oldest preachers in the state of Iowa. He was sound in doctrine, rather solid than brilliant; a good counselor, a warm friend, and fully devoted to his work. His record in Iowa as a faithful minister of the gospel is without a blemish. In this station, I became more fully acquainted with Rev. Wm. Corkhill, the first and for many years the only Bible agent for the state. As he resided here at this time, and was a member of my charge, we enjoyed many pleasant hours together. He was well adapted to this important work, never failing to give to "saint and sinner a portion in due season," *for a little money.* He had talents for great usefulness, and had he been as pious as he was amusing, he might have exerted a vast influence in winning souls for Christ. Not that he lacked devotion to every good cause, but he had been so long accustomed to jesting and joking that self-denial was no longer a virtue. Whilst these remarks are true, very few men inherited a larger heart and warmer sensibilities than my old friend.

Within the bounds of his work he had a very wealthy man, who was a member of our church, but he could never, with all his eloquence, touch the nerve of his generosity. If he gave anything to the Bible cause, it was a mere pittance. And yet no one professed to value religion, its hopes and enjoyments, more than he. Brother Corkhill being so often defeated, felt a little like the farmer toward the boy stealing his apples. After kind words and tufts of grass had been employed to no purpose: "Well, well," said the farmer, "if neither words nor grass will do, I will try what virtue there is in stones." And so felt the agent. He drew a vivid picture of a wealthy man who in company with others owned a large and productive vineyard, and whilst his partners from day to day were out laboring in the hot sun, digging and pruning, that it might bear abundant fruit, *this man* sat on his sofa, beneath the bending branches, in the cooling shade, and every now and then he would pull off a rich cluster, smack his lips, and then say, "*bless God for grapes.*" And thus he continued from year to year, enjoying his soft seat and cooling shade, blessing God for grapes—and at the same time never lifted a hand to assist in procuring them. Then came the application. Many wealthy members of the church, owing all they had to the influence of the gospel of Christ, and under the divine blessing had become wealthy, and to it indebted for the prospect of a glorious immortality; and yet when asked for a few dollars to assist that cause that had made and saved them, they turned a *deaf ear* and an *empty pocket.* Well had it been for Brother Corkhill if his last remedy had been as effectual as that of the farmer's; but instead of this, his last donation to the cause was in keeping with those that had gone before. A ministerial friend of mine being present, went up to the party after the discourse, and asked him how he was pleased with the sermon. His answer was: "That he did very well, but *made a great many blunders*." And thus the hard labor laid out in drawing a vivid picture and a pointed application to reform a penurious man, ended just where it began.

In this station I had also the acquaintance of Henry Clay Dean. Though I had labored with him during the great awakening in Muscatine, referred to in a previous chapter, he now being stationed on an adjoining charge, and seeing him every few days, I had a better opportunity to learn the character of the man. And with this knowledge, I am satisfied that there is only *one* such man in the United States. He preached occasionally for me during the year, and in some instances, in his eloquence, he reached a *sublime grandeur*. This term expresses it, as nearly so as any language at my command. I have heard many of our most eloquent men, but in some of his lofty flights he was not excelled. At one of our camp-meetings at Long Grove, being left in charge of it, I was aware that he desired to preach on Sunday night. Having had a short interview, I said to him: "Henry, if you will preach a good gospel sermon to-night, adapted to the saving of souls, as I know you can, and leave out *Dean*, we will be glad to hear you." True to promise, he started out; his voice, *naturally musical*, rose with the interest of the subject. He commenced with the sinner in his sins; he carried him through all the stages of spiritual progress until he stood upon the Rock, "with a new song in his mouth, even praises to God." He then followed him through all the conflicts and experiences of human life down to the day when he placed his foot upon the neck of the last enemy, and then stood waving the flag of victory over the head of his conquered foe. Then, with one sublime flight he reaches the golden gates of the heavenly city, where he is greeted with the songs of angels and the shouts of saints; and Jesus standing in the front meets him with a shining crown, and says to him: " You have been faithful over a few things, and now I will make you ruler over many. Enter thou into the joys of thy Lord." No pen-sketch can give an accurate idea of the sermon and its effects upon the audience upon that clear and beautiful night, and it was the *crowning glory* of all his pulpit efforts in my hearing. Had he been as devoted and consistent in his life as he was eloquent in his address, he would have been a power for good; but it remains a truth, and that *truth* will forever remain, that nothing can be substituted for a *pure heart*.

We were favored with a good revival influence, during this the first winter of our labors, wherein about fifty professed conversion and were added to the church. Whilst this work was in progress, a colored preacher (or professed to be) came to Burlington, and many of the friends were anxious that I should invite him to preach. I had learned up to this time to be a little cautious of strangers, unless they came well recommended; and as he had no credentials, I was slow to push him forward. But the pressure was such I consented for him to preach. He did very well. In a short time he was requested to preach the second sermon; but in this, the first one was nearly half repeated, when I began to suspect that all was not right. Within a short time I was informed that his liquor-bill was unpaid; which being confirmed, he hastily left, leaving his admirers to square the account. From this experience, I never again invited a strange man into my pulpit unless I knew it to be a clear case. It would be a strange occurrence indeed, as we have counterfeits on almost everything else, that we should not have now and then one in the ministry. A few years after this event I saw him in the northern part of the state, and I was informed that, getting tired of his first wife, he visited our place in quest of a second. Let all who read this profit by the history.

During the first half of this year—in November, I think, I received a letter from Hiram Price, of Davenport, to come to his city and meet some previous engagements entered into before I left. Their daughter Anna had engaged my services to perform the marriage ceremony, when the time came, and I had promised to attend, and now I was to honor my pledge. The young man of her choice was Doctor Dillon, living in that city, of studious habits and of much promise. Having been intimately acquainted with them for the past two years, and Brother Price's family a kind of home, I responded to this call with the greatest pleasure. The marriage ceremony was performed in the Methodist chapel, before a large audience, after which the friends retired to the house to enjoy a season of social entertainment. Rev. A. J. Kynett, now my successor on this charge, was with us, and enlivened the occasion by his cheerful spirit and conversation. In fact, it was one of those pleasant pastimes which occur only now and then in a man's life. Many have been the friendly hours, since that time, enjoyed with Judge Dillon and his kind companion. Seldom did I visit Davenport without paying them a visit, and through the varied changes which have taken place since 1852, I have numbered them with my warmest friends. I little thought that when that young man stood before me and so frankly assented to his marriage obligations, that the period would soon arrive when he would occupy one among the first positions in our nation; but this only shows what can be accomplished by studious application and an honorable course in life; and should he yet be permitted to occupy a seat on the "*supreme bench*," the only comment I should make, is this: "*He is worthy.*"

On my return home to Burlington, from this pleasant visit, I found the citizens much excited by the sudden dis-

10

appearance of a young man by the name of Hawks Griffith, who, it was thought, had committed suicide. The most thorough search had been made, but with no success. The only evidence that he had made way with himself was some missing trace-chains, supposed to have been taken to fasten weights to his body to prevent its rising to the surface of the water. The family was composed of a widowed mother, a grown-up son and daughter; all, the son excepted, members of the M. E. church. This son was a very moral young man, of fine appearance, and a regular attendant at church; and so far as we knew, they were a pleasant and very happy family. We learned after this occurrence that there had been a little difference of opinion between the mother and son as to the propriety of moving to the country in order to lessen the expenses of living, and that this opposition had caused him to commit this act. His person was not found until the coming spring, and then in the Mississippi river; some of the fastenings had been detached and he was floating near the surface of the stream. But O, what an experience for that mother and daughter! For many weeks they seemed almost comfortless, he being their main stay and hope to sustain them amidst the burdens and interests of human life. What a *fearful delusion*, to think that the relations of life will be changed for the better by forcing ourselves out of time into eternity!

The spiritual interests of the society during this conference year were greatly promoted by a higher spiritual life within the church. Sister Porter, from Quincy, Illinois, having united with us, and Sister Moore, with some others, coming out into the full light and liberty of gospel fullness, they became a power wherever they went. I have known very many talented and eloquent women in prayer, but for beauty in language, richness in thought, inspiration in feeling, and in sublime, moving eloquence, Sister Porter stood first. You might calculate when she commenced, that before she closed, you would be carried upward far above sun, moon, and stars, and finally your feet placed upon the golden streets of the New Jerusalem. Many of the unconverted came to our weekly prayer-meeting, attracted by the powerful prayers of that talented woman. But this is not all. That which gave such efficiency to her eloquence of speech *was her eloquence of life.* The same might be said of many others—members of this charge. How often did I realize, whilst laboring among them, with this host of faithful workers, "That the lines have fallen unto me in very pleasant places."

Rev. Wm. Simpson, my old colleague at Mt. Pleasant, being now stationed at Fort Madison, wrote for me to come and assist him in his work. Being nearly seven years since we separated, nothing could have been more agreeable than this reunion of friendship with him and his family. During this interval he had been stationed at Council Bluffs among the Mormons, cursed by the priest, buried a little daughter with his own hands, saved from Mormon wrath by a few heroic Gentiles, triumphed over all opposition and hardships, and left the field with a flourishing society of two hundred and forty members. All this he had passed through since we were co-laborers together for the Master, and no wonder that we were ripe for a brotherly greeting. I remained with him for several days, and the work of the Lord prospered in our hands. Here I met a brother and his companion, an old acquaintance of former days, whom I married six years previous on a distant charge. Although not a professor of religion at that time, he was now a prominent member of this station, and recorder of the county. My reception in this family was heart-cheering, they being warm and zealous members of the cause, and my stay was among the happy events of my life. I trust that, when life's history is written up, the names of Brother and Sister James will be found recorded in the "*Lamb's Book of Life.*" Brother Simpson was one of those *humble, trusting,* happy Christians, and during our acquaintance often said to me that his last song on earth would be, "And we'll cross the river of Jordan, happy in the Lord." We will see how this was fulfilled when I come to record his death. Duty now called me to return to my own heritage, and I left the pleasant little city and its many warm friends, storing up its interesting history among the precious remembrances of the past.

Among the many interests of this year I had a very pleasant experience of a different character. Judge Stockton, the son-in-law of Rev. John Collins of precious memory, was a member of my charge, but being a very humble man, and not inclined to push himself forward, the brethren seemed content that he should attend to his own specific duties unmolested. Upon my appointment to the city, a warm friendship was formed, and I recommended him to the quarterly conference for the office of steward. To the surprise of many of the brethren—and gratification also—he soon became one of our best advisers and most efficient workers in the station; and his own religious enjoyment seemed to deepen and expand as he labored to promote the interests of the charge. And this was not strange, for how can an individual feel much interest in that with which he has nothing to do? If we would see him all awake and alive in any enterprise, let him become a party to its profits; yea, let him go to work earnestly to reach the desired result, and how soon the whole course of life is changed. In the work of the church it is no less true "That he that would win must labor for the prize," but he that would enjoy God must be diligent and faithful in the work assigned him. In no appointment in the state of Iowa did I find a more flourishing Sunday-school than in the city of Burlington. At that date, we had an average attendance of over two hundred scholars, and a healthy religious influence all through the year. Many of our scholars were converted and united with the church. The secret of our success in this department of our work is easily accounted for. Not only had we the very best of teachers, but they were always at the post of duty; and these two good qualities—fitness and faithfulness, will invariably enhance the prosperity of the Sunday-school. I never failed to attend and interest the scholars, so far as I could, with my presence and coun- sel; and as a kind of *token* of their appreciation of my ser- vices, they presented me with a purse containing thirty dollars in cash. I think that I can safely say, that in no one field of labor did I ever secure the confidence and affec- tion of the children to a greater extent than in this sta- tion, and I fondly hope that in that heavenly kingdom, where Christ will know his own, I shall still share the friendship and love of many of those choice spirits to whom I ministered in 1853.

CHAPTER XXII.

Dr. Chalmers paid quite a compliment to Methodism when he called it "Christianity in earnest;" and this idea was seconded by a Presbyterian minister at one of our gatherings, who remarked: "When the Methodist church has anything to do, she goes right to work and does it." This compli- ment is not always well deserved; for "Old Zion," at this date, had needed a new roof for a long time; so much so, that every hard rain endangered our plastering; and if good wishes had been of any avail, long before this the work would have been accomplished. But the time had come when necessity demanded action rather than good wishes, and we went right to work in earnest. After having raised sufficient funds by a *rousing festival*, I called for volunteers to do the work "without money and without price." At the time appointed, they came by scores, tearing off and putting on, which by their hammer and clatter seemed to wake up the whole city, and in two days the old *moss-cov-*

ered roof was displaced, and old Zion had become partly new. We had a time of general rejoicing over this valuable improvement, and some of those who were in doubt as to our success, now came in to share the honor. Seldom, in any experience in the history of the past, have I had more striking proof of what can be done by resolute purpose and prompt action than in this undertaking; and I can here say of the good brethren and sisters of Burlington, that they are hard to surpass when they enter upon the " *home-stretch*."

This city also surpassed any other charge in my pastoral work in the number of weddings which I attended. In one instance I had three in one day, and I was obliged to change the hour to suit the pastor. I was never involved in the same difficulty, however, as in the case of my colleague. After the ceremony he was asked the charge for his services, when he informed the party that he generally left it to the generosity of the bridegroom. But he insisting on the minister's setting his own price, was told that five dollars would be about right. He paid it, but learning afterward that he had paid *too much*, he came back and demanded restitution. My colleague was not a relative of Zaccheus " to restore four-fold," but he gave him to understand that the value of an article was known by the price paid for it, and by this rule all would know that he had a good wife. This new departure seemed to satisfy the claimant, and he went out from the pastor's presence a *wiser* if not a better man. But whilst I never passed through just such an experience as this, I had one of a different character, and fortunate for me had I fared as well. This man came to me manifesting deep concern. He wished to let me into a secret of a very private character, which had involved him in very serious trouble, and he assured me that if I could relieve him I should be well paid. He informed me that the woman with whom he was living was not his wife—that they had not been married—

and that if I would procure the papers and finish the work legally, without making it public, he would be very grateful and pay me my own price.   As he appeared so honest and sincere, I really felt that it would be a virtue to assist a penitent man, even in a dilemma like the present.   And thus I went to work, advanced the money for the necessary papers, and at eight o'clock P. M. I had pronounced them husband and wife.   He thanked me kindly; said he would call at the parsonage the next day and satisfy me well for my trouble.   The next day came and I saw him not; and the next came but he did not appear; but a friend of mine assured me that he saw him on the road with his new wife and a few traps, making great haste for *tall timber*.   When I received this intelligence I said, truly the bird has flown, and I am sold.   Just now I felt very much like attuning my powers of song to this stanza:

" How vain are all things here below,
    How false, and yet how fair;
Each pleasure hath its poison too,
    And every sweet a snare."

This little-counter experience, however, was only the dry branch to a green tree—perhaps I ought to call it a *snag;* and I could well afford to endure it, in view of the fact that all the others were pleasant, and my marriage fees during the year amounted to over one hundred dollars.

The conference year of 1853 is now drawing to a close, and we are looking forward to our next annual session. But a short time before its arrival I was brought down with the bilious fever, and was quite feeble when we started for conference.   Rev. Erastus Lathrop, on an adjoining charge, kindly proffered me a seat in his buggy, and we started for the city of Oskaloosa.   Our little towns were all cities then, for this was the only badge (the name) by which they could have been known.   Our route being through one of my former circuits, of course they must again hear their old pastor; and I was delighted that they had the opportunity. As many of them had traveled for miles to meet me on my way, and my appointment circulated, though feeble, I could not disappoint them. The hearty greeting which I received, after an absence of six years, the joy and gratitude expressed, reminded me of the joyful reunion when Christian friends shall meet in heaven. Oh, there is a bond which binds the lovers of the Saviour so closely together that all the powers of earth cannot break and death cannot sever.

> " Death may the bands of life unloose,
> *But can't dissolve our love.*"

Truly, it was a feast of social friendship and spiritual enjoyment all the way to the seat of conference. As we arrived, who should we meet but Brother J. B. Hardy, the pastor stationed at Oskaloosa, who informed me that I must preach that evening. I plead inability, but to no purpose; preach I *must*, and preach I *did*. But in view of my recent recovery from a bilious attack, it was *too much;* it brought on a relapse, which continued for three weeks. This session to me was almost a blank, inasmuch as I was confined to my room and visited the brethren but once, and this was the morning that Elder Reed spiked the gun of that " young man eloquent," noticed in a preceding chapter.

At the adjournment of this conference session, being returned to my former charge, some kind brother took me in his covered carriage and conveyed me to Mt. Pleasant, where I remained with these kind friends until I recovered strength to return to my work. My reception then was of the warmest kind. From the children greeting me on the street, up to the editors of our city papers, all gave me a hearty welcome. How cheering and *inspiring* to the minister of the gospel is such a reception by the people of his charge, as he assumes the responsibilities of a new year. The work having been divided at our last quarterly conference, Rev. W. F. Cowles was appointed to the new charge, which embraced what is now called South Burlington. David N. Smith was now Sunday-school agent for the conference, and made his home in our city. He was formerly a member of the Ohio conference, was transferred to Iowa in 1848, and stationed here for two years, where his labors were very much blessed. In this relation we had a fine opportunity to form each other's acquaintance. I often invited him to preach, as his labors were always appreciated, and in this way he rendered me valuable service. He was a good preacher, popular and successful in his stations, a genial and cheerful companion, an honest man and a true friend. He has passed on to his heavenly reward. Erastus Lathrop and Samuel Clark were early and faithful workers in their Master's vineyard in this state, and shared in the honors connected with a pioneer life. Brother Clark long since joined his brethren in his home beyond, and Brother Lathrop is still living and laboring in the state of Nebraska. As the division of this city into two stations was a kind of experiment, and its utility doubted by some, each pastor went to work in earnest to build up its interests. A church was to be erected in the new charge, and it required all the tact and energy of the preacher in charge, with our co-operation, to consummate so important an undertaking.

I will right here pay this tribute to Brother Cowles—that in the building of churches he was eminently successful, and had but few if any equals in the Iowa conference. His arrows were all *steel-pointed* and well aimed, but *he* carried a shield of such a character that, however well directed, balls nor arrows could ever penetrate. If there ever was a period in his history when he was in the least discomfited by the logic or the sarcasm of his opponent, most certainly it occurred in my absence; and yet, beneath this seemingly *impervious* armor, there was a kind and sympathetic heart which responded to the warmest sympathies and honored the noblest sentiments. We labored together throughout the year in the spirit of harmony and love, and, so far as it was in our power, contributed to each other's interests. Having sustained a loss in the membership of Old Zion in the division of the city, I felt like putting forth every effort in order to supply the deficiency, and accordingly we started out in our revival work. There seemed to be a moving power behind all our efforts at this time different from that of the winter previous; then it required hard labor to make any progress, but now the good work moved on in the advance, and within a few days we were enjoying a blessed work of divine grace. Among the many young persons coming out into the full light and liberty of the gospel was Charles C. McCabe, now Dr. McCabe, and assistant corresponding secretary of the Board of Church Extension of the Methodist Episcopal church. He was then a young man about twenty years of age, of fine appearance and rare talents, and being fully baptized into the spirit of the work, he became a power for good in promoting the interests of the revival. His dear mother, a precious spirit, died a short time previous to this in the city of Burlington, in the triumphs of a living faith, and left her last blessing upon her children; and now the mantle of the mother had fallen upon "Charlie," her youngest boy, and almost within sight of the grave where her body sweetly reposes, her son was busily employed in gathering jewels for his Master. Brother Cowles was frequently with us during this blessed work, and rendered valuable assistance. It continued about six weeks, during which time about one hundred and thirty persons professed conversion and united with the church. Over one hundred were added to Old Zion, and the remainder to South Burlington. Here were some of the fruits of dividing into two charges. The Lord gave us back our old number besides the large addition to the new station. Our society being so much enlarged, there was a necessity for appointing some new leaders, among whom was Charles C. McCabe. He had exerted such a saving influence among the young people during the meeting, that he was now to assist them in the path of spiritual life.   The only difficulty with our new leader was his popularity.   The room was too small to accommodate the class; and as new accessions came in weekly, the difficulty increased upon our hands.   But relief was near.   Spring returned again with all its genial warmth and beauty, and buds and blossoms betokened delicious fruits and the coming harvest.   Our meetings, too, were full and refreshing, filled with the spirit of joy and prosperity,   But on my mind there rested a *burden* and it required a sacrifice to throw it off.   My divine Saviour, whom I loved and honored, had said to me in language not to be misunderstood: "That young man, the leader of that class, belongs to me.   It would be pleasant for you to enjoy his society and services in Burlington, but I have assigned him to higher positions and greater honors; you must let him go."   Brother McCabe was then in charge of his father's store, who himself belonged to this station, and passing by my room every day, I called him in.   What momentous interests cluster around a few moments of time!   I delivered to him my message from the Lord.   He listened.   I saw by the starting tear that it had found a hearty response in his own heart, and he was ready to say, "Speak, Lord, for thy servant heareth."   I suggested to him what was his duty— to leave his muslins and calicos in the store and go to the "Ohio Wesleyan university," and prepare to preach the glorious gospel of Jesus Christ.   Within a few days he obtained his father's consent, received his letter of dismissal, bade us farewell, attended with our prayers and tears, and started for his Ohio home.   The time, place, and peculiar circumstances of our next meeting I will record in a future chapter.   But, in relation to the present history, permit me to say that among the promising young men of my acquaintance, Charles C. McCabe stood alone.   For untiring zeal, intense devotion to God, power in prayer, eloquence in speech, sweetness in song, and an overcoming faith in Christ, I have not found his equal.   As he shook my hand heartily for the last time before starting away, all the sensibilities of my nature were called into active exercise; and long was he remembered in the prayers of the church in Old Zion, where his sweet voice of song was no longer heard. Inasmuch as I design to prepare a more enlarged sketch of his life for this book, I will defer further remarks.

The labors of the past winter having drawn heavily upon my mental and physical resources, the church very kindly proffered me a release of six weeks to visit my friends and relatives in Ohio. Before starting, I had engaged different brethren to supply my pulpit in my absence, so that my mind would be free during my visit. The railroad having been recently finished from Chicago to Burlington, I was about to enjoy my first ride on the cars, in company with Brother Sweeney, a member of my charge. On a beautiful day in April, we started out to visit old friends and my former home. Our ride was very pleasant until nearing the city of Indianapolis, running at the rate of forty-five miles per hour, when, turning a curve, we ran over five cows that were standing on the track. In a moment two or three of our coaches were jumping on the ties, then the right-hand wheels were plowing in the sand, which resistance turned us up on one side, and here seats, cushions, men, women and children were all piled up together. Such a screaming and struggle to get unwedged I never heard nor saw; but we soon recovered our footing, and in a short time were free from the wreck, standing on terra firma, rejoicing in the consolation. All the damage done to humanity was a bad scare and a few bruises; but the cars were so much injured that new ones were run up from the city to conduct us on our journey. This, my first experience with railroad speed, was not very flattering; but we reached Cincinnati in safety, after which I rode up to Lebanon to visit my old friend, Charles Ferguson, who was stationed in that city. Having been separated for nine years, our meeting was a social and religious treat, and I remained and preached for him on the Sabbath. After the congregation were dismissed, two persons came up to the pulpit and gave me a friendly greeting, who had been formerly members of my charge in Burlington. The following week, by the river, I landed in Portsmouth, where, among my friends, we revived the pleasant recollections of years and events in the history of the past. What an inspiration *in nature*, to revive and cheer the human mind, and especially in its contrasts. When we left Iowa, not a leaf, nor a flower, nor a blade of green grass was to be seen. But here in Southern Ohio, all nature was putting on her beautiful garments and ornaments, whilst convocations of birds were celebrating the transformation from winter to spring. How it reminded me of the sublime effect which must be experienced in our glorified nature when we place our feet upon the golden streets of the heavenly Jerusalem, as we remember earth's days of darkness, sorrow, sickness, poverty, separations and deaths; but now darkness is past, sorrow a stranger, poverty unknown, and friends united, never to speak a *long farewell*. Never in my life before had I seen such a beauty in this poetic language:

> "Lo, upward I gaze, and the glory supreme,
> Which illumines the heights of elysian,
> Shines down through the vale,
> There is light in each beam
> That renders immortal my vision.
> See, there are the towers of my future abode,
> The city on high and eternal,
> And there is the Eden, the river of God,
> With trees ever bearing and vernal."

The few weeks passed in this visit among the friends of my youth, the home where I was converted, and on that consecrated ground where I preached my first sermon, and gathered so many jewels for my Master, were among the happiest of my life; but for a *resting-place*, I have long since learned that among the *last places to find rest* is to visit a former charge.

But what tender sensibilities were aroused as I stood by the graves of a father and a little son of five years. For the space of ten years all that was mortal had been reposing here, whilst the waving spruce and the beautiful rose were paying a tribute to their memory; but the immortal were reposing in that land where the sun ever shines and bliss ever reigns. Stoical must be the man or woman who cannot here find memories to cherish and hopes to inspire. But as I visited the resting-place of *little Susan* (a niece) the next day, how *solemn* the history. She was a lovely girl about fourteen years of age. Attending the last day of school, she went home with an associate to pass the evening. A young man visiting the family had left his pistol in the room as he stepped out to take a little walk. During the interval Susan and her school-mate came into the room, and not conscious of any danger, as they were amusing themselves with it, discharged its contents into her brain. She fell back on the sofa and expired. I was the first one to arrive after this sad transaction, and arranged for the removal of her person. It was a shock of such a character as to overwhelm the parents with grief. Hundreds attended her funeral, and such a solemn occasion I never witnessed. And there, in the little grave-yard at Franklin Furnace, she was buried, and on her head-stone was this little verse:

> "Remember this, as you pass by:
> As you are now, so once was I.
> As I am now, you soon will be.
> O, then, prepare to follow me!"

Fifteen years had now elapsed since I passed through that sad history; and now, standing by that lonely monument, there moved before me a *vision* of the past. I saw her lovely face, always smiling, as she stood by our fireside, or sat at our table, in all the hilarity of youth. I could still hear that merry laugh, and see the sparkling eye. But it was only a reflection from the history of former days; and with this melancholy pleasure I left these wasting memorials and thought of the joy of meeting that amiable youth in the better land. But among the reminiscences of this visit to Ohio was my reception in the village where in other years I had taught their school. Nothing could have been more gratifying than this. The little boys and girls then, had grown up to men and women, and some of them married and settled in life. At the close of my sermon, their welcomes and kind expressions came so thick and so fast that I had no time for a suitable response. It was nothing less than a shower of greetings of such a character that, with my emotional nature, it was as much as I could manage. And in the speaking meeting which followed, so many referred to early impressions received in our school-room that led them to a Christian life, that I was constrained to say: "How precious are the seeds of life sown in youthful hearts!"

There is no lesson more impressive, to show this world of change, than a visit to our *old home* after an absence of many years. Hardly anything looks familiar. The house, the garden, the orchard, the old play-ground have all changed. The familiar faces, so long the title to true friendships, are not recognized, and we find ourselves encircled by a new generation. How often have I realized this in my meanderings through life. But amidst this whirl of change there is one comfort more precious than gold. It is this: The grace of God *changeth not*. The years of time cannot deface it; moth and rust cannot corrupt it; fire cannot burn it; floods cannot drown it; and even death cannot destroy it. Imperishable by time, and lasting as eternity. I have often been led to inquire, whether this life, in its variations, is in any sense a type of the glorious future. Doubtless *there* we shall still be under the law of change, but not subject to corruption or decay, but one of delightful progress, "led on to fountains of living water." When we think of meeting our dear little children on the "shining shore," we entertain the idea that we shall find them just as they were when they left the earth. Perhaps so; we cannot tell; but is it not more reasonable to suppose that, dwelling in the presence and under the care of the blessed Saviour for many years, their immortal powers will be greatly strengthened and enlarged, and their divine knowledge greatly increased? *Who can tell* but that, in some instances, in view of their superior knowledge, when we arrive there they may become our teachers and we the learners! If our children, with our present advantages, can become, within twenty years, our teachers here on earth, will they be less qualified, within twenty years, *with all the advantages of heaven?* My dear reader, let us not fail to go and see.

However reluctant the disciples were to come down from the mount, our Lord had other work for them besides building tabernacles. And though I could tarry with great pleasure, absorbed with such thoughts and fond anticipations as the above, yet the call of duty is heard to come down to the more practical work of life. However joyful the return to visit home and friends, the departure is often shrouded with tender and gloomy reflections. As we go out from their presence, we can but realize that some of these hands we have shaken for the last time; some of these voices of friendship, and cheerful faces, which so often infused inspiration to our hearts, have been heard and seen for the last time on earth. Our next meeting will be among the redeemed in the land beyond the river. Such is the history of human life; and a scrap of such history I am about to make as I leave my dear friends on the banks of the Ohio, and hasten to join others on the banks of the Mississippi. As I returned to Burlington, every spiritual interest was still prosperous, and I entered again upon my work with physical strength renewed. During the summer I attended a camp-meeting at Long Grove, ten or fifteen miles from the city, of the most interesting character. It was a "season of refreshing from the presence of the Lord." One afternoon of peculiar interest, I invited *first* those who were living in the enjoyment of perfect love; then those who were earnestly seeking for it; and lastly, *all* who wished to be saved. Such a time of divine blessing is seldom witnessed. Nearly all of the congregation were seekers, and very many were saved; and among the precious ones at this pentecost, I shall long cherish in my memory Brother Avery and family.

On our return home from this camp-meeting, we stopped for dinner at Wm. Johnson's. He was not a professor of religion himself, but his wife had been a devoted Christian for many years. Having attended the meeting, he had been seriously awakened, and was now under deep conviction. Just before starting, I proposed that we should not separate without prayer; and whilst asking the divine blessing upon Mr. Johnson *especially*, the pressure became *too great*, and he surrendered. He requested us to continue the prayer-meeting for his benefit; and so we called in the neighbors—one of whom was Mr. Leffler, his brother-in-law, and formerly a member of congress—and his companion, with many others; and thus we continued the services until time for supper. When this repast was well over, we renewed the contest until almost midnight, when the bands of sin and unbelief gave way, and heavenly light and holy rapture came into his soul like a flood. In no one conversion, among the many witnessed, did I ever see such a proof of our Saviour's language: " Except ye be converted and become like little children, ye shall not enter into the kingdom of heaven." After his conversion, he was as simple as a child and happier than a king; and we continued our rejoicing until far in the night. " It was meet that we should make merry, for our prodigal brother had come home; he that was dead is now alive, and the lost is found." Great was the rejoicing in the community over

11

this interesting occurrence, as he had long been known as one of its prominent citizens; and so far as I am informed, he still lives in the same house where he was converted, and has not forgotten that memorable hour when saints and angels united in concert to celebrate the glorious victory. A little later in the year, with some of the members of my charge, I attended another camp-meeting in Illinois on the work of Rev. Wm. Haney. This meeting, in the manifestation of divine power, was equal to if not beyond that at " Long Grove," and the influence of two or three devoted females was never more apparent than upon this occasion. Sister Moore, and Sister Porter—referred to previously,— members of Burlington station, in this battle for life, were like a Frazer at Saratoga; their words of courage and shouts of victory in the grove as well as at the altar carried success wherever they went. Defeat was nowhere written upon their banners, and they knew no failure with the presence of Jesus to back them. Scores were converted, and still more professed sanctification through the Spirit; and the notes of victory, through faith, cheered us to the end. The pastor reported about one hundred saved and added to the church during these services; yet the good work did not stop when the meeting closed, but it spread through the different neighborhoods for weeks afterward, and very many souls were " added to the Lord."

During this summer, under the pastorate of Brother Cowles, the corner-stone of the new church (Ebenezer) was laid with appropriate services, and the occasion was one of unusual interest. Brother McCabe, previously mentioned, having left for Ohio, Brother Williams was appointed class-leader to supply his place. I little thought when for the first time I called upon Brother W. to pray in public, that within a few years he would be filling the first stations in our church. As a young man he was quite timid, and needed the influence of his brethren to assist him forward; but this reluctance he finally overcame, and stands to-day

at his post, an honor to the Christian ministry.   But the time
of my " walking about Zion " has passed; my last sermon
has been preached, from " Peace I leave with you," etc.;
the dear friends are all at a social gathering, to which I am
invited to spend the evening, and a memorial of thirty dollars is presented as the last token of their love. The trustees
of the church pass a resolution of thanks for my financial
success; when, full of gratitude to God and hope for the
future, I wave a final farewell as I enter upon new duties
and go forth to other conquests; but such names as Bennett, Hagar, Hisey, Eads, Pew, Clark, Brown, Cooke, Dee,
Sherfy, Sweeney, Scarf, Evans, Leffler, Mac, Jones, Randall,
More, Porter, Smith, and others not named, will live in my
gratitude and affections until mortal life is changed and I
go to live with them in heaven.

CHAPTER XXIII.

Our conference for 1854 convened in the city of Dubuque,
Bishop Ames presiding. Having been stationed in this
city four years previous, it was very pleasant to enjoy a
week in the society of former friends. My home at this
session was with Brother Cook, an old and intimate friend.
Rev. Thomas Corkhill had been stationed here at the last
conference, and took every pains to make the session
pleasant for all. On the Sabbath preceding the conference,
I preached for Rev. Wm. Corkhill, on the Bible cause, and
in the evening the society held its anniversary. One of the
speakers on this occasion started off very finely, but when
about half way through he became confused, and then so
embarrassed that he could not utter one word. He stood
before the vast audience for some time perfectly silent, tax-
ing his memory to loyalty, but it failed to perform its
office. He finally retired with the honest apology that his

speech was memorized, and he could not call up the idea
in its proper order. I am inclined to think that his congregation were about as much embarrassed as he was, and
would have given a liberal collection if that would have
relieved the difficulty. Speakers who memorize their discourses should see to it that this servant is very trustful, for
if that fails, there is no remaining remedy. As I have
already alluded to Rev. Thomas Corkhill, pastor of this city,
I will now present this tribute. He was one of the early
ministers of this conference, and having passed through
the medical course, he was familiarly called Dr. Corkhill.
He is not only an able preacher, but a Christian gentleman.
As a pastor in the many charges under his care he has been
eminently successful; as a presiding elder, faithful and efficient; so much so that his ministerial brethren have honored
him with a seat in the General Conference. True to every
trust, fully consecrated to God, may he long live to honor
the church and bless our fallen race.

Our conference session passed off very pleasantly. The
sermon of Bishop Ames on the Sabbath was not among his
best efforts. The point of main interest was reached on
Monday, in the reading of the appointments, where it was
written: Dubuque district, J. G. Dimmett, presiding elder;
Main Street, A. J. Kynett; Centenary, Landon Taylor. This
last announcement was no surprise to me, as I had previously learned that I was to be stationed here with twelve
members as a nucleus to this new charge.   Old Centenary
was now so improved that it looked like a new church, and
as I had been a witness to many victories around its sacred
altars, in previous years, it seemed very much like coming
home. The official brethren, too, were old Christian friends:
Brother George M. Samuels, Ben. M. Samuels, C. Hetherington, Brothers Robbins, Karrick and Bradstreet. These
were so many favorable presages leading on to a year of
spiritual prosperity, and though our numbers were small,
I was aware that heaven's resources were large. My

opening sermon was from this text: "By whom shall
Jacob arise, for he is small?" Before I concluded, I felt
very much that the prisoner had become a *prince;* having
"power with God and with men, we should prevail." My
colleague, stationed in Main Street, Rev. A. J. Kynett, was
then a young man, with only about three years' experience
in the ministry, and he felt *deeply* the weight of responsibility resting upon him, which he failed not to express in
my presence. Having but small experience, and now filling
one of the most important charges in this conference, he
felt like saying: "Who is sufficient for these things?"
Brother Kynett being still with us, and carrying a sharp
critical knife, I must be careful of my pen. But if it be
true, that the "truth shall make us free," I wish to render
him all the aid within my power. It may be of service to
many brethren of my own conference, and no injury to
Brother Kynett, to say, that in some respects he has been
misapprehended. I remember well when the current of
feeling was very strong against him, in view of the impression that he was an ambitious aspirant for office; but if
that ever was the case, I am certain it was not so at this
date, being placed in a position to know.

During our conference at Burlington, the presiding elder
came to me and requested that I should decide a very important question as to my successor in Davenport station.
He stated "that the choice lay between two brethren, one
of whom was Brother Kynett, and as I was their former
pastor and understood their wants, and knew the men, as a
matter of courtesy he wished me to decide it." I at once
decided in his favor, and I was also aware that he consented
to this appointment with great reluctance. And in the
expression of the same feelings he entered upon the work
in Main Street, Dubuque. I do not know that the doctor
ever gave me credit, by the above decision, in giving a new
shape to his ministerial life, but it is no less true. This
decision of a moment gave a new direction to his entire

history, and I trust that in the *great day* when the books of
this life shall be opened, and their contents understood,
that it will be approved by the Master and honored by his
minister.   Perhaps no two men of the Upper Iowa conference have had a better opportunity for intimate acquaintance and personal knowledge, than the doctor and myself;
and I record it with pleasure, that during that experience
of thirty years, both in our business and social relations, I
have found him ever true; with a heart to sympathize, a hand
to relieve, and a spirit to forgive; in a word, a safe counselor, a truthful friend, and a devoted Christian.   In every
relation, as a servant of the church, he has made an honorable record, and in no one *more so* than in his present
responsible position as secretary of the Board of Church
Extension.

But I must not forget that I am now stationed at Centenary with only twelve members, and I must go to work to
build up the interests of my charge.   But right here occurs
a touching little incident.   I call it *touching*, because it was
truly so, in more senses than one.   Whilst passing along
Main street, Brother Karrick, one of my official members,
called me into a tailor's shop and addressed him thus:
"This is our new minister, and I wish you to do your best;"
and within a few days I stood up before my audience in the
pulpit *in the very best*.   I began to think if these were the
first fruits, that I need not fear for the coming harvest.
Quite a large number of the members of Main Street had
been inclined to say, after their removal from Centenary,
"If I forget thee, O Jerusalem, let my right-hand forget
her cunning," etc.; and now that it had been reopened they
returned to the church of their choice.   In this way we
received an addition of some thirty or forty members.   A
new Sunday-school was now organized, with increasing
prosperity; our house was filled at every service, and as one
item of additional interest, one of the clerks in the land
office was converted under a sermon.   With this growing

interest, when the winter came on, we were ready for work and salvation. And here it did not need hard tugging at the oar in order to a little progress, but the messenger of mercy led the way, and soon we were gathering spiritual fruit unto life eternal. A faithful mother, living not far distant, had said to me: "I have a dear boy in the city of Dubuque, and oh, how glad I would be if you would hunt him up and persuade him to give his heart to God." With some little trouble I found where he was at work at his trade, and I made him a visit. I informed him that I had a message from the Master, and he must obey. He appeared a little discomfited with my positive manner, but promised me that he would attend our meeting, but went no further. In the evening when the crowd assembled, sure enough, he was there. And when seekers were invited to the altar, *sure enough*, he was there. For several evenings he was faithful at the altar, but found no relief. But the time for victory arrived. I called upon Brother Kynett to pray; and had it been revealed to him, the important future of that young man, he could not have been more earnest, nor his prayer more appropriate. He seemed inspired with the prevailing Spirit, and the shout of triumph ascended to heaven: "The dead's alive and the lost is found!" With many others, the mother's boy is saved. A few weeks subsequent, as he was called to leave to return to his own home, I invited him to my room, made known to him my convictions as to his duty to engage in the ministry, "commended him to God and the word of his grace," and he left with his pledge of fidelity to duty. True to his promise, he shortly entered upon a collegiate course, graduated with honor, and for nearly twenty years has been employed in the work of the Christian ministry. He has filled many of the most important charges in the Wisconsin conference and is now stationed at Topeka, in the state of Kansas. That young man was Oliver J. Cowles. This blessed work of divine grace continued for several weeks, which brought up our membership to one hundred and forty. During its progress Brother Kynett labored with me like a brother. A large number of young men were converted at these services, over which Cyrus Hetherington was appointed leader. Days of prosperity were these, and we felt like saying: "Not unto us, but unto thee, O Lord, the praise is due."

As I had rented a room for study in the city, adjoining mine was the room of Mr. Moreland, who had a large class of young men. This was a kind of commercial college, and the teacher was a thorough scholar, but was dissipated. He was educated in Cincinnati and received the best qualification that the Catholic church was able to give. As he had to pass my room in going to his, in some instances I had to assist him to his lodgings; and in one instance he had fallen at his door, and when I found him he had nearly perished. One evening about ten o'clock he came knocking at my door, fearfully alarmed. He cried out: "If you have any pity, *do get up* and help me drive Satan out of my room!" Said I, "Moreland, has he come to make you a visit?" "Yes, yes; hurry; *do hurry*," said he, "for I can't stand it in this way." I repaired to his room as soon as possible, and as I entered, his lamp standing on the table, I at once took in the whole situation. His eyes looked like two balls of fire, and I discovered it to be one of the worst cases of "snakes in the boots." Said I, "Where is he?" "Don't you see him," he said, "on the other side of the table? There he has stood a long time, and I've done everything to drive him away, and he won't *budge a hair*. Mr. Taylor, do help me if you can." Said I: "Moreland, I can manage him without any difficulty. I know just how to do it, for I've ousted the old fellow a great many times." "Have you? well, I am so glad." I then asked him if he had a Bible in his room. "O yes," he answered, "one that my sister gave me as a present in Cincinnati;" and in a moment it was brought and presented to me. It was a beautiful copy of the Catholic Bible, a large gold-leaf cross on the back; and as I received it I assured him that this would *rout him.* "Now, Moreland, take this Bible, walk right up to the table where you see him, and lay it down as near him as possible." Carefully he stepped, almost holding his breath, nearer and nearer, until he reached the dreadful place, when *whack* it went on the table. "There," said I, "Moreland, didn't I tell you so? Didn't I tell you that he couldn't stand the Bible? Don't you see that he is gone?" "Well," said he, "*he has,* hasn't he?" The vision had fled, and his mortal enemy had disappeared; and now I persuaded him to blow out his lamp and retire to rest, assuring him that there was not the least danger of his return that night. To this he consented, and slept until eight o'clock the next morning. After breakfast he came to my room, mortified and ashamed, and begged me not to make public the transactions of the last evening, for if I did it would ruin him in his business. He then gave me his history, and he wept like a child. Said he: "Wicked associates and liquor have brought me to this. Who could have thought, when I left Cincinnati, an honorable and upright man, that I ever would come to this?" I consoled him, entreated him *then and forever* to forsake his corrupt associates and liquor, and former friends and habits, to which he assented and gave me his solemn pledge to become a new man. This was my last interview with him. The next I heard he had drowned himself in the Mississippi; and here his earthly history ends. Upon this sad history I wish to add a few reflections to show the power of faith even upon an insane mind. His first utterances when he came to my room proved this; for said he, "I believe you are a good man, and can assist me." Here, faith was the foundation in the beginning, and when I informed him that I *could manage* him, he was as confident as a child; and when I told him, after he had placed the Bible on the table, that Satan had fled, that positive assertion turned the whole delusion into air. This was my object, to turn the current of his thoughts into another channel, and in this I was successful.   But oh, what a *monument of warning* to all young men to shun the society of wicked associates, and dissipation!   Another reflection: That Satan becomes a *real personage* to men in this condition (even if it be so), does not require a great stretch of credulity, for there is such an intimate relation existing between him and the liquor interest, that if he comes round upon such important occasions to inspect his work, in order to report favorably to headquarters, it is no marvel; but to step out of the house of God, where souls were translated from darkness into light, into such a synagogue of Satan as this, was a contrast realized only once in my life.

But who is this walking up the street—a rather short, portly man, stepping quickly, approaching the Methodist chapel?   It was the day of our quarterly meeting, and certainly it must be our presiding elder.   I was not mistaken; it was Elder J. G. Dimmitt, for many years a prominent member of the old Ohio conference, but now filling this responsible position in Iowa.   When he first came to Burlington city, in 1853, he was attacked with the cholera and his life despaired of, but by almost superhuman exertions, with God's blessing, he was raised up to serve the church for many years.   The temperament of the elder was rather of the phlegmatic; sometimes it required an effort to rise above it.   In warm weather, with a small congregation, the pressure was beyond his control; but on any important occasion, of a nature to call his powers into action, he was truly eloquent.   His voice, though not round and full, was musical, and when inspired in the warmth of his subject became bold and commanding.   In his longest sermons and happiest efforts, he never became hoarse nor weary, neither did any one complain that he preached too long.   I never knew him disconcerted but once in the pulpit upon an important occasion, and that was when six children, at the top of their voices, were all crying at the same time.   His voice rose far above the tumult for some time, when contending with two or three; but when the number was doubled, and the instruments keyed still higher, he paused in the conflict, and yielded up the palm to the victors. With a pleasant remark, he accorded the honor to whom it belonged, until silence reigned and order was restored. Brother Dimmitt at times was subject to great depression of spirits, which seemed to cast a shade upon his ministerial character, but in all my intercourse with him I found him a genial companion and a true friend. Perhaps no man had a profounder contempt for sham than he. When living at Le Claire, at a time when dancing was a popular amusement among the worldlings of that place, a gentleman dressed in the highest style of fashion called on him and introduced himself as Professor A. After salutations, during which the elder took the measure of his visitor, he blandly remarked: "May I inquire of what you are a professor?" I am a professor of the terpsichorean art, sir." "Ah!" said the elder, "you mean to say that you are a dancing master." The interview was not a protracted one. Brother Dimmitt served the church in Iowa not far from twenty years, occupied the most important positions, was two or three times a delegate to the General Conference, and a few years since, at the city of Des Moines, in holy triumph, bade adieu to earth, and took his position among the redeemed in heaven.

My brother, Harvey Taylor, at this time was stationed at Maquoketa, and needing help, I went down and assisted him about one week, which effort was attended with great success. As he had recently married (a Miss Sarah E. Thompson of Tipton, Iowa), this was my first introduction to her, but *after-acquaintance* proved her one of the precious of the earth. During the most of this year I made my home in the family of Brother Kynett, which very much served to create the strong attachment so long existing between us and his excellent companion. And among the precious memories of this year, I should be ungrateful did I not include such names as Amanda M. Samuels, a faithful worker and a true friend, and Rev. James R. Goodrich, a wise counselor and ever ready to lend a helping hand.   In taking a review of the history of this year's labors and successes, I am filled with gratitude to God in view of the prosperity which attended us upon this charge.   Throughout the year it was one of peace and progress, without a ripple on the stream; and in subsequent years, and in other states, I have met with those who were converted in Centenary church in the winter of 1855.   The old chapel has passed into other hands, and the influence of time is written on its walls; yet when the stirring events of this life are all written up, and their results known, what precious fruits will be gathered from the labors of God's people around the sacred altars of old Centenary:

> " Yes, there is one spot, one beautiful spot,
> My heart lingers o'er with emotion;
> Its peaceful enjoyments will ne'er be forgot,
> It's the place of the spirit's devotion.
> I see it outstretched in its loveliness lie,
> Like a garden of lilies and roses,
> More charming to me as it fades from the eye,
> *Than the beauty of Canaan to Moses.*"

CHAPTER XXIV.

This year's history is now concluded, and we meet again in conference session in the city of Keokuk, named after the old Indian chief.   For the first time we are visited by Bishop Simpson, and truly it was an event of rare interest. The bishop then was right in his prime.   We had heard much about him, but now our eyes enjoy the sight and our souls the benefit.   Being chosen for his private secretary, I had a fine opportunity for personal acquaintance, and found his social qualities in accord with his pulpit abilities.

Several of the brethren at this time were talking about locating, and on the Sabbath the bishop shaped his discourse accordingly. He preached from "But none of these things move me," etc.; and such a portrait as he drew of St. Paul could have been drawn only by a master's hand. He traced him through every stage of his history; he marked his stripes, his shipwrecks, his being stoned, the day and night in the deep, how his brethren wept as he was about to go up to Jerusalem, and finally as a prisoner in Rome. At this point he drew a graphic picture such as I shall never forget. He had the old heroic prisoner seated near the prison window, where he could look out and see the instrument of death, and he is intensely interested, by its dim light, in writing to his son Timothy his last epistle. He now invites his brethren to take a walk with him through Byron's "City of the Soul," until they reach the old prison where Paul is confined. Having gained access to the room of the prisoner, he cautions them to *step lightly*, that they may not disturb the old veteran as he is making his last record in time; and as they move up carefully and look over his shoulder, they see the heading of his manuscript: "Perils of waters, of robbers, by my own countrymen, * * in perils among false brethren." And as the eye glances further down the page, they read his concluding remarks, embracing his triumphant faith, and victory over death, as embodied in this language: "I am now ready to be offered, and the time of my departure is at hand. I have fought a good fight; I have finished my course; I have kept the faith," etc. And now some inspiring genius appears, holding an interview with this man of God, inquiring of him, in view of the perils, hardships and tribulations of the past, and the certainty of a martyr's death now at hand, if he is not tempted to give over the struggle and record his defeat. He waits for the answer: "But none of these things move me; neither count I my life dear unto myself so that I might finish my course with joy, and the *ministry* which I have received of the Lord Jesus, to testify the gospel of the grace of God." Here the *climax* was reached, and such a volume of praise as went up from that audience can only be fully appreciated by warm-hearted Methodist ministers. After such a sermon, no locations at this conference. We were entertained in the afternoon with a very fine discourse from Dr. Berry, of Indiana, and another in the evening by Rev. J. V. Watson, editor of the *Northwestern*. But the brethren had ascended to the top of "Nebo" in the morning, and had such a look into the spiritual Canaan, that of necessity they had to come down a little in order to grapple with the realities of practical life. This Christian Sabbath was a high day for the church in Keokuk. This was the last time that we looked upon the pale countenance and wasting frame of Brother Watson. We all felt that he was preaching his own funeral sermon as he discoursed from "For we know that if our earthly house of this tabernacle were dissolved, we have a building of God," etc. And sure enough, within a short time he " ceased at once to work and to live."

This was the last conference at which the whole state of Iowa was represented by our church. The necessary arrangements were made at this session for its division, and at the ensuing General Conference the next May we were divided into the Iowa and Upper Iowa conferences. In the arrangement of the work for this year, I was appointed Sunday-school agent, and Rev. J. R. Cameron was my successor in Centenary. Rev. A. J. Kynett was returned to Main Street, Dubuque. Having made arrangements with Rev. D. N. Smith, former Sunday-school agent, for his team and a quantity of books, I was ready to engage at once in the work, still retaining my home in Dubuque. Dr. Baird, presiding elder of the Pittsburg conference, came to our city for the purpose of taking an excursion into the back counties in view of entering a quarter section of land for each minister on his district. Inasmuch as I had a little

leisure, I proffered him a ride, and he gladly accepted.
The weather being pleasant, the roads good, and the doctor
first-rate company, our trip could not have been more
pleasant. We visited Grundy and Butler counties, with
their nice rolling prairies, and having selected his location,
we returned home. The "land office" being now at
Dubuque, Brother Baird had some hard experience in order
to secure his land. From early morn, until night, great
crowds stood before the door and in the yard. As each
one had to take his turn, those in the rear had to wait hours
before they could be accommodated.

My work in this new relation was to preach on the Sabbath, present the nature and importance of the cause, take
up a collection, and supply books for the Sunday-school. If
the school was needy, in many instances the whole of the
collection was returned in books. In organizing new ones,
I made donations frequently amounting to five dollars; but
one of the pleasantest parts of my work was the privilege
of talking to the children. In this way I made a great many
little friends, and, I trust, many lasting impressions for
good. During the year I organized about fifty new schools
and scattered the books of our "Union" all over the northern part of the state. Wherever I went I met the heartiest
reception from the ministers of our conference, and they
did everything within their power to make the work a success. Richard R. Swearingen being out of employ a part
of this year, I secured his services in assisting me through
the western part of our conference, and he rendered me
very efficient aid. Had it not been one of the coldest winters known in the state (1856), I should have regarded it one
of the pleasant and successful years of my life. But such
a winter! For weeks, in some instances, such was the
severity of the weather that it was impossible to get about;
in fact, it was dangerous to venture out, and hard to keep
comfortable within doors. At West Union, Fayette and
Farmersburg, had I not fallen in with kind friends, I must

have perished. And I still recall to this day, with grateful recollection, the pleasant home I found in the house of Dr. Fuller, at West Union; Robertson, of Fayette, and Webb, at Farmersburg. A young man at that time was living with the doctor, who took much interest in taking care of my team; afterward he became a member of our conference. As they were returning from church one evening, after a sermon by the writer, the doctor asked this young man "What he would be willing to give if he could preach such a sermon?" It seems that this question made a deep and lasting impression upon his mind, which led him finally to serious reflection and positive action. He soon became an authorized minister of the Methodist Episcopal church, and for more than twenty years has been cultivating Immanuel's land in the state of Iowa. That young man was Francis X. Miller. I shall have occasion to refer to him again. How often we are making valuable history when we are the least aware of it! At that time Brother Fuller thought not for a moment of the result of that simple question, and perhaps by him it was soon forgotten; but it was the little mustard seed dropped into good soil: "it sprang up and brought forth fruit unto eternal life." And the same is true in the case of Rev. F. M. Robertson, now a prominent member of the Upper Iowa conference. He assured me not long since, that whilst remaining at their house in this extreme cold weather, in my conversation with him when a boy, that the impressions made upon his mind still endure. And thus it is true:

> "In summer's heat or winter's cold,
> We gather lambs into his fold,
> And know not, when the seed we sow,
> *That fruit therefrom will ever grow.*"

After the weather had moderated, I visited Brother Byam, stationed at Decorah. He had written, requesting me to come and assist him at a protracted meeting, and when I arrived I found it in progress. I remained with him during the week, preaching for him every night, but seemingly with little effect. Myself the judge, I think if I ever did my whole duty in presenting God's truth, I did it here. During the entire services but two young men came forward to the altar, and they were converted. I had been so long accustomed to number seekers by scores, that I must confess I left that meeting feeling that but little had been accomplished in view of the faithful labor performed. This impression remained upon my mind for years; when, at one of our conferences, a stout, hardy young man, of fine appearance, came up to me, gave me a hearty shake of the hand, with "How do you do, Brother Taylor? You do not know me, I suppose? Do you recollect how you labored at Decorah in the winter of 1856, when during the week only two young men embraced religion?" I answered "Yes; and that service I shall never forget." Said he: "I am one of those two young men, a minister of this conference,* and the other is a Baptist minister, stationed at Quincy, Illinois." When the great Richard Watson, then a youth, stood up before the British conference to preach his trial sermon, he announced for his text: "There is a lad here which hath five barley loaves, and two small fishes; but what are they among so many?" Here, in this question of the disciples, was man's limited estimate of God's resources. And how often in the Saviour's employ in the present day, we manifest as little wisdom and faith as did Andrew in the above language. We forget that *one loaf* in the Saviour's hands is equivalent to a thousand. When I saw the small fruit, apparently, as the result of that week's hard labor, compared with the scores which I had previously witnessed, my estimate was like Andrew's: "What are those two young men compared with the many?" But my blessed Lord, who fed the multitude with those morsels, can so multiply the resources and honor the labors of these two faithful ministers that *that week* may be

---

* This young man was Rev. Snyder, of Northwest Iowa conference.

among the most important in my life. From this lesson I learned to trust the Saviour for results, rather than to number Israel. The Rev. Mr. Byam, pastor of this charge, was at this time a young man of more than ordinary talent; and for years was quite successful as a minister; he became eventually state agent of the American Bible Society until the breaking out of the rebellion, when he was appointed colonel of a regiment, and is now located, I think, at Fort Dodge, in the state of Iowa. Rev. J. R. Cameron, my successor in Dubuque, during this year rendered me valuable assistance in sending out Sunday-school books to different points on my work. He entered the ministry at an early period in the history of Iowa—I think an old schoolmate of Dr. Kynett, which rendered their associations very pleasant in the city. A faithful servant of the church he has proved in every interest where he has been placed, and is stationed at Maynard the present year (1881). When the day of reckoning comes Brother Cameron will be ready.

Not very far from this date, and the temperature of the weather about the same, I visited Rev. Joel B. Taylor, stationed at Lyons, his work embracing Clinton and Camanche. He was laboring at the latter place, with a blessed revival on his hands, and being very much worn, my visit was very timely. Although he had written for me to come, I took him by surprise, and a happier man could not be found in the Taylor family. It was often said to me, in passing through the state, "I know your brother Joel, but this is my first acquaintance with you." Though not brothers in the flesh, yet our relationship is very close in several respects. Born about the same date, converted and entered the ministry about the same time, began to preach the gospel in this new territory in the days of log cabins and crust coffee, at war with the same enemy, sharing rich spoils of victory in the same conflict, of the same name, and with titles to the same rich and glorious inheritance in heaven, is it any wonder that we are called brothers? Well, this is

the man whom I met on Sunday morning, just ready to
preach; so that I stepped out of my carriage into the pulpit,
and preached on "Faith and its victories." This was one of
those sweeping revivals which embraced scores within its
influence, and every obstacle for a time seemed to fall before it; and among its faithful workers Sister Taylor was
one of the first. We often do injustice to our female friends
in writing up the history of these miracles of grace. We
honor the names of such a minister or such a brother, when,
if the facts were known, a faithful mother, or a devoted
sister, was the humble instrument in God's hands which
opened the way and led on to success. But when the final
award is rendered, Jesus will know upon what head to place
the crown. I remained with Brother Taylor during the
week, as the interest seemed to increase, and left at its
close with great reluctance. There are no occasions in this
life so well calculated to cement Christian hearts as a genuine work of divine grace, and most assuredly if it creates
joy among the angels, shall it not give heavenly inspiration
to saints on earth! This meeting continued for some time
after I left, resulting in a large accession to the church, and
in giving new life to the cause of Christ.

CHAPTER XXV.

Before I pass on, I may as well take a glance at Brother
Taylor.* In his own conference, where he is so well known,
it needs no pen-sketch to describe the man; but for the
benefit of other readers, I will say that he is of average
height, stoutly built, hair a little curly, and not rapid in his
movements. He has a fine voice, and it was said, in his
younger days, that such were its powers of penetration, that
two or three children, crying at once, could not disconcert

---

* Since the above tribute was written, Brother Taylor has entered into his reward.

him. In later years it has become more round and full, and
possesses great endurance. He seldom becomes hoarse
with hard labor. Very few men excel him in the gift of
exhortation and public prayer. Some of his exhortations I
have never known excelled for eloquence and power, and
when *fully inspired*, his prayers seemed to reach the very
heavens and capture a blessing for every believing soul.
In relation to his education, Brother Joel deserves much
credit in climbing the Hill Difficulty, deprived of the advantages of early culture. When he was converted in Dubuque county, and entered the ministry, the country was
new, but few opportunities for an education, and, like many
others, he carried his library in his saddle-bags, and on his
horse studied the philosophy of salvation. With all of
these disadvantages, he has been successful in his work,
and seldom leaves a charge without making it better. As
an evidence of his wisdom and discretion, in early life he
selected one of the best of companions, who has greatly
contributed to his success in every responsible position.
He has been honored by his brethren with a seat in the
General Conference; and through all of those thirty-eight
years in the ministry, not a charge has been presented, nor
a stain soiled the garments of his Christian character.
May the *winding up of his days be peaceful and serene,
and his sun set without a cloud.*

Toward the close of this winter I took a trip through the
northern counties of the state, and on my way called upon
Rev. George Clifford, who was stationed at Colesburg.
They had recently lost a dear child, and were, passing
through the deep waters of affliction. Being a particular
friend of theirs, my visit was very timely, for there is a so-
lace in trial, coming from the presence and sympathy of a
dear friend. I remained with them for several days, and
accompanied him round his entire circuit. I found him the
same humble, earnest and devoted brother, such an one the
more you know of them the better you like them. But with

all of his good qualities, at this time he was very much depressed in spirit on account of financial embarrassment. He was involved to the amount of one hundred and fifty dollars, which he found, with his small salary, impossible to pay, and he informed me that he must locate to enable him to meet this demand. Having that amount on hand that I could spare, I proposed to loan him the desired sum, and he might pay me at his convenience. In doing this he could continue in the blessed work. At this proposal the gratitude of his heart radiated from his countenance, and I left him a happy man. I am undecided as to which of the two was the happiest, for if at any period of my life I enjoyed the privilege of conferring a favor it was on this occasion. Brother Clifford remitted from time to time until the whole amount was canceled. I record this circumstance, not in the spirit of self-gratulation, but that it may serve as a hint to others to render like assistance in time of need. Brother Clifford is still doing his Master's work as presiding elder of Sacramento district, California, and when he reads this, there will be another "*communion of saints.*"

On my way from Colesburg, descending the Turkey river hills, I passed a point of danger which to this day makes me shudder. In descending a steep hill, before me at the right was a gully some twenty or thirty feet in depth, almost perpendicular. At the worst place the hame-strap of my *near side* animal gave way, which threw the whole load upon the other, and within three steps of the *awful gully*. All I could now do was to trust God and fly to the rescue. I leaped out of my wagon and found that my other faithful animal was *bracing for life*. To cramp my wagon to the right or left, in order to relieve the pressure, I could not, for this would have deprived her of her foothold, and destruction the consequence. I left all, ran up the hill until I found a broken rail, then returned, blocked my wheels, cramped my wagon, supplied a new strap for my other horse, and then pursued my journey. But that *suspense*, between leaving my team and returning with my rail, would not have been repeated with the purchase of gold. Never before did I place such an estimate upon "Fanny" for heroism in the hour of danger, and never did I feel such gratitude to my Lord for deliverance in the face of death. Skepticism may sneer at such offerings, but whilst they are amusing themselves over our credulity, we will be gathering strength and courage from this divine declaration: "The angel of the Lord encampeth round about them that fear him, and delivereth them."

When the huge bodies of snow and ice disappeared, and the ground was relieved of frost, such was the state of the roads that for a time travel was out of the question. Raised in the state of New York, I had heard much about *sloughs*, but it takes a Western man to know their meaning. At this early period, one entire trip through the state would be sufficient to graduate an apt scholar, and all the diploma he would want would be the monumental epistles read and known of all men. Not unfrequently you would pass a hack (if pass you could), foundered in the mud about two feet deep, with three or four rails lying by its side as evidences of their inefficiency to relieve the case. And in some instances, I have seen the ladies riding in the "hack," and the gentlemen alongside, each one with a big rail on his shoulder, ready to pry out of the next slough. This they called "working their passage." And right here, as it comes in so naturally, I must furnish my readers with an amusing episode, in the way of spice. A clerical gentleman and his lady, taking their bridal trip through the country at this time of the year, encountered this slough difficulty in a very practical way. The road being sidling, and they occupying an outside seat on the carriage, a sudden reel of the hack tumbled them both out into the deep mud. This was rather a hard experience for the first fruits of the "honey-moon," inasmuch as they had on their best, and endangered the well-being of a *new wig*, which had been purchased at quite an expense, in order to supply hair where it was not. It was an occasion of so much interest as to wake up the muses, and gave inspiration to this parody:

> "Away went Gilpin, hat and wig,
>   Away went Gilpin, he,
> And landed with his Sunday rig
>   In mud up to the knee.
> He struggled hard and waded out;
>   But, oh! the sight to see;
> His hat was gone, his wig was lost,
>   And very bald was he,
> And said if hacks were such a bore,
> *Such pleasure ends, forever more.*"

Thus you see we had poets in those days who could pluck poetry out of sloughs, and whilst the sufferers were cleaning their boots and recovering their losses, the muses had transformed the whole scene into poetic history. And if it be a fact that the scenery with which we are surrounded gives character to our productions, we are not at all surprised that the above incident should have aroused the muses from their slumbers. But the days of traveling in hacks in Iowa has nearly passed, and the iron-horse has taken its place, and the probabilities are that poetic genius will no longer be taxed to turn such misfortunes into verse. And my friend above says, " Let it come!"

Having such an extensive field of labor in this Sunday-school work, embracing more than half the state, I cannot enter into all the interesting details, neither dwell upon the many stirring incidents of the year; but I must again record with great satisfaction the hearty welcome and salutary help rendered me by the ministerial brethren of our conference. So seldom anything of peculiar interest occurs in presenting causes of benevolence, and in the taking up of collections, that I must step aside a little and note an exception. At this time, Rev. F. Amos was stationed at Dewitt, and as I was to preach for him on Sunday evening, he requested that before the collection was taken he might be permitted to follow the sermon with an exhortation. To this I assented with pleasure. He started out, commending my sermon and the value of the cause in which I was engaged, and the great contrast between our tract and Sunday-school literature and the yellow-leafed trash circulating through the land, and that it was our duty as Christians, and even good citizens, to use every exertion to suppress the one and promote the other. He stated to his audience that this was the work in which the Sunday-school agent was engaged, which was a strong motive why they should liberally contribute. " But," he remarked, " there are other reasons why. Your reputation as a circuit depends very much upon your generosity in this matter, inasmuch as Brother Taylor will report you to conference, and if they hear that Dewitt sent up *a little puny morsel* in a cause like this, they will decide that you are a "small fry," and will send you a one-horse preacher, just as they did this year. Now, if you desire to escape these consequences, I advise you to *shell out liberally*." Such overpowering motives as these could not be resisted, and the result was a first-rate report from the charge. You may recollect that Brother Amos was the man that met Mr. Sanford (Universalist) in a theological fight, and left the field with his colors flying. He still lives in the city of Maquoketa, Jackson county, Iowa, and though he left one arm on the battle-field in the war of the rebellion, he did not lose the dignity of a Christian soldier and a true man. I could still pass over this fruitful field of youthful culture with the greatest degree of pleasure; I could show you groups of little boys and girls around my wagon, pleading with their parents to purchase a book for them that they could call their own; I could refer you to instances where children were the instruments in God's hands in the promotion of blessed revivals; but other fields are before me to cultivate, and I must not honor the one at the expense of the other. But before taking my

leave of this field of labor, I must refer to my first and
happy introduction to Dr. Fuller, afterwards a member of
our conference, but now in heaven. In our last interview
before he left us, he gave me this statement: "I was
practicing medicine beyond Mt. Vernon, and hearing that
the Sunday-school agent had an appointment at a distant
school-house, I concluded I would go and hear what he
had to say. As I entered the room I saw a stranger sitting
near the stove; and soon he began to sing 'From every
stormy wind that blows,' etc. It was new to me," said
the doctor, "and as he proceeded, I saw the tears passing
down his cheeks, and I said, 'we will have something
worth hearing to-day.' After singing, he arose and took
for his text: 'The fear of the Lord is the beginning of wisdom.' I was not only edified, but my soul was very much
blessed, and the influence of that hour has never been lost.
I was then a Baptist minister, but soon united with the
Methodists, among whom I have labored to the present time;
and though nearly twenty years have passed, I cherish the
memory of that afternoon with the greatest pleasure." How
little did I think, and as little did he, in our last interview
on earth, when making this simple statement, that it would
become future history; but here it is recorded, and perhaps will remain and be read by hundreds, if not thousands,
long after our admittance into the heavenly kingdom.
About three years from the time above referred to, he was
appointed my successor as pastor at Sioux City, at my
request, and was very successful in building up the interests of the church. His was an honorable record on earth,
and I doubt not but that his reward will be glorious.

CHAPTER XXVI.

Our conference session was held this year (1856) at Maquoketa, and this was the first for Upper Iowa. Bishop Janes was again with us,—always welcome,—and the writer was elected secretary, with Rev. Elias Skinner for assistant. Brother Skinner was one of the old members of our conference, and a most excellent secretary.   He excelled in correct forms of expression. Being treasurer of the missionary society this year, as well as secretary, I had two men's work, in which Wm. M. Doughty, our book agent at Chicago, rendered me valuable assistance.   I had made my arrangements to continue in the work of the Sunday-school agency, as the experience of the year past enabled me to understand its wants, but a man was wanted for Sioux City district, and no one could be found willing to go.   Several of the older brethren had been consulted, but the honor was of such a character that they chose not to accept it. As the last extremity, toward the close of the conference the bishop sent for me to come to his room in order to see if I could not be prevailed upon to go. As I entered, he informed me that "they had come to a full stop, and could proceed no further in their conference business until they found a man for the Missouri valley; that several of the brethren had been solicited to go, but refused, and now he wished to know whether I was willing." I answered, " Bishop, if this is your *only hope*, put me down."   Such congratulations as then came from the bishop and presiding elders do not often occur in his cabinet, when Elder Dimmitt cried out: " Brother Taylor, *live forever!*" The dead-lock was now broken; the notes of victory had calmed down, and I was booked for the honorable position. I was fully aware that it required a sacrifice to leave many friends, and well-organized society, and travel a distance of three hundred and fifty miles, and then to find no society and but few of the comforts and conveniences of life. But then I knew also that forests could not be explored and new countries settled and cultivated without the courage of the hardy pioneer, and I was willing to accept my share and stand up boldly at the call of duty; and should small rations or hardships intervene, no human being could meet them with greater fortitude or a better grace than a true minister of the gospel of Christ. Such were my convictions; and inspired with the fortitude that Christ *only* imparts, I accepted the perils and awaited the honors. In reading the appointments, when the bishop came to "Sioux City district, Landon Taylor; Sioux City station, Landon Taylor," he paused; then, with the emphasis which *he only* could impart, he exclaimed: "Glory enough for one man!" In relation to my own history, I suppose this might be called a "*new departure.*" So far as territory was concerned, one-fourth of the state was under my supervision, and being presiding elder and stationed preacher also, I was endowed with double honor.

All things in readiness, I started for the "western slope," accompanied by Rev. D. J. Havens, the son of the venerable James Havens, of the Indiana conference. Brother Havens, not being very well, about the third night out, having to sleep in our wagon, passed through a hard experience. Being the first of September, the mosquitoes were without number, and as this peril had not been anticipated, our netting was not on hand. Such a night's rest was not refreshing, and when daylight appeared, my colleague concluded that if this was a foretaste of the bishop's "glory"—referred to in conference—the consummation must be *decidedly rich.* But so far as mosquito experience was concerned, this was but the beginning, for they gathered strength in ratio to the distance, until near Webster City, when we put up for the Sabbath at a Yankee farm-house, where we found protection, and improved it. On Monday morning, starting out on the prairie, Brother Havens in the advance, with a hatchet in his hand, some prairie chickens flew up before him, when he let fly his hatchet and took off one's head. Nothing occurred on our route so inspiring to him as this. Being low in spirits in view of his illness and loss of sleep, this little feat seemed to break the monotonous spell and placed him on a higher plane of enjoyment; and in addition to this, when we reached Sac. City and enjoyed the luxury of a good cup of coffee at Mr. Austin's, where we passed the night, we both felt like new men; for this was the first enjoyed on our way. We were now within one hundred miles of Sioux City, and "rejoiced in the consolation." At this point the weather turned cooler, and two successive frosts swept the crop of corn throughout the western part of the state and closed up our mosquito history for that fall. On our way down the Maple valley we met Brother Black, who had been laboring on this district the past year, and he conducted us to Brother Vandorn's, near Smithland, where we remained over the Sabbath. Here at Smithland, thirty miles from the city, I preached my first sermon on my district, and Brother Havens his opening discourse on his circuit. If the time ever was in my official history, when I could appropriate the language of Cowper, I could do it now without scruple:

> " I am monarch of all I survey,
>   My right there is none to dispute;
> From the center, all round to the sea,
>   *I am lord of the fowl and the brute.*"

It was said of one of our brethren, when raised to the dignity of presiding elder, that he started off singing:

> " This is the way I long have sought,
>   *And mourned because I found it not.*"

But no such mournful review was I tempted to sing during all my authoritative history on Sioux City district. Had I been so tempted at any time, a circle of nearly three hundred miles around it, through creeks and sloughs, and roving Indians, with swarms of flies and mosquitoes, would have changed the meter into this:

> "Better dwell in the midst of alarms
> Than to *reign* in this horrible place."

On my arrival at Sergeant's Bluff, I met Brother Clark, who gave me a hearty reception, and kindly proffered to take me in; and at Sioux City, Brother and Sister Yeomans had always an open door and words of welcome. These two places had been rivals, but Sioux City, at this time, was so far in the advance that its superiority was settled. Dr. Yeomans had been a practicing physician, but was now register of the land office in this place, and a local preacher in the Methodist Episcopal church. The warm reception given me by these brethren greatly contributed to relieve the hard experience whilst passing through the state, and make me feel at home among strangers and in a strange land. As Sergeant's Bluff was more in the country, and I had a team to provide for, I remained for a while with Brother T. Elwood Clark. The fall of 1856 was very beautiful, and within a few days I went to work and put me up an office 12 by 16, and before cold weather I had it finished, using it for a study, bed-room and chapel. Council Bluffs was one hundred miles south of us, upon which we depended for provisions, but the weather had been so pleasant during the month of November that a supply had not been obtained. On the first day of December, winter commenced with snow from the northwest, increasing in severity until the afternoon of the second day, when the climax was reached. To give my readers something of an idea of its character: About two P. M. I started from my office to dinner, about ten rods distant. When about one rod on my way I became lost; not being able to see my hand before me, and the storm cutting my breath, I halted and queried: "Strange, if I should perish within a few feet of my door!". But I thought, "as

I am facing the storm northwest, if I return southeast I will strike my office;" and this happy idea brought me into safe quarters, but dinner was dispensed with for that day. The storm continued for three days, and snow reached the depth of four feet on the level, accompanied with a crust so hard as to bear up a man. This was truly a snow blockade, for no one could travel for weeks, and the people being short of provisions, many had to subsist upon hominy and a few potatoes. Such were some of the honors arising out of my new relation to the church; but I was so much better provided for than many of the settlers around me that I felt truly thankful; for whilst they were restricted to corn and potatoes, we were favored with a little bacon in addition, which was our substitute for butter, for this last article was not to be obtained for love or money. But the time soon came when our larder was exhausted and something *must be done*. The snow is four feet deep, every day the storm is raging, the roads are fearful, and almost impassable, and if we start for Council Bluffs after provisions, we may perish. Such was a true picture of our situation at this time. But there is no other alternative. So Brother Clark and myself, each one with a team, started out upon this perilous journey of one hundred miles. When we met a team *loaded*, we gave the whole road. In that event we shoveled a *side-track* sufficiently large to admit our team until the other went by, then returned to the beaten road. And thus we continued until we reached our place of destination. Having obtained our supply in turn, we faced the storm, which at times was so furious that we could scarcely see our teams, the drifts filling up the road as soon as it was broken, when on the eighth day we reached home, incurring the greatest dangers and the most severe experience of my life. But the peril was passed, the goal was reached, and the material furnished for this page of history. Such was the depth of snow during this winter that in some instances it was dangerous to venture far from home, in view of the hungry wolves. Mr. Little, where we put up for the night, had been out to his grove, about one mile from home, after a load of wood, when his large dog was encountered by several wolves, which within five minutes left nothing but his bones; and the owner had to flee for life, and left his wood behind. And in another instance, a negro had been out a little distance from home, chopping, when on his return he was driven by a pack of wolves into a fence corner, where his remains and his axe were found, with six dead wolves lying by his side.

During this severe winter I did not lose but one appointment, and that was the Sabbath made vacant by my trip to Council Bluffs. Safely housed again after this trip of two hundred miles, it was a comfort to think that we had provisions enough to meet our present wants; but what of many of our neighbors? Many were reduced to the last extremity, subsisting for weeks on parched corn, and nearly perishing for want of wood. But this was not all. The severe frost in September cutting off the corn crop, but little was left for subsistence, and even *that* was very poor. I paid two dollars per bushel for such inferior corn in order to keep my team through the winter. But in the midst of this dreary weather, hedged in on every side by snow-drifts, cut off as it were from the blessings of good society for months. I could realize all that is meant in this stanza:

> "From every stormy wind that blows,
> From every swelling tide of woes,
> There is a calm, a sure retreat:
> *'Tis found beneath the mercy-seat.*"

Through the varied experiences of my ministry I have treasured up this lesson—that friendships formed through the history of perils and hardships in a new country are very sacred and of an enduring character. This idea is embraced by our Saviour when he said to his disciples: "Ye are they which have continued with me in my temptations." Take old soldiers, for example, who have shared

the hardships and faced the dangers on many battle-fields;
let them meet after a separation of many years, the out-
gushing emotions from the memory of past experiences are
beyond control.   The rush of past events turns toward each
other the currents of affection, and for a time the old hero
becomes a child.   The same is true in the maturity of
Christian friendships created in distant lands, and through
the trials of a new country.

From this little digression we will return to our narrative.
There were two or three oases, however, in this wintry desert, that served to break the dreary solitude and awaken up
new interests and pursuits.   During the beautiful fall, two
or three enterprising men came in from other states and
sojourned with us during the winter season, and their presence and cheerful spirits were like sunshine in the glade.
These were Brother E. R. Kirk, from Ohio, and Alexander
and Cornelius McLean, from New York city.   The first two
passed the winter with us at Sergeant's Bluff, and it mat-
tered not whether storm or sunshine, with them "December
was as pleasant as May."   But I have long since learned that
it requires less grace to be cheerful and jovial sitting by a
warm fire than in facing a driving snow-storm from the
northwest.   But such they were, and we were very thankful for it, though backed up by favorable circumstances;
for they served as harbingers of hope in a dreary land.
Brother McLean being a local preacher in the M. E. church,
often rendered me assistance.   He continued with us most
of the year, very much respected, when he returned to New
York, and is now a member of that conference.   Brother
Kirk is now residing in Sioux City, and among its prominent citizens.   Brother Havens having charge of Smithland
circuit, as soon as the weather would permit, I made him a
visit, and continued our meeting nearly one week.   Quite
a number were converted and added to the church.   Among
them was the lady of the house where Brother Havens was
making his home.   Her husband a few months previous,

owning a saw-mill in the town, was caught by his circular saw and killed instantly. He was a man very much respected. His last words were: "Oh, my dear wife!" and expired. His wife was a talented and amiable woman, and during that year her name was changed to Havens, the marriage ceremony taking place at the residence of Doctor Yeomans, at Sioux City.

Having to pay two dollars per bushel for corn, and but little to be had at that, I concluded to raise a patch of my own; and as the spring came on, I made my arrangements accordingly. In the ensuing fall I had enough for my own use and some to spare. Whilst preparing to plant, that fearful history occurred—the *Spirit Lake massacre*. As this account has been distorted, having taken place on my district, I will give the facts as they were. The Indians having camped near Smithland for the purpose of hunting and fishing, occasionally some few would pass through the town. At this time, three or four called in at a small store, with a few ears of corn gathered up in a field thrown out to the commons. A few of the whites, or rather *roughs*, asked them where they had obtained their corn, to which the Indians frankly replied. No more was said, but the whites went out into a thicket, cut each one a hickory, then returned, fell upon the Indians, and chased them into their camp. The males, most of them, being absent on a hunt, the whites gathered up all of their guns remaining, and brought them to Smithland, having made them promise, before they left, that on the following day they would go down and shake hands with the Omahas, another tribe, which the Indians knew would be certain death. When the hunters returned and found what had been done, they started in the night for the Cherokee, and commenced their depredations. Some forty or fifty of the whites were killed and several of the Indians. When I tell you that liquor was the moving cause, my readers will not need any further explanation. I have read several incorrect statements in

13

relation to the origin of this massacre, but this is the first, so far as I know, that gives the true history. If those roughs had behaved themselves, the Indians would have retired, and this sad affair would never have taken place.

As my quarterly meeting was at hand, having to pass through Smithland, and up the Maple valley to Ida Grove, on their trail, I never before witnessed such a state of excitement. The settlers had gathered into the little towns, selected the strongest house for a fort, then fortified to the best of their ability—the males on guard without, and the women and children within.

A Mr. B., on his way to town with many others, boasted what great feats he would accomplish in case of an attack. The party concluded to test his heroism by a little manœuvre. They planned for one to pass through the brush ahead, and wait until the company came up; then the war-whoop was to be sounded. The plan was executed, and the yelp given at the proper time, when lo! he dropped his coat, which he had been carrying on his arm, his hat flew off, and such speed as he made the famed Dexter hardly could have excelled. He never looked back to count the slain, but concluded that for him the only safety was in flight. When the harbor was reached, they handed him his lost apparel and congratulated him on his safe arrival. And thus ended his Indian campaign. On my return from Deni-son homeward, riding on horseback, I made a very narrow escape. The road was along a willow creek, which before me I could see some distance. Directly ahead of me, about thirty rods, in a little opening of the willows, I saw my enemy *sure* enough. The main road would have taken me within eight rods of the place of concealment. "What shall I do?" My thoughts ran fast. Fortunate for me, before I reached them, the road made an inward curve behind a little bluff out of their sight, and at the center of the curve, a ravine ran up to the left, which would take me into the main road, a distance of about a mile. You may

rest assured that I improved my advantage, and Fanny
went up that ravine with the speed of Mr. B. Within a
few minutes I was safe in the main road and out of the
reach of danger, and thanked God for the rescue. Never
since then have I doubted divine interposition in discovering those Indians. At the time, I was thinking about
something else, when one appeared in that vacancy so
plainly that not a place for a doubt remained. This narrow
escape from death, I did not at the time reveal to my own
friends, lest it might increase the excitement, or be attributed to a freak of the imagination, arising from the alarm-
ing state of things then existing. And right here I wish to
present a few thoughts in relation to Indian character.
And inasmuch as I am neither a hater, nor an admirer, what I
write may be regarded as the honest convictions of my heart.
I have no apologies to make for their code of justice, killing
the innocent instead of the guilty; I have but little confidence in their honesty or innocence where occasions offer
to test them; and their cruelty to prisoners is inexcusable.
Yea, I believe them to be treacherous in every sense of the
word, except in solitary instances; and yet I am fully satisfied that their association with the whites, copying their
vices, purchasing their liquor, and swindled by their deception, has had much to do in giving a still darker shade to
their degradation; and as they hold sacred the law of
revenge, is it a great wonder, after being so often deceived and imposed upon through government officials,
that they are brought to *despise government,* and take matters into their own hands! They are a down-trodden and
degraded race, of but little value in the world's history, and
our business as a Christian nation is, not to make them
worse, but to do all within our power to lift them up
to a higher plane; and this can be done only in the exercise
of justice, mercy, and truth.

During the summer of this year quite a number of ministers from the East visited our young city with a view of

investing a little in land for future use. Among these
were Rev. Mr. Lownsberry and Professor Loomas. The
fine opportunity, at this date, for purchasing land at government prices, brought in many ministers from the older
states, by whom we are now well represented. Sioux City
was then a small town of but a few hundred inhabitants,
but it has grown rapidly, and now numbers some eight or
ten thousand, besides being a place of commercial importance. Built on the Missouri river, a kind of railroad center,
and distant one hundred miles from any competing city,
with such an immense valley and fertile country to sustain
it, it must eventually become one of the great leading
marts of the West. Perhaps there is no better representa-
tion of intelligence and enterprise than here. Of one hundred persons attending church in that early period, nearly
all classes of professional men were present, and a fair proportion were graduates from some institution of learning.
To me it was a great pleasure to preach the gospel to such
a class of men and women, for I felt assured that if I presented anything deserving commendation it would be appreciated. From this statement you will discover that though
cultivating new soil, and enduring hardships and privations, we had some *bright spots* along the way, and one of
these was my home at Brother and Sister Yeomans', where
I always found a "light in the window for me." Upon
the return of summer, our table supplies were more plenti-
ful, and once more we enjoyed the luxury of milk and
butter—the latter at fifty cents a pound, and thankful to
secure it at that price. Having made my arrangements to
return to this work the second year, I made ample provision
for my team, and in the latter part of August I started,
in company with Brother Havens, to Marion, Linn county,
the seat of our next annual conference. Near Toledo we
attended a very pleasant camp-meeting on the way, at
which we spent the Sabbath, and here greeted many of our
old ministerial friends. As a long dreary winter makes a

delightful spring by the law of contrast, so my pioneer experience gave an unusual interest to our annual meeting, making friendships more dear and religious privileges more precious. What truth and beauty I now saw in this sentiment:

"Society, friendship and love,
Divinely bestowed upon man."

CHAPTER XXVII.

Bishop Ames is again with us at Marion, and the brethren at their posts. Rev. Elias Skinner was elected secretary, and we were favored with a very pleasant session. As I had no competitors for the office of presiding elder at Sioux City, I was returned without opposition. On my way back to my appointment I had the pleasure of the bishop's company to the city of Des Moines, nearly one hundred miles. He had to meet the conference at this place, and I proffered to take him through in my buggy. I found him one of the most genial and cheerful traveling companions that I had met, and for the first time in my life I had the honor of being raised above a bishop. And this result was reached without any effort on my part or any opposition from him. It was in this wise. His weight was about two hundred and thirty pounds, and mine one hundred and sixty; so when the springs of the seat on his side went down, mine went up, and thus in altitude I was constantly his superior.

Passing along the prairie the first day—full of life—said he: "Brother Taylor, as you have a new buggy, why don't you get a fancy horse?" I answered, "I will tell you after a little while." Within two or three hours we came to one of those terrible sloughs, near Marengo, which required all the skill and strength of my animal to take us through; but Fanny came out victorious on dry land. "I now know," said the bishop, "why you do not want a fancy animal; you do not wish to be left in the mud." Between Marengo and Newton we stopped at a hotel for dinner, and sat down to the table with about twenty boarders. As they began to ply their knives and forks, Bishop Ames called a halt, and said to the landlord: " If you please, we will ask God's blessing upon this food;" which being done, they resumed action, but kept an eye of interest upon the stranger, wondering who and what he could be. Having finished his meal, as he retired into the sitting-room the landlord came to me and with intense interest inquired, " Who is this man that asked that blessing?" Said I, " That is Bishop Ames, of the M. E. church." " Bishop Ames!" said he. "Then my table has been honored with a bishop." Hurrying to the door, as some of his boarders were leaving, he called out to them: " Did you know that we had a bishop at our table?" And thus, until we started, he was communicating the good news to every one he met. It seemed one of the grandest events of his life; and I doubt not that he treasured it up as a precious memorial. From this circumstance I found it to be a losing business to be in the company of a man who in office ranked so much above me, for all the honor I received was reflected from my superior.

At the close of the third day we landed at Des Moines, and there being a camp-meeting at Saylorsville, a few miles distant, I went down to that and spent the Sabbath. Here I found my dear old friend Rev. J. B. Hardy, one among the first preachers of Iowa conference, and one of the men that can be trusted. He is not only a good preacher, but all his powers are consecrated to that blessed Saviour who called him into his service. He is one of those men who need no epistle of commendation from me, for he is a "*living epistle* read and known of all men." I write in the present tense, as he is still living and laboring in his Master's cause. Brother Hardy being presiding elder of the district, he informed me that I must preach on the Sabbath at ten o'clock A. M., to be succeeded by Dr. Jocelyn. By some means neither of us were highly favored in our sermons, and for my own part I felt somewhat mortified. Not so much, however, as a brother minister, who stopped in his sermon, took to the brush, and then went to bed, as a fruit of his failure. No; but I was conscious that my effort was anything but a success, and every preacher knows what that means. Monday morning came, when the elder said, "At nine A. M. you must preach again." And now *mark* the benefits of a failure. Had I made a happy effort on Sunday morning, I should not have felt my dependence upon God, in that *helpless sense* as I felt it now; but this brought me very low at the Saviour's feet, and before I left the consecrated spot in the grove, before service, with my faith I had *grasped* the divine arm, and my motto furnished me upon my knees, "that *no enterprise can fail with God to back it.*" Baptized with this spirit, I ascended the pulpit and preached on the victory of faith. I need not detail the result. This much, however, I can say, that at one period in my discourse the weight of divine glory was beyond any former experience, and such a meeting after the sermon was truly glorious. Brother Hardy and many who read this will remember the hour and appreciate what I have written. Dr. Jocelyn, that blessed man who is now in heaven, what shall I say of him! For years we were members of the same conference; he was one of my successors at Old Zion, in the city of Burlington, and at this time pastor of the M. E. church in the city of Des Moines. It was here, from month to month, that the members of the legislature sat under his ministry, edified and delighted, and room could hardly be found for the crowds that attended. No minister of the gospel ever left our state with a better record than George B. Jocelyn, and the Michigan conference seldom if ever received a more valuable accession. The Albion college, of which he was so long president, was very much blessed and prospered under his faithful labors, and his name like sweet perfume will go down to other generations.

After a delightful season of enjoyment at this meeting, I started onward, and within three days I was welcomed to my old home at Sioux City and Sergeant's Bluff. Rev. C. J. Campbell was now stationed at Sac City, and Wm. Black at Denison and Carroll.   After the arrival of, the former, we held his first quarterly meeting, which was protracted through another week.   Here the Lord poured out his Spirit upon this place, which resulted in the conversion of about twenty persons.   One good feature of this revival, it was married to a temperance society; and as a result, they were like David and Jonathan, loving and assisting each other. There is no use in tampering.   Whisky and grace are incompatible, and the only way of success in religious societies is to deal with it as Putnam did with the wolf—take it *square between the eyes*, and then see to it that there is no danger of its restoration to life.   Before I left this meeting to return home, Brother Campbell complained of a pain in his toe, and on examining it, there was a red, round spot on the fleshy part of it about the size of a five-cent piece. Realizing nothing serious, I started for home, one hundred miles distant, and when I heard from him again he was in his grave.   He tried to send me word, but failed.   It was a case of the erysipelas; continuing to spread, its progress could not be arrested, until physicians decided that the limb must be amputated above the part inflamed.   He finally consented, but the shock was too great.   In the reaction he expired, but died like a Christian.   His remains are now slumbering in the grave-yard at Sac City, reminding us of the spirit of heroism which led him into distant lands to labor and die for the cause of Christ.

Among the number converted during this revival was a young man of promise, the son-in-law of Mr. Austin, one of the oldest citizens of the place, whom we licensed as a local preacher; but in less than one year he was sleeping by the side of Brother Campbell.   Failing to secure a supply for Smithland and Sac City, left vacant by the death of its minister, I saw no other way but to turn the whole district into a circuit, and go round it once in four weeks. In doing this, as there was Brother Black and myself, they would have preaching every two weeks. The brethren at Sioux City and Sergeant's Bluff consenting, we started out upon this new arrangement early in the spring, the distance around the work being about three hundred miles. This being one of the wet seasons, the traveling was perilous. For miles together it was wade through mud and water, through sloughs, and rapid streams, endangering our own lives as well as those of our faithful animals; but not an appointment did we miss, except Carroll, where the crossing was such that it was impossible for us to reach. In some instances we came up to those deep creeks on the prairie, full to the banks, and now our only course was to take a hatchet, lop down the willows standing upon the bank, pile old broken rails upon these, with weeds and grass and driftwood, layer upon layer, until the resistance was such as to bear up a horse, and then pass over. One of our prairies between Ida Grove and Sac City was forty miles across, without a house or a particle of water, which was an exception in our round. The only company to enjoy along this lonely way was now and then a little prairie bird flying up before my horse, or some hungry wolf following upon my track.

In going from Ida Grove to Denison, which was about thirty miles distant, I witnessed one of the most interesting sights of my life. In ascending a little bluff, as I reached the top, before me stood one hundred elk of various sizes. As I approached, they crossed the road a little before me, then formed a ring—the mothers with their fawns within; the males, with their great horns, completing the circle without. There they stood in this fortified position until I was out of sight. This was the grandest array of horned battalion that I ever witnessed, and was worth a journey of one hundred miles to see. I stopped my animal for some time to look into this *living fortress*, but they faced me with a look of defiance, as much as to say: "Come this way if you dare." At Denison, among other good brethren, I must mention the name of Morris McHenry, who at this time was county surveyor, and one of the pillars of the church. He was one of the men who would be an ornament to society in any place, in "the city full or on the desert waste." It was a pleasure to me to see these newly-organized societies of the previous year now taking shape and becoming centers of a strong and prosperous church. During the summer at Sac City I baptized about twenty persons by immersion, at the same service; and here again I realized the value of my method referred to in a previous chapter. These were some of the fruits of the revival during the winter. In passing round our work, in going and returning, we had to pass through Ida Grove, the county-seat of Ida county, where I always received a hearty welcome from Mr. Morehead, the first settler, and principal man of the place.

Mr. Morehead came to this place in 1856, one year previous to the organization of the county, and twice he was compelled to leave on account of the Indians. For many years settlement was very much retarded by the large grant made to the Chicago and Northwestern railroad company, both of which causes prevented its growth; and it was not till about 1870 that emigration commenced in *good earnest*. In 1871 he laid out the village of Ida, which at this date (1881) contains about eight hundred inhabitants, and he made during the last year over $50,000 worth of improvements. The present population of the county is over 4,000, of a respectable and wealthy class, and strongly republican. In 1877 the Maple River branch of the Chicago and Northwestern railroad was completed to this point, since which time settlement has been very rapid, there having been sold last year over 100,000 acres to actual settlers. Mr. Morehead at this time is the owner of 3,000 acres in the county, one-third of which is under cultivation. This interesting scrap of history is from my old friend (through his son), and goes to show what time, patience, and perseverance will accomplish within a few years. At that time there were but a few families and no church organization, but he had been raised a Methodist, and was what might be called a pretty good orthodox sinner. I always enjoyed putting up with him and his kind family, and he was as well satisfied as myself. My bill of fare was always adjusted by his generosity, without reckoning up my debt or credit. My successor, however, did not fare so well.

When leaving the circuit, he inquired of Mr. M. " how much he was in debt." The answer was that he could not tell without looking over the account. So here the settlement commenced.

REV. ———, DR.

To so many night's lodging and meals,	$20 00
Horse-feed in addition, . . .	10 00
Total indebtedness,	$30 00

At this point my ministerial brother began to feel a little streaked, and entertained some doubts whether after this bill was paid he would have enough left to pay his way to conference; and as he was about to adjust his pocket-book in order to square the account: " See here," said Mr. M.; " your credits are to come in before we strike the balance." " Credits!" said the preacher; " I have no credits to offset that indebtedness!" " Yes, you have," said my friend; and here they are:

	CR.
By so many sermons preached,	$10 00
By so many prayers in the family,	15 00
By so many blessings at table, . .	5 00
By one prayer, offered upon one knee,	25
Total, . . .	$30 25

So, you see, after this supposed money peril, my brother came out twenty-five cents ahead, which only gave elasticity to the joke. So far as the *sermons* are concerned in the items of credit, I am not so positive, but the facts are the same; and inasmuch as I received it from the preacher himself, I presume that it is true to history. Little thought my old friend, that some future scribe would record this amusing incident; but here it is, a part of the early history of Ida Grove. Mr. Morehead is still living, and when he reads this he will be twice blessed.

There was a young man of sandy hair and light complexion teaching school at Sioux City during the present year, with whom I formed a very pleasant acquaintance, who has since become well-known throughout the state of Iowa. I was well aware at that time that he possessed the elements that would eventually bring him into public notice, and his subsequent history has proved that I was not mistaken. For many years he has been general agent of one of the most responsible life insurance companies of the West, and perhaps no man has met with greater success. Not only does he possess great financial ability, but above all, he maintains the character of a Christian. He is a prominent member of the M. E. church, and he and his excellent wife reside in the city of Davenport. That young man was I. T. Martin. I must also include among my pleasant acquaintances during the year, Ezra and Joseph Millard, now wealthy bankers in Omaha, Nebraska. They were at that date just starting out in business life, and being young men of principle and good character, they have pushed their way up to wealth and affluence. Among the sad events to record about this time was the death of Brother Brindell, recently from Philadelphia, and an own brother to Rev. G. W. Brindell of the Upper Iowa conference. He had been recently married, and moved out west, near Sioux City; when in the act of cleaning out a well, he inhaled the poison, and at once expired. As he was much respected, the loss was deeply felt. His widow returned to Clinton, where she had been raised. It was here also that I first formed the acquaintance of Rev. Cornelius F. McLean, who has been long a member of our conference. He had taken up a claim in Nebraska, opposite Sioux City; had built a cabin, and was meeting the demands of the law. At his request I went over to Dakota, a little town across the river, and preached, I think, the first sermon in the village. Subject: "Heaven's estimate of one repenting sinner." I had great liberty, but whether there was joy in heaven on that day because of repenting sinners, is not yet revealed. But I went from the pulpit to my home happy in the consciousness of the soul's reward. As soon as Brother McLean could make his arrangements he entered upon the work, and now over twenty years he has been publishing the glad tidings of salvation, fully consecrated to God.

Our young city at this time, like the most of pioneer towns, had its drawbacks, including saloons and gambling rooms, where many a soul was ruined and families disgraced. On one occasion I was called upon to hold religious services over the body of a man who had died with the delirium tremens. As they had no other place, I stood up among the barrels of liquor. I referred, in my remarks, to the probabilities that this man was of respectable parentage, that he had grown up under the influence of religious training, had come out West to seek a home and fortune, followed by the sympathy and prayers of an interested mother that her dear boy might be honored and prospered in a land of strangers. And he himself as he left home was ardent with hope and solicitude that his way would be prospered. But he fell in with bad company, contracted bad habits, became a gambler and a drunkard, and here his earthly history ends in a liquor-shop, with no mourners present but his companions in crime! Whilst I am attending the last services of this young man in this saloon, in the presence of these *monuments of ruin*, interested friends may be praying and hoping that health and prosperity attend him. Then came in the appeal—that the same

company and habits that had brought this man to his
untimely end would result in their ruin also, and that their
only safety was in a life of virtue and temperance. During
these remarks they wept like children; but speak not of
reform in a business which bears the inscription of disgrace
and death.

The summer of 1858 was an exception, in that the rainy
season continued until the last of August, up to the very
time when we had to start to our annual conference, which
caused us much inconvenience. The creeks and rivers were
bankfull and overflowing, and had I not been a practical
swimmer, our trip through the state would have been a
failure. Having finished the last round, we bade farewell
to the friends at Sioux City and Sergeant's Bluff and started
on our way. I had arranged to hold our last quarterly
meeting at the different appointments, the first being at
Smithland, thirty miles distant. Having closed up the
labors of Saturday and Sabbath, without any marked
results, on Monday morning we intended to start for our
new appointment. But before starting, a delegation was
sent, among whom were some of the unconverted, beseeching us to stay another day, as there were a large number of
persons seeking the Lord. Such a motive I could not
resist, and so appointed a meeting for Monday evening.
Surely enough, ten or twelve seekers came forward, professed conversion, and united with the church, who subsequently became faithful members. Passing on to Sac City,
we had a meeting of unusual interest. Those who were
converted and baptized were to be taken into full connection. During this service, in giving them the right-hand of
fellowship, and requesting others to do so, a wonderful
spiritual manifestation attended, which filled every believing heart with joy and rejoicing. This was our last service
on the district; twenty or thirty had been recently converted, and it was meet that our last meeting should be a
pentecostal feast. At its close, I opened the doors of the

church, when six of the principal men of the place came forward, who afterward became pillars in the church.

Our labors have now closed on this district. Monday morning arrives, and a large number of Christian friends accompany us to the river, our place of crossing. Swimming our horses over the stream, we crossed in a small boat, and having hitched our horses to our buggies and waved to our friends, still standing on the river bank, the last farewell, we started for Lyons, the seat of our coming conference. When almost out of sight, I cast a look backward, and still the friends were standing, waving a distant adieu. Such tokens of friendship and affection were *heart-cheering* after encountering the labors, hardships, and perils of the last two years, and it reminded me of the waving flag of welcome that they might be permitted to hang out as a *signal* when approaching the heavenly shores. There is no small event in the history of my ministerial labors that has left a more tender and touching impression than the last greeting of those Sac City friends; and as the husband and father can endure the hardships and dangers of the soldier when inspired by the love of liberty and home, so I felt that these memorials of true affection served to inspire me with still greater heroism in the cause of Him who died for us. And not many hours passed before the occasion was furnished in a very practical form. We came to a large stream, widening out ten or twelve rods, and now what is to be done? Brother Black, my traveling companion, cannot swim, the water is too deep to ford, some of our articles must not be wet, and now I will test its depth by wading through. Carrying our blankets in my hands, extended upwards, I started for the other shore, and found that I could just go through, the water coming over my shoulders. Safely landed, I deposited my load on the bank and then swam back after the second. Thus I continued wading and swimming alternately, until all were over excepting Brother Black and the buggy. Well, what disposition is to be made of them? Fortunate for us, we have a rope on hand, and so I fasten this to the shafts of my buggy, lash the preacher fast to the rear, and Fanny brings all in safety over to the opposite side. It was quite amusing to see a very short man rolling and whirling in the stream, but this was the only hope—too short to wade, and unable to swim, his only *hope* was that of the *rope;* and to this he adhered like a faithful friend. So that beyond the floods, standing on the shore of safety, in his song of gratitude, like Miriam he could sing: " The horse and his rider hath he thrown into the *sea,* but out of all the *rope* hath delivered *me.*"

When I describe the method of crossing in one instance, it embraces our entire water experience, except in cases where the streams were too deep to wade; then I had to swim over in the advance, then my animal came, afterward my traveling companion and appendages. Thus we persevered onward until we came to a long layer of floating logs, lifted up by the high water, and over these we rolled and splashed until at last, the second afternoon, we reached the dividing ridge. If two men were ever glad and grateful for dangers passed, and victories won, we were, when our horses' feet stood firmly on " terra firma." And now, what an appropriate time for a short review. Two years had passed by since I entered upon this work; and though I had encountered hardships, braved dangers, and suffered the loss of many social pleasures, yet I had been honored with the privilege of preaching the gospel where its joyful sound had never been heard, organizing new societies, establishing new Sunday-schools, witnessing the conversion of many souls, and laying the foundation for the future growth and prosperity of the church of Christ. At this point I can furnish nothing more interesting or appropriate than a short extract from a letter just received from Dr. S. P. Yeomans, now residing in Charles City, but then the register of the land office at Sioux City. He says:

" It is generally thought that, to find the heroic in Methodism, we must go back to the early days of our church history; but when I call to mind (as I often do) your trials and privations as you buffeted the terrible winter storms of twenty-five years ago upon the Sioux City work, laboring with your own hands for the support which the scattered membership was unable to afford, I am firm in the conviction that your faith, zeal and endurance in the Master's work were hardly surpassed by the old pioneers of Methodism. As we now look over the field, we are enabled to see clearly that your labor was not in vain. The seed that you scattered in that virgin soil has taken root and already yielded an abundant harvest. The apparently barren field which you then traversed has now become a mighty center of Methodism, whose influence is felt through all Northwestern Iowa and the territory beyond; another evidence of the verity of that grand old promise, ' *Lo, I am with you always.*' "

I am glad to be able to add to this page the testimony of such an able writer as Dr. S. P. Yeomans. In leaving this work my report to conference is as follows: Members, 141; probationers, 36; baptisms, 24; churches, 1; Sunday-schools, 6; scholars, 158; preaching places, 10. The remainder of our trip through the state was very pleasant, and rendered the more so by the pleasant Sabbath spent at Marshalltown, with Brother Henderson. On this day I preached from "Never man spake like this man," and Brother Black gave us a sermon in the evening. The following Thursday we reached Honey Creek camp-meeting, near Marengo, and here I again met my old friend and former colleague, Rev. Wm. Simpson, now presiding elder of Oskaloosa district. I need not say that there was mutual joy, and this was one of the happy events of my life. This was my last season of personal enjoyment with the elder on earth, and the next will be in heaven. On our way to Lyons, from this place, again we enjoy the luxury of a

14

short visit at Hon. Hiram Price's, at Davenport, and preach
for them on the Sabbath. Rev. Linderman, at this date,
was pastor of that society. On the following Tuesday
we all met at Lyons, and thus closes up the history of
Sioux City.

CHAPTER XXVIII.

"And are we yet alive, and see each other's face!
Glory and praise to Jesus give, for his redeeming grace.
What troubles have we seen, what conflicts have we passed!
Fightings without, and fears within, since we assembled last.
But out of all the Lord hath brought us by his love,
And still he doth his help afford, and hides our life above."

What a history has been made by these one hundred and
sixty Methodist ministers during the last twelve months!
Here they all are, to report past progress, and to gather new
strength for additional conquests. Some have passed through
sore trials, some have had to live on small rations, and yet
others inscribe: " The lines have fallen unto me in very *pleasant places.*" But in this diversified history, our *grand end
and aim* has been to win souls for Christ. For *this*, every
book has been studied, every prayer has been offered, every
sermon has been preached, and the results recorded above.
Bishop Morris is again with us, but now shows the marks of
time. During this session, I used every effort in order to
supply my former work with good men; and in this I was
successful, having secured the consent of Rev. George Clifford for presiding elder, and Rev. I. K. Fuller for Sioux City
station. Brothers B. C. Barnes and Glassner were also appointed to this district; good and faithful men. The usual
business of the conference finished, my appointment is read
out for Maquoketa. Rev. G. W. Brindell had been their
pastor the year previous, and left the charge in a good
spiritual condition. Having labored here in revival work

three years previous, I had formed a very pleasant acquaintance; which gave me a hearty reception, and I felt at once
at home. My congregations were large, a flourishing Sunday-school, an intelligent audience, and all alive to the interests of religion. Brother Brindell was recently from
Philadelphia, this being his first station in our conference.
He was a good preacher and faithful worker in the Sabbath-
school, and labored to promote all the interests of the
church. He remained with us several years, a successful
pastor, until his father's ill health called him again to Philadelphia. So soon as he could leave he returned, and since
that time he has filled some of the most important positions
in our conference, and leaves the blessing of his Master in
every charge. This year he is stationed at Osage, and his
labors are attended with the same gracious results. His
pleasant companion contributes her share in all the interests
of the work, and often in feeble health, has cheerful words
for him in every trying hour. Long may they live to reflect
the lustre of a Christian example already bright, until grace
is with glory crowned.

The faithful pastor, like the skillful farmer, commencing
the labors of the year, looks around to see what work is the
most important to do first. By this rule I was governed as
I entered upon my pastoral relation in Maquoketa; and
very soon I found myself included among the number addressed in the language of the poet:

"Do not, then, stand idly waiting for some *greater work* to do.
Fortune is a lazy goddess; she will never come to you.
Go and toil in any vineyard; do not fear to do or dare.
If *you want a field to labor, you can find it anywhere.*"

And my charge was not an exception to the truth embraced in this beautiful language. Our church had been
recently enlarged by an addition in length of sixteen feet,
but the basement was unfinished, without door, windows or
floor; cold weather would soon be upon us, and the main
audience room could not then be made comfortable. The

brethren had been largely taxed in order to finish the upper
part, and seemed reluctant to incur further expense; and so
the matter stood.   But the alternative was before us: the
basement must be finished or religious services suspended
in very cold weather.   After my experience and discipline
in the Sioux City country, I did not need any additional inspiration, but felt the moving impulse of Brother A. at a
camp-meeting which I attended near Burlington, when a
shower had unfitted the altar for service.   He cried out:
" *Straw, brethren, more straw!* twenty souls lost this morning for want of straw!"   It has been supposed that this
exclamation was manufactured, like many others in our day,
but being on the ground, I can vouch for its truth, with the
name of the person.   This brother was very impulsive, and
could not think of the idea of salvation's work being retarded for the want of a little dry straw.   And thus, in the
work of finishing up our basement, I expected that salvation would be our work during the coming winter, and we
needed all the helps within our power; and thus I went
right to work, and in a short time the voice of prayer and
praise ascended from within its finished walls.   The brethren, within a short time, returned to me all the funds that I
had advanced, with their heartfelt thanks, and we all rejoiced in the consolation.   So far as efficient help in the
church was concerned, if ever I realized that I had "a good
heritage," it was here.   Rev. Lyman Catlin, now a member
of the Upper Iowa conference, and his excellent wife,
Brother Martin, our stirring Sunday-school superintendent,
Brother Spencer, our teacher of the Bible class, Brothers
Poff, Stevens, Wright, Barnes, Stimpson, Northup, Fellows,
Gephart and their companions, with many others, a little
host, stood by my side, ever ready to bear a part in pushing
forward the good cause.   My home this year was at Mr.
Millard's, whose wife was a member of our church, and who
spared no pains to make it a pleasant one.   These were the

parents of Ezra and Joseph Millard, so favorably mentioned in my sketch of Sioux City.

Everything in readiness, we went right to work, laboring earnestly for the salvation of souls, and we did not labor in vain. The interest increased gradually from day to day, until we looked upon thirty persons at the altar for prayers at the same time. One evening we had a similar manifestation of divine power as that witnessed on Dubuque circuit, ten years previous. Such was the unity of hearts, and the victory of faith, that they were all converted about the same time. So well assured was I of this, that I requested all the seekers who had obtained a *clear* and *satisfactory* evidence of their acceptance with God during the last prayer, to rise to their feet, when every one arose. It was a grand sight, and the divine glory in the midst made it still grander. Such victories of faith do not often occur, and never, until the church rises to a high spiritual condition. As is generally the case, the blessed work commenced in our Sunday-school and embraced many of its largest scholars. One evening of much interest, I witnessed one of the most interesting scenes of this kind within my ministerial experience. The teacher of a Bible class, having sought and found the "*pearl of great price*," came to me, her face all aglow with holy joy, and asked me: "Will it be right for me to go out into the congregation and invite my scholars to come?" I said to her "Go;" and one after the other she led to the altar, until she reached the seventh, and then she knelt by their side and prayed for their conversion. Bless the Lord for such youthful missionaries! My heart grows warm in giving this interesting relation. I have read and thought much about "ministering angels," and often have I fancied that I felt the brush of their balmy wings, but never saw a closer resemblance of one in human form than that dear girl of fourteen when leading her companions to Christ. And then to see them standing up side by side, all saved and happy, praising God for redeeming love, would require an angel's pencil and angelic skill to furnish an appropriate picture for the mansions of heaven.

When the time of our second quarterly meeting arrived, our presiding elder, Rev. J. C. Ayres, was with us, and his heart seemed inspired with strength anew in view of the glorious work in progress. On Sunday evening his subject was the Prodigal Son, and of all the discourses of his to which I have listened, this was the most convincing and powerful. Brother Ayres came from the Erie conference to ours in its early history. As an efficient laborer in his younger days when a member of the Erie conference, he had but few equals, if any superiors; and during the many years in which he served the church in the state of Iowa, he was the same devoted, able, and honored minister of Jesus Christ. No man in our conference was better acquainted with its doctrines and discipline, and no one better qualified to defend them. He was one of those men that needed no adjectives to portray his real worth, as he embodied nearly all of the valuable qualities of the Christian character. He is still living in Kansas, in a good old age, awaiting his Master's call.

This glorious work—described above—continued about six weeks, and resulted in a large accession to the church. It was here, in Maquoketa, that Rev. Oliver J. Cowles found a companion in the family of Brother and Sister Matthews, who were members of my charge; his parents at this time residing in this village. As one of the results of this revival, it diffused a new interest in our Sunday-school, and from this time onward, until my term of labor expired in this station, our services here were a spiritual feast. In no one appointment in the state did I experience such a continuous spiritual influence as in this place, owing much to the interested superintendents and noble band of evangelistic workers. One of the interesting departments of this school was the *infant class*, at this time under the care of Sister Catlin, numbering about fifty scholars. No one was better qualified for such a position, and no one enjoyed it more. Being present on one occasion when she was asking questions, she inquired: " Who was the first man?" Answer, "Adam." "Well, children, who was the first woman?" "Mrs. Adam," answered a little urchin. The little boy thought of course that if the man's name was Adam, the wife's must be the same. And right here I will present a specimen of the powerful influence of moral and religious teaching upon the minds of children. Being always at Sunday-school, when it was possible, I had a fine opportunity of impressing upon the minds of youth the importance of virtuous habits. One day, coming up the street, I saw before me a group of boys, earnestly engaged in talking— so much so, that I was unobserved. As I approached near, one of the boys, becoming angry, swore very profanely. Looking around, he saw me, and you never saw a boy run to the extent of his powers faster than he did; and he continued until he was out of sight. The other boys stood still and laughed. Said I, " Boys, what made George run so fast?" One immediately answered: " He had been swearing, and when he saw you he was afraid." The next day, in Sunday-school, George was present, and I mentioned the circumstance, when his head dropped. Then I asked the school to give me a passage of Scripture to prove that boys were afraid, and would run when they swore. Instantly one quoted this language of Solomon: " The wicked flee when no man pursueth, but the righteous are as bold as a lion." How often have I thought of this simple circumstance as illustrating human character. He was a boy, it is true, but human nature is as plainly manifest in the boy as in the man. And you may trace the elements of sin through all of its stages and developments, and you will find that it is never to be trusted. If it is there in the heart, it will crop out in some form, and then its results are fear and shame. Take a man who has done you an injury, and not unfrequently he will go half a

mile out of his way to avoid meeting you. Fear and shame
are the fruits of wrong-doing—as much so now as when our
first parents tried to hide away from God in the garden of
Eden; whilst an upright life is always honored with courage
and unshaken confidence. This is the true secret why the
pure man is calm in the hour of death, and happy in the
face of his Judge. Up to this period I had never felt the
least symptom of failure. For more than twenty years I
had been laboring in revival work without attempting
to favor myself in the least, but during this meeting, one
evening, when preaching on the redemption of time, becoming very much engaged, I felt a kind of weakness and giving way in my left side, attended with acute pain. For a
time I was fearful that I would have to give up my charge,
but warm weather coming on I felt much relief.

In the labors of this winter, Rev. Samuel Y. Harmar, of
Sabula circuit, held a meeting on his work which I attended
for some days. It was a season of much interest, and many
souls found peace in believing. When our meeting commenced he rendered us similar service, and our interchange
was very pleasant and profitable. Brother Harmar was
also transferred from Philadelphia to our conference in 1857.
He came out to Iowa to do service for his Master and adopt
it as his home. No one who has seen him once needs any
pen-sketch to describe his person. He is short, thick, and
fleshy, weighing about two hundred and thirty or forty
pounds; quick step, full round voice, a little bald, quite a
poet, and an excellent singer; always cheerful and happy;
and when he begins a protracted meeting he perseveres until
he makes it a success. He has a peculiar gift in becoming
well acquainted with his people, and almost invariably
brings up a good report from all the interests of the church.
When he starts out upon any enterprise he is always hopeful, strong in the faith, and often writes *victory* before the
field is won. In all of my pleasant acquaintance with him,
and *tight places* to which ministers are subject in a new

country, I never knew but one in which he cried for help;
and that was at our conference in Iowa City, when the bed
that sustained him and Brother Knickerbocker gave way
and brought them into such close communion that neither
skill nor physical force was of any avail. Here were about
two hundred and forty pounds on the one side, and one
hundred and seventy-five pounds on the other, tending
more and more to the *center;* and the longer the pressure
the tighter the squeeze; and had it not been that a helping
hand was near, what the result might have been, I write
not. But timely aid was at hand, and deliverance rendered, so that they could now sing:

> " From this peril I am free;
> *Bless the hand that rescued me!*"

Brother Harmar, after a faithful service of twenty-two
years in this state, retired from active labor at the last session of conference in Osage; but his name is engraven with
honor on our church records, and in the hearts of his brethren he will long live in the Upper Iowa conference.

Among the interesting events of this year on this charge
was the licensing of James W. Martin and Stephen Poff
to preach the gospel as local preachers in the Methodist
Episcopal church. How these brethren have improved this
great privilege, then conferred, I am unable to say, inasmuch as my fields of labor since that time have placed
many miles between us. I have reason to hope, however,
that when the Master calls upon them for a settlement—as
he surely will — each one will be able to say, " Lord,
thy pound hath gained five pounds." I must here record
one occurrence of interest which took place during the
revival season of the present year, A young lady who had
recently embraced religion was invited to take a sleigh-ride
of several miles into the country as a pleasure trip. She
willingly consented, not suspecting any decoy; when reaching the place of destination, lo! a splendid dance had

been arranged and was in successful operation. She at once notified the young man "That she was now serving another Master, and should not remain; that she should return home, if compelled to walk the whole distance." This was a kind of damper to her attendant, but he honorably returned the young lady to her own dwelling. This was conduct so noble and heroic on her part, that I took occasion to commend it to the public congregation, and trusted that such traits of character would be appreciated by some one qualified to reciprocate.

CHAPTER XXIX.

About this date (December 13, 1858), I received a letter from Rev. R. L. Collier, now stationed at Davenport, to come down and spend the Sabbath in the city, preparatory to his marriage with Miss Mary Price. She was the daughter of Hon. Hiram and Susan Price, and embracing religion under my pastoral labors, I was selected to perform the marriage ceremony. It was announced in the public congregation to take place at nine o'clock on Monday morning, and an invitation given for all to be present. Long before the time appointed, the Methodist church was filled to its utmost capacity, including the minister and many from Rock Island; and now we await the arrival of the parties. The interval attending this delay of the nuptials is always *pleasantly painful*, and every minister of the gospel knows the nature of the suspense. Why it is so, more than on any other public occasion, may not be so easy to explain, and yet such is universal experience. The party having arrived, the congregation at this point of interest were about to rise up, when I requested all to be seated, that each one might enjoy a better view. After the ceremony was performed, Judge Dillon came to me, commending my

marriage service as a model form; then two or three others;
which made me feel very pleasantly that the occasion was
one most agreeable and satisfactory to all. My readers will
remember that the marriage of Judge Dillon occurred five
years previous, mentioned in a former chapter. Brother
Collier at this date was a very eloquent and promising
young man, possessing popular talents, a fine voice and
very pleasing address. He labored about five years in the
Upper Iowa conference in the very best charges, then transferred his ministerial relation to the Rock River conference,
laboring in Chicago some two or three years. Having a
call from the Unitarian church, he accepted it, where he
labored many years with great acceptance, and is still a
minister of that church. Sister Mary Collier was a model
Christian lady, throwing all her influence to promote the
interests of the church whilst living, and when her Lord
called she was ready; but she never departed from the
faith which at first gave such a lustre to her youthful character. Her remains are slumbering near the old home
where she passed into spiritual life, awaiting that grand
event, when " Beauty immortal shall wake from the tomb." ✗

The winter having passed, in the month of April, a Sabbath was set apart for the baptism of the young people
recently converted. It was a beautiful sight, on Sunday
morning, to see the altar surrounded with those who a few
months previous had found the Saviour on the same spot,
and receive their pledge of fidelity to God. In the afternoon, as some preferred to be immersed, we repaired to the
Maquoketa river, a short distance, to finish up the labors of
the day. I found the water intensely cold, apparently more
so, in view of the temperature of the weather, and one or
two of the candidates could hardly survive the shock. As
I had baptized the last person, and was about starting for
the shore, I looked up and saw one of the old citizens coming toward the stream, headforemost, his hat flying in
another direction, when, *plunge!* he went under the water

a few feet from my side. This last service I had not included in my programme, and it took me by surprise. As it occasioned much merriment among the unconverted I took occasion to administer reproof for such conduct upon such a solemn occasion. But the novelty of the scene, and the suppressed laugh, so outweighed the force of the rebuke, that I have no idea that any one was struck under conviction. I have often read: "Only one step from the sublime to the ridiculous," but never saw it realized as upon this occasion. I afterward learned that the whole plan had been previously arranged, and funds promised to meet all damages. It seems that the administrator of this service, in the early history of the town, had worked for this man to the amount of thirty or forty dollars, but could never get his pay, and that this short method was adopted to square accounts. The following day the party was prosecuted, when the jury rendered a verdict of five dollars damages and costs. If the injured party had been popular in the community, the result would have been otherwise; but this *one item* changed the whole color of the transaction. But not in the estimate of Him " who rendereth to every man according to his work."

In the latter part of April, in view of my incessant labors through the winter, and the injury sustained affecting my side, the church voted me a release of six weeks to visit my relatives and friends in Ohio. This was very timely and highly appreciated. As I had my pulpit supplied by different ministerial brethren, it gave them quite a variety in its ministrations. It was now five years since my last visit to this state, and I found the same striking contrast in the world of nature. When I left the Mississippi, all was still under the dominion of cold and frost; but on reaching Portsmouth, Southern Ohio, the hills and valleys were clothed in green and adorned with beautiful flowers. What an inspiration do such contrasts impart to the soul of man, and especially to the Christian, who sees the impress of God written upon every leaf and giving beauty to every flower; and just in proportion as we bear his image, do we see his glory reflected through all of his works. Not notifying my friends in advance of my coming, I took them by surprise. On the Sabbath I preached for Brother See, at Bigelow chapel, Portsmouth, and addressed the Sunday-school. I was now among my old friends, many of them the religious companions of my youth, who for many years had been kept by power divine, and this reunion of friendships made our communion sweet. At Wheelersburg, nine miles above Portsmouth, and where I publicly consecrated my life to God, they were waiting my return, to welcome me to my former home. And thus, from place to place, over the old consecrated ground that I traveled in my early ministry, it was a continuous feast. When I reached Ironton I put up with Brother and Sister Peters, the friends of my youth, and an ever-welcome home. Toward evening, who should come into my room but Charles C. McCabe. Six years previous, in the city of Burlington, he left my study, followed with my prayers and tears; but now we providentially meet in another state with joy and rejoicing. To me, nothing could have been more unexpected, and nothing more welcome. To be permitted to meet Brother and Sister Peters after an absence of many years, filled the cup with joy; but the visit of Brother McCabe in addition, caused it to "*run over.*" Rev. C. A. VanAnda was then stationed at Spencer chapel, and I was booked to preach on the Sabbath at half-past ten o'clock A. M. Could any occasion have been more inspiring? Perhaps one-half of the audience had been members of my charge or of my congregations fifteen years previous; and many of them converted under my ministry. Surrounded with old and tried friends, as well as ministers of the gospel, with the inspiration of Brother McCabe, it seemed as though I was for an hour raised above myself as I discoursed from "Never man spake like this man." As to the merits of the sermon, it would be improper for me to speak; but as to the state of my mind I can say "My soul mounted higher, in a chariot of fire, and the moon was under my feet." Such a Sunday of reunions and true spiritual enjoyment occurs but a few times in the history of human life, and I doubt not they will remain bright when the pages of this world are transferred to the records of heaven. As Brother McCabe was teaching in one of the high schools in this city, on Monday I called at his room, where I found my old friend Kingsbury, who was now superintendent. He said to me, "Though it has been seventeen years since I heard your voice, as I passed the church yesterday, when you were preaching—though I did not know that you were in Ohio— I *knew it* as soon I heard the first sentence." What a mystery is man to himself. Though according·to the laws of physiology the human system undergoes an entire change once in seven years, yet *that* which constitutes the man is still the same. The eye that saw, the ear that heard, the voice that spoke, twenty years ago, memory lays away carefully in the drawer, and when the occasion calls them out, here they are, as familiar and as fresh as though suns had not risen, and stars had not set. Ah, yes! What God hath made immortal, will endure forever.

In connection with our Sunday services, I ought to have said, and will now say, that Brother VanAnda preached a very fine sermon in the evening from "O Lord, I will praise thee." When dwelling upon silent praise, he presented some grand and sublime thoughts. He had the towering mountains, the waving forests, the old Egyptian pyramids, all vying with each other in their offerings of praise to God. On Monday evening we enjoyed one of those seasons of Christian fellowship seldom surpassed in its spiritual power with clear and intelligent testimonies. In that audience there sat Dan Young, Thomas O'Neal, Brother Hand and Brother Gillam, with many others, whose faces I was looking upon for the last time on earth.

We parted that evening, never again to meet until we embrace each other on immortal shores. It was here at Brother Peters', in Ironton, where Rev. C. C. McCabe first became acquainted with one whom he thought worthy and suitable to become a companion for life. Miss Peters had recently graduated in Cincinnati, and was a young lady of fine appearance, of piety and intelligence. It was not long before her name was changed to McCabe, which consummation I trust neither has had cause to regret during the experience of twenty-one years. Among the many old friends, the six weeks allotted me soon passed away, and in the early part of June I arrived in safety at my pastoral charge in Maquoketa. We passed a very pleasant summer, with great peace and prosperity in the church, and wound up the labors of the year writing success in all of its interests. We will now interest our readers with a sketch of Rev. C. C. McCabe, D.D., assistant corresponding secretary of the Board of Church Extension of the M. E. church.

Rev. Charles Cardwell McCabe was born at Athens, Ohio, Oct. 11, 1836, and is the son of Robert and Sarah Cardwell (Robinson) McCabe. His great-grandfather, on the male side, was a native of the county of Cavan, Ireland, and descended from Covenanter stock. His father was a man of noble and generous impulses, and was for many years a merchant and railroad contractor in the West. He died in Chicago, in June, 1872, loved and respected. His mother was born in England, and came with her parents to this country when seven years of age. She was a lady of high social position and fine literary attainments, whose name was well known as a contributor to the *Ladies' Repository* in the earlier days of Ohio Methodism. Her life as a Christian was characterized by deep piety and benevolence, and as a mother, by unceasing devotion to the welfare of her children. She died in Burlington, Iowa, in 1852, in the full assurance of a blessed immortality. During the first ten years of his life, Dr. McCabe was a very delicate child. Indeed, during all of that period, he never passed what might be called a well day; nor was it till ten or twelve years since that he attained to robust and muscular manhood. He was educated at the Ohio Wesleyan university, which he entered in 1853, remaining four years, and receiving a full classical and theological course. From the earliest dawn of reason he was a believer in Christianity; his heart was touched by the Spirit of God in childhood, and, like Samuel, he was "Lent to the Lord from his birth." He always desired to be a Methodist minister. This was the one and the only ambition of his life.

After leaving college he taught school for two years to pay expenses of his education, his father at that time being in straitened circumstances. On the 5th of July, 1860, he married Miss Rebecca, daughter of John Peters, Esq., of Ironton, Ohio, a lady well-qualified to fill a wife's place in the sphere in which her husband moves. They have one son, named John Peters; a youth of fine appearance and good parts, likely to follow the footsteps of his father. Dr. McCabe entered the ministry the same year in which he was married, joining the Ohio conference of the Methodist Episcopal church. His first charge was Putnam, in that state, where he remained over a year. In 1862 he entered the army as chaplain of the One Hundred and Twenty-Second Ohio infantry, Col. Wm. H. Ball of Zanesville commanding, and followed the fortunes of that regiment until June, 1863, when, during the raid of Lee into Pennsylvania, while with his regiment in the defense of Winchester, he was captured by the rebel Gen. Early, with others, and sent to Libby prison, where he remained four months, his health being most seriously impaired by the rigors of the incarceration. He was exchanged on the 28th of October following. Many thrilling passages might be produced from lectures afterwards delivered by him before vast audiences, on life in that notorious "keep." While yet suffering from the effects of his imprisonment, and looking more like a galvanized skeleton than a living man, at the request of George H. Stuart, of Philadelphia, he delivered many addresses in behalf of the Christian Commission, an organization that accomplished untold good on behalf of the sick and suffering soldiers. Over one hundred thousand dollars were raised for the commission by the efforts of Chaplain McCabe, assisted by John V. Farwell and B. F. Jacobs of Chicago, Wm. Reynolds of Peoria, and M. P. Ayres of Jacksonville, Ill. It was during his visit to Jacksonville that Jacob Strawn, the giant farmer of the West, proposed to give ten thousand dollars to the Christian Commission, on condition that the remaining farmers of Morgan county could be induced to give that much more. The condition was more than complied with; Mr. Ayres sending on one occasion to George H. Stuart the sum of twenty-three thousand five hundred dollars, the result of ten days' work in that county. After the chaplain's return to his regiment, in the spring of 1864, then at Brandy Station, Va., a great revival of religion broke out in the brigade to which he was attached. Meetings were held every night in the open air or in a large tent, and many souls were converted to God as the result. Over-exertion in this great work brought on a relapse of his former illness, and for several weeks he was in a most critical condition. A few months, however, found him again at his post of duty, where he remained until the close of the war, after which he returned to the regular ministry of his church, and in the autumn of 1865 was placed in the pastoral charge of a large congregation at Portsmouth, Ohio. Here, within a short time, he secured the erection of a fine church at a cost of fifty thousand dollars, mainly raised by his own efforts. He was not, however, permitted to remain long at pastoral work. His gifts had fitted him for a broader theater of action and a wider field of usefulness. At the call of his conference in 1866, he accepted the position of centenary agent to utilize the enthusiasm pervading the Methodist body of Ohio during the centenary year of Meth-

15

odism in America, with a view to the endowment of the
Ohio Wesleyan university. This position he held for two
years with the most satisfactory results. In the autumn of
1868, his superior talents as a financial agent were called
into requisition in a national enterprise for the extension of
the church, and the placing of the society for that purpose
upon a solid basis. This position he has held for the past
thirteen years, his headquarters being in Chicago, and traveling not less than twenty five thousand miles annually in the
discharge of his duties. His efforts have been crowned
with marvelous success. Beside his regular work, "the care
of all the [weak] churches," he has been mainly instrumental
in building up a "loan fund" in the treasury of the Board
of Church Extension, which has already reached the royal
sum of three hundred and fifty thousand dollars in cash,
and in subscriptions and real estate over two hundred thousand dollars more. As long as time lasts will the influence
of this movement be felt by the church and by the nation.
It has become a power in the land. It extends a helping
hand to some struggling church seven times each week, and
it is the aim of its officers to aid two churches each day of the
year. Dr. A. J. Kynett, of the Upper Iowa conference, is
corresponding secretary of this most excellent organization.
In his labors in this connection Dr. McCabe has invaded the
territory of the "Saints." He assumed a debt of forty
thousand dollars upon our church in Salt Lake City, and
with the help of his thousands of friends, raised the money
and paid every dollar of it. He has also aided in building
a church in Salem, Oregon, which is by far the finest structure in the state, at a cost of forty-five thousand dollars.
These are the works that constitute his record, and these are
the labors which shall be his monument when the heavens
are no more.

As a lecturer on popular subjects, and especially in behalf of the objects of his mission, he has few superiors. His
style is terse, pungent, and irresistible. His pathos is from

the heart, and goes directly to the heart. It is the logic of human feeling and Christian love, and he who would avoid its application must either destroy God's precepts or crucify his own conscience. There is no escape from his all-powerful grasp. When he buckles on his armor resistance is idle, whether he assails the impenitent heart or lays siege to the purse of the listener. His lecture on the "Bright Side of Life in Libby Prison" was in the greatest demand for years after that dark spot on our national humanity had been wiped out. But, indeed, no place could be without a *bright side* that was enlivened by the cheering presence of Dr. McCabe. Like Paul and Silas in the Philippian prison, he and his comrades sang praises at midnight, and the prisoners heard them, a spiritual earthquake shook the prison, the Holy Spirit descended and opened the prison doors of guilt and fear to many hearts, and the spiritual shackles fell from many limbs. In view of this aspect of the case, well might he dwell upon "The Bright Side of Life in Libby." At the reception of the news of the victory of Gettysburg, the rugged walls of the old dungeon re-echoed the strains of the Battle Hymn of the Republic, led by the chaplain:

" Mine eyes have seen the glory of the coming of the Lord,
He is trampling out the vintage where the grapes of wrath are stored,
He has loosed the fateful lightning of his terribly swift sword,
Our God is marching on.
Glory, glory hallelujah."

Added to all, he is an accomplished vocalist. His singing, which is solemn, sweet and rare, is a cogent illustration of the soothing power of music, even upon the savage breast. He is emphatically the sweet psalmist of the Methodist church, and politically an ardent Republican. The degree of D.D. was conferred upon him by Fisk university of Tennessee, in 1875. His brothers are L. G. and R. R. McCabe, printers, of Chicago, and his only sister, Mary, is the wife of Edward Starr, Esq., of Chicago, Ill.

CHAPTER XXX.

This year (1859) we meet for conference at Iowa City; and being elected secretary, I was assigned the task of transcribing the journals of the four years previous preparatory to the next General Conference. Nothing of unusual occurrence took place at this session, except the election of delegates, which is always an occasion of much interest. The good people of this city entertained the conference with honor to themselves, and with satisfaction to all. At its close, I was returned to Maquoketa station, as my friends had requested it, and now I enter upon the labors of another year. Perhaps very few charges ever presented a more inviting field of labor than this at the present time. No embarrassing debts to meet, no unhappy difficulties to settle, no backslidden church to restore to spiritual life, but wide sail and a pleasant breeze. After my return, and matters were arranged for the coming year, I attended the session of the Iowa conference, held at Muscatine, Bishop Simpson presiding; and being desirous of hearing him preach, I made my arrangements to stay over the Sabbath. His discourse was from "Preach the Word." In effect it was not equal to that at Keokuk, referred to previously, and yet in thought it was not inferior. As I did not take any notes of his sermon my references must be limited. He remarked that the Christian ministry towered far above every other profession, however honorable, in that of its "*wider compass.*" The artist taxed all of his powers to excel in one single art; the mechanic was confined to narrow limits, and bent all of his energies to his trade; the physician spent a life-time to search out the secrets of disease and apply the remedy; all the powers of the lawyer were employed in securing legal knowledge that he might honor his profession, and of the geologist in the examination of the earth's strata; but whilst all these were confined to one single branch of science, the Christian minister, in his theme, embraced *all science.* I aim to give only the idea, but not the language. But there was one presentation of his subject peculiarly beautiful. He stated that after the deepest researches of the human mind, embracing the most gigantic intellects, and the most glowing descriptions in human language, sweeping the whole field of nature and of art, "They were but God's *little thoughts,* let down from heaven to earth, accommodated to man's feeble capacity." After the sermon, Hon. Hiram Price said to me—quoting some of the bishop's language—"Wasn't that grand?" I began to query in my mind, if such be "God's little thoughts," what must be his great ones? If such be the brightness of the page, what must be the glory of the volume?

Upon my return home, riding in my buggy, the distance thirty miles, I concluded to improve the time in studying a subject for the coming Sabbath. In meditating as to my text, *at once* it was suggested to my mind: "This is the victory that overcometh the world, even our faith." Why is it, said I, that this scripture was presented in such a clear and forcible way? The entire arrangement, which I still retain, was presented as readily as the text itself, and long before the thirty miles were traveled, my sermon was all ready for the pulpit, without paper or pencil. When reaching home, in order that nothing might be lost, I wrote out the sketch as presented to my mind, and on Sunday morning delivered it to my congregation. I was favored with great liberty and personal enjoyment, but nothing further was as yet revealed. On Monday morning, Sister Catlin, that blessed sister now in heaven, said to me: " Sister M. wishes to see you; I think she has good news for you." Accordingly I went over to her house. She looked as bright as a morning in May, and welcomed me most heartily. " I sent for you to let you know that my soul was saved yesterday under your sermon. I have been a

member of the church for twelve years, and long sought
this blessing, but never obtained it, and often I have been
almost discouraged. Yesterday, as soon as you gave out
your text, I was at once impressed, '*now is my time;*' and
whilst you were preaching I was praying, and trying to exercise faith; when about half through, the blessing came, and
it was too good news to keep, and I have called you in to
tell you that I am happy in the Lord." I now needed no
interpreter to explain the whole matter, but I saw great
beauty in the language of Cowper: "God is his own
interpreter, and he will make it plain." Should I say here,
that I place a very high estimate upon this text and sermon, no one will think it strange, as I have not the shadow
of a doubt that they were *divinely* given; not only to reach
this individual instance, but perhaps many more yet unre-
vealed; and oh, how encouraging to know, in the work of
saving souls, that there is an unseen power that sanctions
every truth and aids in every effort! And though we are
called to walk by faith, and toil by faith, the shout of *victory*
will be ours at last.

In the various duties now before me, I engaged heartily
in carrying out the wish of my conference in transcribing
the journals for the coming General Conference. I found
it to be a heavier task than I had anticipated, requiring a
portion of my time every day for about six weeks. But
the work was creditably finished, and will remain among
the records of our conference, as a kind of memorial, long
after the writer is in heaven. Having to preach frequently
three times on the Sabbath in this station, when I could
find a supply for the third one, it was very timely. I was
aided in some instances by Brother Catlin; at others, by
some brother from an adjoining charge. One Sunday evening, having such a supply, the brother prefaced his sermon
with a long apology, stating that " he was quite ill in body,
much fatigued with former labors, in no condition to preach,
but would *talk* to them a short time." And this same *inva-*

lid preached one whole hour, as though the elements of mind and matter were warring with each other, and mind's victory depended upon flesh's overthrow. What a want of harmony between the statement and the discourse. In " this *little talk*," to which we were prepared to listen, the gentle breeze had become a gale, and the rill a mountain torrent. In the interpretation I could not escape this conclusion: " Now, gentlemen and ladies, you have a specimen of what I can do when beset with infirmities. What a *tower of strength* would I present were I but in my happiest mood." I am glad that the time has come when this silly habit is estimated at its real value, and by an intelligent people considered but an insult to their good taste.

A young man of my acquaintance, about this time, wishing to honor our rule of discipline in relation to marriage, consulted me by letter as to its propriety. Of course I gave him the wisest and the best within my jurisdiction. My counsel included about three items—First, Will she make you a good wife? Second, Are you ready to enter into this relation? If you can give an affirmative answer to these questions, then—Third, " Strike without delay and take the citadel of bliss." Had I asked the third question, it would have been this, " Are you not already engaged?" In very many instances of this kind, the prayers and counsels come in as a kind of reserve. Whenever I have been consulted in this matter—as I often have been—I have reached this conclusion: He *wants* that young lady. Wanting her, he will be almost certain to secure her if he can. Therefore I will do all I can to help answer his prayers, for a young man's prayers on this subject always follow in the wake of his love. As an evidence of the truth of my remarks, I knew one young man consulting his older brethren, with the license of marriage in his pocket. This whole matter has its illustration in the case of a brother, then a young man, whose name is very familiar in the Ohio conference. Looking around with interest, he found the one at last that was exactly to his taste. Entering her room, when engaged at work, he made known to her the very delicate subject, and wished to know " what she thought about it." She politely intimated that a " matter of such importance required serious consideration and prayer before deciding it." To this he assented most heartily; stating that he " had *considered it well*, and now let us pray." I suppose that this prayer was full of the assurance of hope, for a *direct answer* was received, and through a long life of toil and usefulness in the Master's cause, they were *one* with unswerving fidelity.

On Maquoketa circuit there was a young minister by the name of Brewer, who occasionally changed with me in preaching, *i. e*, I would go out and preach for him in the afternoon, when he would return with me and preach at night. One of his appointments, about five miles out, was at Twiss' school-house, where a minister of another denomination preached also. Caleb Twiss was our class-leader at this point, and he was very much annoyed by this minister, who would attend his class and prayer meetings and assume control, and thereby defeat the design of the meeting. It was right here, after the morning service, when one of these difficulties took place, and the excitement ran high, that I preached for him in the afternoon. Ignorant of the difficulty, and also the name of Brother Twiss, I took for my text: " But my servant Caleb, because he had another Spirit with him, and hath followed me fully, him will I bring into the land whereinto he went, and his seed shall possess it." When quoting my text, I saw a smile all over the audience, but the cause I knew not. The minister being present, as well as the leader, only gave intensity to the feeling. When I dwelt upon the character of the spies, their cowardice and false reports, and commended the *courage, faith*, and fidelity of Caleb, they all thought that I was drawing the picture of their difficulties and presenting its moral. And especially when I came to the application, that we were all *reporters*, either false or true, it was hard for the congregation to suppress their emotions. Had 1 known the nature of the whole difficulty I could not have been more true to history. Meeting closed, we started home, and when fairly out of sight, Brother Brewer laid down upon the grass and poured out the warm effusions of his soul in a burst of laughter. The forces had been so long gathering, that it was meet that they should find relief "in the desert air." How many such waves of merriment started out upon the passing breezes of that afternoon I am unable to say, but the citizens of that place long remembered the "*Caleb sermon*" with its personal applications.

The fall and winter of this, my second year in this station, passed off very pleasantly until our second quarterly meeting, when I found that the injury received in my side the year previous had become so painful that I should be compelled to give up my charge. This was a new, and the hardest trial of my life. My faith and grace had been tested in many ways, but here was a new experience, and it was *some time* before I rose in triumph above it. But even here I found the "grace of God sufficient." Before my resignation, however, we enjoyed a very pleasant repast in what we called a "tea meeting," accompanied with refreshments, and two or three addresses from different ministerial brethren. Brothers Kynett, Brindell, and Professor Wheeler from Mt. Vernon college, were the speakers on this occasion. Brother Kynett being the principal speaker on a similar occasion the year previous, and Brother Brindell their old pastor, they assigned the main speech to Professor Wheeler. I shall not say too much when I state that he did honor to the occasion. It was not only a season of *rare* social enjoyment, but of financial success, netting about one hundred dollars. Doctor David H. Wheeler was for several years at Mt. Vernon, Iowa, honoring his position, when, at the breaking out of the rebellion, he was appointed

by the government consul to Italy. Returning to the
United States, he was elected to the chair of professor of
languages in the Northwestern university, Chicago, Illinois,
which position he held until he was called to the editorship
of the *Methodist*, in the city of New York, which responsible
post he has held for the last six years. It may be truthfully said of Doctor Wheeler, wherever he has been tried,
that he has proved to be "the right man in the right place."
After my resignation of the charge in Maquoketa, some of
my Methodist friends preparing to go to the Rocky mountains in the spring, requested me to accompany them.
Believing the journey across the plains, and the mountain air, to be the very thing I needed, I consented to bear
them company. So on the thirteenth of March, 1860, we bade
our friends adieu in the city and started for the land of
gold. I said to my Christian friends when starting, that if
any evil reports came back as to my ministerial character,
not to credit them, as I intended to honor God in the desert
as well as at home among the sacred influences of the
church.

CHAPTER XXXI.

We were thirteen days on our journey through to Council Bluffs, and found the distance to be three hundred and
fifty miles. Before we left home, we agreed that we would
not travel on the Sabbath unless it were absolutely necessary,
which pledge was kept sacred. The weather continuing dry
and warm, we were under the necessity of remaining almost
four weeks at the Bluffs waiting for grass upon the plains.
But to me this was not a barren season, as I found here quite
a number of old friends of other years. Among them
were Hon. Thomas H. Benton, Doctor Golliday, pastor of the
M. E. church, Ezra Millard, of Omaha, and a number of
others. In fact my stay here was one of the most interest-

ing character. Once I preached for the doctor and went
with him to a very interesting wedding. Nothing is truer
than the language of Cowper: "There is mercy in every
place." Yes, and there is true enjoyment in every place,
if our hearts are right in the sight of God. Having been
honored by my company with the office of cook and finan-
cier, I spared no pains that I might manage the one and be
well qualified for the other. April 23, we left Council
Bluffs and started out upon the plains. The monotony of
traveling for several days was broken only by Indians begging for something to eat. They are the most incessant
beggars I ever saw, and had we listened to their calls, our
larders would soon have been empty. We had to make
one exception, however. Whilst eating supper one evening,
the Pawnee chief called upon us with his two wives and
requested something to eat. I gave him some bread and
meat in his hand, but he shook his head, pointing to our
dishes; so, after we had finished, I had him and his squaws
set up to the table, which they seemed to enjoy most
heartily. On his neck he wore a medal, with the inscription: "James Buchanan, president of the United States."
I asked him, by signs, where he obtained it. He pointed
toward Washington. I asked him its worth, in dollars.
(He knew the meaning of dollars). He lifted up his hands
twice, numbering his fingers and thumbs, making twenty
dollars. I asked him how he reached Washington city.
He gave me first, a *journeying* motion; second, a puffing and
paddling; and lastly, *whew!* As much as to say, part the
way on our ponies, then on a steamboat, and lastly on the
cars. As he left us, he bowed very gracefully, and with his
charge was soon out of sight. The Pawnees are a small
Indian compared with the Sioux, and yet such is their per-
fection of discipline in riding their ponies, and shooting on
horseback, that they are more than a match for them on the
battle-field.

From Omaha to Denver, we passed through four or five

tribes, and we found their appearance, their habits and traits of character about the same. Their wigwams are the same in structure, their clothing of the same material, and their adornments after the same fashion. As we passed through their towns, the young Indians would come out by scores, almost naked, begging for something to eat. I had read in my youthful days about female beauty among the Indian tribes, but during this trip I came to the conclusion that it was more fanciful than real. They were in the habit of stampeding the horses frequently, which gave them a better opportunity for stealing them from their owners. They did this by creeping up slyly near to the place where they were feeding, about dusk, then suddenly flutter a handkerchief or piece of cloth, which would scare the animals, when *away* would go a dozen at a time. Before they could be secured, the Indians would overtake them and bear them away. We had one experience of this kind through the plains, but fortunately our horses did not admire Indian character, and they escaped out of their hands; but it delayed our travel nearly a day. We were constantly hearing evil reports, how emigrants had been waylaid and murdered, but it was all in the distance.

In one of our companies, a little in advance of us, there occurred an amusing incident, similar in character to that related as occurring near Smithland, Iowa. In the company they had one of those *braves*, who boasted what great things he would do should the Indians attack them. They concluded to test his heroism in a very peculiar way. Sleeping in a light-covered wagon every night, they so arranged their camping-ground that *his* was left on a sidling place. About ten o'clock at night, when he was sound asleep, three or four of the company upset his wagon, accompanying its fall with a terrible yell, when our *brave* left all and sought safety in flight. Having left his pantaloons in the wagon, when all was still and the danger past, as he supposed, he returned. Having notified his comrades of the disaster which had befallen him, they assisted him in righting up matters until the return of daylight. When the morning returned, among the missing articles were his pants— nowhere to be found. This being the only pair on hand, and they gone, his only recourse was a substitute. So, having a few empty flour sacks, he took one for the body, then sewed on one for each leg, with strings for suspenders, and holes cut in the sack for buttons, and now he is ready for travel. There being no danger of friction, and plenty of fresh air, he had what might be called a *"wide berth."* They had traveled but a short distance when they met some Indians, who were so amused at this new suit that they jumped up and cried out, " Wah! white man, wah!" I need only to say, when the joke was ended, that his comrades delivered up his pants and revealed the whole tragedy; but his zeal for another fight with the Indians never again came to the surface.

As we approached nearer the Rocky mountains, we were not very favorably impressed with the humanity of our emigrants, in witnessing the skulls and bones of the buffalo as they were scattered over the plains. On one occasion, stopping our team, I counted no less than seventy skulls within a circle of about fifty rods. And why were these animals slaughtered at this rate? Not for the meat, neither for their hides, but just for the pleasure of seeing them struggle and die. When will the sons of Adam learn to pray: "That mercy I to others show, that mercy show to me." During the warm season, these buffalo come by hundreds to their watering-places, and this is the time that the hunter takes advantage of their necessities. What a shame, to shoot down such a noble animal of God's creation, just for the satisfaction of seeing it kick and die!

We were delighted, however, with another inhabitant of the plains, and very well able were they to take care of themselves. They are not as large as the deer, and yet they outstrip them in the race. If I mistake not, there is

no work of the Creator, in animal form, for fleetness, which
comes up to the antelope. No swift-winged bird can overtake him, or well-trained "iron horse" can keep up with
him. He seems peculiarly constructed to distance all animals in his flight, and laugh at man's endeavor to capture
him as his game. The Indians, however, have two methods
by which they now and then obtain one, and both of these
are by stratagem. One is to conceal themselves in the
grass and wave a red handkerchief suspended to a stick a
few feet high. Seeing this, they approach near, curious to
know what it is, when the bullet brings him down. Another
method is to form a line on the plains, of several miles in
length, with their swiftest ponies, then one or two drive the
herd toward the line. When it is reached, the first hunter
on his pony chases him to the second, the second to the
third, and so on, until the last hunter is reached, when the
antelope becomes so exhausted that he falls an easy prey.
When decoyed by the first method, their flesh is very tender and nice, but when run down—like venison—it loses its
peculiar flavor. Like the buffalo and the Indian, their
march is westward, and in a few more years they will belong
only to the history of the past.

To the traveler passing over the plains for the first time,
the *prairie dog* is quite a curiosity, but two or three days'
acquaintance removes the charm of interest, and we think
no more of his presence than of the birds that fly over our
heads. I have read much about their mechanical genius
in laying out cities in proper form and order, but in all of
my investigations among them I have seen no exhibitions of
this kind; and I am inclined to think if such evidences of
canine skill were ever witnessed, it must have been about
the time when Indian squaws were beautiful. It is an
interesting sight, however, to stand in their presence some
bright morning and hear hundreds barking at the same time,
standing like the squirrel upon their hind feet. I learned
this lesson practically, long before we reached Denver

City, that in every enterprise of life—however promising—
there are many failures. Frequently on our way, we would
meet some returning home with downcast looks and discouraging reports. They had seen the elephant, and were
satisfied. One covered wagon had a large horn pictured
upon its side, with a man's head coming out of the little
end, written underneath: "Coming out of the little end of
the horn." I was very forcibly reminded that this journey
in its various manifestations was but a type of the successes
and reverses of human life. Some, with the same opportunities, would go there and succeed, whilst others would
fail and return home empty-handed. Another fact was
forcibly impressed upon my mind, that this was a real *ordeal*
to test the value of human character. A man may stand
upright and appear of genuine worth, amidst all the influences and restraints of church and home; but if you wish
to ascertain the real elements of his character, take him
out upon the plains where he has to depend upon his own
resources; then if he acquits himself like a man, you need
not fear to trust him in any position in life. What a prize
it is, to find a man true to himself, true to his fellow-men,
and true to God under all circumstances in life.

The first indication to us that we were approaching the
Rocky mountains, was the appearing in the distance, seemingly but a few feet above the horizon, of what we supposed
to be a "thunder-head." It resembled this, nearer than
anything else, about one hundred miles distant, and as we
approached nearer and still nearer, it grew higher and
wider. "Long's Peak" is the *first* that we discover of the
great snowy range, and at that time this was numbered the
highest among the peaks. As we approached within thirty
miles, these mountains presented the grandest sight that I
ever looked upon. At this distance they appear to be only
some fifteen miles away, owing, probably, to two causes: their
magnitude and the clearness of the air. How many times in
approaching them did I stop to *wonder, admire* and adore.

I thought that if these were but the outer indications, upon a small scale, how great and powerful must be that *Being* who created worlds upon the top of worlds innumerable. I thought of Isaiah's lofty flights, when he had such " mountains in scales, and the hills in a balance," and I did not wonder that even inspired writers, after considering the greatness and glory of God's works, should be constrained to cry out: "What is man, that thou art mindful of him?" If the comparison were between different bulks of matter, we might hide ourselves behind some mountain-rock as unworthy of notice, and be tempted to think that in the divine estimate we should be entirely forgotten. But when we consider that one human being, bearing the image of God, in point of value outweighs worlds of matter, and that the same interest is taken in us by the Supreme Being as though we were the *only one created;* taking this view of the subject, rocks and mountains may stand aside. What imparts a grander view to these mountains is the relation that they sustain to each other: rising like towering steps one above the other, until you reach the great *snowy range*, which seems to look down from its superiority upon them all, as much as to say:

> " I sit a queen upon this pile,
> Look down upon your dust and smile;
> And you shall own my lawful sway
> *'Till rocks and mountains* melt away."

When we were within a short distance from Denver, we were overtaken by five or six hundred Shians in battle array, on their way to fight the Utes across the mountains. They were all painted, well armed, and feathered off in true Indian style, mounted upon their ponies, doubtless intent upon certain victory. Their prophet, or *medicine* man, gave them this assurance before starting, for he is a great man among them. The medicine man, they think, can perform wonders; not only foretell victories, but that he can control the elements. We have a scrap of history right in

point. In a severe drouth upon the plains, the tribe blamed
their prophet, inasmuch as he controlled the winds and
rains, for suffering such a calamity to come upon them.
Such was the pressure that he saw something must be done
or he would lose his prestige as a true prophet. So, upon a
certain day he made a great display of "fire-works" to con-
vince his brethren that the clouds would now obey his call!
Surely enough, the next day there came a thunder-storm,
when the lightning struck a wigwam and killed two or three
of the tribe. Enraged at this, he was arraigned before a
council of Indians for permitting such a sad event to take
place, and demanded his reasons for it. In his defense he
stated that "they all knew that the medicine was a very
fine thing, but in that instance he had made it a *little too
strong*." This, I presume, was perfectly satisfactory, as the
writer gives us no further particulars. When we arrived at
Denver City we found that these warriors had left their
squaws and children in camp at that place, that they might
be secure in their absence. In a day or two they returned
to the city, having secured three prisoners and a large
number of ponies. The next night after they arrived, they
burned one of their prisoners, an old squaw, and such a
parade, and such music "of a melancholy sort," I never before heard, and hope never to hear again. It was a kind of
mixture of the horn, tambourine, piping and the human
voice. I suppose that this was a kind of sacrificial dirge in
celebrating their victory over the Utes, but we were informed that the victory was on the other side; yet this
would take away the reproach of a defeat. This sacrifice
of the old squaw would not have been suffered by the citizens of Denver had they known it beforehand. The other
two prisoners were boys about ten years of age, who were
purchased by the whites and sent on to the city of Boston
to educate. After our arrival at this place, we pitched our
tents for a few days' rest, where we were surrounded by
Indians, male and female; and Pocahontas had no de-

scendants here, I am sure, or she would have taught them
better manners than at meal-time to catch and eat the
vermin out of the heads of their own children.   Here was
another specimen of " female beauty among the Shians and
Arrapahoes," and such was its influence upon our remaining sensibilities, that, as *soon as possible*, we placed ourselves in a position where "distance lends enchantment to
the view."

The city of Denver at this date (1860) had a population
of about five thousand, and might have been called *in truth*
a great gambling depot.   One entire street was set apart
for that particular interest, and seemed to be recognized by
its citizens as any other branch of trade.   In company with
a friend, a resident of the place, I visited quite a number
of them for my own satisfaction.   Here were tens of thousands of dollars in gold piled up in heaps upon their tables,
inviting the unwary to come up and try a hand.   When we
wished to visit the postoffice, we had to take our place in
the rear of the vast crowd pressing up, and wait sometimes
from one to two hours before our turn came in regular order.
If a man were in a hurry, and had plenty of money, sometimes he would buy out the privilege of some one in the advance and change places with him.   The distance between
the city of Denver and the gate into the mountains proper
is twenty miles.   Here at Golden City we left our teams
and wagons at the "Correll house," and with blankets and
provisions on our backs, we started in to survey the land of
gold.

CHAPTER XXXII.

Before reaching Mountain City, some twelve thousand feet above the level, there was any amount of puffing and blowing, especially in ascending a hill; and we could hardly tell the reason why, until our well-experienced philosophers reminded us of the lightness of the mountain air when compared to that of the plains. It was quite amusing to see the broad-shouldered, thick-chested stalwarts plying their lungs for more oxygen, when the stripling passed on his way, looking back and laughing over their imbecility. Upon one occasion we had not only a fair test of the powers of endurance, but a little *spice* to cheer up the mountain scenery. Several of us, of different sizes, started up one of those mountains, nearly a mile in height, for a little recreation. Being of medium size, sound lungs, and naturally active, I had a little ambition not to be outdone; so up the mountain I made my way. It was not long before quite a number were in the advance of me; but I remembered "Addison's Hill of Science," of school-boy days—how Genius made a failure and Application gained the prize; and so I toiled on, until one and another, and another had stopped in order to take in a new supply, whilst my own was not yet exhausted; and whilst they were replenishing, I was still advancing, until I saw those below me, who had at first "derided my slow and toilsome progress." In this ascent I was much assisted by an occasional rock projecting from the surface; and when this was reached, after hard toil on the hill-side, I could stand secure with *firm footing*, when, with strength renewed, I pushed my way still upward, where another rock seemed to beckon me onward to its sure support. Not only in this way did I gain the ascendant of all my company, but it furnished me facts for a rich and beautiful application. It taught me this: That not all of

those who start out upon the heavenly way, who at first are
the most promising and run the fastest, in the end are the
most successful.   The next lesson impressed upon my mind
was, that it is not wisdom in any important enterprise in
this life to exhaust all of our energies in the first setting
out, so that we have nothing to fall back upon, and thus
create a necessity for flatting out, which is always weaken-
ing and mortifying.   But the last *moral* furnished from this
occasion was both practical and spiritual, as well as beautiful and sublime.   We began at the *foot* of the hill, and our
advance was on the *ascending plane*.   And thus it is with
every soul that treads the heavenly way.   No starting half
the way up the hill, but all must start from the same place;
and not one single move forward from this point, but what
elevates the character and dignifies the man.   Again, the
higher our *ascent* the *wider* the view and the *brighter* the
prospect.   What so expands the mind and enlarges our
views in relation to all that is beautiful and sublime, as a
high position in the *life divine!*   Let the love of the Saviour
fill the soul, and it gives a moral grandeur to all of our
views, and an enrapturing delight to all of our enjoyments.
Finally, in our ascending progress towards heaven, though
attended with toil and danger, our weary footsteps often
find *the Rock*, upon which we can stand and feel secure.
And oh, what a comfort it is to us to know that the most
and worst of the ground has been traveled over—that the
last difficulty will soon be surmounted; and then, on its
summit, we will raise the flag of victory, with this inscription: "The battle is fought and the victory is won."

   In traveling through the mountains, I expected to see it
teem with life—with its birds, reptiles and insects; but
what was my surprise, that no warbler was to be heard, no
serpent's trail could be traced, no toad nor frog disturbed
the pearly waters, nor the song of a cricket or mosquito
enlivened the passing hours of the night.   If St. Patrick
had ever crossed the ocean, with his long pole, we would

be tempted to believe that he visited this place and made a clean sweep. The first Sabbath after leaving the plains we attended church at "Methodist Gulch," where a Brother Fisher preached; and imagine my surprise, when, after the sermon, he announced my appointment for the ensuing Sunday. We remained for class, including eighty persons, and such testimonies exceeded anything I had ever heard. Here were ministers, exhorters, stewards and old class-leaders—a host; and we enjoyed truly a mountain feast. Having selected our transient home, our company is now composed of Brothers Northup and Nims, both formerly members of my charge in Maquoketa, Iowa. They went to work, and soon we had a cabin "all fitted and furnished." The *furnishing* part was easily reached, as we had spruce boughs for a broom, spruce boughs for our bed, and our *musk* was mountain spruce. If changed into verse it would read:

> " Spruce, roughly hewn, composed the floor,
> And boards of spruce made up the door;
> Above, below, and all around,
> *Could not one stick but spruce be found.*"

But the Sabbath is at hand, and I am fifteen miles away from my appointment. What is to be done? I have no horse, and no clothing suitable for the occasion, as I left them behind at Golden City; but the appointment is out and I *must fill it*. So, rising quite early, I started through the woods for my place of destination, and precisely at the time I reached the log chapel. Brother Fisher met me near the door very heartily, when I asked him if the people would receive the gospel message from one so rough as I. Said he: "If the message is right, they will not see your clothes;" and so I proceeded to the work before me. The house was not only filled, but the yard also, when I announced for my text: "So much as in me is, I am ready to preach the gospel to you." I thought then, and still think, that I never addressed an audience that more fully appreciated the words of life. Though having traveled fifteen miles that morning, I preached one hour without weariness, and if the congregation were as much blessed in hearing as I was in preaching, the hour spent was not in vain. The most of them more than one thousand miles from home, with all of its interested associations, I could reach many tender chords at once. After the audience were dismissed, a large number greeted me who had been my old friends in the state of Iowa. After refreshments, as duty called me home, 1 returned, happy in the consciousness that I had been abundantly rewarded for the travel of thirty miles on foot through the rocky forests. Our mountain home was on "Gold Dirt lode," fifteen miles from Mountain City, with the great snowy range looking down upon us. Upon this lode I purchased two claims for seventy-five dollars, in which my partners were to share equally with myself in the profits after the purchase money was repaid. We had on our claim a butcher's shop, in which we were peculiarly favored, and found it a great convenience. Shortly after our arrival, a man came into our vicinity and started a saloon; but the miners gave him twenty-four hours in which to leave, and he improved them well. Among our near neighbors was the son of Dr. Charles Elliot, so well known in the history of Methodism. He was a true man, and such elements were appreciated in a land of strangers. Shortly after our cabin was built, some *spruce being yet left*, on a beautiful eminence I erected a " bower of prayer," and consecrated it to God. And, oh, the sacred seasons enjoyed there! In the hours of devotion, how I loved to sing, as I often did:

"Sweet bower, where the pine and the poplar have spread,
    And waved with their branches a roof for my head.
    How oft have I knelt on the evergreen there,
    And poured out my soul to my Saviour in prayer.

    How sweet were the zephyrs perfumed by the pine,
    The ivy, the balsam, the wild eglantine;
    But sweeter, O sweeter—superlative, were
    The joys that I tasted in answer to prayer."

Among the numerous causes of failure far from home, there is one depressing genius that visits nearly all. There is no head so gray, nor youth so sprightly and vigorous, but that he pays a passing tribute. Upon some, it is true, he confers a double honor, as they can bear it. His benefits are quite peculiar in one respect, and similar in nearly all cases—that after his respectful attendance, his subjects are ashamed of his character and personal impositions. Would you know his name? It is familiar to all. "Home-sick" is the familiar name, but nothing less than hope's reaction reduced to reality. Away from home, left to depend upon his own resources, facing now the practical realities of life, fancy and imagination take their leave, and there is nothing left but the real. And now past pictures of former friends and home rise up to his view, and he longs to see the land he left behind. Hardly anything makes a man feel more worthless than when under this depressing influence. It undermines his courage, warps his judgment, and makes the man a child; and not unfrequently, before you are aware, he has raised the flag of retreat, and with hasty step is making his way home. The only remedy for home-sickness is to *set your teeth*, stout it out, until the fever passes off, when in a short time a healthy reaction will take place. In this respect I had decidedly the advantage of my company. The "world" being my "parish," I felt as much at home among the mountains, in the discharge of duty, as on my charge laboring for the salvation of souls.

My next religious season was the regular quarterly meeting, when Elder Chivington preached to a large multitude near Mountain City, seated on the hill-side. Oh, what a scope was here for the exercise of all the powers of the mind! Poetry, philosophy, eloquence, and song might have gathered inspiration to unfold their richness upon the one hand, and to have sung their music on the other. We were not bordering upon Mount Sinai where the glory surrounded Moses, but we were standing upon Mount Zion—if not with harps in our hands, with the presence of our Saviour in our midst, and the accents of praise upon our lips; and from this distant standpoint, I fancy that I yet see the towering cliffs, the stately pines, the clear atmosphere, and hear the stirring songs, all uniting together and saying: "All thy works shall praise thee, O Lord, and thy saints shall bless thee." The Rocky mountains are opening extensive fields for missionary operations, and, thank God! our men are upon the ground, counseling the miners from the hill-tops to the gulches to secure the "gold tried in the fire, that they may become rich;" and one I heard say before I left, that "the richest prospect he ever struck in the mountains, was the prospect for glory."

Shortly after this quarterly meeting, Elder Chivington needing a supply for Denver, came up to our cabin and wished me to fill the appointment until he could find a man for the place. I complied with his request, until I was released by a minister from the East by the name of Allen, when I returned again to our mountain home.

During my absence at one of our appointments, in company with Brother Nims, my other partner remained at home, and he was under the necessity of baking his own bread. Not being a practical baker, he gave it such a consistency that, when he took it out of the pan, it would neither cut, break, nor twist; and being a little doubtful whether it would digest, he ventured not, but in full bulk he set it up against a mountain rock that it might be tempered down by the summer rains. When we returned home from the meeting, there it stood, awaiting the softening process, and though the rains fell and the dews moistened, it bent not its back and bowed not its head. The next quarterly meeting came round, but the loaf changed not, and when I left the mountains on the first day of October, it was still bidding defiance to the storm and tempest. How long after this, it stood a monument of resistance, I cannot say, but during the months of my acquaintance with it, for *durability* it took the premium. The baker never let me into the secret of its permanence; but he is still living in Maquoketa, Iowa, and should any of my readers have use for such an article, I can recommend his as genuine.

In one or two instances during the summer, such was the interest to hear the gospel that the people sent a messenger a distance of fifteen miles to engage me to give them preaching on the Sabbath. It was quite a distance to walk (go and return) thirty miles to deliver one message, but I reasoned that if they felt such an interest to hear it, I should not feel less to deliver it. At one of these distant appointments a Brother Williams, from Rock Island, was present. He was an old acquaintance of mine at Davenport, and hearing that I was going to preach in the gulch, came some distance to attend service. That forenoon, the brother of the late J. V. Watson preached, and Brother Williams, supposing it to be " Landon Taylor," was seriously disappointed and mortified to think that his old ministerial friend had so " backslidden in the mountains." We were invited to dinner at the same place, when the brother made known to me his painful conviction, still laboring under the mistake that I had preached in the morning.* He seemed to think it a *great pity* that Methodist ministers of long-standing could not come to this land of gold without losing the spirit of the gospel, and intimating that among the *last* he could have suspected of backsliding was his old minister. I received the reproof from him very kindly, assuring him that even good men were not always alike happy in their pulpit efforts, and as I had an appointment that afternoon at two o'clock, I might be able to lessen the reproach. I must confess, after our previous talk, that I had a little ambition to excel, so we walked over together to the service at the appointed hour. Having come down from the

---

* This mistake arose from the resemblance in our persons—ten years' absence, and his error as to the hour of my appointment.

Nebo of expectation in the morning, the ascent now was all in my favor; and as I proceeded in my discourse, I saw that he was gathering new inspiration under a mixture of faith and surprise, until he reached a point where suppression was no longer a virtue, and he *praised God* that the gospel of Davenport which he heard ten years previous "*had the same old ring* in the gulches and on the mountains." By this time Brother Williams had learned that his criticisms in the morning were without edge, and presented me an approving apology. In this very amusing and yet enjoyable interview, I learned the value of Davy Crocket's motto: "Be sure that you are right, and then go ahead!" On my return home from this meeting, passing through the tall forests, and by the side of the pure waters, I was led to admire the young Indian's valedictory when leaving college to visit his forest home:

> "Let me go to my home in the far distant West,
> To the land of my youth, which I love the best,
> Where the tall cedars are and the pure waters flow;
> *To my home in the forest, white man, let me go.*"

The last quarterly meeting that I attended in the mountains was but a short time previous to my starting home. In the quarterly conference—some of whom were my Iowa friends—they proposed to the elder that if I would remain and take charge of the work that I need preach only once every Sabbath. The proffer certainly was very kind and appreciative, but I felt that my work was not yet finished in the Upper Iowa conference, among those dear brethren where I had toiled and gathered sheaves for the heavenly harvest, from pioneer days up to that period; and so I had to decline the honor. But the rich experiences and seasons of Christian fellowship enjoyed among those dear friends, in Nevada and other kindred places, are so deeply engraven upon my memory, and cherished in my affections, that the hand of time will never obliterate them; and through the coming ages, could it be possible that some intrusive hand should proffer to blot them out, I would say: " Stay thy progress; let these memorials stand, accumulating brightness with the history of future experiences; as well as a grateful tribute to my divine Lord and Master, for his amazing goodness to me in the land of gold."   Having decided to start for Maquoketa about the first of October, and the time now drawing nigh, I looked for some providential door to open that I might dispose of my interest in our claims.   I had not the least doubt but that if it was my duty to return to my conference, a wise Providence would open and prepare the way.   Whilst waiting this opening, surely enough, Mr. Elliot came to me one morning, proposed to buy me out, and within ten minutes the sale was consummated; which, after paying all expenses, left me about five hundred dollars for my summer's trip.   This I considered extra, as I had calculated that if I returned home with renewed health and vigor, I should be well paid; but in this case—like Solomon asking for wisdom and understanding, when the Lord added the rest—I was enabled to praise God for renewed physical strength, and he " had doubled all my store."   And this was not all.   I had gathered upon my journey and in my short stay so many interesting items of history that these would have squared the bill of outlays without anything beyond; but when these *three items* were added together, and *grace crowning them all*, I felt to say: " Thou hast increased my greatness, and comforted me on every side."

When reaching Denver City, after leaving the mountains on my return home, I found Mr. House, who had been one of our company out, and arranged with him to convey me to my adopted state.   This was very pleasant, enjoying the company of an old friend; so, on the first day of October, 1860, we started upon our journey home, a distance of one thousand miles.   In taking a farewell of our mountain home and my friends I left behind, nothing came with tenderer sadness to my heart than my *bower of prayer.* Truly I felt all that is expressed in these lines:

> " Dear bower, I must leave thee, and bid thee adieu,
>   And pay my devotion in parts which are new,
>   Well knowing my Saviour is found everywhere,
>   *And can in all places give answer to prayer.*"

The weather was unusually pleasant as we started from Denver, and remained so during the entire month. We arranged in our travel to arise at three o'clock A. M., start out at four, and stop at five P. M. This gave us twelve hours' travel, and time to rest. In adopting this rule our team remained fresh and vigorous, and averaged forty miles every day. In our company was a man by the name of Green, who had passed the summer in the mines, and had saved about enough to pay his way home. On our way, we called a few minutes at one of those so-called ranches—truthfully, gambling shops—when, everything being " well cut and dried," they induced Mr. Green to try his hand at " three-card monte." His last ten dollars were taken from him in a moment, which left him almost penniless, and he far distant from home. Our sympathies were not very deep in his case, as we had cautioned him to beware of such sharpers. He continued with us for some days, and then left us, as best he could to pursue his way; but we could not forget his name—*Green.*

Upon our return trip, we saw what I had never before seen. There were three spots upon the sun's surface, apparently as large as a silver dollar, which remained for several days. The weather—a little smoky, and the face of the sun quite red, we had a distinct view. Whether this phenomenon was confined to the plains or not, I am unable to decide; but to us it was a new thing—not under, but upon the sun, and of much interest. I had another new experience. Whilst in the mountains, owing to the want of oxygen, if any difference, I *lost*, rather than *gained* in flesh; but now upon this return I averaged nearly one pound increase each day for thirty days. In approaching Iowa, when sufficiently near to discover the distant bluffs and groves, a very pleasing sensation was produced. Though absent but a few months, there came a rush in connection with all the endearments of home. Here before me was my adopted state; the land that I loved; the history which I had made, and the strong friendships formed and long cherished; and *here I am*, about to enter into the same fields and re-enjoy like precious seasons of communion. In such a position as this, what reflective mind cannot enjoy this poetic sentiment:

" You may value the friendships of youth and of age,
And select for your comrades the noble and sage,
But the friends that most cheer me on life's rugged road
Are the friends of my Master—the children of God."

Filled with such emotions, I was not at all surprised that the army under Xenophon, when they came in sight of familiar scenes upon their return home, should cry out *"The sea! the sea!"* And then, how natural in such experiences to look away from earth, to the time when we shall catch the *first view* of the celestial fields—ever green—and the flowers ever-blooming; and as we approach the immortal shores, to see the signal-flag hung out to welcome us to our eternal home. Will it not be joyful and transporting?

I was not in the least disappointed, after reaching Iowa, in the kind reception meeting me upon every hand. As we put up for the Sabbath at Brooklyn, I went out in the morning to preaching, not knowing who was the pastor of the charge. I soon found that it was Brother Wilson. After he had started out in his sermon, I was discovered, and I saw that he was evidently embarrassed; so much so, that he called me out. I requested him to finish his sermon, when I had a very favorable opportunity for improvement. His father's funeral sermon I had preached when he was but a boy; the family home was one of my stopping-places fifteen years previous, and in that time he had grown up, and was now a minister of the gospel. These were among the references made in closing after him, and for one I enjoyed the surprise richly. In the afternoon I went with him to one of his appointments and preached for him, and renewed a friendship which will last forever. This Sunday evening was the first, since I left Maquoketa, that I had slept in a confined room, and it was attended with embarrassment. I had read of such experiences in the history of travelers, but never knew it practically until now. The contrast was such between tenting in the open air, and that of confinement in a close room, that I seemed at a loss for an element to breathe. The following week we arrived at Maquoketa, my old charge, where welcomes and salutations to me were of more value than my Rocky mountain gold. My friends were not apprised of my approach, until I entered the Methodist church at the hour of lovefeast, where I had the opportunity of telling them that through all the opposing influences which had attended my campaign, " I had been kept by power divine," and stood before them in the freedom of spiritual life. The next week I had the privilege of voting for Abraham Lincoln for president of the United States, which I had included in our hurried journey across the plains. Brother Kendig was now in charge of Maquoketa station, and was a very faithful and efficient pastor during the year. He was elected chaplain at the breaking out of the war, and occupied this position among the Iowa boys during the memorable battle of Pea Ridge, in Arkansas. After a term of service he returned to his pastoral work in the Upper Iowa conference, where he continued very successful until he was transferred to New England, and is now stationed in the city of Boston. Brother Kendig, everywhere, is the same untiring laborer, and success attends him wherever he is stationed. In the very honorable position which he now holds as a Christian minister, we have a most striking example as to what a man may become by untiring perseverance in the cause of

Christ. After spending a few weeks very pleasantly in visiting my friends, I was appointed to a new and interesting field of labor, which will be embraced in our next chapter.

CHAPTER XXXIII.

My last chapter finished up my Rocky mountain history. As I had written to my presiding elder, whilst there, to release me from active labor another year, at our annual conference at Dubuque I was left without an appointment. But upon my return, my health had so much improved that I was ready upon the first opening. I did not have long to wait. Rev. E. C. Byam, who had been stationed at Iowa City, having been appointed state agent of the "American Bible Society," left the charge vacant, when I was selected to fill the place. I was well aware that such changes—as a rule—were not very favorable to the successor; but as the request was unanimous by the official board, I proceeded at once to the work assigned me. I entered upon it the more cheerfully, inasmuch as I was aware that my church associations would be of the most agreeable kind. Here was Brother Spencer, president of the Iowa State university, a man that would do honor to almost any station. Here, also, was Rev. Alcinous Young and family, with whom I had lived for two years in the city of Davenport; also Brother A. Hart, a local preacher, with whom I had formed a pleasant acquaintance; so that my introduction was like going home. My reception was all that I could have desired. Within a few weeks the parsonage was all fitted up, Brother Mandeville, a local preacher, and wife were engaged to occupy it, and with them I passed a very pleasant year.

Brother Mandeville was subject, quite frequently, to seasons of mental depression, popularly called "the *blues*,"

and it was quite amusing, sometimes, to see how easily the
remedy could be applied. Whenever I found him in this
mood, I would manage in some way to raise a *good hearty
laugh*, and in no one instance did I fail to produce a reaction where the laugh was a *success*. It reminded me somewhat of David's music driving the evil spirit away from
the person of Saul. Though in this process of mental
relief I did not herald the object in view; had I done this,
the remedy might not have proved so effectual. From this
amusing experience I was brought to this conviction: that
very many of the sad and gloomy hours in this life are the
result of looking at ourselves—of pondering over our own
ills—until we imagine that our case is desperate. In this
state of mental gloom, could we be induced to leave our
melancholy reflections and launch out into new fields of
thought, or take lessons in the school of cheerfulness, sanctified by faith and prayer, this depressing genius would
find a welcome home somewhere else. Some of my readers
may have read the history of Rev. John Smith, a Wesleyan
minister of England, whose companion was seriously
afflicted in this way. At times she imagined that she was
about to die, and would say to him: "Johnny, I'm going
to leave you this time *certain*, and you must do the best
you can when I am gone." This declaration was repeated
again and again, with greater assurance, until his sleep was
seriously disturbed. At the worst stages, he concluded to
try an experiment, to see if he could not break the spell.
So the next time the delusion came on, when she asserted
that her *time had come*, instead of pity and sympathy, as
usual, he began to praise God that "Maggie was about to
get rid of her troubles at last by going home;" and the
more she asserted it, the happier he seemed to get; blessing the Lord for the happy exchange. This was more than
she could bear—shouting over her departure; when she
became *very angry*, and declared she "wouldn't die *any-
how*, that he could not get rid of her that easy;" and right

here the *evil genius left*, and this was the last of this experience during life. This is an extreme case, it is true, and
yet it furnishes us the groundwork as well as the remedy
for many of the same class. I suppose that musicians call
the above a kind of *interlude*, and so I will return to
personal history.

Rev. Alcinous Young was a minister of such prominence
that this is the appropriate time to pay a proper tribute.
He joined the Pittsburg conference in the year of our Lord
1828, when having served the church faithfully for seventeen years, he emigrated with his family to Mt. Pleasant,
Iowa—then a territory—in the spring of 1846. He united
with the Iowa conference at its first session in Muscatine,
and labored with us about thirteen years; then took a superannuated relation, which he sustained to the conference
until March 30, 1876, when he left the world of labor for
one of rest and reward. His end was triumphant.* Brother
Young was a man to be trusted. Perhaps few men in the
ministry of our church applied themselves more diligently
to the work in hand than he. Especially was this the case
in the earlier part of his life, and thus he secured a thorough
knowledge of God's Word. He was a good thinker, a
sound preacher, and a successful debater; and at times his
discourses were accompanied with great spiritual power,
and gracious revivals attended his labors. Being a member of his family for two years, I had the very best
opportunity of learning the striking traits in his character;
and whilst he was not free from the infirmities of his brethren, I am happy to state that he was a true Christian minister. When residing at Davenport, he gave me two or three
remarkable cases of history connected with his labors which
should not be lost.

He had been stationed at Wellsburg, Pa., and what was
unusual in his history, the entire year passed away without
any revival of religion. Upon his return the second year

* He died at the residence of his son, Hon. J. B. Young, in Marion, Iowa.

17

he was very much discouraged. The first Sabbath after his return, he made from his pulpit the bold declaration "That no man, sincerely inquiring for light, could read the Bible and pray in secret earnestly and sincerely for guidance three times a day for two weeks, and not at the end of that time experience a change in his views and feelings upon the subject of religion." A young man, president of the infidel club, and two other members, agreed to try the plan, as Brother Young had promised to make a public exposition of the matter from his pulpit, in case such effort was made and proved unsuccessful. Two weeks rolled round, and neither of the young men had read the Bible or prayed in secret during that time. They were resolved, however, to have some fun at the minister's expense, and accordingly agreed to tell him that they had complied with the terms of his proposition in every respect, but had experienced no change in their religious views and feelings. They started for the parsonage, but on their way two of them suggested that "they ought first to have complied with the terms proposed, and that to go to the pastor with lies in their mouths would be so dishonorable they would go no further." The president of the club said that "he would see the fun out," and proceeded to the house. He knocked at the door, and in a moment was seated in the family circle. He seemed to be greatly agitated, and remarked that he wanted a few minutes private conversation. The children were sent into an adjoining room, when he asked Brother Young to pray for him. A chapter of the Bible was read and earnest prayer offered. When he rose from his knees he told the minister of all that had occurred, and said: "When I knocked at your door, God knocked at my heart." That was the commencement of the greatest religious awakening known in Wellsburg. The young man above referred to afterward became a faithful missionary of the Cross. Hon. J. B. Young, son of the elder, now residing in Marion, Iowa, by my request, gives me the above facts, which correspond with the statements made by the father to the writer when I resided in his family at Davenport, in 1852.

Another fact, still more remarkable, which goes to prove that Christ will defend his own. A young minister made it his home on his charge at the residence of one of his stewards. One of the family, a young man, by some means took offense at the minister and determined on revenge. So, as he was about to start to one of his appointments, the young man slipped into his saddle-bags quite a number of bank bills, unperceived, and when the minister left, pretended to have missed his money, laid it upon the preacher, and finally had him arrested. He was soon overtaken by the officer of justice, when he, in conscious innocence, delivered up his saddle-bags to be searched. What was the minister's surprise when the amount of money, as described by the young man, was taken out from among his books! Of course here seemed proof positive of the crime of theft, and the result was a trial before a committee of ministers, and he was expelled from the church. He received his sentence of expulsion very meekly, attesting his innocence, but stated to them: "In less than one year, the Divine Master whom I serve will vindicate my character, and you will know that I am an innocent man." Was the prediction fulfilled? Within this time the young man who preferred the charge was taken sick, and his attendants said *he must die*. He begged for life, and said he "*could not die*," and finally requested this expelled minister to be sent for. He came; when, in the presence of witnesses, he confessed his crime, asked the pardon and forgiveness of his injured minister, when the Lord, in mercy, prolonged his life. But what of the expelled preacher? It is easy to imagine. He was at once restored to his former position, and such a wave of honor rolled back upon him that it was almost overwhelming; and through all of his future days, he remembered, with grateful heart, *that hour* in which his faith found expression in these words: "The Divine Master whom I serve will vindicate my character." What a losing business it is to fight against God. Whilst that youthful evangelist rose so much the higher when his fidelity was revealed, the *stain* left upon that young man's character, by this revengeful act, could never be wiped out. It would follow him as a part of his earthly history through all time, and unless erased by a divine hand, continue in the records of eternity.

This charge to which I was appointed pastor this year (1860–61), in some respects was the most eventful in my history. During my pastorate, that terrible war of the rebellion had its commencement. Such was the disturbed state of the public mind, for months previous to its consummation, that it was almost impossible to interest the people upon any other subject. The pastors united in their efforts to promote the interests of religion, but the Southern war cloud seemed to cast a shade over all of our spiritual prospects. Whilst these meetings were in progress, the tidings came from day to day of the secession of state after state from the Union. Such a state of things was not very favorable to the promotion of our work, as it betokened the fearful calamity which was just at hand. The day that the news flashed over the wires that Fort Sumter had been fired upon, was one of the greatest excitement in Iowa City that I ever witnessed. From street to street people were running as out of breath, spreading the panic to a still higher pitch, and the military calling to arms all that would volunteer. Within a very short time we had two companies formed and ready to go out in the defense of the "Stars and Stripes." This drew quite heavily upon our church, inasmuch as a large proportion belonged to the station. The members of the Methodist Episcopal church being loyal to the government, with few exceptions, contributed its full share in maintaining our national existence. She gave over one hundred thousand brave soldiers during the war for the defense of our republic, and the first soldiers that fell in their country's cause were members of the Methodist church. The military field has been so largely occupied by able historians that but a mere glance can be expected in a work of this kind, but I am fully persuaded that the *generation* who lived to witness that rebellion, and the *soldiers* who fought so bravely to conquer it, lived in one of the most eventful periods of the world's history, and were engaged in one of the most important conflicts of any age. Embracing the glorious results attending the freeing of a race in bondage, their education and elevation to Christian principles, the reflective influence of this great nation upon other lands and governments in their coming history is without a parallel in the records of time.

For the space of two or three months, as our city was a kind of military camp, we were favored with all the paraphernalia of war; but the time came when music and drill found a practical reality on the battle-grounds of Wilson's Creek and Pea Ridge. There is a vast difference between the honors conferred in preparing, and the solid realities in fighting and marching. But the one contributes to lighten the other. Oh, what a *power* there is to inspire courage and endurance in the hardships of war, in *the thought* that interested friends at home are praying and expecting that my record will be crowned with honor! and my return home will be welcomed the more for my virtue and fidelity in the testing hour. Brother Nobles gave me an account of a touching scene in the cars, as a regiment was about leaving for Missouri. The trains were in waiting, when there came in a venerable-looking couple in search of their son just starting South. He was sitting a short distance from him, when the aged parents came up to give their last blessing before starting. "Well, Jake," said the mother, "you are about to leave us to go to fight for the Union. It is hard to give you up, my boy; but remember you go in a good cause, to save your country. And now I have this to say to you, Jake, before you start—*don't disgrace dad and I.*" With these parting words, and a mother's kiss, the venerable parents left the cars, whilst the son was bathed in tears. How I thought of the *power* of those few words from that mother during his entire campaign. When in his long wearisome marches, sleeping on the cold, damp ground, and encountering the chilling storms, the mother's words, "Jake, don't disgrace dad and I," sounded to him like *clarion notes* above the storm, and inspired him with courage afresh. And in the hottest of the battle, when the wounded and dying were all around him, and death facing him, the words of that mother, like an inspiring angel, came to his rescue, and led him on to nobler deeds of valor. And when his term expired, and once more he returned to his family dwelling, what a scroll of honor to hand over to his over-joyed parents: "I have honored my station."

A short time previous to our "Boys in Blue" starting to the seat of war, we had an interesting sermon preached to them in our church by President Spencer; at the close of which I presented to each one a copy of the New Testament, with appropriate remarks, and commended them to the God of all grace. It was one of the most touching scenes that I ever witnessed, to see hundreds of soldiers leaving for the bloody fields of war, taking, many of them, a last farewell of the friends and relatives they were leaving behind. What a stigma is this to a Christian nation—the more it is considered, the more revolting it looks,—to settle difficulties with the *price* of blood! And the party which is the most successful in the work of slaughter and suffering is considered the one entitled to the greatest honor. What a comment upon enlightened humanity, and what a crown of honor upon the gospel of peace! It is a species of barbarism befitting the darkest days of the world, and bears no relation to the Light of life and the Prince of peace. And yet, when a nation's life is endangered by its enemies, this seems, at the present, the only remedy.

As unpleasant as it is, I must here record the sketch of a

young man who came to Iowa about this period. Mr. G.
was born and educated not far from the city of Auburn, in
the state of New York. He was of Methodist parentage.
Being in good circumstances, and the only son, they spared
no pains to qualify him to fill the first positions in society.
He gradually rose in their confidence, graduated with
honor, and became county superintendent of public schools.
At the close of his term, being a young man of enterprise,
he concluded to come West. Two years previous to this
date (1861), he arrived in Iowa City and applied for a position in the State university as teacher. There being no
vacancy at this time, he concluded to go to Council Bluffs,
Iowa, hoping that some door might be opened which he
could enter, suitable to his qualifications and tastes. Not
meeting with such opportunity at once, and being unfortu-
nately thrown into the society of the dissipated, within a
short time he gave himself to drink and to gambling, and
within a few months the last dollar out of eighteen hundred
which he brought with him was gambled away. Here he
was, among strangers, without money or credit, and, I might
add, without friends, for gambling friendship ceases when
the purse is empty. Ashamed to write home to let his
hopeful parents know how he had disgraced himself, he
made every shift and turn to pay his way. In this pitiable
condition, character, money and manhood gone, he found
his way back to Iowa City, and at this date was tending a
saloon for his board, among the Germans of the place. One
beautiful morning of spring, a messenger came running up
to the parsonage, and wished me to go with him *quickly*, as
some man had just committed suicide in one of the saloons.
I went in haste, and such a spectacle I never saw before:
Lying flat upon his back, his person and the floor covered
with blood, his throat cut from ear to ear, mouth and eyes
wide open, grasping the razor still with his right hand, and
such a *look of despair and horror* would almost have made
Satan turn aside. As soon as possible I hastened from the

scene, and though twenty long years have intervened, the *horrible image* then presented is as fresh as on the morning witnessed. To my surprise, the owner of the saloon called on me in the afternoon to hold religious services in the room of the victim; and if ever I realized all that is meant in Jonah ii. 2, I did when offering up that prayer. Having learned, during that day, something of his former history, as contained in my sketch, for humanity's sake, and for the respect due to his parents and relatives, with a few Christian friends, as far as possible, we gave him a decent burial, when the painful task devolved upon me to write on to his honored father and mother, giving the sad history of their once promising and beloved son. The hearts of those parents were so broken that my letter was never answered. But, oh, what notes' of warning came back to us from the sad history of Mr. G., and especially to every young man traveling the same road of gambling and dissipation! When he left the parental roof, had a sketch been handed him, giving a true history of his disgraceful progress and fearful end, he would have *revolted* at the idea; and yet the course pursued was just as sure to reach such a result as that a human hand will be destroyed in the burning fire. Let all young men who read this mournful end, profit by his example.

When our different regiments left us for the fields of strife, how great the contrast. It resembled the stillness of the calm after the storm. No longer were to be heard the sound of the bugle, the roll of the drum, or the shrill notes of the fife, but seeming peace and tranquility reigned; but the interest *now* was transferred to *human hearts.* I think that in no one station in Iowa did I enjoy more liberty in my pulpit efforts than in Iowa City. Our sermons, of course, were shaped to meet the exigencies of the times, and as every family, almost, was represented in the war, the tender sensibilities of the heart were easily roused into action. It is well-known also by many ministers who have served this people, that the social element in this charge is of the first order, which greatly contributes to assist in the work of the pastor. If I had any criticisms to present in relation to the membership, it would be in reference to the length of their prayers at our weekly prayer-meetings. This criticism would apply also to many other charges. Some of the *old brethren* seemed to think that unless their prayer was about such a shape, and such a length, embracing the past, the present, and the future, that its value was greatly diminished. In this way, unless much time is occupied, but few could take part; and the interest of this important means of grace greatly lessened. These remarks only apply to a few, and in my different charges I have labored to correct this evil, but have found it a very difficult task. When habits of this kind are formed, it seems almost impossible to induce them to leave the old beaten track, though they are aware that it defeats the design in view. There are others, who seem to depend upon their long prayers and frequent repetitions to make them *happy*, instead of using the private season, as they should have done before they left home. As an illustration: A Brother E. never thought the prayer-meeting *a success* unless there was about so much demonstration. In a word, he estimated the meeting by the amount of amens and hallelujahs offered. During one of our prayer-meetings, I discovered that he was using his best endeavors to reach this point, and by his demonstrations *was sure* he had reached it and was rejoicing over it. About this time I dismissed the meeting, when he came up to me with a kind of disappointed look and remarked: "Brother Taylor, I am sorry you dismissed so soon; if you had held on a little longer I should have received the blessing." I said to him: "Brother E., I supposed by your notes of joy that the enemy was defeated, and that you were rejoicing over the victory." "Oh, no," said he, "I was just getting ready." Often since that time have I thought of that brother's shouting over his preparations for a triumph, and queried in my mind, if such were his manifestations in the " green tree," what would they have been in the "dry." Whilst dwelling upon this subject, allow me to say, that if we would have our prayer-meetings a success, our prayers, our songs, and speeches should be short (not abruptly so), and all alive with spiritual interest. They should not always run in the same old *groove*, but they should be varied according to circumstances; and in this way a skillful pastor will always find elements of interest. Anything else but *"dragging their slow length along."*

Our presiding elder on this district at this date, was Rev. Samuel Pancoast, who did all within his power to give success to the cause. He was formerly of the Philadelphia conference, and was transferred to the Upper Iowa in 1858. He was a very good preacher, a close student, very genial and frank in all his associations with the preachers of his district. He remained with us about twelve years, when he returned to his old home in Philadelphia. Sister Pancoast had quite a taste for poetry, and was a contributor to the *Ladies' Repository*. Some of her productions were very creditable. Iowa City at this date was the home of Governor Kirkwood, now (1881) a member of President Garfield's cabinet. He was loyal to the backbone, and threw his influence *wholly* into the cause of the Union. He had no apologies to make for secession, and hardly any patience to exercise toward its sympathizers. Sitting by him in the cars, on our way to Davenport, one of these apologists for the rebellion threw out some remark which made the governor angry, when he gave the intruder a curse instead of a blessing. Two or three days subsequent to this, I met him in the city, and as he greeted me cordially, he remarked: " Mr. Taylor, I have an apology to make to you. That *impudent* Irishman made me mad on the cars by his rebellious remarks, and it was more than I could stand. I was taught better than this—to swear in

the presence of a minister, and I offer my apology to you."
Of course it was cheerfully accepted, and in view of the
aggravating circumstances I had already cancelled the
fault; but this little act of his, in this instance, gave me
such an estimate of the man, as I could not have had if
the matter had passed by unnoticed. It proved to me that
the element of sensibility and respect had a place in his
heart, and by him were cherished, though human passion
had for a moment assumed control, and all that was wanting was time for reflection to restore the equilibrium. I
met the governor often, upon different occasions, and found
him always the same frank, sensible, and kind-hearted man.

One of the interests of this station was the privilege of
a frequent visit to Widow Carlton's, who lived about two
miles from my home, within the suburbs of the city, and
Carver Thompson's, about seven miles in the country.
Sister Mary Jane Carlton was the daughter of Rev. Alcinous
Young, and widow of Judge Carlton, who died several
years before. This being the home of the father, and a
kind of Bethany for every lover of Jesus, in the midst of
war's commotion, how sweet to retire for a season to this
sacred retreat, to enjoy the communion of friends and think
of that land of peace where foes never disturb and strife
never enters. Long shall I cherish in memory the sacred
hours enjoyed there, with some now enthroned above. But
a few months passed, the term of service having expired,
when the soldiers residing in this city, and the surrounding
country, returned from the field of conflict. This return
was celebrated with all of the honors and interests of the
occasion. Many a heart which had throbbed with hope, a
few months previous, upon their departure, had ceased to
beat, and their bodies now rested upon the battle-field.
Many a fond hope for a son's or a brother's return was now
blasted; and this, for them, was an occasion of sorrow
rather than joy. But to the survivors, the citizens lavished
their richest favors, and made them feel that to the brave

the reward was sure. Many of these re-enlisted and served
during the war.   I had now been pastor of this station
about eight months, and during that short period, what
pages of history had been made, what tears had been shed,
what family relations had been severed!   Such an amount
of crime had hardly ever been crowded into so short a compass; but the conference year closes, and we all prepare for
its coming session as though cannon had not boomed nor
fields been stained with human gore.   Rev. A. J. Kynett favored us with his presence and assistance the last
Sabbath, and we parted with these dear friends without a
note of discord during the year to disturb the spirit of
harmony and love.   Our next chapter opens with a new
field of labor.

CHAPTER XXXIV.

Having just taken our leave of Iowa City, we meet for conference at Marshalltown to report progress and learn our
destiny for the coming year.   Here was Bishop Scott, who
is always wise in his counsels and respectful in his decisions.   At this session are about one hundred and twenty
Methodist ministers, and all loyal to the Union.   Here is
history worth recording.   Rev. C. G. Trusdell is now pastor
of this station, and he is very successful in making satisfactory provision for the conference.   During its session I
was consulted as to my willingness to go to another station
and make room for a minister who was anxious for the position.   Not willing to make my own appointment, I was
somewhat reluctant in giving a positive answer; and yet I
could see no reason for my removal, as I had served them
only eight or nine months, and the charge had prospered
in my hands.   I had now become acquainted with the
people and they with me; hence, I was better prepared to
serve them successfully by our short acquaintance.   But I

saw the *coming wave* and concluded to let it have its *swell*. The appointments were read, and I was appointed to Cedar Falls station, and Rev. R. L. Collier my successor at Iowa City. As soon as possible, I made my arrangements, took the stage across the country a distance of fifty miles, and reached my charge about dark. The weather being quite · chilly in the fall, and the long ride, I took a severe cold, which renewed the old difficulty in my side brought on at Maquoketa. The friends at Cedar Falls received me very kindly, and my introductory labors were as promising and acceptable as on any work in the conference. But in the very beginning of my labors, the *acute pain* returned, and though I did not mention it to the brethren for fear of discouragement, I felt that without relief my stay would be short. What made my introduction pleasant was my home at Brother Philpot's, an old Ohio Methodist, with his pleasant companion, and Brother and Sister Wilson of Ohio boarding in the same family. Certainly my reception was all that I could ask, and friendly society all that I could desire. Our congregations were good, our class and prayer meetings well attended and spiritual, an intelligent community, and a very prosperous Sunday-school. But all these would not avail without health and strength to perform the work assigned me. I could not think of leaving them without a pastor, so I continued my labors until spring, thinking the warm weather might produce a favorable change. During the winter I was, for the first time in my life, afflicted with sore eyes, so that for weeks I was unable to read. During this time I visited Brother Ridlington, who was engaged in a series of meetings at Waterloo; and whilst assisting him, one of his members had a valuable eye-water, which, with one application, restored my eyes to soundness. It acted like a charm. In the morning when I arose I felt like a new man. I was richly repaid in this restoration for all the assistance rendered the pastor. This was my first introduction to Brother and Sister Miller, who resided in this city; as I put up with them the most of the time during my stay, I found this a very pleasant home. The meeting was a decided success, and my renewed acquaintance with Brother and Sister Ridlington gave a pleasure to this revival season which has been remembered and cherished as one of the bright spots in my history. A little occurrence here which was new to me: Having preached a sermon especially to the young people, I was requested to repeat it the following evening, with which I complied; but a sermon, like a story—however good,—loses much of its relish in its repetition. Though in this instance I revised and enlarged, the spirit of interest was less ardent. Since that time I have been more intimately acquainted with Rev. Joseph Ridlington, and I have found him *true* in all the relations of life — a good faithful pastor, and a successful evangelist. The experience of twenty-five years in the work is a satisfactory test of his fidelity to the Master. He has been blessed with a companion who has been to him like the *right arm* to the workman, ever ready to pull or push that the work may move on to success.

The winter of 1861–62 was a very severe one, and our railroad from Dubuque west was blockaded by snowdrifts for days at a time. This was a kind of drawback which was not very patiently endured, as the war news was so very exciting that every mail arrival was thronged with anxious inquirers. Hardly a household but what had a son, a father, or a brother, in the army; and every other interest stood in the background compared with this. It seemed at that time that we lived on excitement, and that scarcely anything possessed interest unless infused with the spirit of war. Long shall I remember the thrill of joy that went through my own heart, as well as that of others, when sitting at the dinner-table, Brother Shepherd Wilson came in and brought the tidings that " Fort Donelson was taken!" The Iowa legislature was then in session, when the news flashed over the wires, and such a jubilee I suppose was hardly ever witnessed. No business could be continued under such joyful pressure. Both houses adjourned; and they gave vent to the greatest demonstrations of rejoicing. They cheered, they swung their hats, embraced each other, and some of them wept like children. Well, it was meet and right, for this victory opened the door into the very heart of the rebellion. One of my old Sunday-school scholars said to me shortly after the occurrence: " Though on Saturday—led on by General Smith,—we gained a position in the very face of death; yet, when on Sabbath morning we marched into the fort, and our regiment—Iowa Second—was assigned the *honorable position*, *it was the proudest hour of my life*." Another interesting event of this year was the visit of Hon. James Harlan, United States senator, who addressed the citizens upon the great interests of the nation. His audience was numbered by thousands, and the address was a very able one. One remarked to me: " I was not aware that you had such eloquent ministers in your church." During the spring, the friends consenting to release me for a few weeks, in view of the state of my health, I visited Chicago to hear Parson Brownlow's opening address. He had just been released from rebel bondage, and he gave us in that speech a history of his own sufferings and that of his brethren before his release. The history was horrid in its details, and I did not wonder at the joy and satisfaction by him expressed, when at last he found such kind relief in "Abraham's bosom." After visiting some of my friends, I returned again to my charge and remained with them until our quarterly meeting in the spring, when by mutual consent I was released and Rev. L. D. Tracy, formerly of the Wisconsin conference, was appointed to fill my place. It was quite a trial to close up my labors upon the charge at the end of six months, as I had now become attached to the people; but duty called, and I obeyed. Before winding up my labors, however, I must state a very sad occurrence just before my departure.

A citizen of the place who had frequently attended our service had been in former years addicted to habits of dissipation. By the efforts of the Good Templars he had been induced to join them and take the pledge of total abstinence, and he became quite zealous in the cause. For several years he was faithful and true, and no one apprehended any danger of his return to his cups. His companion having made some domestic wine, placed it down cellar, and at this date was visiting some friends in the East, whilst her husband remained at home. During her absence he concluded to test the qualities of the wine, perhaps little suspecting the effect upon him. Here was the fatal step! No sooner had he tasted it, than there sprang up all the powers of the hidden viper, and the first known, he was staggering through the streets of Cedar Falls, a drunkard. In this state of intoxication he came to one of our religious services; and witnessing his degradation, no language could describe my feelings. Last week a *man* and an *honored citizen*, but now fallen below the brute. What a spectacle! and all this just by tampering with a little currant wine. Within a short time he was in his grave. He died of delirium tremens, and it might have been truthfully inscribed upon his tombstone: " Here lies the victim of domestic wine." Since that event I have been brought to see the danger of this enemy to human happiness in any form. It may be sugar-coated and called by some respectable name; but like Satan in sheep's clothing, its character is not altered. Alcohol in domestic wine or cider, is alcohol still. It will make drunkards as easily behind the cupboard as in the saloon; and the more so, in many instances, in view of the fact that the reproach is removed; and I have not the least doubt that there are thousands of sons from Christian households in these United States, that took their first lessons in drunkenness at the

cider-barrel or domestic wine-keg. He is wise who under-
stands these things, and who is resolved to show his " faith
by his works."

Having a supply to fill my place, in visiting Chicago I
passed one or two days very pleasantly with Rev. R. L. Collier, who was now stationed in the city. The friends in
this station had requested his services, and the bishop had
honored their wishes, and Iowa City was supplied by
another minister. Whether this event in the order of Providence was any indication of the want of divine approval in
my removal from Iowa City, I leave my readers to determine. To say the least, it was rather a strange occurrence.

A few weeks' rest from responsibility and labor, and the
return of warm weather, so renewed my health, that by the
request of Brother Kynett, now presiding elder of Davenport district, I supplied one round of appointments whilst
he was engaged in the sanitary work. This change was
very pleasant, as it took me over much of the ground where
I had labored in former years, and furnished me with a
pleasant interchange with ministerial brethren. One of the
most interesting appointments of this round was at Maquoketa, my former field of labor. Two regiments were about
to start for the field of conflict, and they met here to enjoy
a kind of farewell ovation before starting. As they had
expected the presiding elder to be present, to furnish an
address, I knew that I was *booked*, and within a few short
hours, collected all the material to be in readiness. As I
came in at the last, I had a little the advantage in time, and
hundreds being my old hearers and friends, I had the
advantage in sympathy. It will not be considered egotistic
for me to say, that if I ever made a success on the platform,
I made it then, for such *inspiration* would bring out the
man if there were anything in him. Judge Burris, from
Davenport, upon this trip was my traveling companion, and
preached for me on the Sabbath. He was also one of the
speakers on Saturday, as he was always ready for every good

18

work. On Monday, as we returned home in our carriage, the good friends of the town, as we passed through, came out waving their handkerchiefs for nearly half a mile as a farewell token. Such friendly salutations do not cost much, but they are, when compared with gold, *of purer worth.* Said the judge, when we had passed the final token: " I could hardly desire any higher honor than this, such a response from true-hearted friends." At this distant hour, as I seem still to review the scene, I am inclined to write: " Sacred to the memory of those that I loved." At the close of this round upon the district, as Davenport station had been left vacant by the appointment of Rev. J. G. Dimmitt to the office of presiding elder, I was requested to fill out the time until conference. To this people I needed no epistle of commendation. Ten years previous to this, their character and my fidelity had been mutually tested, and I went to work at once to strengthen the weak places and to encourage the faltering; and although the war with its attendant evils, with other changes, had altered the spiritual *status* of the charge, yet human hearts and God's grace were still the same. I labored faithfully during the few months of the remaining conference year with increasing congregations and interest, and deeply regretted that I could not comply with the request of the elder to serve them the coming year. He urged it as far as prudent, but I had resolved upon spending one year of rest in Vineland, New Jersey, and I was excused. The next chapter will embrace some of the interests of that place. We will now introduce our readers to Dr. A. J. Kynett, corresponding secretary of the " Board of Church Extension of the M. E. church."

Alpha J. Kynett was born in Adams county, Pennsylvania, August 12, 1829, the youngest of a family of eight children. Five—three brothers and two sisters, still live. The parents were Methodists—the mother, the daughter of a local preacher in Maryland, and one brother a local

preacher by the name of Henry Peterson. The father
for many years was a class-leader and steward, and his
house a preaching-place and home for the old-time itinerants. Rev. Samuel Clark, afterward of the Iowa conference, John Baer, and George Heildt distinctly remember
the family, and especially the devout mother. In their
early history, the family removed to Ohio, Trumbull county,
the Western Reserve; then, in 1838, to Rush county,
Indiana. After four years' sojourn in Indiana, having sustained the loss of their property by a bad title, they gathered up all their effects and emigrated to Iowa territory,
Des Moines county, in 1842. After reaching their place of
destination, their small flocks, household goods, and fifty
cents in cash, were their only capital for building a new
home. The father being a mechanic, by the assistance of
his sons, worked at his trade in the winter and rented lands
through the summer, and in this way accumulated enough to
enable them to enter government land and make a farm of
their own. In due time, a good farm-house was erected
by their own hands; other buildings and improvements followed, and within a few years they enjoyed a pleasant
home among the pioneers of the West. This was the
family homestead for many years, when the father of
Brother Kynett, after an illness of some two weeks, died
in Christian triumph on the twenty-ninth of June, 1856.
His old pastor from Pennsylvania preached his funeral
sermon from "The righteous shall be had in everlasting
remembrance." This was the first breach death had made
in the family, except those who had died in infancy; but
was soon followed by the death of the youngest sister.
After this change in the family, the son purchased the
homestead of the older heirs, perfecting the title in himself, then placed it at the disposal of his mother and faithful sister who remained with her, and continued to be the
family home until 1865. At this date, the most of the children having removed to Mt. Vernon, Iowa, the old home-

stead was sold and a new home provided for them, by the same hand, at that place, where they resided until the death of the mother, which occurred June 10, 1869. She passed away in the full assurance of faith.

The early school privileges which the subject of our sketch enjoyed were of a superior character at Western Reserve, which a New England population always provides. In Indiana they were fair and faithfully improved. In Iowa, owing to the newness of the country, and the necessity of continued labor, there was some interruption, but every opportunity was employed, until an old English graduate of Oxford university, and a superior teacher, took a school in their district, became specially interested in the youthful student, who was soon regarded as the best scholar in the neighborhood. About this time Foster's letters on Calvinism, addressed to Dr. Rice, were being published, which awakened a profound interest in the community, intensified by the fact that the prevailing sentiment was Calvinistic; and many were the discussions out of school hours in which teacher and pupil shared with their neighbors. The logic, theology, as well as philosophy of Foster's letters were keenly relished by the young student, and tended to form the habit of thought at this period of mental discipline. His services as a teacher were soon in demand, and about one year was devoted to this calling, whilst the higher studies were pursued out of school hours.

All the children of the family, as they came to mature years, under their faithful parental training embraced religion, and became members of the Methodist Episcopal church, and handed in, when they came to Iowa, on the same sheet of paper, certificates of membership. It is not strange that impressions of duty as to preaching the gospel, which had followed him from childhood, should return with intense power. It was not strange that all of his plans of studying law in Burlington had been thwarted, and that he should have been induced to enter into a *solemn covenant with God* " to go forward in the way which he should make known and open before him." Within a short time after this covenant he was called to service as leader of a class, then licensed as an exhorter, and next to preach the gospel of Christ. This was on Yellow Springs circuit, Des Moines county, Iowa. The presiding elder, Isaac I. Stewart, and the preacher-in-charge, Joseph McDowell, conferred together, and as he re-entered the church, said to him: " You are now a Methodist preacher, and for two things should be always ready—to preach and to die; so you must preach to-night." Within less than an hour he stood in the pulpit preaching his first sermon on 1st Peter iii. 18, under a most simple and natural arrangement—1, The sufferings; 2, Their vicarious character; and 3, The object sought—to bring us to God. Thus he continued to teach during the winter, and on Saturday and Sabbath to assist the preachers of the circuit at distant places, and in their revival efforts. One new appointment, at the mouth of the Iowa river, after two or three weeks' continuance, resulted in the conversion of sixty persons—nearly the whole neighborhood. Another was held in a community where Universalism held almost uninterrupted sway, when the young preacher discoursed from Job xxxvi. 18: " Because there is wrath, beware lest he take thee away with his stroke: then a great ransom cannot deliver thee." The effect of that sermon was not soon forgotten. With the close of his school came a new and unexpected opening. A former minister of the circuit, Rev. James C. Smith, and an intimate friend, had been appointed to Dubuque circuit. The work being too large for one man, he desired a colleague, and after conferring with Elder H. W. Reed, wrote to his old parishioner. But here arose a new difficulty. Such an extensive field as this to which he was invited required a good horse, and all his funds acquired in teaching were not sufficient to procure one. But right here his oldest brother proposed to loan him *his* until conference; and thus every difficulty removed, the young itinerant mounted his horse on the 14th day of April, 1851, and started out to enter upon new history. The experience of this young herald of the Cross in leaving old home and its sacred associations and launching out into untried paths was very much like that of his brethren; but God had opened the way and he went forward without fear, meditating on Matt. xix. 29: "And every one that hath forsaken houses, or brethren, or sisters, or father or mother, or wife or children, or lands, for my name's sake, shall receive an hundred fold, and shall inherit everlasting life." After four days' travel, he joined his former friend, now his colleague, at the house of John Paul, which became a home to him whilst on the circuit. On the Saturday following, at the quarterly conference, he was formally employed the remainder of the year by the presiding elder, Henry W. Reed, who has ever proved himself to be a true and valuable friend. This was one of our wet seasons in Iowa; bridges were swept away, and not unfrequently the young itinerant had to swim his horse over swollen streams—a good introduction to the service. Three months finished up his labors on this large circuit, when he returned to his old home. His brother standing in need of his horse, his friends counseled him to resume teaching until he could enter the conference without embarrassment; and at this date there were fears lest his health might fail him, being considered a good subject for consumption. But at the ensuing session, held at Davenport, in August, 1851, Bishop Waugh presiding, all of these facts were presented, considered and overruled, and he was admitted on trial, in a class of seventeen, and appointed to "Catfish," a station near the city of Dubuque, composed largely of English. He had hoped to be a junior preacher, and his field of labor nearer home, but his brethren knew where his services were the most needed, and, like a dutiful son in the gospel, he was to do the work assigned him. These English friends had the reputation of being a little hard to please, and in view of his youthful appearance some apprehensions were at first entertained that he might not be able to meet their demands; but these fears all passed away, and they were anxious that he should serve them the second year. They thought, however, that one of the necessary qualifications of a preacher was to be poor, that he might be humble, and though the wealthiest congregation in the conference, their estimate of "table expenses" was the actual cost of board and washing, and the disciplinary allowance of "quarterage" one hundred dollars. No danger of "waxing fat" on this line; and as one of the results of this humility, the charge was favored with a good revival, a new chapel was erected at "Center Grove," and at the pastor's suggestion, "Catfish" was changed to Rockdale, which it still retains. At Burlington, the seat of our annual conference of 1852, he was appointed to the city of Davenport, as the writer's successor, where his labors were very much blessed. During this term of two years' service in this city, the new church was built on the corner of Fifth and Brady, all the interests of the station prospered, and at the close of his term, Sept. 10, 1854, he was married to Miss Pauline Gilruth, born at Ann Arbor, Mich., Feb. 25, 1835, and educated at Berea, Ohio. Brother Kynett's next field of labor was Main Street, Dubuque, embracing 1855 and '56, at which place I made his house my home, where a friendship commenced between us which will know no ending. Reference free and full having been made as to our ministerial relations in a former chapter, I will here add that the interests of the charge were well sustained throughout his entire term, and especially the reputation of the pulpit; and I think that I am justified in saying that in no two years of his ministerial life was his progress more marked in this respect than at Main Street, Dubuque. Perhaps it was owing, in part, to having a young and valuable wife to assist him. There were some prophetic sons inclined to predict that as he had now reached the highest appointment in Upper Iowa conference, he would seek a place in some other; but such invitations were declined, and the fall of 1856 finds him stationed at Iowa City, where his labors were attended with more than ordinary success in a very gracious revival which extended into all the churches. At the close of the first year he was solicited to take charge of Iowa City district, but declined in view of his wife's health, which at that time was very poor. In 1858 he was appointed to Lyons, where, as to popularity and success as pastor, perhaps he reached the highest point in his ministerial relations, and suffered no abatement to the end of his term. Next we find him in charge of Davenport district, sustaining himself also in this relation, until the war of the rebellion broke out, when he was appointed as one of Governor Kirkwood's aids; and whilst attending to the work of the district, assisted in recruiting, organized the State Sanitary commission in connection with the United States Sanitary; and in this relation several times visited the army at Vicksburg and other places, secured two steamboats from the government to carry supplies to sick soldiers, whereby many lives were saved and thousands provided with comforts, ignorant of the men who served them. In this commendable work he was attacked with the prevailing form of disease, which came near ending his own life. At the conference of 1863, held in Davenport, he was elected to General Conference—the last of the delegation; but since then (except the last), at the *head*—a compliment to his work of church extension. In the fall of 1864, the Conference Church Extension society was organized, and his consent obtained to act as first secretary if the preachers should pledge three thousand dollars themselves and cordial support. This done and he was appointed. The imperiled churches the first year were relieved, great improvement in church architecture secured, and new interest in church building; and in 1866 a conference loan fund was created, which has aided many churches, and now amounts to nearly fourteen thousand dollars, including a late bequest from Samuel Rounds of Cedar Falls, Iowa. In this relation he served the church until June, 1867, when being appointed by the bishops to fill the vacancy occasioned by the death of Dr. Samuel Y. Monroe, he resigned, and entered upon his present position as corresponding secretary of the Board of Church Extension, to which he has been well-nigh unanimously elected at each succeeding General Conference. Whatever may have been said by some as to his elevation to the office of bishop, I should regard a change of this kind a great misfortune to the church, and even to himself, as I am well assured that there is no position in which he could be placed where he could exert such an influence *for good* as the relation which he now holds; and the success which has attended this benevolent department of the church confirms this statement beyond a doubt. This conviction has its foundation in the following reasons: First, He saw the necessity of such a work on his own district, and originated its organization. He introduced the matter to the General Conference, and followed it through all its stages in that body. Then rescued it from ruin on the death of Dr. Monroe in 1867; secured some needed modifications by the General Conference in 1868, and conducted it successfully. Second, In 1872 he secured a thorough reorganization of it, taking the election of its managers out of the perils of a *town meeting* and transferring such election to the GENERAL CONFERENCE—a movement which resulted in a similar change, at his instance, in all of the benevolent societies of the church. This must be regarded as a very important measure. He also organized our plans for a " Loan Fund " for church extension, first in the Upper Iowa conference, and after in the parent board, which had reached, January 1, 1881, the sum of $358,523.28, from which churches are aided only by loans. And, finally, he secured the publication of the *Church Manual*—a very important document for every Christian minister. Before concluding

my sketch, it will be appropriate for me to say that his
honorary title of D.D. came unsolicited from the faculty of
the Ohio Wesleyan university on the eve of his appointment to his present position, but with no reference to it, as
it was not then known; and up to this date the question
may arise in the minds of some, which of the two reflects
the greatest honor—the institution upon the *man*, or the
man upon the institution.   We think, however, that it can
be truthfully said, as due to his efforts, and his assistant,
under the blessing of God, that very seldom in the history
of church enterprises has any one reached such a position
of importance in the same time as that of church extension
in the Methodist Episcopal church.   And it is the earnest
prayer of the writer that the good work already accomplished may be but the prelude to a brighter day and a
richer harvest, until every true worshiper may be able to
say: "I was glad when they said unto me, 'Let us go into
the *house* of the Lord.'"

CHAPTER XXXV.

For many months I had been convinced that I required
rest from ministerial labor in a milder climate, until my
physical energies were restored; but I had not decided as
to the desired locality.   Whilst inquiring in my mind as to
the desired haven, I took up the *Chicago Tribune*, and saw
a short notice of Vineland, with its climate and advantages,
and at once decided to spend one year at that place.   So,
at our coming conference at McGregor, I was granted a
superannuated relation for this purpose.   The locality I
knew to be favorable, as it was half-way between Philadelphia and the ocean; and one day's ride took me through in
safety.   On arriving, Mr. Charles K. Landis, the proprietor
of the place, met me on the cars, and proffered me a ride

over the premises; but as it was Saturday, and I wished to spend the Sabbath in Millville, five miles distant, I postponed my ride until Monday. As I called upon one of the stationed ministers, I was heartily welcomed; the more so, as I was from the West, and on the Sabbath I agreed to preach for him at half-past ten o'clock A. M., but stated that I should not preach but one sermon, as I had visited New Jersey for rest and recuperation. After my discourse in the morning, the pastor notified the congregation that I should preach again in the evening; and with all of my vetoes to the contrary, he would not budge a hair. What my ministerial brethren may think of such liberties I cannot say, but I felt that it was far from being a compliment —even if so intended—and an abuse of ministerial respect. If he were well-pleased with the sermon, after what had passed he should have secured my consent at least. I began to think if this was ministerial law in the New Jersey conference, I should be a little cautious in the future as to *loyal subjection.* Monday morning I returned to Vineland, when Mr. Landis met me with his carriage, and gave me a long ride and a fair view of the place and its surroundings. The town itself was then small—in the fall of 1862,—a little larger than the "Jefferson City" referred to in my work, but five or six houses would include the whole of the buildings in the town proper. Having made my survey, and suited myself, I purchased twenty acres on the line of the railroad, about one mile north of the town, at twenty dollars per acre. Upon this I built a neat little cottage, costing, when finished, about five hundred dollars, and before cold weather it was all completed and ready for occupancy.

During this improvement I made it my home at the regular boarding-house, and for some time I was engaged with Mr. Landis as a kind of private secretary, writing and sending out circulars in every direction. I found Mr. Landis, in every respect, honest, upright, and much of a gentleman, in all of my relations with him. Whilst at the boarding-house I became acquainted with a man from Ohio, having come to make Vineland his home, who remarked to me that "If we could only keep saloons and liquor out of the place it would be the most desirable thing in its society and improvement." To this I most heartily assented. When within four or five months of this time, he had put up a building, started a grocery, and was the first man to retail liquor on the premises! Mr. Landis and myself consulted about this temperance question, and a meeting of the citizens was called to decide in reference to it. Speeches were made by him and others, and this was the hardest man to fight upon that occasion. During my remarks, in winding up, as Mr. R sat right by my side, I stated that "he was the last man that I should have thought of to oppose the cause of temperance, in view of his record upon our first acquaintance," and then quoted *his language*, and appealed to him for its truth. I think I never saw a man *wilt* as soon as he did when I exposed his true position, and this was a complete settler. When the vote of the citizens was taken at that meeting, it was almost unanimous in favor of keeping the liquor interest out of the town; and to this day, it affords me much pleasure that all of my influence during the year was exerted in that direction. The results of this early movement will be given upon another page. It was easy to predict, even at this early history of Vineland, that it had a prosperous future, for at almost every arrival of the cars newcomers were on hand to see what interests and attractions it had for them. And thus day by day new purchases were made, new improvements started, and the *coming city* at a distance seen. Perhaps no one man in the state was better qualified to carry on to success such an interest than Charles K. Landis, and certainly no one could have had a stronger motive than he, to reach the *highest point* within the compass of human enterprise.

For some time after my purchase, we had no place for

religious services, and as a result we were without preaching; but as soon as the point could be reached, our schoolhouse was finished, when the Presbyterian minister and myself alternated each Sabbath. Our ministerial relations were very friendly, and we did everything to promote the spirit of unity and peace. There being now ten or twelve members of the Methodist Episcopal church residing in the place, I took the legal steps to organize them into a society, and thus we were prepared to build upon the proper foundation. I am not quite certain that I preached the first sermon in Vineland, but I am positive that I preached the first after our church organization. I served the church as pastor the most of the year after our organization, the membership continually increasing, when I arranged with the elder to make this one of the regular appointments on the circuit, and thereby I was released. I did this in view of the possibility of returning to my own conference at the end of the year. I cannot too highly commend the generous spirit of Mr. Landis in appropriating a lot to each Christian denomination for church purposes; in doing so, these monuments of beauty and architecture are a great ornament to the city. Besides this, they silently speak, but no *less eloquently*, to every Christian man and woman: "Here you may find a home, and worship around your own altars." Nothing speaks more forcibly as to the taste and character of a people than these commanding memorials of mercy and truth, and they exert a powerful influence in promoting the interests of the place. During the year the proprietor selected a spacious lot for the Methodist Episcopal church, and in company with him we measured and staked it off, and it is now adorned with a beautiful house of worship. From these historic items, I suppose that it may be truthfully said: "That when the full history of Vineland is written up, the writer will come in for a place." During the winter, the pastor at Millville for whom I preached sent word to have me assist him in protracted services. I honored his request and remained with him several days. My home at this meeting was at Rev. Garrettson's, a local preacher, a relative of Freeborn Garrettson, of precious memory; and if not mistaken, he possessed some of the same spirit. Whilst preaching upon the redemption of time, the good work commenced, and went on from week to week until about two hundred embraced religion in that station. During its progress the pastor of the other charge sent for me to come and assist him. Not wishing to show any partiality, I went at once, and soon both charges were favored with a wonderful work of grace. This blessed revival went on in both charges for some length of time, until about four hundred persons were received into the church. Seldom have I witnessed a more thorough work than this. I now felt, though not laboring in my own conference, to say: "Now, thanks be unto God, which always causeth us to triumph in Christ, and maketh manifest the savor of his knowledge by us in *every place*." Whilst residing in Vineland, a distance of only four or five miles, I found these stations a very pleasant resort. Upon the return of spring, I attended the New Jersey conference at Burlington. Our learned and talented Bishop Thomson presided, and on the Sabbath I had the privilege of listening to one of his discourses upon the evidences of Christianity. This was the last conference that I saw him. In a short time he entered upon his reward, but I am well assured that the church has been blessed with few nobler men.

Learning at this session that the colored people were engaged in revival services in the city, I had a curiosity to attend one of their meetings. I had heard so much in relation to their singing and preaching that I wished to go and see for myself. So, in company with a local preacher, we entered the church just at the close of the sermon. The inspiration of music soon reached its highest point after we took our seats, and the old church resounded with songs and praises. The singing was led by a chorister, and he seemed inclined to have his own way. The colored preacher would call him to a halt occasionally, and cry out: " Bredren, let us change de exercises!" when he would break out anew and make the old house ring again. As well as I was able to judge, the chorister composed some of his songs as he went along, for they were *newly coined*, and strangely measured. He seemed to have a thorough knowledge of the weak places of his *Satanic majesty;* and his principal drive seemed to be to do him all the injury within his power. I was well aware that he was not invincible, but they seemed to have a method of putting this master spirit to flight, which to me was entirely new. My readers will be interested to know some of their methods of foiling this wily adversary, as embraced in song. Here is one:

> " The way to make the devil run,
>   Is to shoot him with the gospel gun.
> CHORUS: — *The Lord is my shepherd, I shall not want,*" etc., [four times repeated.]

Here another:

> " The way to spoil the devil's nest,
>   Is to shout like a Methodist.
>   *The Lord is my shepherd, I shall not want,*" etc.

The above is but a specimen of their military tactics, and should I say that they embraced new features of success, I should be true to history. In my theological training I had read of " Satan's kingdom, Satan's devices, the snares of Satan, that he was the god of this world, going about" in the work of destruction; but that of being a " *nest-builder*," to me, was a new scrap in religious history. But to them it was a small matter whether the sentiment was or was not orthodox, so that it would *jingle*. Occasionally, when a pause was reached in their swaying and songs, the colored pastor would cry out: " Come, bredren, let us bring de boat ashore; 'tis time to close; we'll want to worship another night;" when the singer would start off again with something new, with renewed enthusiasm. Having remained until past ten P. M., to witness the landing of the boat, and it seeming to us no nearer the shore, we started for home, having secured, within a few hours, material for days of amusing and interesting meditation. The cup of my curiosity was now full, and all that remained was to profit by past experiences. But I am fully persuaded, with all of the amusing things and extravagances in their religious exercises, many of them will shine in the heavenly kingdom.

Having now a pleasant cottage home, I went to work in preparing for the useful and ornamental; for the blessing of health cannot be secured so successfully in any other way as by plenty of exercise in the open air. And thus I prepared my garden for its crops, my flower-beds and walks for beauty, my ornamental trees in proper order, and within a few months truthfully I could say:

> " My little cot's with herbage crowned,
>   And beauty's smiling all around."

Being a great admirer of flowers, I took especial pains to cultivate this department, and therefore secured every variety which I could obtain. Such was my success that many came quite a distance to see my well-selected varieties and engage seeds for the coming year. My garden also produced its abundance of Irish as well as sweet potatoes; so that, like David and Jonathan, beauty and plenty were blended together. A very pleasant event of this summer was the visit of Judge Burris and companion from Washington City. They were my old Christian friends, and members of my charge at Davenport, and nothing could have been more inspiring. They remained with me for two days, and they seemed like the renewal of past history. They still reside at the capital, " filling up, I trust, the measure of their days with usefulness."

It was while here at Vineland, the first days of July, that the great battle of Gettysburg was fought, which had much to do in the restoration of the Union. During the progress of the war, I never felt as much interest in the success of our arms as I did during this terrible conflict, and never did I pray so long and earnestly that God would give us the victory. The success of our arms upon this occasion, as well as the surrender of Vicksburg about the same time, sent through the nation such an inspiration of hope, that they were signals to the crowning victory. For the first time in Vineland was the Fourth of July celebrated, and the recent victories just achieved gave additional enthusiasm to the occasion. Mr. Landis and the writer were the principal speakers, when the entertainments which followed reflected credit upon the ladies of the place. Had I intended to make this my permanent home when I purchased, I could have had but little inducement to sell out with the expectation of finding one more to my taste; but feeling that my work was not yet done in the Upper Iowa conference, my health having improved during the year, as the time of its session came on I felt like entering anew upon my work. There was only one thing in the way. My ready means were invested in the place, and there was a necessity that I should find a purchaser in order to be ready for ministerial work. But it was my honest conviction that if duty called me to efficient labor a wise Providence would prepare the way. Acting under this conviction, the season passed away until within a few days of our conference. I had now *just time enough* to transact the business of the sale, and not one day to spare, and no purchaser as yet. This was the suspense of faith. The afternoon of the last day arrived, the time being about one o'clock P. M., and as I looked out of my window I saw a man in the distance approaching my place. As he was nearing my house some unseen visitant seemed to say: "That is *your man*, who comes to purchase your home." When he entered my room, *at once* he made his business known; without one word, gave me the price asked, and within five minutes the sale was completed.

19

That same afternoon the writings were drawn, the money
paid, and the next morning I was ready to start for Iowa.
As I visited Mr. Landis to pay him the balance due on the
place, he looked a little surprised, and in fact expressed it,
with his regrets at my leaving; and *my heart* responded
"*regret*," for our intercourse through the year had been
pleasant; but the Master who called me required continued
service until my work was accomplished.   The facts above
stated, at first view appear a little like romance, but every
syllable is *true to the letter;* and the *occasion* furnished the
nicest little *test* of God's faithfulness, and *personal trust*,
within the range of my history.   Had I not been brought
to a *point* in time, the divine interposition would not have
been so manifest.   Had the test-time been enlarged to
months, the event might have been attributed to chance;
but being brought into the compass of an hour, we see the
movings of an unseen hand.

Before taking leave of Vineland I will enter upon a brief
review.   I have already stated that during my residence
the place was in its infancy, and the *stand* taken by Mr.
Landis and its citizens to make it a temperance town.
Through the untiring efforts of the former, and the enterprise of its people, it has continually prospered, until it now
numbers a population of ten thousand inhabitants.   It gives
me pleasure to state, also, that the *firm stand* taken in its
early history to keep out whisky-saloons and grog-shops has
been faithfully maintained.   By my request, the proprietor
sent me a few items in reference to its past and present history, which I will here record.   " By a fundamental law of
the township, the question of ' license' or ' no license' is sub-
mitted to a popular vote at every spring election, and thus far
only twenty-five votes have been cast for license.   The tract
has several railroad stations; one hundred and eighty miles
of splendid roads, streets and broad avenues lined with
shade trees; many fine residences; fifteen church edifices; a
fine high school and numerous other schools.   The tempera-

ture is about that of North Carolina, with little snow in winter. It now has four shoe factories, three button factories, steam mills, foundry, machine shop, one glove factory, pocket-book factory, and extensive manufactories of clothing. A building association, a saving and a national bank have been established, and six trains arriving and departing for Philadelphia and New York every day." And now for its temperance and moral aspect, given by the overseer of the poor: "Though we have a population of eleven thousand, for a period of six months no settler or citizen of Vineland has required relief at my hands. During the entire year, there has been one indictment, and that a trifling case of assault and battery, among our colored population. So few are the fires, that we have no need of a fire department. There has been only one house burned down in a year, and the police expenses amount to but seventy-five dollars." He says: " I ascribe this remarkable state of things—so nearly approaching the golden age—to the industry of our people and the absence of King Alcohol." What a *record* is this for a young city of ten thousand inhabitants! Well might the writer call it " an approach to the golden age." It stands without a parallel in the history of the United States, if not in the history of the world. This shows what can be done by *men* and measures. But this is not all. " The home example," says Mr. Landis, " has been such that the neighboring cities of Millville and Bridgeton, which previously could number liquor saloons by hundreds, and were often the scenes of disorder and crime, have abolished them with the same favorable results as in Vineland. The example has also spread to other townships of the state, and over one-half of all the townships in the great state of Pennsylvania." If the facts above stated, from the best authority, should contribute to aid in the least in paying a proper tribute to this young city, with its faithful workers, and aid in the cause of God and humanity, I shall be happy in presenting my readers this full page. And I most earnestly hope and pray that the commendable history of Vineland, in its influence for good, may spread from city to city and from state to state, like the leaven in the meal, until this *unmitigated curse* of drunkenness shall find a page only in the history of the past. I now bid a short adieu to this city and its many friends with my parting benediction: God bless you!

CHAPTER XXXVI.

Having everything in readiness, I took the cars in Vineland on Tuesday morning, and on Wednesday I reached Davenport, the seat of our annual conference. Here I was conducted to the residence of my old friends, Brother and Sister Morton. One year had passed since, as pastor, I left its consecrated altars to seek for health and vigor in an Eastern clime, and now I return bringing back to Iowa the precious boon. Bishop Ames, my old traveling companion, gave me a hearty welcome, and as a kind of episode introduced me to my ministerial brethren. This was one of the sessions that I really enjoyed; and how could it be otherwise in the society of such Christian friends. One of the pleasantest interviews connected with it, was a meeting, by invitation, of all the old pastors of the city at the home of Hon. John F. Dillon, who at this date resided in the place. Very few men enjoyed such a social gathering more than he and his excellent lady, and none were better calculated to give it interest. Among the pleasant remarks passed, said Brother Dimmitt to the judge: "Why is it that you think so much more of Brother Taylor than the rest of us?" "A very good reason," he answered: " he is the only man that ever married me." Sister Dillon was the oldest daughter of Brother and Sister Price, a particular friend, and engaged me to perform the ceremony a year before the event; and

since that time, not a link in the golden chain of friendship
has ever been broken; and I trust, that as by its power it
has kept us unaltered on earth, it will bind us the closer in
our glorious reunion in heaven. As stated in a former chapter, Brother Morton has reached the better land, but Sister
Morton is still watching and waiting to join precious spirits
who have entered into rest.

My field of labor for the coming year had been decided
before I left Vineland, as Brother Kynett, the presiding
elder of Davenport district, had written me previously; so
when the appointments were read, and I was assigned to
"Clinton station," I was not taken by surprise. This was
a smart little village at this date, about one thousand inhabitants, and a great lumbering center. Brother R. Norton
was my predecessor; a *true man*, and I found the church
in a good healthy condition. Having visited the people
once or twice previously, I was not a stranger, and at once
I found a home in the family of Brother J. C. Young.
Brother and Sister Young were the parents of Rev. E. K.
Young, of the Upper Iowa conference. The health of my
brother, Harvey Taylor, having failed, I wrote to him at
Wyoming to come to Clinton and start a harness shop. He
acceded to my proposition; so when he came, I made my
home with him. I found here many noble-hearted brethren
and sisters, and for the spirit of enterprise and intelligence
the town would compare favorably with any previous station.
This year embracing the very heart of the war, and the one
in which the heaviest drafts were made, every other interest
seemed subjugated to this. But notwithstanding this heavy
pressure upon us, the cause of religion prospered during the
entire year. Brethren J. C. Young, W. H. Lunt, and Simon
Shoecraft were our class-leaders—Brother Lunt, our Sunday-school superintendent, and Shoecraft principal in our
high school. These brethren took right hold and worked
like men; then here was Brother Dunn, Brother Ham, and
many others whose hearts were enlisted in the good cause.

Among the friends of the church, Mr. Wm. H. Young and his excellent companion were ever ready with their hearts and pockets open to render assistance. As a specimen of the spirit of Mr. Young, who conducted the largest mill interest of the place—when one of his hands threw out some disloyal remarks, he *soused* him into the mill-pond in order to cool off his Southern ardor, and dismissed him. When taking up the missionary collection, I proposed to all those present who used tobacco to donate the amount of their tobacco bill yearly; when he said, "Put me down ten dollars;" but after a little consideration, thinking it not enough, he added two dollars more. Mr. and Mrs. Young at that time possessed all the desirable qualities of the Christian save the "grace that bringeth salvation." This they did not profess to enjoy; but I trust that when this short memorial shall be read by them, coming from their old pastor and friend, the *one thing* then lacking, may be now secured. How true it is that nothing can be substituted for the " *Light of life.*"

Having an appointment about three miles in the country every other Sabbath, on that day I had three sermons to preach. From one of these I was often relieved by my brother. Shortly our winter revival services came on and continued about four weeks with much interest. A large number were converted, and we had a general " refreshing from the presence of the Lord." Brother E. K. Young, then stationed at Davenport, assisted for several days and contributed much to the progress of the work. Rev. S. N. Fellows, then stationed at Lyons, also preached once or twice with good effect. Brother S. Shoecraft, having charge of our graded school, rendered us valuable assistance, in view of his influence among the young people. I was never more impressed in my life with the importance of Christian influence in the school-room, than during this meeting. The teacher has the power, in a great measure, to infuse his own spirit, and stamp his own image upon the hearts of his pupils, and impressions thus made in early years have their influence to the latest day of life. Rev. E. K. Young at this date had but just entered the ministry, and his history was yet in the future. But the elements were there, and needed only time and application for successful development. Since that period (1864), those years have been furnished; and though small in stature, in ministerial rank he stands upon a level with many of his brethren who have strength sufficient to carry *two big* D's. A resident of the country seeing so many " Co.'s " attached to other names, concluded that the Co.'s were a very numerous family; and should *eminent men* multiply in future years, as rapidly as in the past, every pastoral charge will have its own doctor as well as pastor. My dear Brother Young has not as yet, I believe, shouldered this cross, perhaps thinking that it is not a necessity to give prominence to his popularity as a minister of Christ. Rev. S. N. Fellows has not, however, been so fortunate. But notwithstanding the *burden borne*, he has managed to make for himself a first-rate reputation as professor in the Iowa State university. Brother Fellows is a safe man, filling with honor every position of trust in which he has been placed in the Upper Iowa conference, and such *honorary titles* set about as lightly upon his spirit as the top-knot upon the head of the blue-jay. During the winter season, Brother Fellows protracting his meeting in Lyons, I satisfied the claim against me by preaching several times for him, and in so doing formed a very pleasant acquaintance with the members of that charge.

Upon the return of spring I concluded to hold a series of meetings in the country, but there was a serious difficulty in the way. Some old grudges remained of a *stubborn character*, and I found that these must be adjusted before we could expect a work of divine grace. So I started out early in the morning, and visited the parties; the next day prevailed upon them to come together, and we so far succeeded as to have a show of victory. Upon this basis we commenced our revival services, and within a few days the altar was crowded with penitents. Thirty persons embraced religion and united with the church; many of them faithful to the present day. Such was the interest for weeks, there was no room for the revival of old feuds; but in a few months I learned by experience, that after all our efforts, the *lion* had been *caged* but not conquered. He would stand before the gates and growl, and show his teeth; as much as to say: " Were it not for this cage you would catch it." This, figure well represents the spirit and action of those who profess to have settled old difficulties, and still cherish in their hearts the spirit of revenge. Unless the evil spirit *is cast out*, and the spirit of Christ takes its place— *i. e.*,—real forgiveness and love,—there is no hope of permanent peace. If Satan is permitted to remain, it will not be long before he will lead off into some sinful work.

Mr. E., within the bounds of one of my charges, had a *pique* against his neighbor, Mr. Elijah Frampton, and was determined to cultivate this spirit to the fullest extent. Attending one of our quarterly meetings, he became deeply convicted for his sins, and came forward as a penitent seeker. But pardon and peace did not come. He renewed the effort, with no better success; and thus he prayed and wept until nearly the hour for closing, and no light yet. One of the brethren knowing his difficulty with his neighbor, said to him: " Mr. E., perhaps there is something you are cherishing in your heart, not willing to give up, that God requires at your hands before he will bless you. Think if there is not." " I know of nothing," said he, " only I have said I would not forgive Elijah Frampton." " Well," said his adviser, " you must surrender this if you would find salvation." One more struggle, and Mr. E. was on his feet, and his first utterance of praise was this: " Glory to God, I have forgiven Elijah Frampton." And now Elijah was the first man he wished to see. This is what grace will do for a man if he will permit it. It will lay the " rough paths of peevish nature even, and open in each heart a little heaven;" but this cannot be done until we become willing—yea, *anxious*—to change occupants. All that a man has to do, if he prefers the fruits of darkness instead of peace, is to choose his master, and he will not fail.

When I returned to the city after this revival in the country, to take a little rest, as we sat at the dinner table, we we were startled with a sharp clap of thunder, and knew from its character that some damage had been done. We were the more surprised, as the little cloud that passed over indicated anything else but a messenger of destruction. But a few minutes passed, and the tidings came: " Mr. L's smoke-stack has been struck and leveled to the ground." I was aware that he had been pushing things to get ready for business, and that some of the brethren had been counseling him for working on the Sabbath, informing him that he would lose more than he would gain. But such was his *anxiety* to hurry through, that in this instance he had overstepped his own convictions, as he was generally an observer of the Sabbath. The event was a remarkable one, as given me by one of my old friends present. Said he: "We had just sat down to dinner—not five minutes since we left the stack, when the lightning flashed, and the report followed. For a moment we were all stunned—not a word spoken—when Mr. L. said to his wife: 'Will you look out and see if my smoke-stack is all right.' She returned in a moment and exclaimed: 'There is nothing left of it!'" Said Mr. S., who gave me this relation, " If we had remained five minutes longer, every one of us—six or seven in number—would have been killed." He further stated to me: " This is the last Sunday-work that I shall do, let the urgency be what it will." Here was one thousand dollars scattered in a moment to the four winds. One of the friends who had chided him for his violation of the Sabbath, remarked to me, "That the angel having charge of the city came along with his *big gun*, and as he came in sight of that *stack* partly built on the Sabbath, he took a dead rest, gave it a centre shot, and knocked it all to flinders." So you see this was about all the sympathy manifested by the people for his loss of one thousand dollars. He proceeded at once to rebuild, but no more of its work was done on the Lord's day. How true it is that nothing is gained by slighting the commands of God.

I was visited this spring by Rev. Wm. Lease, who was stationed at Sabula. He came upon a little business matter, which opened the door to a more extended acquaintance. Subsequently I met him at his own home, where I found a very pleasant family and a hearty welcome. While enjoying the benefits of this social interview, he made one remark of *such value* that I retain it to this day; and I sincerely hope that the statement then made may be as true in 1881 as in the year 1864. The statement was this: " Mrs. Lease and myself have fully resolved that the ' honey-moon ' shall last to the end of life." I then said to myself, what a *noble resolve*, and what an influence will it exert upon these promising children. Having a kind and loving example always presented before them, they will grow up cherishing the same pacific spirit. Should this resolve be faithfully carried out, I should consider it a great honor to be invited to his golden wedding; and I hereby request an invitation, promising the best speech I have for the occasion. But before that time, the writer, as well as the subjects, will doubtless have reached that land where they " neither marry nor are given in marriage, but are as the angels in heaven." Brother Lease has been laboring in our conference about twenty-four years, gradually rising in the confidence of his brethren, until he has reached one of its most honorable and responsible positions, *i. e.*, presiding elder of Davenport district. May his increasing light find its final consummation in *perfect day*.

Having been fully Westernized by many solid experiences, my only son living having recently graduated at Ann

Arbor, Mich., I wrote him to come to Iowa, having encouragement that he could secure a position as principal in
our graded school. He accordingly came, and within a short
time was employed at Lyons, where he remained during
one year. Continuing in this relation as teacher for two or
three years, he concluded to study medicine, when, after
taking a thorough course, he located at Wheelersburg, Scioto
county, Ohio, where he is still a practicing physician. He
married the daughter of James S. Folsom, of French Grant,
Ohio, who is well qualified to fill "her place in all the relations of life. During my feeble state of health, induced
by pneumonia, I made my home in their family for more
than one year, and found my stay very pleasant. Moving
along upon the wave, having had no permanent home for
more than forty years, it is pleasant to find such a Bethesda
"in age and feebleness extreme."

In the midst of my pastoral labors on this charge, I received a letter from Marshall, Henry county, Iowa, from
Sister Simpson, bearing the intelligence of the death of her
husband. My readers will bear in mind that Rev. Wm.
Simpson was my first colleague on Mt. Pleasant circuit. Our
last meeting was at Honey Creek, on my way from Sioux
City to conference, six years previous. But now the "silver
cord had been loosed and the golden bowl broken." As he
was licensed to preach in the year of our Lord 1837, he
had been preaching the blessed gospel for thirty-seven
years. He was one of the first members of the Iowa conference; "having raised the standard of the Cross upon the
battle-fields of Michigan, Wisconsin and Illinois" in years
previous. He preached the first sermon in Keokuk, Iowa;
when in 1850 he volunteered to go to Council Bluffs mission. Here the inhabitants were nearly all Mormon and
Indian. In this Mormon city he preached the first gospel
sermon; was cursed by the priest, but was forced to remove
the curse by the manly and heroic conduct of a few Gentiles. He remained upon this mission for two full years,

when he reported at the close two hundred and forty members. During five years of his ministry in the Iowa conference, he filled the office of presiding elder, and in every position he was the same noble-hearted and true man. In our labors together on Mt. Pleasant work, he often said to me, as referred to in a previous chapter: "When I am dying, I expect my last song to be, 'We will cross the river of Jordan, happy in the Lord.'" I will here present to my readers a short extract from the pen of Rev. Thomas Corkhill, an intimate friend, as to the closing scene: "A few hours before his death the pain subsided, and he rested quietly until the time of his departure. Beside his couch stood a few faithful friends, who had ministered to him in his affliction, and now waited to witness his triumph in the final hour. Steadily the tide of life was ebbing, and the darkness of the grave drawing near. His wife and children were the only objects of solicitude now. The great work had already been accomplished, and like the apostle he was ready to be offered. Two sons stood upon the battle-field; three younger members of the family stood beside his bed. Looking upon the face of his wife, he said: 'Educate these children; train them for God.' Feeling now that his hour had come, and that he stood beside the chilling waters, he raised his voice in *full melodious strain* and sang:

> "'We'll cross the river of Jordan,
> Happy in the Lord.'"

This is the first instance in my work where I have given the details of the Christian's triumphant death, because of the space they would fill, in testimonies so abundant; but Brother Simpson being my old colleague and particular friend, I have thought it due to his memory. Brother Corkhill, upon the occasion of his death, composed a few appropriate lines, which I here record in part:

"Thou art gone to the grave, where thy fathers are sleeping,
    Where sorrow and grief shall oppress thee no more.

Though kindred and friends by thy grave may stand weeping,
Thy labors and conflicts forever are o'er.

"Thou art gone to the grave; but at Jordan's dark billow,
Thy soul not its darkness nor chilliness feared;
Serene on His bosom, thy head thou dids't pillow,
While the crown and the palm in the distance appeared.

"'In joy most triumphant, in ecstasy holy,
We'll cross the cold tide,' was his dying acclaim,
'And with spirits redeemed—with the meek and the lowly,
Possess them in heaven, through Jesus' name.'"

If justice to other charges would allow, I would be pleased to enlarge upon my labors in this station; but I cannot extend the one without slighting the other. But there is one thought upon which I wish to dwell before taking leave of this city. How often on horseback, in my previous labors, did I ride over the very ground upon which the town is now built, when not a house nor an inhabitant was to be seen, but now and then a prairie chicken came sailing by, as if looking for a place to light. And a little further on were a small cluster of houses, called Lyons, where by the roadside was to be seen a little shanty, and on its sign written, "Cakes and Bier." I thought the orthography of the last word very appropriate, inasmuch as it sustained a more intimate relation to death than life; so when properly defined it meant "Cakes and Death." This frontier signal remained there for some years, but was finally displaced in the onward march of improvement. But now there is no further use for the horse and his rider over these bare prairies, for the old iron horse is master of the situation. "The sound of the church-going bell" had not then sent one musical wave o'er its uncultivated wastes, nor the sweet invitations of the gospel thrilled the human heart. The mighty machinery that now rolls out its millions of feet of lumber in twenty-four hours, *then* existed only in the ore, and its present stately dwellings were then waving in forests of pine. Thousands that now crowd its thrifty streets had not seen the light of *day*, nor the railroad's rapid travel ever marked its way. Passing through this growing city at this date, and then going back in its history nearly forty years, it seems for a moment more like romance than fact. And yet these stately towers and massive walls proclaim on every hand its truthful history. And the man who daily walks its streets may yet live to witness as great a change in the future as in the past.

> " O may its crown of glory be
> Full consecration, Lord, to thee;
> Then shall its walks and piles resound,
> *With peace and plenty all around.*"

With this historical tribute, I wave a friendly adieu to Clinton City and its sacred interests, looking forward to the day when eras and periods existing in time will be lost in the annals of heaven.

CHAPTER XXXVII.

We meet this fall at Waterloo for conference, our loyalty to the Union symbolized by the waving of the Stars and Stripes. How natural it is for the man who loves his God to love the country God has given him! I regard that doc-trine sound: " If a man love God he will love his neighbor also," for the greater includes the less—and no less true that he will love his *country also;* for the laws governing both are the same; and especially a country with "every blessing blessed." As I looked at its colored folds waving gently in front of the Methodist church, I felt in my heart like saying: " That star-spangled banner! O, long may it wave, o'er the land of the free and the home of the brave." Bishop Scott was again with us in the spirit of wisdom and love. This session was marked as the beginning of our " Church Extension Society " in practical form. At this conference it was regularly organized, its officers appointed, and a subscription taken up amounting to some two or three thousand dollars. An address was made by Rev. A. J. Kynett as to its object and merits, at the close of which I followed with some remarks; but what was still better, with my subscription of one hundred dollars. Other brethren then followed, until the results were reached as noted above. I suppose as one of the rewards of this dona-tion, I was appointed the first treasurer, with Hon. Hiram Price president, and Rev. A. J. Kynett corresponding secre-tary and general agent. This child of promise has continued to grow and take on strength from year to year, until it has become one among the first benevolent interests of the church, and its influence is yearly increasing. With such men as Doctor Kynett and his assistant, C. C. McCabe, to manage the society's interests, I am not surprised that it has attained its present importance; and from recent indica-tions, it has only just started out upon its mission of mercy and love. From the success which has already attended the efforts of its secretaries, I am more than ever con-vinced " that we have the *right men* in the *right place.*"

As I had intended to take a rest at the close of this year, and being interested in the right kind of a man for Clinton City, I waited upon Bishop Scott personally and secured the man that I desired. We were upon the point of build-ing a new church, and as Brother Trusdell was fully com-petent, the bishop appointed him my successor to that charge. My first acquaintance with Rev. C. G. Trusdell as a minister, was rather peculiar and interesting. I was then Sunday-school agent for the conference, and went with him to his first country appointment. Whether my pres-ence, as an older minister, had any tendency to embarrass him, I cannot say; but one thing I can say—when fairly into the merits of his discourse, he lost *daylight* and began to feel around for thoughts; and as nothing but vacancy appeared, he sat down, leaving the remainder of the service in my hands. Brother Trusdell at this time had not been in the cavalry service—as he was afterwards,—else he might have turned a *short corner* and given the enemy a back-handed lick, and in this way covered his retreat. But instead of this, he very meekly and calmly surrendered the pulpit and took his seat, as much as to say: "Gentlemen and ladies, there is no use of talking—I have made a failure and you all know it." He could not say, either, as an old minister whom I once heard under similar circumstances. After tugging hard to get through, he remarked at the close of his sermon: "Well, brethren, I have *got through* and I *am glad of it;*" for Brother Trusdell was *not through;* he had called a halt, and stopped, just when he wanted to go. But there was one feature of this failure that I really admired. Though deeply mortified, he acted like a man; he did not climb a tree, or take to his bed, but he bore the cross without a groan, and waited patiently on his seat to see what disposition I would make with reserved forces. Being an old tactician in this line—as an old member of this conference will affirm who once saw me tested—I began in the outset to speak well of his sermon, commending its sentiments and its brevity; never hinted to them that it was a failure—glad that he did not call it such—and in my exhortation I had such liberty and light that we came out in the end victorious. The short sermon gave me ample room for an exhortation, and before we left, we wrote success upon our banners. After dinner we had twelve miles to Iowa City, our home, when we had a long encouraging talk, which gave new inspiration to the young preacher, and to which interview Brother Trusdell has since often referred with heartfelt gratitude and satisfaction. Even in this appointment to Clinton he was young in the ministry, but he had the manhood, with a fine business talent, and during the year erected a commodious church, which is still their house of worship. Not only was the church completed, but the station prospered in all of its interests. At the close of the second year he was elected to the legislature from Clinton county, which position he filled with honor; then again prosecuted his work in the ministry, a part of the time as presiding elder, when he was transferred to Chicago. After a term of service in that city as pastor, he was elected to fill 'the very responsible position which he now occupies as " superintendent of the Relief and Aid Society," for which his eminent business talent so fully qualifies him. May his shadow never grow less!

It was during the spring of 1865, a short time after General Lee's surrender, that the heart-chilling tidings flashed over the telegraphic wires that President Lincoln was assassinated. I was then at work in my garden upon a little place near the city, when the messenger brought the tidings. I think such a *shock* I never experienced. It seemed to affect my whole nervous system. The next day (Sabbath) union memorial services were held by the citizens of Clinton and Lyons, with appropriate addresses, whilst the spirit of deep mourning was manifest upon every countenance. Previous to *this*, he had been estimated as the *Nation's favorite*, but on that memorable morning, the fact was engraven upon every American heart: " The Nation's Martyr." The summer of this year passed very pleasantly in the society of my old friends on this charge, and I used my influence as a retired pastor to hold up the hands of my successor without claiming part of the honors.

I must here state a little circumstance which occurred upon one of our charges, as related to me by the pastor. One of the members of the church, very low with consumption, sent for him to administer comfort. He went at once—for he was the man to honor such calls; but after entering her sick-room she was under the painful necessity of requesting him to retire. Having smoked a cigar that morning, she was unable to endure the odor from his person. With his keen sensibilities, how must he have felt

20

returning home unable to administer comfort to the dying because of indulging in a filthy habit! He made this statement to me with tears, and assured me that this painful occurrence had wrought a perfect cure.

At our ensuing conference at Tipton, meeting the state agent of the American Bible Society, Rev. Mr. Jones, and he being very anxious that I should enter upon this work, I consented, and within a short time received my commission from New York. I was well aware that this position would give me more exercise and less hard study, and thereby contribute to my general health as well as enlarge my sphere of usefulness. In this I was not mistaken. During the years employed in this interest, I had not a sick day, and what a field it opened before me for usefulness! Not only did it furnish a fine opportunity for extended acquaintance among our ministers, and the pleasure of rendering them assistance, but it brought me into intimate relation with the ministers and members of other churches; as the blessed Bible was the *friend* of all, and all equally interested in its circulation. Such a work as this is well calculated to enlarge our charity and good will towards other branches of the church, and narrow down our sectarian views in reference to our own. Some of the pleasantest acquaintances formed and most sacred hours enjoyed in this service, were with those of the same " household of faith," though known by a different name. And never was I introduced so practically to this fact: that the more we become acquainted with each other, the *less* of the spirit of selfishness shall we cherish. The *Bible* furnishing such a broad " platform " that all can stand upon it, and a *heritage so rich and full* that all can invest in it, and hopes so *immortal* that all alike can cherish—like the Stars and Stripes to different regiments of the Union, we can all rally around this standard, *God's precious truth*, and feel that we are heirs to the same rich and glorious inheritance. I entered at once upon this work after my appointment, and as the

Apostles after having obtained their divine commission commenced at "Jerusalem," it was meet for me at this juncture to grasp the weapons of this warfare where I first laid them down. It was at Maquoketa where my health first failed, and where for a season I was laid aside, and *here* I preach my first Bible sermon as agent of that society. Here I found Rev. W. Frank Paxton and his excellent companion stationed at this place, who gave me such a hearty welcome in my introduction to this work that the recollection is precious to this day. How different the effect of such a reception upon human hearts, than that of a cold shoulder and a closed door! At once I felt at home, and during my stay, if the work had been his own, he could not have manifested deeper interest; and as a result the efforts were crowned with success.

Perhaps upon no future page shall 1 have a better place for a short sketch of Brother Paxton than here. He was born and reared in Gettysburg, Penn.; graduated at Pennsylvania college, a Lutheran institution of learning in that place, in 1855. He taught two or three years in Baltimore Female college, and joined the Upper Iowa conference in 1858. Eight years he has served the church as presiding elder—four on the Fayette and four on the Davenport district, and one year as agent of Cornell college. Sister Paxton is of pure Yankee stock, born in Great Barrington, Mass., and was married to Brother Paxton in Waterloo, Iowa, in 1860. Three daughters and one son now constitute the younger members of this household. Since that meeting in Maquoketa, our pastoral work being contiguous, I have ever met with the same warm greeting in my associations with his family, and always consider it a great pleasure to enjoy their society and hospitality. As a preacher, his flow of language is easy, his words well chosen, his sermons well arranged, and rich in thought, and in many instances reach the standard of genuine eloquence. In listening to his discourses, no one will doubt but they have passed through the ordeal of hard study. As a man socially, he is genial in his spirit, warm in his attachments, and enduring in his friendships. Brother Paxton is now in the prime of life—many years of usefulness prospectively before him, and should his future record bear a proportionate comparison with the past, he may yet reach a position where his divinity may be crowned with "doctor." Should he ever reach this point, I doubt not the honor will be patiently borne.

In leaving Maquoketa I passed on to the circuit traveled by Rev. James H. Todd. He lived in the town of Andrew, then the county-seat of Jackson county. He had written me to visit his charge, present the Bible cause, and assist him in protracted services. I gladly acceded to his request, and remained with him during the week. Here was another instance of remarkable memory. He would listen to a sermon, and the next week preach the same, almost word for word. Had he been as eminent in piety as in memory he might have shone a star of the first magnitude; but lacking this, his ministerial history has been more like the comet than the planet. Whilst I remained with him, I used all of my influence to induce him to raise a high Christian standard, and labor to excel in the "excellency of the knowledge of Jesus Christ." But I have found in my experience that some men are very much like a peculiar kind of timber—you may line and hew and plane and shape it to your notion, but in a short time it has so warped and sprung out of shape that you are forced to abandon it altogether. Thus it is with some types of human character. If we could keep them under the press of religious influence all the while, they might be able to maintain their Christian integrity; but just so soon as they come in contact with other influences, they so *crook up*, or *flat out*, that there is no suitable place for them in the spiritual building. And just so long as human hearts are under the influence of sinful passions, we shall find just such subjects and experi-

ences.   I have often thought that Father Gruber's *penitent*
fitly represents this class above named, and his prayer a
complete fit in every respect.   Meeting one of them at the
altar, at camp-meeting, and knowing that he professed conversion anew at every big meeting, this old veteran preacher
concluded to offer a *sharp* and appropriate prayer.   Thus
he told the Lord all about his penitent, how many times he
had professed religion, and how many times he had backslidden; how he had abused mercy, again and again, and
"here he is at this altar once more, seeking for divine
favor."   The old elder then prayed to the Lord, "if he saw
in his infinite wisdom that grace could not keep him, *to kill
him* and take him right home to heaven; for if he did not
go there from a camp-meeting it was very doubtful if he
would ever reach there."   The subsequent history of this
man I cannot trace, but I venture to say that in memory's
store-house that prayer of "Father Gruber" long held a
place.

It can hardly be expected that in a work so extensive as
that of the Bible agent, he could embrace all the facts
and incidents occurring, for this would require another such
a volume; but the opportunity of advocating such a cause
as this for three or four years, to half of the population of
Iowa, was a privilege which I regard as among the *first*
in my ministerial life.   As my congregations were generally
large and intelligent, the inspiring motive would often lift
me above myself, so that I felt that I stood upon an eminence not only elevated in position but influential in its
consequences.   How often did the Divine Master honor his
own word and send the promised blessing down!   Associated with me in the Bible work as helpers, were Rev. Z. D.
Scoby, G. W. Jenkins, Levi H. Hale, and Rev. S. W. Ingham.
These were faithful and industrous men, and rendered me
valuable service in promoting the interests of this cause.
It is to me a pleasant and grateful reflection to this day,
that I ever found the members of our conference and min-

isters of other churches ready to co-operate with me in my visits to their several charges, and the friendly aid furnished me yet stands a memorial of interest in the book of remembrance. At our institutions of learning, also, the first at Mt. Vernon, Rev. R. Norton and President King gave me an open door and a wide field, and at Fayette, Brother P. E. Brown and Prof. Brush contributed to make our meeting a complete success. At Waverly I found Rev. F. X. Miller waiting on the platform for his presiding elder, D. N. Holmes; but as he did not come, I was elected in his place; and thus the transformation from a Bible agent to a presiding elder was soon effected without injury to either party. It was here that I first met Rev. John W. Clinton, at this quarterly meeting at Waverly. He was then teaching school at Janesville, and just initiated into American usages. During the progress of my discourse on Sunday morning, he appeared for a while to assume the attitude of a *sharp critic*, but in a little time I saw the big tear coursing down his cheek, and then I knew I was safe. How many times, under similar circumstances, have I seen the pencil drop, when the spiritual *thrill* reached the heart and the tears unbidden flowed. And thus it was with him. His *critical mischief*, which a few moments before I could see written all over his countenance, soon changed into reflective soberness, and the boy became a man. It has always been my delight in the ministry to capture critics in this way, for they invariably deliver up the pruning-knife and become my fast friends. All this I realized in his case; for within a short time I stood in his own pulpit at Janesville, inspired with his confidence and the prayers of his people. Fifteen years have passed since that introduction, but, like his ministerial progress, our friendship has grown into maturity, and the chances are now that it will last forever.

At Waverly I made my home at Brother and Sister Miller's for some weeks, he furnishing me a horse and carriage for my Bible work; and in this relation I felt very much as though it were my own home.   The face of Sister Miller reflects domestic sunshine wherever she goes, and " blessed is that minister who is in such a case."   Brother F. X. Miller was very popular and successful in Waverly, and in the sphere of usefulness in the Upper Iowa conference he has made an honorable record.

At Decorah I met Brother R. Swearingen, who dates back to my early acquaintance in Iowa.   I knew him when a boy in experience, when I reached out to him a helping hand, and now he reciprocates by helping me in my work.   He no longer needs the leading hand of his elder brethren, as when I first knew him, but he stands forth, in battle array, a hero in the defense of truth, capturing his enemy's artillery, and then shelling them in their flight; and had it not been for one *drawn battle* in his theological campaign, he might have stood forth a champion in the fight.   But even with this short halt, in his onward march, Brother Swearingen stands to-day a living witness as to what may be accomplished by steady perseverance.   He has received the highest honors within the gift of his conference, and such are his powers of endurance that they have been borne without serious injury.   I trust that when the Master calls, the "shock of corn will be fully ripe."   Though it would afford me great pleasure, I have refrained from mentioning the names and pleasant associations with ministers of other churches.   In a work of this kind a proper tribute would take up too much space; but though passed by in silence, they still live in my confidence and affections, and I soon expect to hail them as brethren and fellow-laborers in a purer clime.

It was during my labors for the American Bible society that I was induced to make a small purchase of real estate in the state of Michigan.   My only sister, Olive, living near Benton Harbor, and my mother wishing to visit her, I accompanied her to the place.   This was at that season of the year when the vast peach orchards of that vicinity were in

full bloom. Hundreds of acres through which I passed
looked like one continuous bouquet, and I was perfectly delighted with the sight. At that time the peach crop was
very profitable to the grower; so in the latter part of the
summer 1866, in company with Perry Perkins, an old friend,
we made a purchase of about seventeen acres at Heath's
Corners, within two miles of Benton Harbor, and two and
a half from St. Joseph. The year following I erected a
house on my twelve acres, and since that time I have called
this my home. Brother Perkins built also on his, and resided in the state for several years. He finally sold out and
returned to Colesburg, Iowa, where he now resides. Such
was the character of the Bible work, keeping me constantly
on the move, nearly all the time away from home, that I
had but little time for rest or social enjoyment, and no time
for study; so I concluded to ask a release, which the parent
society granted six months after my resignation. I was
succeeded by Brother Chambers, a member of our conference. In the fall of 1869, I entered again into the pastoral relation, and received my appointment at LeClaire,
with Rev. Emory Miller for my presiding elder. The work
and interests of this station will furnish history for our next
chapter.

CHAPTER XXXVIII.

As I sit down to enter upon this chapter, March 25, 1881,
I am reminded of the changes in personal history within a
short time. Only a few days since I was writing a short
tribute to Rev. Joel B. Taylor, in this volume, expecting
soon to see him in his own home; but to-day I am recording
his removal from us. A few days later, he was conversing
with me by letter, encouraging me in my task, and perhaps
at this very time some dear friend may be penning his

obituary. A long life he gave to the service of his Master, and now he has passed on to learn something about the other side. Twenty years previous to my appointment at Le Claire, when stationed at Davenport, I visited this little town to preach the funeral sermon of one of its oldest inhabitants, Brother Taylor then being their pastor, but now I am introduced to new scenes and new friendships. The little group of houses has grown into a thriving village, and the few citizens are multiplied to hundreds; but it matters not; the minister's work is not to draw a map of changes, but to save souls. Yes, wherever he drives his stakes and pitches his tent he writes upon his canvas, "I am here to seek and save that which was lost." With this motto, I entered into the work of this charge, and within a few months the chapel and altar were crowded with interested hearers and anxious inquirers. The means employed to reach gracious results in works of this kind may be various, but the elements of success are always the same. "Not by might, not by wisdom or human eloquence, but by my Spirit, saith the Lord." If I ever depended upon this divine agent, it was here in this effort at this time. The meeting continued for some weeks with little abatement of interest, and quite an accession was made to the church, and all of its interests advanced. Brother Emory Miller, the presiding elder of Davenport district, residing here, rendered me valuable aid, as well as Rev. J. H. Rigby, laboring upon an adjoining charge. Their ministerial assistance was not only highly appreciated, but their social friendships gave sacred relish to many a passing hour. Often, when weary with study at Sister Brotherlin's, my pleasant home, would I step into Brother and Sister Miller's, where an open door and a hearty welcome were always in readiness; and the children, catching the same spirit, seemed to regard my visits as a kind of cheerful ovation. What can be more pleasing and appropriate for those who profess to be training for heaven, than the cultivation of such feelings and habits here, typical of that pure and holy society into which we shall enter, made up of those who "walk with the Saviour in white." Certainly there should be a close correspondence between the earthly and the heavenly kingdom.

The friends of my acquaintance all know of my attachment to children; and this reminds me of a remark made by Brother Miller to me as we were returning from Sunday-school where I had addressed them. This was his remark: "Brother Taylor, the secret of your success in talking to children is because *you love them.*" A truer remark could not have been made; and because of this I treasured it up in my memory. Is it not this *love* which gives inspiration to our efforts and leads us on to success? If a man love his companion he will spare no pains to minister to her happiness; if a man love his neighbor, in many instances he will serve him at his own expense; and if a man love Christ, not unfrequently will he *plant the Cross* in sickly climes, whilst at its foot he finds a grave, upon which we read this inscription: "Let a thousand fall, before Africa shall be given up." How often have I thought of the impressions made upon the minds of those children which Jesus took up in his arms and blessed. Those *too young* to remember it, as they grew up to years were informed by the father or mother that the world's Redeemer honored them thus. I doubt not that this was the *crowning event* in their life's history. I am sure, were this true in my own case, I would *tell it* whilst living, lisp it when dying, and praise him in richer strains for it with an immortal tongue. In this charge we had a very prosperous Sunday-school, with an excellent superintendent, Brother James Davenport. And this was one of the secrets of its interest; his whole soul was engaged in its success. Many were the happy hours passed in its delightful exercises, and many of its scholars during our revival became subjects of saving grace.

This charge at this date had but two appointments—one in the village of LeClaire and one at Pleasant Valley, five miles out in the country, where I preached every Sunday afternoon. Here we had some noble brethren, a very good chapel, and an interesting Sunday-school. On the way out to this appointment, lived Sister Stone, whose husband was taken very sick. He was a very pleasant man, but, like many others, he was a stranger to saving grace. On my way I called to see him from time to time, and labored diligently to lead him to Christ. Brother Miller also visited him with me, and prayed with him; but he found no rest in believing. Calling on him again, I saw that he must be saved soon if saved at all—and I proposed to Sister Stone to unite with me *once more;* for this was the last and telling hour. Before prayer, Mr. Stone being very low, I urged upon him the necessity of a total surrender into the hands of an All-Mighty Saviour; and here was one of those peculiar manifestations not often experienced in ministerial history. As I began pleading for his salvation, such were the exercises of my mind that I could not close my prayer without a clear evidence that he was saved. And *that witness* came as *clear* as the noon-day sun. When I arose from my knees he was rejoicing in the knowledge of his sins forgiven, and shortly died in the blessed assurance of eternal life. In this case I had another evidence of the folly of prolonging a preparation for death until the dying hour.

Brother Rigby, whose name is mentioned above as one of my helpers during our revival, had but just entered the ministry. This was his first year in our conference. Having graduated at Mt. Vernon, and there received his license to preach, I was permitted to hear his first sermon, and now he sustains to me the relation of colleague, as we were mutual helpers to each other. I was an *old* minister and he a *young* one, but such was his congenial and flexible spirit, that I could not have felt any more at home in company with a man of my age. Though a good scholar and deep thinker, he put on no airs, no assumption of arrogance; but he was meek and humble, ever ready to receive instruction, even from a child. With such a spirit, you will not be surprised when I say that he improved rapidly as a public speaker during the year, was very much beloved, and his labors abundantly blessed. This truthful tribute to his memory, I give with the greatest pleasure, and in looking to the future assign him one of the prominent positions in ministerial rank.

Until my present relation to our presiding elder, I had but little personal acquaintance. I had heard him preach but once, when I was stationed at Iowa City, but I was aware that he was moving on the ascending plane. Now our present relations were such that I had a fine opportunity to know the man. Brother Miller was wise and very skillful as a preacher. In his ordinary efforts there was nothing marked nor unusual—a little slow constitutionally in his movements; but upon important occasions, when the interest was such as to draw him out, he excelled. He had a discourse all ready and prepared for such an assembly, and seldom failed in the object in view. In some instances he rose to an elevation in sublime eloquence that I never knew surpassed by our most eminent men. In his perorations he often reminded me of Castelar, the Spanish orator, for beauty and effect. His skill was manifest in another respect. He often preached the same sermon to different audiences, but in almost every instance I noticed that it was revised and enlarged so that it appeared in quite a new dress. He is a good scholar, a close student, and possesses a very comprehensive mind. And yet with his *rare* talents, no minister in the conference has less display. His brilliant mind is so tempered by the spirit of humility, that one would think that he considers himself the "least of all saints;" but when the lion is roused he stands forth a champion for the truth. He has been gradually rising in the confidence of the brethren of the Upper Iowa conference, until he has reached the highest honors within their gift;

and such are the elements in his character, that I have reason to believe that the light will not decline. He is stationed this year at Iowa City, one of my former charges, where I trust he will be still gathering laurels to perpetuate his name and enrich his mansion in the heavenly home.

During the summer of this year (1870), the preachers of the district all repaired to the feast of tabernacles in the grove near the town of Camanche. These gatherings may well be called *feasts* of spiritual enjoyment, when we go to them for this purpose; but how easily defeated, when for mere pleasure or pastime. Being called upon "to fire the first gun," I discoursed from "Ye shall receive power after that the Holy Ghost is come upon you." We had an interesting prayer-meeting after the sermon; but shortly after the preachers had retired to rest in their tent, some of the fastenings gave way, and all slid together in a heap. In the merriment that followed, I found that even Methodist ministers were very much like other men, if not a little more so, when they gave loose reins to laughter, and when they were bent upon a little spree. I was glad *that evening* that the *glee club* was confined to the ministers, and that they were the only ones affected by the sudden catastrophe; and though not a profitable means of grace, they understood the secret of praying out. This sudden reverse of the order of things had a dissipating effect upon the minds of the ministers, which I think was not fully regained for some days. At this meeting we had one or two very able sermons on the Sabbath, and we were very forcibly reminded of the importance of appropriateness in the selection of subjects. In fact very much of our success depends upon this. One of our ministers took for his text on Sunday afternoon: "And the city lieth four-square." I suppose the speaker did his best for about one hour, but no one was interested; and if the sinner had depended upon that sermon to learn his way into the kingdom of grace, he would have groped his way in the dark for a long time.

After the discourse, a very sensible sister said to me: "What do I care whether the city is square or round? we came here to learn the way of salvation." How hard it is to divest ourselves entirely of the idea at these interesting gatherings, that we must preach a *big sermon*, that the ministers and members may know that we are of some importance; when, if we had taken some plain and practical subject, and bent all of our energies to save perishing sinners, nothing would have done so much to raise us in the estimation of all present. When God is fully honored in the presentation of a sermon, it requires no critic's glass, or doctor's verdict, to reach a just decision; the Spirit is its own interpreter, and this will make it plain. I am here reminded of a simple statement given me by an aged minister who had the privilege of hearing John Summerfield and Henry B. Bascom in the city of Philadelphia on the same Sabbath. Summerfield preached in the morning and chose for his text: "Where two or three are gathered together in my name, there am I in the midst of them." "When he closed," said the minister, "the whole assembly were in tears, and completely under the dominion of that 'breathless awe that dares not move, and all the silent heaven of love.' As the congregation were passing out, one said to another: 'What a sermon! Did you ever hear anything like it? What angelic sweetness, and what a feast for the soul!'" In the afternoon Bascom stood in the same pulpit and poured forth torrents of eloquence—of which he was master, until the vast audience were almost lost in astonishment. When passing out of the church, one hearer said to another: "What a man!" Another said "We have but one Bascom." And yet another, "He is the most eloquent *man* I ever heard." Here, then, was the difference. In the first, the *man* was lost in the sermon, and *Christ only* was seen. In the second, the sermon was lost *in the man*. Between the two we are not at a loss to choose our model. Blessed is that minister who can truthfully say: "But I

labored more abundantly than they all; yet not I, but the
grace of God which was with me."

During seasons of special effort, when the church is putting forth all its energies for the salvation of souls, how
often are we brought to witness exhibitions of judgment as
well as mercy. It was so here at this camp-meeting. In
the height of its interest, a young man who had been attending its services only to mock and revile, must needs
show his defiant spirit to all gracious influences by starting
out upon a horse-race near the camp-ground, when his horse
stumbled and fell, and sent him into eternity in a moment.
What a spectacle! Only a few hours before, he was seated
near the altar listening to calls and invitations of the gospel;
but now, by his associates in crime, he is borne to his last
earthly resting-place, where the sound of the gospel is not
heard, and mercy's offer is not given. What a warning is
this to all who " slight the force of gospel truth."

> " When every means are tried in vain,
>   The Spirit strives no more with man;
>   Then full of guilt and fear and pain,
>   Death strikes the blow, the sinner's slain,
>   *And sinks to endless ruin.*"

In the varied services of this year, I attended several
quarterly meetings for Elder Miller, he filling my appointments in the station. One that I attended at Low Moor, I
doubt not, had much to do in shaping my labors for the ensuing year. Rev. J. B. Taylor was on this charge, and this
being his third year, the people became interested as to
their coming preacher; and as the service of the meeting
was one of much interest, the members asked for my appointment as his successor, of which I was notified at this
camp-meeting. Not that I had anything to prefer against
the good friends at Le Claire, for we enjoyed a year of prosperity, and our relations were of the most pleasant character
from first to last; but the presiding elder yielding to the re-

quests of the official board at Low Moor, with my consent the change was made at our ensuing conference, and my next chapter will embrace its history.

———

CHAPTER XXXIX.

As the vessel starts out upon its conquests on the ocean, no one can predict its history. The storms that it will encounter, the enemies that it will meet, the rocks to which it may be exposed, its reverses or successes, no historic pen can write. Thus it is as we start out upon the history of a pastoral year. Its trials, hardships, joys, sorrows, conflicts and victories are yet to be experienced and understood. But there is no safety in casting anchor and waiting for calmer seas and clearer skies; but like the storm-bird that arises only when facing the storm, thus, whether in season or out of season, we are to press on, until the rainbow of hope signalizes that the tempest is behind us, and the bright and shining heavens before us. And what a cheering thought, that no cloud is so dark but that light is beyond it, and no danger so threatening but that Providence can control it. In this respect all fields of ministerial labor stand upon the same level, and the sentiment of the poet holds true in them all: "Joy to find in every station, something still *to do or bear;*" and whether in the desert waste or in the city full, Christ must be honored, the gospel must be preached, and souls must be saved. This was the banner which I bore in entering upon this new field of labor, and the inscription thereupon written: "So much as in me is, I am ready to preach the gospel to you." And is it not strange that though these old truths have been repeated over and over again, for thousands of years, the interest is not lessened nor the power diminished! And this truth will forever remain, so long as man has spiritual wants and the gospel only can supply them.

After passing a few rounds on this charge of three appointments, I commenced a series of meetings at what was called Hatfield's School-house, and I pressed the siege from day to day, and from week to week, until the close of the third week, and then wound up with little visible success. During its greatest interest, I learned that a husking-bee and a dance following at night was to come off, and knowing its deathly influence upon the interests of the meeting, I visited the lady of the house and besought her, in view of the cause of Christ and the credit of her family, as well as the community, to desist from the dancing, assuring her that I would use all of my influence, and turn in and husk corn myself through the day, if she would stop the dance. She promised that she would, and I faithfully kept my word, and the corn was husked. But to my mortification and her shame, the dance came off, after all. Is it any surprise to my readers that the gracious Lord withheld his blessing after such a base violation of sacred obligations? I have witnessed many *mean* things in my life, but this was one for which I have no apology. Never was time more faithfully spent, neither the gospel more pointedly preached, but, like Alexander in the work of the Apostle, " she did me much evil; the Lord reward her according to her works."

At the close of this meeting I found a very pleasant home for the year in the family of Brother and Sister Kistner, who were old members on this work. How often the spiritual progress of the pastor's labors are retarded, and that *seriously*, by being obliged to turn aside to grapple with financial interests. It was the case here. A new chapel had been recently built, and it was reported when I entered upon this charge that all of its indebtedness had been met, and the field was clear. But in less than six weeks the officers came and threatened to levy upon the church unless a claim of about four hundred dollars was immediately satisfied. This was rather a *backset*, after a few faithful brethren had been so heavily taxed previously; but there was no retreating from this obligation, and so I called a meeting of the brethren to see what could be done, Brother Joel B. Taylor, their former pastor, meeting with us. At this meeting we divided the amount into thirty-dollar shares, of which the pastors took each one, with the brethren, and a committee appointed to raise the balance. This was the work of most the entire year, and when we saw the end, we felt like thanking God and taking courage. My appointment at Low Moor was rather peculiar in another respect. It contained a strange and fearful history, never to be forgotten by the inhabitants who witnessed it, and often referred to with as much interest as though it had just passed. It was here that the terrific tornado passed through which nearly destroyed Camanche and New Albany in the year 1860, and its effects were visible on every hand. If ever conversation flagged, the citizens could find some inspiring incident in connection with that storm. Rev. S. C. Freer, who was then stationed at Camanche, writes me that he had closed his sermon at a country appointment, and as he started for home he saw the danger approaching. His animal, as if infused with the spirit of the coming event, made double speed, and reached home sooner than usual. He had just put away his horse and buggy, entered his house and sat down, when the destroyer came. The kitchen was blown down, the barn demolished, but the horse was not injured. The buggy under the shed adjoining the barn was not disturbed, and though *in great danger*, "not a hair of their heads was injured." Had he come from his appointment at the usual rate of traveling, he would have been in the very path of the storm, and escape impossible. The house nearest to *his* was blown to atoms and everything destroyed but a rifle. "A German, keeping a store in the place, with more or less liquor, said to a young man leaving for safety as the storm was near: 'Old God is going to do some of his fancy work now;' when in less than one minute the building was in ruins, only two of the family escaping. He was one of the last taken from the ruins in the city, and his body found lying upon a barrel of whisky. Twenty-nine persons were killed and eighty wounded at that place. Many families in the best of circumstances in the morning, before sundown were left destitute and homeless." The different pastors along the line of the track took especial pains to gather interesting items, and among them was this: that of about two hundred killed and badly wounded, not one devoted Christian sustained serious injury. I had just returned from my trip to the Rocky mountains when this report was made by the several pastors, and the providence was so remarkable that I noted it down. How true it is that "He that dwelleth in the secret place of the Most High shall abide under the shadow of the Almighty. A thousand shall fall at thy side, and ten thousand at thy right hand, but it shall not come nigh thee." This was the faith of the Psalmist, and this is the faith of the writer. It is as easy for the Almighty to preserve the Christian in the *storm* as to protect Daniel in the den of lions. And that his preserving care was seen at that time in the deliverance of his saints, no one acquainted with the circumstances can deny. In addition to the case of Brother Freer and family, I will note one or two others, among the many.

Brother Kistner, with whom I boarded for the year, seeing the tornado approaching, proposed to his wife, recently confined—occupying the bed-room, that they should all go down cellar as the safest place. "No," said Sister K., "all come into this bed-room. God can save us here as well as in the cellar." Hardly had they grouped together when destruction came. The barn, the house, all but the bedroom were scattered in a moment to the winds. Though their room was shattered much, and its floor covered with debris some five or six inches in depth, the shell of the room still stood as a protection from the blast, and not a soul received the least injury. The little babe, but a few days old, was whirled out of its mother's arms and buried amidst the rubbish, but it was recovered safe and sound. After the storm it was found that the ruins of the barn filled the cellar, with their horse in the midst, looking very wishful for freedom, but uninjured. This proved the wisdom of the mother's decision, as divinely directed. One more, no less striking.

Rev. Mr. Williams (I think this is the name), stationed at New Albany, Illinois, like Brother Fre'er, had been out to a country appointment, but returned home when the storm was past. Hurrying as fast as possible, with intense interest, when he reached his residence he found naught but a pile of brick. As he rode up, what must have been his feelings, as he supposed that his wife and children were buried in the ruins. Almost overwhelmed with the pressure, a voice came out from beneath the brick-pile: "Husband, do thyself no harm; we are all here." Sister Williams was one of those consecrated women, *who fully trusted God*, and when she saw their condition, she said to her children, "we will take refuge in our large wood-box in the room and cover it over, and the falling brick will not injure us." She did so, and when her husband arrived—as she had been listening for his horse's footsteps—she was as safely housed as if in her cozy parlor. I need not say that those brick enclosing the precious treasure, flew rapidly, until freedom and affection met there and embraced. And who dare say that Sister Williams was not directed by a kind and wise Providence. These were some of the interesting relations of remarkable deliverances, during my labors among this people; and yet notwithstanding this terrible visitation, the ungodly seemed rather hardened than improved.

When a young man, residing in the state of New York, I

witnessed what few have the privilege to see. It was one of the grandest displays of the origin of tornadoes which can be imagined. My grandfather's residence—my home— was on an eminence overlooking the Chemung valley for a distance of seven or eight miles. On either side of this valley was a range of hills running nearly east and west. I suppose, by some means, at this time (the first of June) that the air became overheated, beyond that of the sur- rounding hills, and the colder air rushed in to supply its place. The first indication of anything unnatural, was about five o'clock in the evening, the weather being very sultry, when we saw those light swiftly-flying clouds com- ing from different points of the compass, meeting within about one mile of our residence. As they met, they formed at first a small black *cloud*, which was in constant commo- tion, from the different currents of air. As these swift ones increased, the cloud became larger, and if possible blacker; the currents seemingly contending for control, until it attained to the size of a large thunder-cloud. The whole family by this time were out in the yard gazing upon it with *fearful dread*, as the outskirts of the cloud seemed to reach our dwelling. The doors and windows were made secure, when all at once, the *irregular movements* within the heart of the cloud seemed to grapple with each other for the mastery; and after a fearful tussle the cloud took a *spiral motion*, and was making its way to the earth. I should calculate the time about one minute, from the com- mencement of the circular motion before it struck the ground, when the *sharp, terrific* roar began, resembling a thousand cars in motion at the same time. As soon as it reached the earth it seemed to overwhelm itself in its clouds of dust carried upward, and in its mighty struggle for the mastery, it would weave to and fro; not as yet attained to any definite course. During this struggle, it crossed the Chemung river, scooped it out, when striking Mr. Kress' barn standing on the bank, in a moment it became like chaff. Boards, shingles, rafters and timbers were seen by us flying through the air, some of them almost over our heads. At last the west wind prevailed, when it took an eastern direction, and for miles swept almost everything in its course; but fortunately it soon spent its force, and the damage was small. Though I have been requested, this is the first description of it prepared for public print. I presume that the cause is about the same in all phenomena of this character; but happy is the man who, witnessing its *mighty tread*, steps out of the way.

The Rev. S. C. Freer, who so narrowly escaped death at Camanche, is one of the old ministers of our church. Converted in 1834, licensed to preach in 1840, and joined the Erie conference in 1841. He belonged to the same class of Bishop Kingsley and others, now nearly all passed away. He was transferred to the Upper Iowa conference in 1856, and upon almost every charge his labors have been crowned with success; at LeClaire, Vinton and West Branch, eminently so. When he goes to a charge it is to do work for his Master, and he is not satisfied until he sees the fruits of his labor; and now at Laporte, in the sixty-fourth year of his age, he preaches three times on the Sabbath and teaches one Bible class. Like many of our brethren, he has been blessed with a companion who has contributed to his success. May his mantle fall upon those coming on to fill his place. Rev. Isaac Newton being stationed at Camanche the present year, Brother Miller wished me to attend the quarterly meeting in that village. I think that on the Sabbath was one of the blessed seasons of my ministerial life. As I discoursed from "Godliness is profitable unto all things," at times I seemed to stand upon the very borders of heaven, where the spicy gales and divine rapture sweetly blended; and the congregation catching the same spirit seemed to move upward in harmony with the theme. Such days of blessing are not easily forgotten, neither by the preacher nor congregation. , More than one year afterward,

a Christian lady said to me: " I shall never forget the sermon of that day." No; those hours of divine refreshing are
so deeply imbedded into our spiritual nature that we
remember them when everything else is forgotten. And
often have I thought, that among the exalted privileges in
heaven will be that, in the society of saints, of sacredly
reviewing earth's history, and talking over the sweet hours
of holy joy and communion experienced when glory
crowned the " mercy seat." What contributed very much
to the interest of this meeting was the privilege of enjoying the society of Brother and Sister Newton, whose friendship and hospitality I had shared in days gone by. In the
memorable winter of 1856—the severity of which tried
men's *bodies* as well as souls, he hailed me a brother
beloved in the northern part of the state, and when the
mercury had gone down to thirty below zero, I found that
his "loving kindness changeth not." And through subsequent history, I always found a warm place in his house
and in the affections of his family. Was it strange that I
had unusual freedom in the pulpit, meeting again a fellow-
soldier in the contest for *life?* Thirty years has Brother
Newton been standing in the ranks of his brethren in the
good fight of faith in the state of Iowa, his garments un-
tarnished and his progress unchecked, and the prospect
now is that he will come to the harvest *ripe* for the inheritance of the saints in light.

And here again, as the conference year passes, and summer crowns the husbandman with stacks of grain and fields
of corn, we meet on the old camp-ground to raise the gospel standard, and battle for the truth. Since we last met on
this consecrated spot, twelve months had rolled around, and
the destiny of millions had been settled forever. But
whilst life prolongs its precious light, the duty of the
Christian minister is clearly presented: "We must work the
works of him that sent us, while it is day: the night cometh
when no man can work." This camp-meeting opened with

every indication of success. The first sermon was attended with the *unction* from on high, and the place seemed to be honored with the divine presence. The family of our presiding elder being sick, we were deprived of his assistance, and the charge of the services devolved upon Brother Newton and myself. Such was the interest at the close of the week, that the vote was unanimous to extend it one week longer. We had no such casualty to contend with as in the year previous, but all things moved forward pleasantly and successfully. The elder was able to be with us on the Sabbath and preached a sermon of great interest from " But if the light in thee be darkness, how great is that darkness." Upon this occasion he excelled, rising higher, in grandeur of thought and real eloquence, than at any other time, in my presence, during our ministerial relations. The people were delighted and blessed.

The good order that here prevailed, and the respect shown to the cause of Christ, was noted by all present; to which blessed result our wise committee of arrangements greatly contributed. Every other interest seemed to be lost in the *great one*—that of bringing poor, perishing sinners to the Saviour. Four or five of the members of the Rock River conference were with us, and in their plain presentation of truth they honored the gospel which they preached and the conference to which they belonged. In military phrase, it was apparent that the ground was well chosen, their guns well aimed, and their arrows steel-pointed; in addition to this, there was a power behind all which carried conviction for sin, and salvation through faith in Christ. There is one great ruling principle which ever holds good in the gracious work accomplished at our camp-meetings. In fact, it seems to be a divine *law ever prominent*, that our success in the salvation of souls will be in ratio to the sacrifices we make and the *interest* felt. Uniting these two elements (and they are not hard to unite), and then our prayers and efforts all tending to this result, we may rely as confidently that Christ will honor the means as that he hath appointed them. For the Master delights to smile upon his own cause. But on the other hand, if we repair to these sacred retreats that we may enjoy a good social time with our Christian friends, and the luxury of listening to a few able sermons, merely for our own personal enjoyment, we shall leave these groves, "God's first temples," in about the same spiritual condition as when we found them, and sinners unsaved. But these urgent impulses of the soul sent up to heaven with strong cries and tears for the salvation of our friends are never, *never* turned aside. The "effectual fervent prayer" is the one that is honored in heaven. Many times had Jacob prayed, and many mercies received, but it belonged to that eventful period *alone*, when *help must come, and God only could give*, that the silence of solitude was broken: "I *will not* let thee go, except thou bless me." Was ever a prayer offered up to God in this spirit unheeded and unanswered? Ah, it is when we unite our ignorance with his wisdom, our weakness with his strength, our entire helplessness with his almighty power, that the divine annunciation comes to the ear of the soul: "Thy name shall be called no more Jacob, but Israel; for as a prince hast thou power with God and with men, and hast prevailed." How truthfully and sublimely embodied in this language:

> "In vain thou strugglest to get free,
> I never will unloose my hold.
> Art thou the Man that died for me?
> The secret of thy love unfold.
> Wrestling, I will not let thee go,
> *Till I thy name, thy nature know.*"

Brethren, here is the secret of spiritual victory. It is not a hard matter to prevail with God and exercise power with men, when we meet him at his own appointed place, and carry out the conditions of his own appointed means. This is the point at which human effort ends, and the grace of Christ gloriously triumphs. I never saw this truth more fully exemplified than at our camp-meeting.

A Mr. B., the year previous, had a remarkable conversion. His light was so brilliant, and his rapture so great, that he could say: "I could not believe that I ever should grieve;" but in the hour of temptation and trial he lost his confidence, and with it his enjoyment. Months had passed, but they had afforded him but little spiritual comfort, when he came to our camp-ground to see if he could not be once more restored to his former enjoyment. At once he came to me, as I had assisted him the year previous, and I saw that he was struggling in the shades of unbelief. After learning his real situation, I proposed that we sit down together, and that he should tell me all about his former experience, his convictions, how he was led to Christ and found him precious. So he started out, giving me the details, and as he progressed step by step, I discovered that his soul was taking in the spirit of his past experience. At times his feelings almost overcame him, when he would recover and proceed until he reached the time and place where the darkness gave way and light from heaven shone upon him. At the moment when he reached the joys of pardon, I saw that he was on the brink of the kingdom, and I said to him: "Brother B., do you not think that Jesus' power and faithfulness is the same now as last year, and that he has the same interest that you should *now* be saved as at that time?" He paused a moment and answered: "Yes, I know he is faithful that promised." This little admission was the hand that turned the key; the door flew open, the streams of gratitude and love poured into his anxious soul, and the joy was unspeakable. All was silent on the camp-ground, preparing for dinner, when this shout of praise went up, which continued so long and so loud that many left their boiling pots to listen to the voice of triumph. He went from tent to tent, telling his friends and neighbors what a Saviour he had found. A happy man was he from that blessed hour, and the last I heard from him his tent was in the "Land of Beulah," where the Sun always shines. In this interesting restoration there is a lesson of instruction. I requested him to relate his former experience, knowing that if I could succeed in getting him on the *gracious path*, it would lead all his thoughts, sympathies and faith to the Saviour; and when he reached the point of blessing, he was so near the Master that the hand of faith could reach him. This was one of the most simple, and yet the most successful transformations of this kind that I ever witnessed, and I relate it for the benefit of others who may be engaged in the same work.

I think that there is a hidden law in the process of association, though powerful and successful, yet hard to be explained. It has its lesson in the practical workings of every-day life. As the association of names will often bring up to the memory many of the occurrences of life, so the association of happy hours and divine blessings in the past will empty their cups of joy into the bosom of the present. A dear old brother of mine, now in heaven, gave me this interesting fact touching his religious life: He was converted at a camp-meeting on Brush Creek circuit, under the ministrations of Rev. John Collins of precious memory. For about six months he walked in the light of peace and happiness, but, like the case above related, he lost his hold on Christ, and darkness was the consequence. For months, like the man deprived of sight, he felt his way without any visible guide or spiritual comfort. "Oh," said he, "that I could once more see old Brother Collins! I believe I should find relief." Brother Collins was to be seen now, at the same place, forty miles distant; when he started on horseback to see his old minister by whose influence he had been saved. Toward night, as he was approaching the camp-ground, and nearing the preacher's stand, the first man he saw was Rev. John Collins who took him into the church; and as soon as he saw his face, quickly as an electric flash, the long-lost blessing came, and on his horse, his eyes filled with tears, his heart leaped with joy, and the song of gladness went forth from lips of praise. Not that there was any blessing on the face of the minister, but seeing the old veteran once more brought all of his thoughts and feelings to the very *gate* of blessing, when the Holy Spirit shed the rich supply. Oh, what a boon was this! Forty miles he had traveled in order to secure this *pearl*, and before he dismounted from his horse, Brother Story was richer than the king upon his throne. After enjoying the meeting through the Sabbath, he returned home to his family, through the woods a good part of the way singing in spirit:

> " Now rest, my long divided heart,
>   Fixed on this blissful center, rest;
> Nor ever from my Lord depart,
>   *With him of every good possessed.*"

Camanche! What a memorable spot! Only a few years previous the messenger of *destruction* swept through this place, carrying terror and death in his hand; and very near this beautiful grove were gathered up the bodies of the slain. But in his stead here are the messengers of *mercy* heralding this great truth: " He that believeth in me, though he were dead, yet shall he live," and very many are fleeing from the . face of the destroyer and taking refuge beneath the shadow of the Almighty. Here on this hallowed spot we meet Rev. J. H. Rhea, " a workman that needeth not to be ashamed, rightly dividing the word of truth, giving to saint and sinner each a portion in due season." Brother Rhea at this date had been recently transferred from the Central Illinois conference to ours, and was comparatively a stranger, but through the ten succeeding years he has established a ministerial character which ranks him among the honored of his brethren. He has filled our best appointments during that time, and stands among us to-day with a growing reputation, and I doubt not but that in the final award he will have very many " stars in the crown of his rejoicing."

 'Another dear friend I welcome during this spiritual feast; and what gives value to his friendship, it had been tested. He stood firmly by my side when "warring with principalities and powers;" his position in the front, ever ready to assist, with encouraging words and a helping hand. For nearly two years in Maquoketa he was my right-hand man, wise in his counsels and preaching by his life. He was admitted to the Upper Iowa conference in 1865, with fewer words than any member of my acquaintance. When his name was presented for admission, Brother Kynett called upon me to speak to his case: " No discount on Brother Catlin," was all that was said and all that was needed. In the several relations of life, whether as teacher, merchant, local or traveling minister, he is the same safe, prudent, and true man; his words ever seasoned and his example ever pure. The present year he is stationed in Bellevue, adding value to his former reputation.

And I must not omit the name of Rev. Geo. W. Rogers. He was a young member of the conference, stationed at Grand Mound. At three o'clock P. M., that hour marked *sluggish* in the preacher's diary, I see him standing in the pulpit, with my old friend Earhart of Pleasant Valley in front. Brother R.'s subject is faith. The weather is warm, the audience dull, some fast asleep, their faith not strong enough to keep their eyes open. I listened attentively to the discourse and thought many things; among them *this*, that in the days of our Saviour on earth, the hardest devil to cast out was the *dumb devil;* and considering the *sleepy one* a first cousin, as the elder said I must exhort after the sermon, I was at a loss how to proceed. Strategy was a necessity, but even this was hard to call into requisition under the pressure of a hearty dinner and ninety degrees heat in the shade. But the sermon closes and there is no backing out. I took for my starting thought, an old saying—(new to

many just opening their eyes): " Blessed is the man who
first invented sleep;" and as many present had been *won-
derfully blessed* during the last half hour, they felt a deep
interest in everything pertaining to their personal welfare;
and as I advanced, presenting the different features of this
patrimony, their eyes flew open and the mouth enlarged,
when soon " nature's kind restorer " had not a place to set
his foot.   Before I knew it, we were all breathing the air of
victory.   I was aware that there must have been some hidden virtue in David's harp to expel the evil spirit from the
person of Saul, but I never realized that there was so much
virtue in a smile as upon the present occasion.   Having
succeeded in breaking the lull and securing their attention,
I was favored with very much freedom and enjoyment in
closing the exercises.   Elder Miller and Rev. R. W. Keeler
who were present, congratulated me on my success in master-
ing such a difficulty; and though it began with a singular
maneuver, it ended with a spiritual triumph.   Brother Rogers,
who passed through that severe ordeal, was a particular
friend, a blessed young man, and highly appreciated the
assistance rendered.   As his eye runs over this page, memory will recall the peril and pleasant deliverance.   Such is
the history of human efforts in waging war with the powers
of darkness.   Brother Keeler was with us during these
services and preached with his accustomed ability, but as
he will have a notice in our next chapter, I will pass him
for the present.   This camp-meeting from the beginning to
the end was a decided success, and wound up to the satisfaction of all who attended it; and in the day when earth's
doings shall be fully revealed in the great future, it will be
known that the influence of that labor bore a part in adding
to the number of those who will be permitted to " sing the
song of Moses and the Lamb."   After such a season of
holy and heavenly fellowship, how solemn the separation.
No more to meet, many of us, until, disrobed of mortality,
we meet in the mansions of light, in the home of the

heavenly Bethany, where the Marthas and Marys in the presence of Jesus find a sweeter rest and an eternal home. How many of us who sang and prayed and rejoiced during those weeks of refreshing, will unite in that land of purity and love to *adore Him* who hath called us to such bliss in heaven to share?

As I returned to my pleasant home at Brother and Sister Kistner's, after this meeting, with the other members of the family, I was attacked with the scarlet fever, which very much prostrated my system, and disqualified me for my usual labors. The youngest member of the family was taken to the home above, and some of us were in a fair way to follow, but the Divine Master had other work for us to do, and so kindly lengthened out our days; but the severe ordeal through which I passed will not soon be forgotten. As the conference year was drawing to a close, I was convinced that I would not be justified, in my state of health, in returning to the charge; so at our annual conference held at Clinton, I requested a release of one year from labor, and was granted a superannuated relation. At the close of the session I repaired to my pleasant little home in Michigan, near Benton Harbor, my brother Harvey Taylor having moved there the previous year. Here in my brother's family, whose companion's face was always sunshine, in sight of the beautiful lake, with its rolling waves and waving sails, the passing night and pleasant day glided imperceptibly away. Like the former fields where I had labored and gathered jewels for my Master, here also on Low Moor circuit, friendships had been formed and attachments created which the hand of time cannot deface and the ravages of death cannot destroy. The pleasant history there made during the years 1870 and '71 will extend onward in its delightsome progress to the day when " friends shall meet again who have loved," and then its pleasant memories will be cherished still as we go on to higher honors and richer joys. Oh, what a meeting that will be, when from the pastoral charges of former years the thousands of faithful ones come up to heaven to greet their faithful minister who assisted them to secure the prize! Some of the precious ones to whom I then preached have entered into rest, and others soon will follow; but room abundant still remains for us who later come, to sit down at the *first table*, when our Lord himself will serve us, and glory crown the heavenly feast. Unto Him who hath exalted us to such immortal honors, be praise, and honor, and thanksgiving, now and forever. Amen!

CHAPTER XL.

Who will say but that there is something in a name, and especially so in olden times when they portrayed the elements of character. Often have I been led to inquire whether, in heaven, I shall still be called by my familiar name Landon. In this world how often, as my brethren and sisters have given me the kindly hand and called me by name, has it afforded me pleasure. How much more so, than as if they had stiffened up and called me Mr. Taylor. But whether on the golden streets, as I meet these loved ones, they will greet me thus, I cannot say. With my present views and feelings, it would be pleasant there. But then I have thought that if divine grace could so transform a Jacob, that infinite wisdom saw it best to change his name to Israel—the supplanter to a prince—is it not reasonable to suppose that in the change from sinners saved, to glorified saints, that a *new name* may accompany our new nature? In Revelations iii. 12, it is said of those who overcome: " I will write upon them *my new name*," and then we read of those " whose names are written in the Lamb's Book of Life." I am fully satisfied that we must wait until that time before we fully know, and yet it is very pleasant to dwell upon those things now, which soon are to become a part of our history. Sister Young, the companion of my old friend Dan Young, who was a devoted Christian, as she was dying, uttered a few words of untold interest. To all human appearance she had passed away, as she ceased to breathe: " Oh, that I could hear her speak once more!" said Brother Young: "Can you not so far bring her to consciousness that I may hear her voice again?" said he to the physician. Said the doctor: " I will try." The effort was successful, and here is what she said: " Oh, doctor, why did you bring me back! I was just about to receive *my new name.*" As soon as these words were uttered she passed from earth to heaven. Whatever changes, however, are made in our heavenly home differing from this, one thing is certain: " That we shall be satisfied when we awake in his likeness." This short introduction brings me to "Wyoming," of historic importance. How, in my school-boy days—as I was reared not far from the valley—I read its thrilling history. My youthful nature was all alive in sympathy with their trials, sufferings and death, and as I come to its namesake, by the law of association I am carried back to all the events of its touching history.

As my year in Michigan rolled around, my health greatly improved, and toward the close of summer I decided to enter upon the labors of another year. Having everything in readiness, I started for Vinton, where our conference was to be held, taking Clinton City in my route. Here I found Rev. James H. Rhea, the pastor of the station, who welcomed me to his charge, and had me booked for his pulpit on Sabbath morning. What an additional impetus it gives in our reception to a place, to know that there is some *assistance* to be rendered. I tell you it often strengthens the grasp and expands the chest when we receive help at the needed time. Whether this had any effect upon the doctor at this period, I cannot say, but the hearty greeting was appreciated fully, and his pulpit supplied to the best

22

of my ability. The general class in the afternoon of that day was a season of unusual interest. Meeting these Christian friends to whom I ministered eight or nine years previous, through the din and smoke of war, but now under the canopy of peace, seemed to intensify the pleasure of this spiritual reunion. Very seldom have I passed a more delightful hour; and what gave additional interest to it was the privilege of meeting Brother and Sister Yeomans, who were the lights of my heritage in a land of strangers. Yes, in a time of comparative destitution, in the reign of snow and ice, and exposed to the ravages of a destroying foe, these two companions of the wilderness provided food for the body and comfort for the soul. Is it any wonder that the flame of gratitude and love should rise unusually high in meeting such friends at the altar of saints at Clinton, who together in Sioux City, fourteen years previous, shared the perils of a pioneer life? But holy days and Sabbath bells with their sacred associations must be left behind as we repair to the seat of our annual conference. Here we are provided with a very pleasant home; my roommate, Rev. Elias Skinner, one of the old members of our conference, and now presiding elder of Anamosa district. A pleasanter home we could not have found than in the family of the "Squire," and we well knew how to value the honor. Shortly after our arrival, a couple called at his residence to get married, and as I was the oldest minister present, I had the pleasure of performing the ceremony. In this way, for the good of society, we confer a double benefit: that of diffusing light and also of binding them together. As a token of respect to our landlady, I handed over to her the wedding fees, and felt it a pleasure to be able to confer a *small favor*, where we were receiving such tokens of their hospitality. Who should I meet at this place but one of my old friends and member of my charge, from Vineland, New Jersey. He was one of the original members in its organization, heard my first and last sermon in that young city, and now we meet a thousand miles distant to exchange greetings and renew friendships upon Iowa soil. My visit with him and his family was a social ovation, and we lived over again the history of the past.

At the close of the session, receiving my appointment at Wyoming, I went immediately to my station and commenced the labors of a new year. Nearly twenty years previous I visited this town, when Sunday-school agent, and preached in a school-house, when it was in its infancy; but now it has grown to the stature of a thriving village, with its shops, stores and bank, and still looking forward to years of greater wealth and prosperity. Almost every place, however small, has a proud and commanding future, and only needs the hand of time and the march of progress to develop its rich resources into a prosperous city. This is almost the universal verdict, and in this coming inheritance Wyoming claims her share. Many of these brethren with whom I come to labor have known me for many years, and now all that remains is to mark out the ground and enter upon its cultivation. The Rev. B. C. Barnes was my predecessor on this work, and discharged his duties as a faithful pastor. This is the record of Brother B. in his relations to the Upper Iowa conference, aiming at all times to do the work of a faithful minister of the gospel. Upon one occasion, however, when I visited his charge as Bible agent in the northern part of the state, we found more than our match. At one of his appointments, the house filled with interested listeners, the "Amens" coming thick and fast, and the inspiration of the speaker raised to the highest point of interest, we looked at its close for a very liberal collection, when, lo! as its contents were revealed, we found that all of their generous enthusiasm had been expended in loud responses to the preacher. In vain we looked into the bottom of the hat for Bible money, for it was not there. When I considered the offering, and the strength employed to secure it, I felt much like saying: "Why all this waste of thought and moving eloquence to open hearts and pockets, when no return is made but simply the old hat!" But I must correct; a few dimes were there, just enough to show the character of their generosity. As we went out from that assembly, infused with the spirit of their liberality, we could not suppress the hearty laugh, and the old home saying: "An ocean into tempest tossed to waft a feather, or to drown a fly." At the next conference I asked Bishop Ames to send Brother Barnes to Hopkinton, when he was granted a kind release.

I found a very pleasant home at Wyoming in the family of .W. Brainerd, and Persons, who spared no pains to minister to all my wants. The society at this place was very much like others—it needed *faithful pastoral work* in order to prosper, and this duty I endeavored to discharge in the fear of the Lord. At the beginning of the year we enjoyed a very pleasant ministerial association at Delhi, Rev. Elias Skinner chairman. The subject assigned to the writer upon this occasion was "The *Happiness* of Heaven." With my limited knowledge I did what I could to enter into its realities, and before my essay was concluded, we felt that we were tasting some of the joys of the coming bliss. In no one instance did I ever realize such a holy rapture in reading the subject assigned me as at this time, and for a season we seemed upon the very borders of the heavenly land. Long since have I been satisfied that what constitutes our happiness on earth, will be the same in heaven. The only difference will be the capacity to receive, and the full fruition possessed. God is the soul's portion, the only element of bliss in this world below, or in our heaven above, and that soul that is *filled with God is filled with heaven.* Oh, that all might know this joyful truth! The greatest interest in our subjects of discussion at this association arose from Elder Skinner's essay on home amusements. The elder in his essay took the broad ground that ministers

had a *higher calling* than to spend their precious hours in
playing "croket," or in like amusements. This view of the
subject came in contact with the habits of some of the
brethren present, and elicited a warm debate for and against.
Some one of the speakers inquired, "that if, in the heat of
discussion upon this subject, a book agent should come in,
having the life of 'Paul and Silas' to sell, with a picture in
front representing them out on the green playing a game of
croquet, if they would not regard it a *slander* upon those
good men? If so in relation to them, is it any less so in its
application to us at the present day?" In this discussion
another sharp point was brought out. One of the pastors
present, fond of this amusement, a short time previous had
been called upon to labor with one of the young men of his
charge for playing cards. Whilst urging the matter warmly
and kindly upon the young convert, he was met by this
home thrust: "That it was no worse to play a game of cards
for pastime than a game of croquet." This was the *nail*
that spiked the preacher's gun, and he went out from the
young man under the pressure of defeat. And now, having
given some of the leading features in that discussion, I will
volunteer a few honest words from the writer. As to the
harm in these amusements, there is, and will be, a difference
of opinion among ministers, and, I may add, an *honest difference*. But so far as my own views and feelings are concerned, the whole matter turns upon these two points:
First, Is it the most profitable way in which we can spend
our time? for our time is our estate; and, Second, In so
doing, do we suffer a loss in our ministerial influence? If
one or the other, or both of these be true, then I should not
feel justified in their indulgence. The Christian minister
has no more right, in the light of the divine law, to pursue
a course to lessen his influence with his people, than to in-
dulge in habits which will destroy his grace, for in doing
good to his fellowmen, one is as important as the other. If
I had any counsel to present to my dear brethren whom I

must shortly leave, I would lay this down as a rule in every act of life: "Is this the course my Master will approve when I stand before him to render my account?" If we honor this rule, we shall not go far astray.

At the close of this session, the family of the elder being sick, I accompanied Brother Ward to Colesburg, to assist at his quarterly meeting. In starting out from Delhi, with a spirited colt before his buggy, in passing down a hill, the horse began to kick and run, and when we reached the foot, giving the horse a short turn to the left, Brother W. took a rolling fall, landed safely on his back, and left me in charge of a running horse and a broken buggy. This was one of the *perils* not in the list of the apostle, as he did the most of his traveling on foot; but as the horse's heels, at every kick, came near my head, I was interested in a sudden halt, and so reined up my charge to a picket fence. In this way I stopped his progress and saved myself; but a part of the day was spent in repairing our carriage. This loss restored, we made our way to Colesburg in safety, where I found my old friends, Brother and Sister Perkins, who had left Michigan and were now living again at their old home. How pleasant the meeting, and how precious the hours spent during our Sabbath services. I chose for my subject at half past ten o'clock A. M., "But this one thing I do, forgetting the things that are behind, and reaching forth unto those things which are before," etc. This was a season of spiritual enjoyment to all who waited upon the Lord, and I felt at its close that large blessings often follow in the wake of temporal disasters. Brother and Sister Ward contributed their influence, with my former friends, to make this among the pleasant seasons of my life, and on Monday morning I returned to Wyoming, with larger history and a warmer heart.

In this station I formed a very pleasant acquaintance with Rev. Mr. Baird, pastor of the Presbyterian church of this place, who seemed quite anxious to unite with us in a union meeting during the winter. At our second quarterly meeting I presented his request to the members of the quarterly conference, and receiving the approval of that body, as well as of the presiding elder, we commenced our services, one week alternately in each church. The meeting was one of much interest, and continued four or five weeks, resulting in the conversion of many souls. There was not one note of discord during this entire meeting, but it soon became apparent to me that our Presbyterian friends had the influence in the community, and were much the best workers; and these two elements in their favor resulted in their receiving nearly all the converts. This was no affliction to me, as I knew that my reward was sure, but it was quite an affliction to many members of our church. Brother Baird pursued a manly and Christian course from first to last, and I closed up the labors of the year with the kindest feelings toward him and his family. During our services a Roman Catholic was converted, which added much to the interests of the work. His little daughter, about ten years of age, and the father's pet, came out to preaching and became very much interested. Upon returning home she reported to her father what an interesting meeting we had, and finally secured a promise from him that he would attend the next evening. He came, according to promise, and the first night he was so interested that he required no further persuasions to attend the house of worship. Within a short time he was converted, and the family became members of our church. At the close of the conference year they were still faithful in the cause. Such fruits as these are worth weeks of toil. The wife of this Catholic was an intelligent lady, and afterward became a Bible-class teacher in the neighborhood to which they moved.

In this charge we had quite a number of faithful workers and an interesting Sunday-school. Brother Pixley was our banker, Woodford our editor and Sunday-school superintendent, James A. Bronson our teacher of the Bible-class,

W. Brainerd and Daniel Brainerd our merchants, Rev. A
Bronson an old veteran preacher, Brother Bradshaw our
dentist; and thus we were well represented in all the interests of the city; and add to these very many others, with
a noble class of women, and this will give a kind of outline
to the character of the charge. Rev. L. Hartsough, being
stationed at Epworth at this date, held a kind of winter
camp-meeting in his station, to which several of the preachers
of the district were invited. I attended it and remained
with him for several days. It was a very profitable season
to the preachers and to the people. Here was Brother T.
Thompson, who attended my ministry in Muscatine twenty
years previous, and that I assisted in quarterly conference
to become a herald of the Cross; glad that he has never be-
trayed the confidence of his brethren. This was the first
opportunity to hear him preach the gospel since I cast that
vote, and I listened with pleasure and profit. Here was
Brother *Dove*, whose wife was converted at Old Centenary,
Dubuque, when I was pastor, who combined also the bold-
ness of the *eagle* when he set out to secure his prey.
Brother F. X. Miller was present also, bringing the finest of
the wheat; and Rev. H. W. Reed, with his words of wisdom.
Many of those present I ministered unto when they were
children, and now we meet to magnify redeeming grace in
riper years. This was the last friendly communion season
that I enjoyed with Elder Reed among these friends, and
the next, in all probability, will be in heaven. Doctor Johnson was then quite feeble and waiting the Master's call, but
now he is enjoying the *pure air* of a healthier clime. My
home at this meeting was with Brother and Sister Johnson,
the warm friends of earlier years, and the comfort of de-
clining age. Many have been the happy seasons that we
have enjoyed together on earth, and happier ones await us
in the better home. We leave this precious season of grace
and repair to our own charges, conscious that many stars
have been added to the crown of rejoicing.

But scarcely had we reached home and burnished our armor for aggressive movements upon the enemy's ranks, before the bugle notes are sounded for a raid in another quarter. Rev. R. W. Keeler, the old commanding officer, for years, of the Master's forces, sees a weak place somewhere in the enemy's fortifications, and he calls for reinforcements to assist in capturing the foe. He was now stationed at Fourteenth Street, Davenport, and as this had been my old battle-ground, and many victories achieved, he called upon me to assist him to gather new laurels and gain additional honors. How could I refuse when such a field was open and such interests at stake? Well armed and equipped, I honored the call and made my way to the city, and when I arrived I found Dr. Rhea and Brother Hartsough on the ground, "strong in the Lord and in the power of his might." My first sermon at night was founded on these words: "Him that cometh to me, I will in no wise cast out." The blessed Spirit attended the word, and among the seekers were some of the children of old Brother Donahoo, formerly a member of the old Ohio conference, and my pastor when a youth. What clusters of interesting history gathered the first night. That father who ministered to me when a boy, now in heaven, to his children I am now ministering, and assisting to enter into the kingdom of grace. And the angels who were present that evening did not return home with a blank message, but with songs of joy and triumph. Brothers Hartsough and Rhea also preached in the spirit of their mission, and the interest increased at every service.

On Sunday night I preached from, " Behold, now is the accepted time," etc. Whilst presenting the plain and pointed truths of the gospel, I felt " strong in the strength which God supplies through his beloved Son." Whilst urging the great importance of present action and the folly as well as the hazard of death-bed repentance — nearly always spurious — as an evidence I referred to an event of

recent occurrence on Lake Michigan. Under a sudden gale
the boat went down, leaving the cabin and about fifteen
passengers hanging to the wreck. In the darkness of the
night they floated on the rolling waves. When morning
returned, seeing no hope of deliverance, they all cove-
nanted together that if Providence would save them from the
wreck, they would serve him for life. Within a short time
deliverance came, and they were landed at St. Joseph,
Michigan, and returned to their homes. Now for the
sequel. Not one of that number kept his pledge, but pursued the same sinful course. Repentance professed under
the pressure of expected death—as a rule—rarely produces
fruit to eternal life. It was an interesting sight to see the
number of young men at the altar that night, and eternity
alone can fathom the results. Brother and Sister Keeler,
with many other good workers of his charge, spared no
pains to make this meeting a success. And a success it
was, and as I left these kind friends and returned to my
home in Wyoming I was reminded of that truthful sentiment, by us so often sung:

> "But if our fellowship below,
>   In Jesus be so sweet,
> What heights of rapture shall we know,
>   *When round the throne we meet.*"

Rev. R. W. Keeler, D.D., came from New York conference to the Upper Iowa in 1856, and during that twenty-
five years he has been filling the most responsible positions
in our church—the most of this time as presiding elder of
a district, in which he has acquitted himself with honor.
He is an able minister of the New Testament, and secures
the confidence and affection of the preachers and the members of his work. In two or three instances he has represented us as a delegate to the General Conference, and
sustains an honorable relation to all the interests of the
church. And though he has been laboring for thirty-five
years in the Lord's vineyard, his "natural force is not

abated and his eye is not dim." He enjoys a good hearty laugh, and looks not with indifference on a good dinner. The blight of dyspepsia has never disturbed his slumbers, and the smoke of despondency never colored his dwelling. He lives to enjoy life, and I trust to enjoy God; and favored with such a devoted companion, I see no reason why his pathway should not be pleasant, and the fruits *peace.* This year (1881) he is stationed at Fayette, the seat of the Upper Iowa university, still adding to former honors and extending the sphere of his usefulness. May the *evening* be pleasant, and his sun set without a cloud. When spring returned, the brethren felt the importance of improving our basement, as it had long been in the *rough,* and by the expenditure of seven or eight hundred dollars we had a beautiful room, an ornament to the house of God. Before leaving the charge, I left with them my donation, which, upon my return, will ever entitle me to a reserved seat in the temple of worship.

In the month of May I received a letter from Rev. James H. Gilruth, that his father was fast sinking, and wished me to be in readiness, when called upon, to attend his funeral services. On the second day of June, 1873, I received a telegram that on that day Rev. James Gilruth was transferred from earth to heaven. I proceeded at once to his residence and endeavored to improve the occasion in the choice of the following words: "For none of us liveth to himself, and no man dieth to himself: for whether we live, we live unto the Lord; and whether we die, we die unto the Lord; whether we live, therefore, or die, we are the Lord's." After the services at the house, we all repaired to the beautiful cemetery, near the city of Davenport, where our aged father and friend was deposited to await the summons of the trump of God. What a life and what a history was this! His parents came from Scotland in an early day and settled on the banks of the Ohio river, in Scioto county, Ohio. It was then a wilderness; without society or any of the blessings of a Christian or civilized life. For many years the sound of the gospel was not heard, the advantages of education not enjoyed, and " society, friendship and love, divinely bestowed upon man," was confined to a limited few. The mortar was their mill, corn-meal was their flour, and cold water their coffee. Their festivals were on Christmas enlivened with their stories of hunting and fishing; and their nightly music the hoot of the owl, the howling of the wolf or the scream of the panther. Growing up in his early days under these influences, without any church organization, Brother Gilruth became a wild youth and delighted in amusements and feats, often at the expense of his own friends. At the age of nineteen or twenty, possessing great physical strength and activity, on his way up the Ohio river, on horseback, he overtook a Mr. Webb,—the family well-known to the writer,—who was a large, bony man; and he riding a small pony, the boy proposed that he should take turns with his animal and ride half of the time. This proposition met with a quick response from Mr. W.; one word brought on another, until a banter was given by Mr. G. for a test of their strength in an honorable fight. I call it *honorable*, because they had agreed that nothing unfair should take place, and that when one cried enough the other should desist. The terms agreed upon, *at it* they went, and for a long time victory seemed to quiver in the balance; the *boy* had the advantage in activity and muscular power, but the man, in age and skill in the contest; and in this way the battle raged till both were completely exhausted and very glad to adjourn. Thus it was a drawn battle, and in after years, in his ministerial life, how often was he heard to say: " This was the turning event of my life; had I come out victorious, it would have spoiled me, but receiving such a *backset* from the brawny fist of that son of the wilderness, I had no further ambition to repeat the history."

Often, as herald of the Cross, have I rode over the very

ground where this battle was fought, and preached the gospel in the house of Mr. Webb, of Lawrence county, Ohio. Shortly after this event Bro. G. married a Miss Kouns, a Christian lady of the same county, who lived but a short time, and on her death-bed secured the promise of her husband that he would seek religion and prepare to meet her in heaven. James Gilruth was not the man to violate his pledge; and on her grave, a short time after her death, he was brought out into the glorious liberty of the children of God. Such was the change—the lion having become a lamb—that the church set him right to work, and as far back as 1819, he entered the old Ohio conference as a traveling minister. When I was appointed a class-leader in French Grant, his mother, a noble-hearted and intelligent Scotch woman, became a member of my class in 1837, and continued such until her death.. In his visits to his mother and brother William who lived near, I first formed his acquaintance and listened to his discourses. On one occasion he rose far above himself in spiritual power and effect, when he referred to his father (now dead) and mother sitting before him, and how he would undo some of his past history, in his conduct toward them, if he possessed the power; but the past was *unalterable*, and all that remained were confessions for its follies and redemption for its future; and here his tears fell like rain. The mighty man became a child, and the soul that hardly ever knew fear, for a time was humbled to the dust. A few years subsequent, his aged mother left for the church triumphant, and the son hearing of her illness, made all dispatch to witness her departing hours and receive her last blessing. But he was too late. On the day after her burial, I met him hurrying to the old homestead, and was the bearer of the message that his mother had departed. And there together, the minister and class-leader took time, each to shed the tear of sorrow for the loved one gone. As years rolled round, and I became a co-laborer in the work of the ministry, whilst stationed at Davenport, Iowa, Brother Gilruth, with his family, came to that city, intending in the vicinity to spend his days. I received their letters of recommendation and they all became members of that charge in the spring of 1851.

During his labors in fitting up his home in the country, a few miles from the city, he often preached for me, but age and experience had modified his manner very much compared with sermons in his younger days. He had now learned the same lesson as my brother minister in Ohio. When asked the reason why he was less boisterous and loud than in former years, answered that "He then thought it was the thunder that split the tree, but he had since learned that it was the lightning that did the execution." And so thought, *practically*, Brother Gilruth, for the mountain torrent had become the clear and quiet stream. Six or seven years from this date, having his home matters satisfactorily arranged, he applied for admission into the Upper Iowa conference, at Marion, when I was called upon as an old friend and acquaintance to represent his case. Being presiding elder of Sioux City district at that time, Bishop Ames inquired of me if I would be willing to receive him on my district. I responded yes, and he was admitted, and continued with us until the day of his death. After he entered the ministry in Ohio he formed the acquaintance of Miss Westlake, to whom he was united in marriage, who still survives him, and now resides with her daughter and her son-in-law, Brother and Sister Kynett, in the city of Philadelphia.

Of this aged veteran of the Cross, pages might be written. Fifty-four years had passed since he entered upon the work of the ministry, and more than forty in the active field. Hundreds, if not thousands, had been saved during that period as fruits of his labors, who are now enjoying with him the fellowship of heaven. Such a man physically, as he was in his prime, very few men have been per-

mitted to see. He was literally a giant in strength and
activity. Brother Church, of French Grant, Ohio, and fel-
low-soldier of the same regiment in the war of 1812,
informed me that he could outrun or throw down any man
in the army, seemingly with the greatest ease. To give the
reader a further idea of his wonderful powers: at Brush
Creek Forge, a large iron which two men had carried out
into the yard on a bet, Brother G., wishing to hitch his
horse, with *one hand* set up against a stump and made it
a hitching-post. In two instances, men came quite a distance to test their strength with his, and returned home
conscious of their inferiority. But time levels all distinc-
tions, and soon the giant lies as helpless as the little child.
The journey of eighty years brought him to the same gate
through which we all must pass, and when he came to enter,
a gracious hand conducted him safely through; and thus
ended his history on earth to commence in heaven. In this
rather *extended sketch* I have felt justified, not only in view
of his ministerial history, but in my relations to him and
his family; and I doubt not but this tribute to his memory
will be read with interest by thousands of his former friends,
and his name will be perpetuated by his valuable book—
" Man's Infallible Guide, both for His Faith and Practice."

Like many other charges, Wyoming had a country appointment, about three miles out, in the vicinity of which
there lived a noted skeptic, who, like most persons of that
class, concluded that he could demolish the Christian religion if he had a fair chance. So he met me at one of my
appointments and invited me home for dinner. I was aware
of his object, and so I went well prepared. After dinner
he squared himself for battle, but I proposed that our discussion should be respectful and fair, and no vulgarities
should be employed during our debate, to which he
assented. He commenced with much self-assurance, as
though there was only one side to the question. He seemed
to think it very unreasonable that God who had all

power should require ages to bring into maturity what he
could accomplish in a day; for instance, the enlightenment
and conversion of the world.   I stated that his power does
not conflict with his wisdom; and that his wisdom assures
us that in almost every department he honors the law
of gradual development.   As an illustration, he might
have created for the forest, *full-grown trees*, but he has
been pleased to furnish the oak from the acorn.   He might
have furnished us *at once* the full-grown man, but he has
seen it best to begin with the child.   A few such facts disconcerted the champion, and he took a new departure.   He
next dwelt upon the mysterious conception of our Saviour,
as an argument against his divinity.   I replied that this was
the strongest evidence of its truth, for if with our limited
capacities we could have mastered the whole idea, we might
have doubted its reality; but this is like many other things
to which we assent *fully*, though the methods of their being
are all unknown to us.   But the most unpleasant occurrence of the hour to him was my quotation from Rousseau,
magnifying the person of Christ.   This was such a *home-
thrust* that it made him angry, when he violated the rule
that we agreed upon to govern us in our debate.   I
reminded him of this, when he wound up the discussion by
remarking: " That if we could not agree upon religious subjects, we were friends in politics, and this last element
' covered a multitude of sins.' "   Some of his objections
reminded me of the skeptic's attack upon Uncle Elisha
Warner, in the northern part of the state.   " You believe,"
said he to Brother Warner, " that Elijah was translated to
heaven, do you not?"   " Certainly, I do," was the answer.
" But, Uncle Elisha, do you not know that it is a fact in
philosophy that a man cannot live beyond two or three
miles up in the air? he would freeze to death.   What say
you to that?"   "What do I care about your philosophy,"
said Brother W.; " Elijah took his own fire with him and

burned his way through." This was a *settler*, and the infidel after this gave him a wide berth.

But I must bring my remarks to a conclusion, so far as
this city is concerned, as I have devoted already about
twenty pages to this chapter. I trust that when the events
of time shall be known and fully revealed, that my labors
and efforts to promote the interests of this charge in 1873
will be approved by the Master; and should this be the
crown that I shall secure in that great day, it will outweigh
all human interests and rewards. Winding up here my pastoral labors of nearly thirty years in the territory and state
of Iowa, it imparts an unspeakable pleasure, that during
all that time I have preserved a clear conscience and
have had an eye single to the glory of God. Oh, what
riches can be compared with the riches of divine grace!
What honor can measure up to the honor that comes
from God! It might be proper here to say, that at
the ensuing conference held at Dubuque, I consented
to receive the relation of conference evangelist for the
coming year, and in this work I continued until the spring
season, when I repaired to my home in Michigan to enjoy
the quiet of domestic tranquility. It affords me much
pleasure, however, to recall the interesting seasons passed
at Blairstown with Brother Bargelt; Sabula, with Brother
Manning; and Camanche, with Brother Waite. And though
we did not realize all that we could have desired in the
salvation of souls, the faithful labor performed will not be
forgotten in the awards of the crowning day. At Sabula,
however, we had a time of refreshing from the presence of
the Lord, and the fruits of that meeting are still to be seen.
Since retiring from the regular work, and making it my
home the most of the time in Michigan, I have been laboring in the good work, as my strength would permit, cultivating new fields and adding new friendships. What a
comfort it is to know that in every station there is something to do, as well as something to suffer, and that *warm*

23

hearts, noble and *true*, are everywhere to be found where Jesus reigns victorious. And when standing on the immortal shores, and numbering the precious spirits *there*, coming up from different charges, I shall not set aside the valued friends I have learned to prize in the state of Michigan. My next chapter will include some of its history and interests.

CHAPTER XLI.

In passing from Iowa to Michigan about this time, I ran a very narrow risk of my life. No money would induce me to encounter the same experience, and nothing but God's protecting care brought me safely through. The same God that preserved Daniel stood by me. The facts are soon told. I arrived in Chicago about four o'clock A. M., and a hack took me at once to the depot of the Michigan Central. As the train for Michigan started early, I supposed that a number of persons would be there in waiting for a passage; but when I arrived, I was the only person to be seen. Descending from the hack and walking to the waiting-room, I heard *quick steps* behind me, and as I entered the door and closed it, my pursuer made an effort to push it open. I braced myself against it, and said to him in *defiant tones,* " that if he opened that door he did it at his peril!" This checked his efforts, and soon the step of the policeman was heard, when he made good his retreat and I was relieved. I learned that morning that a new reinforcement of these scamps had just come from the South, and this doubtless was one of them. Had I not quickened my steps, or had I permitted him to enter, I should have been at his mercy. But I had committed myself to the Lord, and he was " faithful that promised." I never think of this rescue without feeling a heart to praise the Lord for the deliverance.

In setting out upon my labors in this state, I was reminded that human nature was everywhere the same; the restraining influence of God's grace, and the enlightening culture, making the difference. Not long after my purchase near "Heath's Corners," a small Methodist Episcopal church was organized, and Rev. J. P. Force was appointed pastor. I was one of the original members in this organization, and our pastor being young in experience, he looked to me for counsel and assistance. It was my highest joy to contribute all the help within my power, and in our united efforts through the year an attachment was created between us and his family which will endure forever. During the winter months I assisted him about two weeks at "Hull's School-house," in a revival of great power. Some who were saved at that meeting have entered into rest, whilst others are filling their places in the church of God. I often think of that precious season, and the souls that were brought out into light.

It was during this year (1868) that the building of the M. E. church in Benton Harbor commenced, which has had such a *marvelous history.* I am satisfied that no church building in the state of Michigan, of the same age, can rival it in historic importance; and the determined and persevering efforts of Rev. E. A. Whitwam, assisted by a few faithful brethren in the charge, in erecting a beautiful house of worship upon the ruins of the old one, *deserve all praise.* To this church, under the pastorate of Brother Force, I contributed at first, fifty dollars, with the understanding that a house should be erected, costing about seven thousand dollars. But instead of this, when dedicated, it had reached the vast sum of eighteen thousand; and thus its singular history was continued, until the good Being, offended and insulted, sent his fiery darts into its tower; and in an hour all of our false pride was left hanging to the smoking wreck. At the recent dedication, the balance of the indebtedness remaining was about five hundred dollars; one-third of which I propose to meet if the brethren of the charge will pay the remainder during the present conference year. This point reached, we shall have a monument of worship, an ornament to the church and to the city, and one that will extend its blessings to future generations.

Our pastors in this city, up to the present time, have been Brothers Force, Jacokes, Worthington, Hall, Prouty, Gosling, Starks, Sparling and Whitwam, men whose talents and virtues I delight to cherish. In fact my ministerial acquaintance with the preachers of Niles district has been of the pleasantest character. The presiding elders, Hall, Olds, Robinson and Boggs, have commended themselves by their labors, and secured a name for fidelity to the Master which will live in the church long after their transfer to heaven. Brother Robinson has gone on to test its golden streets and sing its new song a little in the advance of his brethren; but soon his fellow-laborers will hail him on the other shore. One of the pleasant and profitable seasons of labor in Michigan was at Pipestone, in connection with the pastor, Brother Steele. I found him laboring under embarrassments, but a man of *pure worth*, and our united efforts were crowned with great success. About the fourth sermon, when discoursing from these words: "Blessed is that man that maketh the Lord his trust," the clouds gave way and victory came all at once. In a few minutes the altar was crowded, and our service was crowned with clear conversions and shouts of praise. From that evening the work moved forward without much effort, and at the close of the second week we all rejoiced over our complete success. At this meeting new friendships were set in motion, which will last, when we have no farther use for the sun or moon, for the Lord himself will be the light of the city. I seldom have left a meeting with greater regret, and but few with greater satisfaction, for I was aware that very many had entered into life who would shine in the coming kingdom like stars, forever and ever.

But what can exceed the pleasure of our annual gatherings or feasts in the grove? Several of these have I attended since my residence in the state, and they have been like the spicy gales to the weary traveler, or like springs of water in a thirsty land. At Crystal Springs, how striking the emblem! Here are the pure and abundant waters pouring forth from the fountain, whilst the heralds of salvation are crying, in the name of Jesus: "I will give unto him that is athirst, of the water of life *freely*," "and he that drinketh of the water that I shall give him, shall never thirst." Oh, what multitudes, during those years of refreshing, who came to those tents thirsting, have gone away with a full cup and a grateful heart! Old Sister Currier, whose prayers and testimonies often raised us upward to that pure and holy clime, is heard no more. Brother Burns, who preached us all up to heaven upon that memorable morning, has reached a land where sinners are not found and sermons are not needed. Elder Robinson, who swayed his scepter of love over the camp-ground, has now exchanged it for a crown. Brother Bliss, who sang so sweetly a few years since, is now attuning his powers to sweeter music in loftier strains. Brother Joy, who discoursed to us so eloquently last year, upon his glorious theme, will soon know what is meant by this beautiful language: "In thy presence there is fullness of *joy*, and at thy right hand pleasures forevermore;" and Brother Boggs, who moved among us so pale and infirm, will soon reach a clime so healthy "that the inhabitants never say they are sick." I have mentioned several names, but, oh, what precious memories come up to my view from those unmentioned names that are written in the " Book of Life!" A few more revolving years and we shall transfer our " camping-ground " to the groves of bliss. During the winter of 1876, Brother J. P. Force, now stationed at Lawton, wrote me to come and assist him in protracted services. We had labored together harmoniously and successfully at Benton Harbor, and now he desired my services at Lawton.

I was not indifferent to the call, but proceeded at once to the spiritual battle-ground. I remained with him not far from two weeks, preaching every evening, the good work gradually progressing, when I returned home to take a little rest, preparatory to other labors. Within a few weeks the Macedonian cry came up from Porter, another appointment of his work, and, with armor on, I hastened to the conflict. Here also the gospel was "the power of God unto salvation," and before the meeting closed, scores were brought out into spiritual life. The pastor reported as a result of our united labors, at the two appointments, one hundred and fifty saved and added to the church.

On my way from Porter to Lawton, in company with Brother Force, the day being cold and stormy, I became so chilled that when I reached home I was attacked with pneumonia, which came very near closing up my days. For several weeks I was not expected to recover, but as warm weather approached, I came up gradually until I was so far restored as to be able to visit Ohio, the residence of my son. It was to me a source of great satisfaction that my campaign of ministerial labor had such an ending as that at Lawton and Porter; and had my Master then called me, I should have raised the notes of victory and ascended in triumph. But my work was not done. In the month of June I returned to Michigan, but feeble in health, and in the coming winter I was prostrated with a second attack. The second one brought me so low that at one period of my sickness my pulse ceased to beat, and angelic music seemed to charm the departing occupant; but at this point the Divine hand arrested my progress to the home celestial, and the pilgrim, leaning on his staff, left " foot-prints " again upon the sands of time. But, with my partial restoration, it was an effort still to live, and in the spring I sold out my effects and started once more for Ohio. My relatives and friends in Michigan, as they shook my hand upon my departure, never expected to see my face again in the flesh, and my impression was the same; but instead of this, my Father granted me a kind reprieve and lengthened out my days.

Ohio—what sacred memories linger around these groves, and what enchanting scenes witnessed along its streams. It was here, in early life, that I consecrated my being to God, and here he placed upon my heart the seal of divine approval. More than forty years had now passed since my name was recorded in the church, and the value of a Christian life had been tested to my entire satisfaction. It was a solemn thought, that here, in Wheelersburg, the residence of my son, only one grown person remained besides myself, who occupied its dwellings in 1834, when I came to Ohio. But this was a part of its present history.

For many years I had been anxious to visit once more the land of my nativity, the home of my childhood in Elmira, N. Y., but I had delayed to the present. Everything now being favorable, in the month of May I took the boat for Pittsburg, and in a few days reached the thriving city. I reached it, not to be greeted as a familiar friend or brother, but to be treated as a lonely stranger; for among the multitude of the friends of my youth, but *one* recognized my countenance and called me by name. My own aunt, living in the city, could not call up my history until I reminded her of our relationship. But this done, her heart was filled with gladness and her eyes suffused with tears. "No one," she said, "is more welcome than yourself." This was Aunt Olive, the oldest of the family living, being now about eighty-two years of age. My cousins, Joseph H. Barney and Luther L. Barney, with their families, all had been born and raised since I left this youthful home. What a change! The house where I was born I could not find, for stores and mansions now took the place of the humble dwelling where I first saw the light of day. But when I went to Chemung, and visited the old residence of my grandparents, with whom I passed thirteen years of my youth to manhood, the change was still more apparent. I asked permission, and passed through all the rooms in the house—the one where we played, the other where we slept; the cellar where the cider was kept, and the apples stored away—but all how changed! I then visited the garden, and orchard, and old fishing ground where I caught such nice strings of fish in my boyhood; but the hand of time had taken away all of their familiar looks, and I felt lonely indeed. Could I have met old "Watch," our domestic dog, as he used to meet me in my youth, it would have been quite a relief; but old "Watch" was not there; and after hours of travel over the old farm, I sat down on the fence, and, like the Psalmist, "I wept when I remembered Zion." I then, with careful tread and silent awe, entered the family grave-yard, where reposing was the dust of my grandparents, loved and honored more than fifty years ago. What visions of the past, what tender recollections, like little waves beat upon my heart; and at that moment, could I have entered their room and have seen them seated in the old rocking-chairs, as they once sat, I would have given *gold;* but *far* in the history of the past *was that honor,* and now I must make the most of the vision, and hope for the future. As I left this little mound so sacred, I thought how appropriate these lines:

"How painfully pleasing the fond recollection
    Of youthful connections and innocent joy,
Whilst blest with parental advice and affection,
    Surrounded with mercies and peace from on high."

But, in the midst of all these changes, united to painful and melancholy reflections, God's stars which illumined my pathway in childhood were shining with the same lustre; the sun had not withdrawn one of its rays, and the moon was still shining all the same; and when in the bower I knelt for prayer, his love was just as *real* and *precious* as though the old farm and buildings had stood in all of their pristine glory. Oh, what a world of comfort to the weary traveler home, that whilst change and decay are written upon every earthly object, Jesus and his grace are the

same "yesterday, to-day, and forever." After my visit to
Chemung, I proceeded to the residence of widow Taylor,
in Breesport, wife of my brother Geroge. This brother had
been dead many years, but the widow and two children
were still residing in the place. I remained three days with
them, enjoying the hours pleasantly, when I returned to
Elmira, the pleasant home of my cousins. My last visit was
to Ashland, the home of Mr. and Mrs. Roberts, the latter an
old schoolmate and warm friend. She knew me at once,
and here, with my aunt, the day passed pleasantly away.
Two weeks had now passed, and waving a final farewell, I
returned to Ohio, blessed in body and enriched in experience. I may not enjoy another such a repast with them on
earth, but a richer one awaits us in heaven.

Upon my return to Ohio, I enjoyed a fine opportunity of
extending my acquaintance in our ministerial associations.
At Haverhill, my early home, we enjoyed one of this character, which was truly a season of refreshing. Surrounded
by many of my old scholars, and the influence of ministerial
brethren, the hours passed pleasantly away. Rev. S. M.
Bright was the presiding elder of Portsmouth district, and
conducted the exercises with much ability. During the
year another session was held at Wheelersburg, where I
resided, still more interesting than the former, owing to a
larger ministerial attendance. During these two ministerial
gatherings, I formed a very pleasant acquaintance with most
of the ministers of the district, viz.: Revs. J. W. Peters and
T. R. Taylor of Portsmouth; Revs. J. F. Williams and J. S.
Postle of Ironton, D. Stover of Beaver, J. R. Tibbles of
Burlington, D. C. Thomas of Hanging Rock, P. Henry of
Lawrence, J. P. Pillsbury of Lucasville, and T. M. Leslie
of Piketon. With Rev. S. M. Bright, the presiding elder of
the district, and H. Berkstresser, the pastor of the Wheelersburg circuit, I had formed a previous acquaintance.
Rev. W. F. Filler of Portsmouth circuit, I include in the
above list. It was very interesting to me through all of

these exercises to mark the *sameness* of Methodism every-where. Though it had been over thirty years since I left Ohio, my spiritual birthplace, and I had been laboring with new men and cultivating new fields of labor, yet the old *Methodist alphabet* was just as familiar to me as though rivers had not rolled nor mountains rose between. Oh, how transporting the thought, when standing on the tower-ing cliffs of Colorado, that the same gospel truths that brought its multitudes to Christ in Scioto, in the early his-tory of my ministry, were still salutary to save in that far-off land of gold. These ministerial associations are not only means of grace, but of mental culture; they bring the pastors and the people into closer relationship, and seldom close without a blessing to the church and community where they are held.

During the latter part of the summer we were all startled with the solemn tidings that Brother Carr, the minister on Wheelersburg circuit, was drowned in attempting to water his horse. He had preached the evening previous at Powells-ville, and the following morning, with his child in his arms, mistaking the proper place, he was precipitated into deep water and drowned before any one was aware of the catastro-phe. The little babe was observed floating on the stream, and thus signalized the fate of the father, and was dis-covered in time to save its life. The memorial services were conducted by Rev. J. W. Peters, at Sciotoville, and his remains interred in the beautiful cemetery at Wheelers-burg. He was a young man of much promise to the church, and such was the unexpected occurrence that we could hardly realize the painful reality.

> " Let sickness blast, let death devour,
> If heaven must recompense our pains;
> Perish the grass and fade the flower,
> *If firm the word of God remains.*"

Such was my state of health during the fifteen months that I remained in Scioto county, that I preached but four

sermons. The first was for Brother Peters, in Portsmouth—
a very pleasant service; and twice for Brother Thomas; the
first at Hanging Rock, and the other at Haverhill. What
contributed very much to make this Sabbath at Portsmouth
a pleasant one, was the welcome home at Brother Ewing's,
brother-in-law to my son, and also the many old friends
present, to whom I had preached in former years. At Hanging Rock I met Brother and Sister Henderson, of precious
memory. Brother Henderson was one of my old associates
before either commenced a religious life; but now we meet
again, not to revel in sinful pleasure, but to bow at the
Saviour's feet, and magnify saving grace. Here I shall
never want for a pleasant home. At Haverhill I preached
from " But this one thing I do: forgetting those things
which are behind and reaching forth unto those things
which are before, I press toward the mark for the prize of
the high calling of God in Christ Jesus." Though the day
was warm, that communion season will not be forgotten.
My further acquaintance with Brothers Peters and Taylor
at Portsmouth only served to strengthen our friendship,
whilst for Brothers Berkstresser and Thomas there were
" lights along the shore which never grew dim."

One of the interesting events of this year (1878) was the
golden wedding of Mr. and Mrs. Boynton, of Haverhill.
This occurred on Christmas day, and was an occasion long
to be remembered. The writer was notified about a week
previous, and as he was expected to act as chaplain for the
company, the song and speech were all in readiness at the
appropriate time. Mr. Asa Boynton and his companion
were among my first acquaintances in French Grant, Ohio,
after my arrival in the state. For several years his children attended my school, received the most of their education under my tuition, and it was meet that I should be
honored as chief speaker upon an occasion of such importance. Nearly one hundred were in attendance to celebrate
the history of this marriage relation. But alas! before the

next Christmas rolled around, Mr. Boynton had been removed from the family circle to enter upon a *different relation*. Such is the history of human life; and happy is the man who is ready—having on the wedding garment.

The next service I attended after this was the funeral of Mr. Wm. Gilruth, the brother of Rev. James Gilruth, whose sketch is given in a former chapter. He was upward of eighty years—born and died on the same farm. I had known him for forty years, and in the winding up of such a life, it was a pleasure for me to state that his firm reliance and trust were in the Almighty power to save. Five years previous I attended the memorial services of the elder brother in Iowa; and now in Ohio, I stand by the younger and see all that is mortal consigned to the dust. Thus our strong men pass away. My health having greatly improved, and duty calling me again to Michigan, I decided to return. So in the month of June I left the pleasant residence of my son, in Wheelersburg, with its many sacred associations, and once more in health, greeted my many friends who had looked upon my face, as they supposed, for the last time. Before I left Southern Ohio we enjoyed for two or three weeks our strawberry feast, and when I arrived in Michigan it had just commenced, so that I enjoyed at least six weeks the luxury of this queen of berries.

As I returned to the residence of my brother Harvey, now residing in Pipestone, Berrien county, I missed the familiar face of one who had been for years the angel of the household. Storm or sunshine, sorrow or joy,—that countenance moved serenely through all the vicissitudes of family history, without a cloud upon her brow or a murmur from her lips; but she is not there. The vision remains, but the mother has departed. Ella, the oldest daughter, with Mattie and Allie, are now standing up in order to bear the burden and share the responsibilities of the loved one gone. *Very few* left in the same relation would do it better, and yet it is not easy to supply a faithful mother's place. The boys are Harvey, Willie and George,—all still at home, save Willie, who has launched out to make a fortune in the land of gold. Having passed the summer and winter in the family of my brother, in the spring I resumed my place at my pleasant home two miles south of Benton Harbor, at Heath's Corners, where I have resided the past year (1880–81) in one of the most pleasant localities, and favored with the best of society.

My sister Olive, and her husband James Jackways, a local preacher, live within four miles of my residence, and with them I often enjoy the luxury of a pleasant visit and a rich spiritual repast. It was here (at Heath's Corners), on the sixth of December last, that I commenced the work of writing up the history of my life and labors, and now the second day of May, I am nearing the close. Whilst engrossed in this important work, my mind has been very pleasantly relieved by three or four letters from Kata and Wesley, my grandchildren in Ohio. They are quite juvenile in experience, and this made their letters the more interesting. A copy of the younger would be of interest to my readers, but I will reserve this for another chapter, adding, that it is a capital arrangement to induce children to begin early in writing to their friends. In addition to these, I received a letter from a cousin, David Landon, living in Parma, Jackson county, Michigan, whom I had not heard from for nearly fifty years. He is the son of Ezekiel Landon, of New York, the brother of my grandmother, Anna Landon, who gave me my name, referred to in the first chapter of my book. But I am reminded that my record of Michigan has already embraced about fifteen pages; and as much as I should delight to extend it, with an interest that will not die, and a friendship which will reach beyond this life, I leave with its many valued spirits the precious heavenly benediction: "The God of love and peace be with you."

CHAPTER XLII.

The company of children and youth I have delighted in since the days of my boyhood. How often in riper years have I gone back and strolled along through the meadows, the orchard and the groves, where my little hands plucked the first flowers of spring, and where, by the stream, I caught strings of little fish, and as I presented them at home, received the honor of a successful fisherman. But for the cleaning and preparing them for the morning meal, it would have been sport all the way through; but this service took off a little of the gloss, which was borne with patience, in view of a *fishing day* to come. I have heard men frequently say that the days of their childhood and youth they did not enjoy; but this I could never say, for I had so many pleasant playmates, and such a good home, with kind parents, that I love to dwell upon its scenes and pleasures. There is one thing, however, which is true and natural to all children, and were it not for this, I think they might be happier than they are. Can you tell me what this is? If not, I will tell *you*. Most all young persons are very anxious to become men and women. "Oh," the boy says, "that I were a man!" This is the height of his ambition. But could the boy and girl lie down at night, and find themselves men and women in the morning, what would they do with themselves? They would have the *body*, and that would be all. Would it not be amusing to see them carrying around a large body, but no experience? no discipline, no education, no muscular power? In fact, it would require more care and expense to provide for them in this condition than as if they remained children in size. Do you not know, my dear young friends, that it requires all the training and discipline of youth in order to become well-developed men, as much so as the growth of the body?

You have seen young pigeons; long before they can fly they have a *large body* and *small wings*. Now, should they attempt to fly at this time, you see that their weight would bring them to the ground; but let them remain in their nest until their feathers are grown, then they can fly with safety. And thus would it be with young persons, could they be men and women at the age of children; they would not have the knowledge or judgment to guide them in safety through the experiences of life.

But this is not all; should these young aspirations be gratified, we should be left without any children in the world, and this would result in great injury. Only imagine, for a moment, a world without children and youth. No little pattering feet tripping through our rooms, no playful sound nor hearty laugh coming from that little group of boys or girls, to give inspiration to the passing hours; the merry glee and joyous hopes have all been transferred into manhood, and now every school-room and play-ground is forever vacated. What a state of society we would have, if little boys and girls could at once become men and women. We that are older need the thrilling influence of joyous childhood as much as you need our knowledge and experience to teach and guide you in the path of safety and obedience. My dear young friends, if you but knew it, you might be the happiest beings in this world, as you have but little care and anxiety, the most of it resting upon your parents; and all you have to do is to eat and sleep and grow, and then to become wiser and better every day, until you can stand up honorably by the side of those who have been so much interested for your welfare. Did you ever think that it is not standing up six feet high, or weighing one hundred and fifty pounds, which makes the man, but it requires something grander than these to make the *true man*. The great poet, Dr. Watts, says:

> "I must be measured by my soul:
> It is the *mind that makes the man*."

I was called upon the other day to make a short address to the Sunday-school; and though some of the scholars were quite large, I presented some simple things quite new to them. I inquired why it was that every one of them that morning had brought their "looking-glass" with them. They were a little surprised, and looked around to see one. Not being able to see the article named, I asked them what they were looking out of. One answered, "My eyes." Then I explained that the eye was nothing more nor less than a small looking-glass, upon which (retina) the picture of the object was formed, which we call seeing; just as our *face* is reflected, standing before one of our large mirrors. The scholars seemed delighted with this simple view of the subject, and all acknowledged that the eye was a wonderful contrivance. I then asked them what they intended to do with their *drums* that they had brought with them. They saw the point at once in this second question, and located it within the ear, and that unless this drum were perfect the hearing could not be good; that a crack in our *musical drum* would spoil the sound, so a *crack* in the drum of the ear would occasion deafness; that very much of our enjoyment in this life depended upon sight and sound. I charged them further with bringing their "*receiving drawer*" with them. Not one of them was innocent of this charge; and now I wished to know *where* it was concealed. Not one dared to speak, and such a *looking* one at the other you have seldom seen. To help them a little, I stated that it was unlike anything else, for the *drawer* was never so full but that it could contain more. One little boy concluded that he had found the key to the answer, and he cried out, "The stomach!" Some seemed to think that it was possible to fill the stomach, though in some cases quite difficult, and they concluded that it must be something else. So, after several attempts, one said, "*The memory;*" and thus the guessing ended. Then I dwelt for some time in showing them the value of this faculty. Without it we could learn nothing. If we could not remember anything, nothing would remain with us and the mind would become a blank. Without this, we would not know our own friends from strangers, and the thief and murderer could never be detected. By this one power of the mind we discover how much we are indebted to our Father in heaven for our happiness and improvement. In this little storehouse we begin, at a very early age, to lay by many precious articles, and when we wish to see them again, all we have to do is to pull out the *little drawer*, and here they are as bright and fresh as ever. This reminds me of one of my young friends in Iowa. She had been collecting and laying aside in her drawer choice pieces of calico of different colors, until she wished to make them into a fine quilt. When this time arrived, there they were, *cut* and *shaped* and quilted in the nicest form; and these little scraps became one of the comforts and ornaments of the household. And thus it is with the *precious little* scraps of life that we lay aside in our memory. We may not wish to use them *but little* for many years, but after a while we have some important work to accomplish and we cannot succeed without looking over the little drawer and examining the precious material that we stowed away. There is another item of interest in laying up treasures for the memory—that the sooner we begin in life, the *fresher* and more *real* they are when we wish to call them into use. Should any of my youthful readers ever engage in writing a book, as I have been doing this winter, you will then know that it is much easier to remember what you learn in childhood and youth than in riper age. The reason of this is, that when young our minds are active, and impressions upon the memory are easily made, and thus they become a part of our nature. Your paper will stick to *soft wax*, but it will not to a *hard board;* and it is as true that your young hearts will retain early impressions, whilst old persons are not affected by them. A few years since I cut the first letters of my name with my knife in the bark

24

of a young tree. Years passed on, and I had entirely forgotten it. But after a while I passed by that tree again, and
what did I see? Large letters had been formed by that
little incision, in the growth of the tree, and now I could
see "L. T." for some distance. So it is with early memories: they grow with our growth and strengthen with our
strength, until they exert a strong influence in shaping our
character for life.

You see by these remarks, my dear young friends, how
important that we treasure up in our memories in early life
those things which are *true* and *pleasant*, instead of those
of an opposite character. When I was a little boy, I frequently fell into the company of other children, who would
relate stories about ghosts and frightful things seen in
graveyards; until I was so influenced that I hardly dared to
open the door, or pass at night the home of the dead. This
unpleasant feeling remained with me until I was nearly a
man grown, and often I would tremble in passing these
places at night. This was all wrong, and it only shows the
unhappy influence of false impressions. How dearly did I
pay for such marvelous tales through all of my early history, and oft-times I made a show of bravery by whistling
in the dark; but "when I became a man I put away child-
ish things;" and soon I felt no more concern in the cemetery than in my father's orchard. I wish to say to my
young readers that these ghostly tales are all false, and if
you are followers of that which is good, you are as safe in the
night as in the light of day. The importance of treasuring
up good things in our memory in early life is clearly seen,
in the fact that they often shape our *future history*, and
things well learned at that time are not easily forgotten. I
very well remember, when a child, that a minister at my
father's house took me up in his lap, spoke kindly to me,
and said: "Before I put you down you must spell Con-
stantinople." It was a long word, but he continued training me until I mastered it, and I never forgot it. Though

I had not yet learned my letters, I was able to spell this word, and I never forgot the name of Selah Stocking, who taught me first how to spell. And a little later I made my first speech, on the last day of school, among the orators of the occasion. That speech was never forgotten. Shall I repeat one or two of the verses:

> "Large streams from little fountains flow,
> Tall oaks from little acorns grow.
> You'd scarce expect one of my age
> To speak in public on the stage,
> And if I chance to fall below
> Demosthenes or Cicero,
> Don't view me with a critic's eye,
> *But pass my imperfections by.*"

Here you have a part of my first speech, which has remained with me more than sixty years, and I think in the heavenly company will not be forgotten. This little item of early history shows the endurance of early memories, and though time may change the face, and age may impair the system, these treasured memories lose not their precious contents.

No historic fact more forcibly shows the power of early impressions than in the war of 1759 between the English and the French. During its progress, the Indians in the service of the French came into the colonies and captured many of their children. Among them were two daughters of a widowed mother. For many years she had heard nothing from them as to their fate. When the war closed, which lasted about nine years, the captives were to be returned, and the day was set when the parents were to meet the commissioner at a certain place and claim their children. There were about two hundred captives present,—arranged in two rows,—with their faces inward; and then the father or mother would examine one row on the one side, and then the other, in order to recognize their loved ones. The widow's turn came who had lost her little girls eight years

previous; but with all her *intense interest* her daughters were
not to be found. Almost *overwhelmed* with grief, she was
about to give them up for lost, when the commissioner
remarked to her: " Your children may be present, but have
grown out of your knowledge. If you can think of a verse
which you were accustomed to sing to them in their childhood, they will be likely to remember it." She thought of
the song which she sang to them at that age, commencing
thus: "Alone, alone, yet not alone, in this wide world of
wo;" and scarcely had she finished one verse before the
oldest daughter rushed toward her sorrowing mother. "My
mother! my mother!" she cried, and soon the two daughters were in her arms. Though they had failed to remember the singer, they had not forgotten the song.

The above fact truthfully illustrates the power there is
in early memories, and the moral force which they exert
upon the young mind; and in some instances, a few kind
words spoken at this time have been the turning point to a
glorious history. The great Dr. Clarke, when a boy, was a
dull scholar. His teacher would often call him *dull* and
stupid, which inspired in him but little courage. A neighboring teacher looking over his class one day, told him that
he would "yet *make a man*," and all at once it gave him
new inspiration. From that day the youthful Clarke entered
upon a new life, and soon distanced all of his youthful associates, and finally became one of the most learned and
devoted men in the Wesleyan connection. All he wanted,
was not a pulling down, but a raising up; and in this way
we may lend a helping hand to many a struggling spirit.
If you can induce boys or girls to believe that they are of
little consequence, and can never amount to anything, they
have but little ambition beyond; but on the other hand, can
you induce them to raise a high standard of human character, and work to that point, it is astonishing how much may
be accomplished in a short time. I would then say to my
young friends, " never be discouraged." Though you may

not possess the same talents of others, you have those which your Father in heaven sees it best for you to possess; and if you improve them *well*, in the rewards of the coming day, your crown will be as bright and your mansion as rich as though greater gifts had been bestowed. He is not the most richly rewarded to whom the *most is given*, but the one who improves the best *what he has*.

We are never to forget that our business in this world is not only to shine upon others, but to assist them in shining also. The diamond in its native state is often rough and uncouth, and before used it has to be polished, and sometimes at the expense of thousands of dollars. Queen Victoria has a very *costly one;* its value about one million of dollars. To polish it properly, cost the vast sum of thirty thousand, which she paid to the jeweler; and all this to decorate the crown of a mortal who is soon to pass away. In like manner we are taken in the *rough* in this world, and need much polishing; even before we are prepared to fill our places with profit, we need a great amount of brightening; but there is a *jewel* down in the rough which gold cannot buy and thrones cannot purchase. At the first thought you may be tempted to envy the queen, in view of her wealth—even to say, "Oh, that I were as rich as she is!" but you are in possession—shall I call it a diamond? Yes, you are in possession of a diamond of *greater value* than all the precious ornaments of Victoria. That *soul* of yours cannot be purchased with silver or gold, or *precious stones;* but in its redemption it cost the *richest gift of heaven.* The blessed Saviour gave his life as a ransom price, and now your great business in this life is to be so shaped and educated—yea, *polished*, that you may not only be prepared to fill an important place here, but to shine in the heavenly kingdom like the stars forever and ever. My dear young friends, I wish to impress upon your minds that the present life, with all of its blessings, is not given you merely for self-gratification or vain show for a few short years; but to prepare for a better and nobler destiny in the home beyond this. And what is so grand and praiseworthy as to see a talented youth bending every energy which the good Being has given him, to excel in virtue and goodness here, that he may be the better qualified to share the honor and the bliss in the coming ages. You have passed by the nursery when the trees were small—just taking shape for the future. It was an interesting sight to see the tree in its incipient state, and to mark the care of the nursery-man in shaping them for the orchard. But how much more *interesting* and even *grand* to pass by the orchard in its maturity, crowned with blossoms, and then bending with golden fruit. And thus it is pleasant to see the indications of promise in children and youth; for nothing adorns the character like early piety; but to see manhood and womanhood crowned with the fruits of right-eousness, and maturing for immortal honors awaiting them in the glorious home beyond, is both beautiful and sublime. Every day that you live is doing something to shape your character for better or for worse. Every bad habit which you form, whether swearing, lying, stealing, gambling or drunkenness, will contribute to make up your earthly history, which an angel cannot alter and eternity cannot change. How many boys there are who think it very smart and man-like to chew or smoke tobacco, when they scarcely take a thought that they are contracting a habit which will cost them a thousand regrets in coming years, and if they live to advanced age, will cost them quite a little fortune. Then think of the precious time spent, as well as money squandered, in smoking or chewing, and to what profit? To debase his manhood, poison his system, pollute his mouth, and often his face; very revolting to persons of good taste. Besides this, the use of tobacco creates a perverted appetite which often leads on to drunkenness and ruin. My dear young friends, this picture is not overdrawn, but it is a plain statement of facts. If I were assured that this counsel would induce any of my youthful readers to shun this pernicious habit, I should feel richly rewarded for the interest that I have taken; for rest assured, that every word of caution has been written that your character may be the purer and your life the happier.   And now it is for *you* to decide whether you will become a noble man, and an honored woman, or be carried on by the influence of corrupt society and bad habits until reformation is almost hopeless and your usefulness almost blighted.   Yes, it is for *you* to decide whether your life shall be a glorious success or a shameful defeat.   Remember this, and to assist you I will underscore it: " *That nothing can be substituted for a good character.*"   You may be called cunning — you may be called smart, you may be called brave, or you may be called wealthy or honorable, or even commanding in appearance, but the day in your history will soon come when nothing will stand by you but a sincere heart and an upright life. And how much often depends upon the decision of a moment.

A traveler on horseback, on a new route, was passing by a flat-topped rock, and near the center he saw a little bubbling of drops, as though there was a struggle in the water beneath, as to which way it should go.   The stranger noticing it, took his finger and directed the little which had accumulated upon the top until it dropped down along its side.   The circumstance was entirely forgotten, when, in a few years, passing that way again, the few drops directed by his finger had become quite a small stream issuing from the rock, still retaining the same channel which he marked out for it many years before.   And thus it is with youthful decisions.   There comes a time in youthful history, when the drift of human life needs a little aid to start it in the right direction.   In a word, when there seems to be a struggle in the mind which way shall be preferred, *the path of life* or the *road to death*—a very slight influence at that time will decide the matter.   Like the finger upon the rock, a kind word from a dear friend, or a *right decision* for virtue or truth, at that moment, decides the soul's destiny for a glorious immortality. What great pleasure would it afford the writer did he but know that all of his youthful friends who read these lines, would decide *now* for Christ and for heaven.

A valued friend of mine gave me this very interesting fact which occurred in his youthful days. In company with about twelve young persons, male and female, they started out, one Christmas evening, for a jolly sleigh-ride. Having traveled several miles, they came to the forks of the road, and stopped, in order to decide which one to take. After discussing the question for some little time, my friend said to the driver: "The left-hand road will take us to the ball, some three miles distant, and the right-hand one will take us to a religious meeting of great interest. Now," said he, "I move that we go to the meeting and do what we can to save our souls, instead of going to the dance." Said another: "I second the motion;" whereupon they all moved off in the direction of the scene of spiritual interest. Before they returned home the next morning the entire number had embraced religion, united with the church, and two of these became eminent ministers in the church of Christ. In this instance, how much depended upon a right decision. Had they decided to take the left, and passed the night in revelry and mirth, it might have resulted in spiritual ruin; but this *moment's decision* for Christ and for heaven enrolled their names in the "Lamb's Book of Life," and settled their high and glorious destiny forever. Think, then, how important it is to choose that "*better part*," which will bless you through all the revolutions of time and ultimately give you a seat at God's right hand.

I remember well, in my school-boy days, what satisfaction it gave me when I received a ticket from my teacher, headed "The Reward of Merit." What inspiration it gave me; and as I returned home, how proudly I presented it to my parents; and here a double blessing was conferred upon me. This little incident had its lesson. Since that time, how have I considered it as a simple yet truthful illustration of heavenly rewards for a life of love and obedience to God. If it were a pleasure to present a ticket of commendation to our earthly parents, showing forth our good behavior, what will be the satisfaction and the joy, as life's labors are all finished, to go up to the Divine Master and present to him for his approval the certificate of a *faithful* and *holy* life. And if the encouraging words from our natural parents sent such inspiration to our hearts, what joy and rapture shall we experience when Jesus smiles and says to us: "Well done, my boy—well done, my little girl; thou hast been faithful over a few ,things, I will make thee ruler over many. Enter thou into the joys of thy Lord." Oh, I trust that thousands of my dear young friends, who have been so much interested in reading this chapter, intended expressly for them, will meet me in that blessed land where we shall be rewarded according to our works. And now, with my earnest prayers for your success in life, I bid you farewell.

CHAPTER XLIII.

There is a curiosity as well as a charm in being introduced to works or characters of great antiquity. And especially is this the case where the object of interest occupied an important place in the world's history. It is in accordance with this law that there is such a solemn and reverential awe felt by us in visiting the sepulchers of the patriarchs and prophets. We seem to be standing almost at the other end of the history of our race, and communing with those who talked face to face with God. What an interest clusters around every step taken by the traveler as he visits those consecrated spots sanctified by the presence and prayers of Jesus and his apostles; and even the old churches and parsonages where such men as Wesley and Whitefield lived and labored are precious memorials of history. And could we enjoy the privilege of a personal introduction to either of these great and good men at the present day, a voyage across the Atlantic would not be considered too high a price that we might enjoy the satisfaction. These valuable interests and remembrances would soon be lost to us altogether were it not that the pen of the historian has kindly transmitted their record, and we are now sharing the benefits of their lives and influence.

Such is the motive of the writer in presenting a few brief *sketches* of our aged ministerial brethren in the present chapter, and though I have not the privilege of presenting a Wesley or a Fletcher, yet I have the honor in giving those *elements of character* which endear those great names to us. Yes; men filling the same position, honored by the same Saviour, engaged in the same work, and awaiting the same high and holy destiny. And though their monuments may not tower so high, nor their lamps shine so brilliant, yet their history has been immortalized by the good accomplished and the crown secured. What can be more sacred in thought or rich in experience than to stand by the side of those aged and faithful veterans worn out in the cause of Christ, and to hear their testimonies of praise for mercies past, and joyful expectations of the life to come. "Tell Brother Taylor," said an old pilgrim living at Mt. Pleasant, Iowa, in his eighty-fourth year, "that I am *all ready*, waiting for the summons." Yes, Father McDowell, you "have fought the good fight and kept the faith," and when the jewels for your Master shall be numbered in heaven, such accessions as Adam Miller will not be forgotten. And although age and infirmities may weaken this house of clay, old and tried friends may have all passed on to the spirit land, and all that earth has in store to satisfy human cravings may be nearly exhausted, yet the immortal

nature is gathering ripeness and a fitness for a purer home
and richer joys. Oh, what a period in the history of the
Christian that will be, when we shall be " clothed upon, and
mortality shall be swallowed up of life!"

Among the number included in this brief chapter, I will
first notice Rev. Michael See. Whether his angelic name
had any influence upon his Christian character I am unable
to determine, but as far back in the history of Iowa as 1845,
he joined that conference, and was a member of the same
class with the writer. Sustaining this relation, I had a fine
opportunity of becoming well acquainted with the man.
The first time I saw him was at a camp-meeting near Burlington, Iowa, as he ascended the pulpit to exhort at the
conclusion of a sermon. " That is *Michael See*," remarked
a minister near me, " and now you will hear a stirring
exhortation." It was not long before I was convinced that
he was correctly reported, and though it required no critic's
glass to discover that he had not " been brought up at the
feet of Gamaliel," so far as human expressions were concerned, yet it was no *less evident* that he had been " tarry-
ing at Jerusalem " until he was " endued with power
from on high." Very soon it was apparent to all present
that everything else was lost sight of, and his soul was all
aflame for the salvation of the lost; and before that service
closed the notes of victory went up to heaven from many
sinners saved. Though not enjoying the advantages of a
good education in early life, he possessed those important
elements of character which qualified him for usefulness,
and these he employed very successfully. Had his mind
been improved by early culture, sanctified by divine grace
as it has been with his limited advantages, he would have
shone among the first ministers; but using well the talents
which God gave him, the best part of his life, many will be
the stars in the crown of his rejoicing. As noticed in a
previous chapter, Michael See, John Harris and Landon
Taylor alone remain to represent the large class of twenty-

five members who united with the Iowa conference in Burlington in 1845.   Brother See is now approaching his three-
score and ten years, sustains a superannuated relation to
his conference, and rejoicing in the hope of a happier country and more exalted honors.

I now have the pleasure of introducing to my readers
Horatio W. Houghton, one of my presiding elders when
engaged as agent of the American Bible society.   He is
about my own age, born October 22, 1812, the difference in
our ages being only one month and fourteen days. (So far
he is my senior.)   He was born in Springfield, Vermont,
and when only five months old, by the death of his father
was left an orphan.   As he grew up to years he learned the
art of printing of his brother Horace Houghton, lately
deceased, who published the *Galena Advertiser* for forty
years.   He was sensibly converted in 1835, while editing a
paper in his native village.   After spending a short time at
the Biblical Institute at Newbury, Vermont, he joined the
Providence conference in 1844, where he labored successfully thirteen years.   Family circumstances demanding his
residence in Northwestern Iowa for a season, he came to
the state in 1857, and was readmitted into the traveling
connection at the second session of the Upper Iowa conference, held in Marion.   At this conference he was stationed at Lansing, where he remained two years; then
appointed presiding elder of the Upper Iowa district
four years, when he was again returned to Lansing.   He
was honored by his brethren to a seat in the General Conference of 1864, and for twenty years he has been a trustee
of the Upper Iowa university.   After traveling Dubuque
district from 1864 to 1868 he was stationed at Epworth,
where he supervised the building of their beautiful church;
personally purchased, raised the money and paid for the
Epworth seminary, which had been built by our people and
had passed out of their hands.   Since which, that institution has been in successful operation and has been con-

stantly increasing in usefulness. In October of his third year in Epworth he was stricken down, caused by a diseased liver, which unmanned him for years, the effect of which will continue to some extent to the end of life. Since that affliction he has resided at Lansing, serving the church one year as pastor; and at New Albin organized the church and erected a comfortable house of worship, besides doing missionary work in destitute places. In the responsible fields of labor to which he has been assigned, he has been favored with a very intelligent and devoted companion, who has been to him like a *right arm*, and in some instances filled his place in the pulpit when he was unable to serve. Brother Houghton is one of those frank, honest-hearted men whose spirit can be known at the first reading, and whose judgment is of the first order. Instead of pandering to the defects of any of the ministers on his district, when duty required he would kindly tell them of their faults and counsel them to change and improvement. In fact, he is a wise counselor and a never-failing friend, and I doubt not but there are scores in the Upper Iowa conference, grateful to God for his salutary influence during the twenty-four years that he has lived and labored with us. It needs no skillful scribe to record his fidelity, or pencil-sketch to ornament his character, for they have been engraven in the hearts and confidence of his brethren by a *long and useful life;* and when the faithful ministers of the Upper Iowa, and other folds, shall bring in their sheaves in abundance in the presence of the Master, Brother Houghton will not come up empty-handed. And as I now linger around the borders of his valuable history, my soul exults in the prospect of that day when we shall be crowned heirs of a glorious immortality.

There are many honored names among the aged ministers in Iowa that I would be pleased to notice in this chapter,

but as space will not permit, I must close with the following tribute to Dr. Brush:

Rev. Wm. Brush, D. D., was born at New Fairfield, Conn.,
Feb. 19, 1827. In his nineteenth year he was converted at
Amenia seminary, New York, while pursuing his preparatory course for college. He entered the Wesleyan university in 1846. After remaining there one year, he entered
the sophomore class in Yale college, and in three years
graduated among the first of a class of about one hundred
students. Four weeks after his graduation, he was married
to a Christian lady residing in Rome, N. Y., of superior mind,
deep religious experience, and in full sympathy with all the
interests of the Methodist Episcopal church, and who has
been to him a congenial and efficient life-companion. In
the spring of 1851, he joined the New York conference, and
after preaching there seven years, was transferred to the
Upper Iowa, and stationed at Dyersville. During his second
year in that charge, he was elected president of the Upper
Iowa university, and remained in charge of the institution
about ten years, during which time the university gained a
fine reputation for scholarship, and its financial condition
greatly improved. On resigning the presidency he was
appointed presiding elder of Charles City district. In his
fourth year in that relation, he was transferred to the West
Texas conference, to take charge of a large district. Here
his work was arduous, and attended with great responsibilities, and mainly occupied in planning and laying founda-
tions; yet many societies were organized and churches built
under his supervision. He not only gave a new impetus to
our colored work, but did much to mould the policy of our
church for a hopeful future on other lines. When Dr. Brush
entered upon that field of labor our branch of Methodism
was not represented by a solitary church among all the
English-speaking white people of Texas; now we have a
vigorous and prosperous conference covering the whole
state in the interests of the white population. After eight

years of hard toil and sacrifice, he returned to the Upper
Iowa conference, and is now (1881) stationed at Maquoketa.
The doctor was honored by his brethren, at four different
times, with a seat in the General Conference, and served
eight years as a member of the book committee; and last,
but not least, he has furnished a son, Rev. F. E. Brush, A. M.,
B. D., a member of the Upper Iowa conference, now stationed at Decorah, who bids fair in ministerial rank to rise
above even his worthy predecessor. Dr. Brush is one of
those genial, large-souled men who will take you at once
into the warm embraces of his Christian confidence—not to
betray you, but to hold you with a firm grasp to the end.
He has never taken any lessons in the science of deception
or hypocrisy, but his frank open countenance is a standing
index of the honesty of his heart. In truth it may be said
he is a *bundle of energy*, and when he enlists in any good
cause, he is a living illustration of St. Paul's motto: "But
this *one thing I do*, forgetting those things which are behind
and reaching forth unto those things which are before, I
press toward the mark for the prize." The doctor is a large
man, quite fleshy, his weight about two hundred and forty
pounds, and by the law of collision, one would be led to
suppose that the flesh would usurp control of the spirit; but
instead of this, it seems to impart inspiration to his zeal;
and may this tireless energy continue until glory shall
crown the warrior at home.

CHAPTER XLIV.

The first setting out in any laudable enterprise in this life is generally attended with hope and cheerfulness, whatever may be the final result. And this interest is heightened when the object sought is of great importance. We have seen the stately vessel as she started out of port, enlivened with the sweetest music, though about to encounter the perils of the deep. We have seen the regiments in starting out to the field of conflict, inspired with the waving of flags, and martial music, though hundreds of those brave men will find a soldier's grave. And thus it is all-important that *hope* and *courage* should stand side by side, whether we enter into victory or suffer defeat. These two elements of our nature we cannot dispense with; for whether we struggle with hardships, they are our pillars; or whether in successes, they remain the same unfailing friends. Under the inspiration of such feelings and motives, about forty-five years ago I made a start for the heavenly country. I was then without knowledge as to its character and progress, and without experience as to its spiritual rewards. Like Abraham, it was a kind of sojourning in a strange land, for a season "dwelling in tents and tabernacles;" but my faith embraced a better country, and with hope and cheerfulness I journeyed on. It was not long before I learned that the soldier must be disciplined, the scholar must be studious, and the Christian must be firm. That if worldly enterprises require patience, hardships and perseverance in order to success, much more so in securing the crown that never fades. It is true that the maturing process that brought me out into the clear sunshine of spiritual enjoyment was strange to human reason but thorough in its work; so much so, that when the haven was gained, I was brought to wonder that the way had been mysterious. From this personal ex-

perience I learned an important lesson—that Christ sends
not his disciples out into the vineyard except they "tarry
first at Jerusalem, to be endued with power from on high."
The complete spiritual victory which I secured on the 30th
day of November, 1841, not only solved all past problems,
and pointed out the path of duty, but qualified me for the
great work now opening before me. Passing through the
deep waters, I could now sympathise with the suffering;
through the different stages of spiritual progress, I could
encourage them on to certain victory—salvation, *full* and
free, "through faith in the blood of the Lamb." Oh, what
an hour was that in my own Christian progress, when every
enemy was foiled, when every cloud was gone, and when I
stood upon an eminence so bright and glorious that all the
gloom of earth was beneath me, and heavenly rapture and
divine joy my continued portion!

Such was the state of my mind when I launched out into
this *great work* of laboring to save souls for the kingdom of
Christ. With me, it was no myth, no speculative problem,
but it was solemn reality, tested in the *crucible* of certainty,
and every converted man and woman stood as monuments
to the truth of the saving power of the gospel of Christ.
Such was the confidence in which I commenced my ministry
in Scioto county, Ohio, in 1841, and this confidence was not
misplaced. Wherever I labored, the blessing of God attended in the salvation of precious souls, and many are the
witnesses still living in my old fields of toil, that Jesus has
power to save. After devoting about four years to this
blessed work in Ohio, where I consecrated myself to his
service, at the call of duty I left all, that I might cultivate
Immanuel's lands in new territory further west. And
though home and friends were dear, about to leave behind
me, and not a familiar face in the land before me, in the
summer of 1845 I stood upon the soil of Iowa, in the city
of Burlington, and there, with a faithful few, I pledged my
fidelity to God to be his for time and eternity. It was here

25

in this little village, at that time, that I united my interests with a few other kindred spirits to endure the hardships, poverty and privations of a new country, that we might labor to impart to others the riches of God's grace, and honor the Divine Master who had called us into this work. With this noble band of workers I then started out to make new history in a new country, and share with them its perils and triumphs. And thus we have traveled on, laboring and enduring for the Master, one falling here and another there, until the first enlisted soldiers nearly all have passed from labor to reward. Only a few of the old veterans who bowed with me at the altar of Old Zion in 1845 are now standing on Zion's walls proclaiming a risen and exalted Saviour; and a few more years will close up the history of the last of those pioneers who first proclaimed salvation to a few scattered sheep in the wilderness. Their lonely monuments are still to be seen scattered over the state of Iowa, in silence speaking, but the fruits of their toil still remain, and will endure till the marshaled hosts of earth shall be summoned before the Judge of the quick and the dead. The old workmen have been buried, but the Master "has carried on his work" by filling up the ranks with men imbued with the same spirit, who have caught the falling flag, and even raised it higher and waved it more triumphantly than the fathers who first unfurled it to the breeze.

Thus the *little company*, at first, has been increasing from year to year, until there remains not a settlement in the *great state of Iowa* that has not been honored by the gospel message and inspired with its songs of salvation. Standing, as it were, a living witness of its growing history, as well as a laborer in the work, how it cheers my heart at this date—though laid aside from active labor—to stand upon an eminence so exalted and glorious as that attained by the devoted ministers of the Methodist Episcopal Church. No one is so well qualified to judge of the success of an enterprise as the man who has stood at both ends of its history. By this rule, I may be considered a competent judge, in comparing its present with its past. The little band that assembled at Burlington in 1845 numbered about twenty, embracing the territory of Iowa. Now (1881) we have four conferences in the state, numbering over five hundred traveling and more than that number of local preachers. Then we had but four or five houses of worship, and those very inferior; now we have two hundred and forty in the Upper Iowa conference, the most of them ornaments in church architecture. We numbered in membership at that time about five thousand, and Sunday-school children three thousand; now our membership in Iowa is not far from eighty-five thousand and our Sunday-school children not far from seventy-five thousand. At that date we had a little conference seminary at Mt. Pleasant, for years struggling for existence. Now, in its stead, in manly form, stands the Iowa Wesleyan university, an honor to that part of the state. In addition to this, we have our noble institution at Mt. Vernon, Cornell college, with its admirable president and corps of faithful workers, among the first institutions of the West. Then we have the Upper Iowa university, at Fayette; Albion and Epworth seminaries — all filling their places with honor and conferring lasting blessings upon our rising race.

When I united with the Iowa conference it was truly the day of log (and sometimes sod) cabins, *corn-bread* and *crust-coffee;* but now, through the spirit of Yankee enterprise, the cabin has become a mansion, and wealth and luxury have succeeded poverty and simplicity. Preachers of the gospel in the M. E. church at that time—so far as salary was concerned—shared in the destitution of the first settlers. My own salary for the first year in our conference was thirty-five dollars. The second year it was advanced to fifty dollars, and for seven years' faithful labor I received

a little less than seven hundred dollars. At that date
I had but little use for the money precept: "If riches
increase, set not your heart upon them." But at this period
of our history, as our church has become wealthy, our ministers are paid a fair salary, and stand in this respect on an
equal footing with ministers of other churches. With
many of the older brethren, I have traveled on from our
first history through all the stages of its privations, its
growth, its prosperity, never missing but one conference
during all of its practical work. I have lived to attend the
memorial services of nearly all of my older brethren, and
many of those younger than myself, and though three years
since I thought I had a transfer to the conference above, my
Divine Master reversed the order and informed me that he
had a work for me to do: to review the old battle-field once
more, record its conflicts, and victories achieved by grace
divine, and give to the church and the world some of the
trophies of redeeming love. And here I am to-day, May
26, 1881, telling what great things the "Lord hath done
for me."

And now it occurs to me that my present position in connection with the ministers of the Upper Iowa conference,
in some respects at least, is like that of Moses standing
upon Mt. Nebo, before his ascent to heaven. How true it
is, that there is sometimes a point of interest in human history when the *joy experienced* outweighs the perils of a
whole life. Such was the experience of Jacob near Kidron's
brook, when the prisoner was changed to a prince. Such
was the reward of Joseph, when exalted to become the
ruler of the land of Egypt. Such was the joy of Columbus
when first his eye discovered a new continent; and such was
the rapture of Moses upon Mt. Nebo, as he reviews the
past, surveys the earthly Canaan, and awaits his ascension
to heaven. How vividly portrayed by a modern writer.
Standing there in his elevated position, having a
glimpse of the city of Jericho, the land of Naphthali,

Carmel's Mount, and Hermon's hills of green, as well as the giant form of "Lebanon on high," the poet continues:

> "Such was the *land* which from that sacred height
> The prophet viewed: but lo! what sudden light
> Bursts from yon cloud just hovering o'er his head!
> Far down the mount its glorious beams were shed—
> It was the angel come to bear away
> *His weary spirit to the realms of day.*"

With one turn of his person he could look back to the Egypt from whence he came; the Red Sea of deliverance from his enemies; view the map of his travels and experiences for forty years in the wilderness; and adore the divine presence and guidance all the way through; and now he is about to wave a final farewell to earth's conflicts and take his seat with God's princes in the Canaan above. Would not such a position as this, awaiting his transition to heaven, more than compensate him for the trials of the wilderness for forty years?

Moses was not the last one of God's servants who after the close of life's labors has stood in an elevated position, "viewed the landscape o'er," witnessed the "*sudden light* from the bursting cloud," and awaited the angel visit to bear his soul away. Nay, verily. Such has been the privilege of many a faithful minister, after the wilderness had been passed, the warfare ended and the victory secured, to occupy an eminence as *honorable*, and enjoy a *bliss* as sublime, as he who "chose rather to suffer affliction with the people of God, than to enjoy the pleasures of sin for a season." If my readers will allow me to mark some points of resemblance, without the charge of egotism, touching my own relation to the church, and especially its ministry, it may assist in its application. Forty years had passed before commencing this *personal history*, since I began the Master's work in leading on the hosts to heaven. An ordeal of severe discipline was necessary to qualify me to be con-

vinced of my duty, and then to enter upon it successfully.
My way has been marked by God's pillar of a cloud by
day and fire by night, and especially *his presence has been
with me* to impart victory in every trying hour, and a heart
to magnify his grace in every soul saved.   And a Caleb and
Joshua are about all that are left of my brother ministers*
(in Upper Iowa) who started with me to the heavenly
Canaan.   And shall I say *too much*, when I add that the
joy and satisfaction now felt in view of past successes,
present honors and future glories, repay me well for all
trials endured.

The question has often been presented by friends acquainted with my past history, "If you were permitted to
repeat your life, with your present knowledge of all your
past experiences, would you choose a new path or adhere
to the same history?"   My answers have been prompt and
without the least hesitation: "Had I my life to live over
again, the only change which I could wish to make, would
be to enlist in the service of Christ earlier, and labor to
secure greater success in winning souls for heaven."   And
as for privations, exposures, and trying experiences—which
are often numbered among those to be dreaded,—these are
the minister's *diamonds* which will cause his crown to
shine when the rewards of ease and luxury are forgotten.
The rich jewels gathered from year to year in my pioneer
history, are so *precious*, that I have laid them carefully
aside; yea, of *such value*, that gold cannot buy; and I doubt
not in the awards of our heavenly inheritance these offerings of personal suffering and endurance for *"Christ's
sake,"* will secure the highest honor and the greatest bliss.

For forty-one years, as my family relations have remained
unchanged, for a home I have been dependent mainly on
others; yet I have found many a pleasant Bethany, and
thousands of willing hands and warm hearts to assist and
cheer me on my way; and now as the autumn approaches

---

* I am now the only one remaining in the Upper Iowa conference.

and the green leaves begin to fade, I realize more than ever, that I *shall never die;* but closing my eyes to the earthly, I shall open them to gaze upon scenes more transporting and faces more heavenly and divine. It might be well to say at this point, that the *victory* gained and *bliss* secured in 1841 have been continued and enlarged down to the present hour, and during the last winter I seemed to be standing upon the very borders of the heavenly land.

And now there remains with me *one ambition*, I apprehend of a higher grade and purer worth than any of its antecedents: that the closing up of my earthly history may have such a halo of glory attending it, that it may reflect a brightness over the past and shed its glory into the future. I have stood with these feet at the foot of the Rocky mountains as the descending sun left his golden tinge upon every tree on the mountain-side; and that *towering cliff* seemed to reflect back its grandeur to every human eye and to every object in nature. Such a sight as this was both beautiful and grand. But with these feet I now stand upon an eminence more imposing and sublime. Yea, at the foot of the Cross of Christ, whose glory gilds the earth and brightens heaven; and as I am soon to pass away from earth's labors and conflicts, my last prayer shall be that this *light* may illumine the passage from a world of sin to a heaven of blessedness, where the "Lord himself shall be our *everlasting light* and the days of our mourning shall be ended."

www.ingramcontent.com/pod-product-compliance
Lightning Source LLC
Chambersburg PA
CBHW051525100726
47898CB00005B/1580